H

H

by r merey

H

Typeset in Minion by Robert Slimbach, and Scala Sans by Martin Majoor.
Original graphics and layout by Hazel Ang.

TABLE OF CONTENTS

One...*The True Princes*...2

Two...*V Falls in Love*...15

Three...*He's Gonna Change My Name*...22

Four...*Atsuko Adds Her 2,000 Yen*...41

Five...*The First Post-Op*...58

Six...*The Water Trade*...69

Seven...*The Gucci Bag*...81

Eight...*The Second Post-Op*...98

Nine...*The Foolish Virgin*...112

Ten...*Two Procrastinators*...131

Eleven...*Aya Falls Out of Love*...150

Twelve...*The Woman from Heaven and Hell*...160

Intermission...*Ako Tells the Tale of O-Yasu*...170

Thirteen...*V Gets Fucked*...175

Fourteen...*The Crossing of the Lion Cubs*...202

Fifteen...*The Infernal Bridegroom*...221

Sixteen...*Everybody Hates V*...238

Seventeen...*Down and Out in Kyoto*...262

Eighteen...*The Rough Trade*...278

Nineteen...*Beautiful World*...285

Twenty...*La Vierge Folle Reprise*...310

Twenty-One...*The Life of an Amorous Man*...344

In Closing...353

Glossary...362

DEAR READER,

This story is light, but not always easy to read. It examines fetishization, infidelity, youth worship. The commodification of relationships. One reader has called it a delicate balancing act; a study in nuance in an era when nuance is dead. Another has suggested that I change the afterword to a foreword, to offer incoming explanation and avoid misunderstanding. I considered the idea, but it felt like spoon feeding. Still, I acknowledge that this book requires a level of trust—one that I have potentially not earned from you yet, and one that some may never see fit to grant. For those who stay, my aim is not to gratuitously provoke, but to serve a certain point. Thank you for reading.

I WROTE THIS FOR NO ONE.
I DEDICATE THIS TO NO ONE.
BUT IF I HAD TO WRITE IT FOR SOMEONE,
IT WOULD BE FOR A CITY.

(2004)

ONE

THE TRUE PRINCES

They say the Kamogawa is a sacred river.

That is precisely why he liked to sit next to it. I won't claim he *knew* that's why he liked it—in no book had he ever read, as you are reading now, that the Kamo is as sacred as the land it splits and that this holy water runs north to south, spilling over the low, flat bank until you could have felt the kami wet your feet. It wasn't knowledge, only instinct, or maybe he hoped the waves would wash away his sins? But no, he wasn't one for sin, and neither was anyone else around him. They didn't come to the water to pray to it, but to enjoy it, and each other, and to see the birds that pick through the reeds, and to hear the boiling sound that rises onto the bridges and the long promenade until it infects the teenagers burning the night with sparklers. Affects everything. The temples beyond, the machiyas, and their upstairs so dark, those shadows could stop a heart dead. Grey-black in the winter, green in the summer, a blade at midnight, shattered mirror at noon—the Kamo ran the blood of an entire city.

Which is why our story starts by the river. On a hot spring afternoon. With V. I won't tell you where he came from, how he got to the Sanjou Bridge that day, or why his name is only one letter—these details are irrelevant and would probably only bore you. I'll just say that V sat by the Kamo and chewed his nails. He got not a few looks as he did this, for his stare off into the distance had the clean, magnetic expression of a person who has completely surrendered to the world and will now deny himself nothing.

Certainly not the public pleasure of biting his nails.

He was a tallish youth with a well-cut face and a look that was difficult to render. Whether it hid a deep soul or a cheerful vacuousness—impossible to say. The crowds shuffled past him on the walk, and glances flicked over him again and again as he glowed with the innocent charm of someone who is completely absorbed in the higher realms of life. A contemplation of the divine. Looking at him as he was, those going by couldn't help but wonder what fine thoughts ran through his head. Such noble concentration! But while it was an aesthetic meditation for sure, in those moments by the holy river, he was not concerned with purity, serenity, sanctity, nor any other person, man or woman, who might have noted his presence, their impressions of him, or their opinions—

V was fully engrossed in the profound sublimity of high school girls.

His unwavering attention was arrested up on the hill, past the river's boardwalk, where the banks ended and the streets began. There was one building in particular that incited a local controversy; it alone was spangling and new in a cluster of splendid old temples, and the side of the structure's polished surface gleamed like a glittering cube torn from the future. ⌈An eyesore, just like downtown's Kyoto Eki!⌋ is what many locals deemed it, and the arguments to tear it down or let it be swirled endlessly, but if V ever cared about the frail balance between the city's old and new architecture, it wasn't now. He didn't even see it, only lwhat was in front of it.

Six young girls, dancing in the fading light.

They careened around, their moves half-random, half-dreamy, to a song that wasn't playing. It was a public slumber party. He observed them dancing, those six girls,

3

with careful consideration: D— blazers hanging off their thin, sparkly shoulders; makeup vigilantly applied; hair cut, straightened, dyed, styled, whipped, whipping—perfect. In his infrequently philosophical moments, V was convinced that this entire country propelled forward on the steaming desire to placate its true princes: these sloe-eyed, little vicious girls. What was it about them? And yet the world fell to their feet.

And he would have gladly fallen with it.

But not that day. Falling required a tender patience to bridge the gap between whatever he was and the elite class who stood at the apex of everything good in modern life. High. School. Girls. And if you think that is hyperbole, he wasn't in the habit of employing them, but he could only imagine all the idols, pop-stars, fad-pundits, fashion designers, cell-phone companies, trinket wizards and manufacturers of anything *sugar* fighting to capture Her attention. And if she was even *pretty* in the bargain? And if she was even a bit *narcissistic* in the bargain? Plunging into that kind of affair required a wallet of steel with nerves to match, and though V was often reckless or naïve, he was seldom both at once.

Yes, he knew what was good for him. At least, that's what he told himself. So why was he even walking up that way? Well, but it was the direction he had to go. Obviously, he could have tried to curb his own stupidity, but who can curb the direction they must travel? Not even God could, so certainly not V. Though some part of him did acknowledge that moving past the girls would require a certain finesse. After all, they were acquaintances of a sort. Even if he'd never spoken to them, they did share this bank. So it would be prudent to walk by in a way that preserved his good standing. Or at least, drew no attention.

Not rolling by slowly.

Not unapologetically staring.

Dear god, not *appraising*.

The Arch-Prince called out:

"What are *you* looking at?" She said *you* like others say *fuckwit*, and the slightest annoyance prickled him. *Oh, I'm supposed to understand that.* Points for guts, but he chalked her a hot little pain in the ass who probably had a whole harem of boyfriends wrapped up in a thick web of girly mind-magic so potent, those sad bastards couldn't know if they were coming or going.

「I don't speak English,」 he murmured, and a ripple of admiration moved through the little group to grate him even further—the dog had risen on its hind legs. And spoke! 「Anyway, I was just wondering what you're doing here.」 His voice was low, fluid; he spoke well, no accent; but his word choice was soft. Too soft. They tittered mercilessly.

「Mireba wakaru.」 The Leader had little patience for foreigners, and if they couldn't even speak English, get out. 「We're dancing.」

「All right. I see that. But why here?」

「Because this building is like a mirror and we can see ourselves move. Any more questions?」

「Just one. Can I see it?」

「...What?」

「The dance. Wouldn't it help someone to see it?」

The Leader wavered. Bit her lip in confusion. Nan ya koitsu? She tossed her hair with a snap to break her neck, and the move said, 'I'm done with you,' but he ignored the hint. As she figured he would. Here was the problem with foreign boys in general, even the cute ones had the subtlety of a dog mounting your leg. As a whole, the group was half-flattered by his attention and half-wishing he would put an egg in his shoe and beat it.

She turned to the others. A mess of giggles and shrugs. The Leader turned back.

「All right. You can watch it *once*.」

They flowed out into a pattern, she counted off. Perhaps he had been right. Their moves did tighten with an audience; their synchronization improved. The girls smiled, ignored him, locked eyes with each other, fell in love with each other in the darkening mirror of the building— The music that wasn't playing stopped. They bowed, he clapped, called out. Jouzu jouzu. By now, the sky had gotten dark. Cell phones flipped out, messages flew to mothers, study partners, boyfriends.

Oh, I really have to go.

But I should go too.

See you tomorrow then?

And then they were gone, just like that. The girls dissolved, their ghost reflections melted in the mirror of the building. Jya ne, jya ne. See you. The brasher ones waved to him too and V waved back, then walked over to a low stone wall. The atmosphere lay stripped without their presence, that numinosity, and he absorbed the scene into himself. There had been girls, a group, to be exact. They were off-limits (perhaps the best kind) and he had approached them, engaged them and managed to part without undue production or selling his soul. Progress, he thought wryly, taking out cigarettes and matches and he watched the fireworks that had started to smoke up the twilight. The girls were a good enough distraction, but anytime now, he'd be getting a message from Rodrigo and not a second too soon: His stomach licked his back, from the insides.

「You know those will kill you, right?」

At the sound of her voice, V turned slightly. He'd classified them all during the dance ritual: the Leader, the

Studious One, the Brat, the Nondescript One. But he didn't remember this girl. Had she even been amongst the dancers? She must have been. The girl stood, looking less extraordinary without her entourage and a little out of place. Too-big navy blazer, pleated long skirt, scuffed loafers. Fist of tie at the throat. She'd fit so seamlessly before; now he watched her fumble with her keitai. Shift her weight foot to foot. Short, pale, soft, round, standing at a distance respectful of his space. But staring at him nonetheless.

And he let himself stare back. V may have never seen this girl before that afternoon, but he knew her well. She was a familiar theme in his life; a contagious melody he could never quite get out of his head; a vector, like hundreds of other vectors, slightly varied but ultimately pointing in the same direction: tepid heartbreak, idle drama, above all, *problems he did not need*, but when she took out her phone and started to dink with the keys— pretty, polystyrene fingers, her lips bitten in the message, she licked them, then relaxed, parted, shining, her hair, falling in her face, refracting, the light off the tiny screen, her eyes black as coke (the stuff you burn, not the stuff you snort); no, darker than that, what's darker than carbon? He considered. A night without stars? A sky without moons? She looked up at him, connecting with his gaze, and in that moment, her fuel-colored pupils cracked his nerves straight open and—

V ripped a match.

The girl's hair hung into her face and she flicked a strand over her shoulder. While she texted, his eye moved to the clean cord connecting the sweep of the jaw to her collarbones. A line, he determined, to ruin yourself over.

「So that means you want one,」 he cracked and the girl snapped her phone shut.

7

「Sure. Why not? Everything that's good kills you.」

He looked at her sharply. 「I suppose so, ojousan.」

The girl came closer, pulled a cigarette from the offered box and bowed primly, bending at the waist. Her 「thank you」 was crisp and polite. V struck her a match as well and moved over to give her a light in the wind. He glanced at her, to signal that she should lean closer. The girl did, and his eyes over the tiny flame stunned her. *He has eyes like a cat,* she thought, wanting to stare more, but drew back instead. Offered her hand neatly, western-style.

「My name is Ayami, but my friends call me Aya. Nice to meet you.」

「The pleasure is mine. My name's V.」

What a strange name, she thought then, not in her repertoire of English textbook names, but then she remembered: He'd already clarified that he didn't speak it. Mystifying, as, in Aya's mind, English and westerners were inextricably linked, but then again, there was something mystifying about him.

She couldn't place his age; obviously older than herself, but young. He was soft-spoken, even by local standards, but his voice was low. Almost rough. Hair the color of high noon. Dasai athletic coat. Woefully unchic. But not a tourist. She was sure of that, not even because he spoke her language, but because of the way he stood against the wall. Fitting into the scene, comfortable with it. No, it was more than that, he belonged to it. And it belonged to him. He smoked, lightly bored and horribly hungry—Aya glanced back over by the building to where her friends had been before. The spot was so empty.

She swallowed, took two steps forward, then walked her two steps back.

「So... then. ...Where are you from?」

Silent until then and draped against the stone, V side-glanced her, then took the cigarette from his mouth. It was an elegant gesture, cut from the dead certainty of her aim.

「From nowhere, really. So you can pick. Where do you want me to be from?」

His face was poised, but his voice still cracked. Could he have possibly been nervous too? The dissonance made her shyness snap.

「I... I don't know! ...Are you French?」

「I've lived in France. Is that close enough?」

「Hey, that really doesn't answer my question! You know, my friends and I made a bet earlier.」

「A bet? About where I'm from?」

「No, it was about something else.」

「I see. And what did the loser have to do?」

「Come here and find out where you're from. I've never seen you here before, but the others say they have. A lot.」

「Of course. There isn't a better spot in the whole city.」

「You think?」 Aya scrunched up her face. 「I wouldn't say it's anything special.」

「Then you're lucky if you think that.」 V breathed out smoke. 「Because I've been to many places, and this spot feels holy or something.」

「Holy?」

「Am I using the right word? Like, being out here cleans you somehow. I'm out here so much, I must be cleaner by now too. I *must* be. And if you come here too, you must be as well.」

Aya laughed, her hand in front of her mouth.

「You're an odd bird, huh?」

「Says the girl talking to me on a lost bet.」

「Well, I'm not the one who had all kinds of theories about you. That was Yumiko. The girl who talked to you first.」

「Theories, hmm. And? Anything good?」

His eyes shone and Aya shrugged.

「Depends on what you think is good, I guess.」

「Tell me one.」

「Well, she thinks you're some kind of foreign perv here to prey on young girls. It confused her so much when you couldn't speak English. She was dead sure you're Australian.」

V stared.

「Prey on them? As in I eat their hearts? Seduce them?」

「Something like that.」

「And what do you think, ojousan?」

Aya's cheeks blushed now the slightest. She flailed for a few moments, and when he saw she would not be answering, said firmly:

「Yumiko-sama should know that us peasants may like to look at the moon, but we'd never dare try to touch it.」

「And what is THAT supposed to mean?」

「Also, I'm not Australian. That part is *very* important. ...Anyway, it was wonderful talking to you. Goodbye.」

Aya's mouth turned down—

「Goodbye? But I just got here!」

「Well, you've completed your mission, and you shouldn't talk to strangers. It's dangerous.」

「I don't, usually! I was so anxious coming over once the others had left, my hands were shaking! But you're a lot easier to talk to than I expected.」

「People say that.」 He conceded. 「I could have a great conversation with a rock myself. But if you're not going to go, then I definitely should.」

「You want me to go so you can go talk to a rock!?」

「I would much rather talk to you than a rock, but then, what I want to do and what I should be doing are hardly ever the same things.」

Aya ground her cigarette out on the stone next to

them and flicked it smartly into the gloom. Her voice had
gained some confidence.

⌈Too bad, because I was going to ask for your advice
about something I think… you might know a lot about, but
I was thinking we could go somewhere else to talk.⌋

⌈MY advice?⌋

⌈You sound so shocked. Do you give bad advice?⌋

⌈I don't think I'm qualified to advise about anything,
really. And I don't know you at all.⌋

⌈We could change that. We could go to a café, or
something.⌋ Seeing the expression on his face, she waved
her hand. ⌈Oh, stop *worrying*. I have a boyfriend, and I
don't care about any of *that*, anyway.⌋

V exhaled loudly, wondering, why was he doing this?
Was he doing this? And when had anyone ever admitted to
caring about any of *that*? Aya turned to him. It was hard to
make out much more than two shining eyes in the furry
dark creeping up the river side.

⌈Or you're not interested at all, now that I told you I
have a boyfriend.⌋

He sighed.

⌈Look.⌋ Rubbed out his cigarette on the stone,
inwardly cursing Rodrigo for not having called yet. ⌈I
didn't mean to give you or your friends the wrong impression. I am here often, I have noticed your friends here
before, and it seems they've noticed me. I think that's fine.
You can tell them tomorrow that I'm the kimoi foreigner,
or the pervert who eats girl hearts, whatever story suits you
the best, but I really don't want any trouble.⌋

⌈You're saying talking to me is trouble?⌋

⌈Oh yes.⌋

⌈But why?⌋

⌈Because girls are trouble.⌋

⌈But we're just talking.⌋

「Talking is NEVER just talking.」

「So you'd rather be talking to a man?」

「You know they're even one thousand times *worse*. Men... are beautiful. And horrible. Don't you think? Which is why I only go for women. Maybe you should too...?」

「Are you being serious now?」

V pulled out the next cigarette.

「Omoikkiri.」

Aya sat next to him. Swung her heavy bag onto the wall and buried her phone in it, amongst a Snoopy notebook and some volume that appeared to be a diary.

「I don't think you're being serious at all. And I don't have jyuku until eight.」

What does she want? He wondered then. Or was that a stupid question? Possessed of a wide range of talents, some random, many useless, the one he had consistently profited from anywhere he went was an uncanny ability to tap right into what others expected of him. Certain people especially. V had been born double-cursed: he worshipped beauty—and despised mind control. And though they could easily degenerate him into a coked-up fox running amok in a well-stocked coop; render him absolutely stupefied with their hothouse innocence, he avoided younger people because it seemed a vindictive god had once made those polar elements in them forever inseparable. A joshikousei drunk off her own power had to be put down hard, and while V was potentially many bad things, he was never cruel (and only *rarely* masochistic).

Looking at this Aya looking at him though, that resolve eroded steadily. Her kind face was uncharacteristically blank to him, but in it, he recognized something of himself. A slaked remoteness. Clarity. He saw then that he needn't worry, because she wasn't looking for currency.

Just novelty. And that was the one commodity V had plenty to spare.

Here we go again.

His rationality and desire raced head to head and he knew it was a damned fight, for rationality had never, ever won. This day, it had an even smaller chance at the elusive victory, because he was sure by now that he wanted her and, once that was determined, it was good as lost. She was an innocently good girl, though not inexperienced (that much he could tell), but most importantly, she radiated the characteristic he felt was most conducive to pure love: a sheer lack of cunning.

They both stood up to leave and his height cleared the girl's by a casual American foot. She gathered her things, and her glossed lips parted to reveal a smile he hoped she would never fix.

V loved crooked teeth.

And straight ones.

Aya raised her hand, and he was afraid for a moment that she would take his. Instead, she started to dance again, miming a microphone.

He hardened his voice:

「What now? I thought we said this is it.」

And she tutted like a study hall proctor.

「You keep saying you have to go, staring at your phone, but you're still here. So why don't we go to a café? Or even better! Karaoke?」

He frowned.

「Us alone, in a small, dark room? Sounds improper.」

「Spoken like a true ero-gaijin.[1]」 No longer shy at all, she completely disarmed him. 「Who said this is a date? I bet you can't even sing at all.」

He stopped with a jerk and Aya looked up, startled.

「What's wrong?」

[1] Pervy foreigner.

13

The dread lifted and V smiled. How could he explain to her the sudden and perfect joy of remembering that the gods loved them?

「I just remembered something. Never mind. But hey. Before we go...」

「Yes?」

「Just to warn you—uta ga meccha umai no yo.」 [2]

She tmiled back.

「You don't look like a singer. You look like a liar.」

They started to walk away—

A young man and his prince.

It was the first time Aya had ever made a big move.

The first time she'd tried to talk to a foreigner.

But maybe it was a night for firsts, and extremes and superlatives because a group of older girls walked by; they giggled, they whistled. V's stride didn't break the slightest, and Aya did something else she'd never done before: wondered if she might not be walking with the H-est person she'd ever met.

[2] I sing wicked good.

TWO

V FALLS IN LOVE

E xactly three hours later, Aya's keitai vibrates violently.
Once. Twice. She opens her eyes, wondering if she fell
asleep. It feels like a nap, the kind she takes when she's
been studying too long and needs a breather. Then she
remembers, grabs her phone fearfully. Flick. The neon
display blazes the dark room, and she's relieved. The time
is all right. Late, but not fatal. Her eyes quickly scan the
messages. Kiriya, asking why she wasn't at jyuku. Yui said
you were in school, where did you go? Yui, asking if Aya
could stay a little later in school tomorrow. I need to
borrow your notes. The last text is from her jyuku teacher.
Aya snaps her phone shut without reading it. Opens it
again. Taps a quick note. Not that her teacher would ever
write her mother, but this way he won't be concerned. She
lays back down, phone on her chest, yawning.

Next to her, V hangs in that place between sleep and
wake, prone like a fish washed up with her on the same
side of the Kamo. The rabuho³ room spreads around them,   ³ love hotel
marbled and outrageous. Sometime in the last thirty minutes, complete dark has fallen and all she can see now is
his outline, bathed in the light pouring from the bathroom.

「Are you... asleep?」 she asks.

V stretches.

「No. It sounds like someone really wants to talk to
you though. Your mother, your teacher, and your best
friend, all wondering where you are.」

She smiles.

「My boyfriend. My classmate. And my teacher. But I'm always late after jyuku, so it's fine.」

He turns on his back now, eyes still closed, when Aya reaches over. Her voice is a finger pointing in the dark.

「So... How much do you think it costs?」

「What then?」

She sighs deeply.

「What you just did to me.」

Instant paralysis. In doom and satisfaction and unable to sort out where one ends and the other begins. He damns a flawed radar that could normally spot a cherry girl, a black aura, or just plain trouble, 100 kilometers off. Aya sits up next to him. The unlit room tints her dark and confusing, and he can't possibly imagine the sweet girl of the last few hours will now morph into a 45-kilo extortionist or douse him in a maelstrom of emotional blackmail, but then again, all speculation is moot because he remembers he knows next to nothing about her. V's sex-scorched dendrites will him to either speak nonsense, make excuses, brush her off coldly, or hold her while she inevitably weeps.

And if none of that works, to let her hijack him through guilt, for as one who plays by luck and impulse, there are only two things he can claim right now with utmost certainty: 1. It had been worth it. 2. He absolutely deserves whatever is coming. *Because you know better than to fuck with these girls—all wide-eyed innocence until they crisp you at the business end of a bubble-gum blow-torch.*

So he closes his eyes and waits for her to hunker over and eat his heart out with a serrated spoon—but Aya is laughing infectiously before he can even forfeit the price. She slugs him on the shoulder.

「Hey, calm down, I was just kidding. It was a joke! I do *that* all the time!」

Which "that," my darling, screwing or giving me a god-damn heart attack? He stays frozen, scared to even touch her, and her eyes narrow mischievously. Aya straddles him, her small hands on his shoulders, her hair hanging in his face. It tickles his nose.

「Relax, will you? Always joking this whole time and can't even take a joke.」

Clicking on the light, he sees then that she seems neither traumatized nor malevolent, just run manic with an affectionate energy. She kisses him dizzy, then points to their bedside clock, and his drained head spins with her shiny talk. The numbers flash the seventeen minutes left before they enter the next hour.

「You really should have seen your face. It was too funny. Anyway, we have about fifteen minutes left. I want to take a bath.」

He nods, struck, and starts to get up, but she won't get off of him. Calmed now, the pitch of her energy blurs, and her voice becomes faded and soft.

「Don't go yet. Can't I look at you first?」

「Like I could move anyway. God, you scared me half to death.」

His voice is still a bit shaken, though not a reprimand, and Aya smooths herself down on him.

「Me? Scared *you?*」 She seems openly pleased with herself while he struggles to hide foolish relief.

「Yes, *you.* I was sure you'd throw the mother and the father of a scene.」

「Don't worry. I...」 Aya whispers something into his ear, but whatever charming, mollifying thing it was, it flits straight through his brain because he determines that her hair inexplicably smells like ripe apricots, and V is again awed by the power that, to him, seems monopolized by girls—the ability to trap the essence of flowers, fruits, sun and air, on their bodies. Not only to trap the scents, but improve them somehow.

「You smell good,」 he says simply, more to himself than anything, and she smiles.

「So do you. I was a little worried at first because I'd always heard that foreigners smell like a dead body when they sweat.」

His eyes narrow from her blunt statement, though he has heard something similar many times before...

「I guess some of them smell, sure. Not everyone though.」

「You're lucky then, that you don't. And your skin is so nice.」

「Not as nice as yours.」

Aya keeps her arm close to his; with her other hand, she runs her fingers along his arm, up to his neck, and back down again, something between massaging and petting, until he feels uncharacteristically embarrassed by her attention. Self-consciousness quickly shifts to excitement though and hating the clock, V wraps the covers around himself, turns, and mutters into the mattress.

「Didn't you want to take a bath? I would stay longer, but I really don't want you to get in trouble.」

Aya's answer is to leap out of bed and immediately flood the tub with water so hot, he feels he'll be boiled alive when they slip into it, even as she splashes comfortably. No matter how long he lived here, he could never get used to the sheer *heat* of the ordinary bath. It cooks his insides and makes his head swim in a pink haze. The tub itself is not the normal deep-soak tub, but a free-standing porcelain claw foot model, filigreed, curlicued, and they sit across from each other in it, steaming, while she chatters and puts her feet up on his shoulders. One on each side. They stay until the very last possible moment, finally dashing out to sloppily dry themselves in towels, dripping water all over the room. 27 seconds V spends, fishing out a hair clip she has somehow managed to wedge between the headboard and the wall.

With exactly two minutes left, they throw on their clothes and fall into the corridor. Weaving over to the desk in the lobby, he is vaguely grateful for the frosted glass that separates him from the face of the concierge— It allows V to watch the last of his money get pushed down the lust industry's gullet with a certain detachment, but coming out onto the evening street, it all feels so light. Free and unconvoluted.

There they stand by the canal just off of Sanjou, and he glances down into it, at the pea green hair moving over the tiled bottom, lit up by the street lamps. Willows hang into the water, and students blaze along the narrow banks on bicycles, end-bloom cherry-petals stuck to their hair. A cherry blossom petal sticks in Aya's hair as well, and he touches her to get it off—an excuse. The water looks very clean and very cold despite the air's inertia, and they can sense the coming rain. Its viscous pressure fills the sky— that, and an unspent possibility.

On all levels, it is breaking up.

「I should go now.」

Their voices ring out, simultaneous, and she flushes.

「Do you have a keitai?」

「Yeah, it's prepaid though.」 It feels like confessing something to her. Perhaps his financial instability? 「But sure, I'll write you if you want me to.」

「Why would I not want you to? Here, let me take a picture of us before you go. I've never been with a kinpatsu before.」

V himself has never been with a school girl before, but to say so strikes him as crass. He says nothing; she flips open her phone, and they stand away from the love hotel, near the canal, their faces glaring and unnatural in the camera's flash. She retakes the picture three times before she is satisfied (the complaint always that her face looks too broad next to his), and then promises to send it to him over the phone.

「Sorry, but I really do have to go now. I did miss jyuku, you know.」

And then Aya is off, before he can even say a proper goodbye. There is no kiss, no hug, no peck on the cheek. No handshake. What does he feel as he watches her run away over the canal, her D— bag flying in the darkness? Whatever it is, he doesn't try to categorize or isolate it. The emotion is likely similar to what he feels after eating a nice meal, going to a good spa, or seeing a beautiful sunset—it lives only in the moment of its enjoyment. As ever, V accepts any gift the universe deems fit to bestow on him, but does not ask for more. For that would be tempting the fates. He cannot remember all the Ayas, and Ayakos, and Ayakas, Ayumis. They recede into the past like she does into the dark, running, dissolving into a flow of favorite foods, incompatible blood types, unusual perfumes, styles of hair, odd snatches of conversation, scars, memorably strange moles, irrelevant details coruscating together in an immense cosmic river of Girl, and any spot he stepped into (gently) both like every other and also entirely original.

Regardless of what happened between them earlier, he imagines that a week from now, he will hardly remember her. She may text him sometime—he may never hear from her again. The probability erases nothing. *I did miss jyuku, you know.* Such an honest farewell! The philter some asked you to swallow as soon as you were upright again, Aya had not uncorked and put to his lips— *A girl after my own heart*— Jaded now, but then she had let him release—

what? Her fragility? Yes, but his as well, and that is a rare thing, so how could anything else matter?

For these last few hours, V had been in perfect love.

He turns down the Pontochou and returns parallel to the Kamogawa, slipping past the drunken izakaya hoppers and the marqueed soaplands. It is a late and rainless dinnertime, but the pavement still glistens with a feel of clean, and on it he is another shadow walking home past well-groomed young men in shrill suits guarding shifty pleasure spots and older men in drab suits gulping ramen under low awnings. The crowds come and go, the massage girls get married, age, die, and are replaced. Younger people, younger buildings; signs and establishments move as changeable details of scenes that never change, and that's all he asks for, really. To have these streets be near and the river. He wishes for the river's constancy.

What a strange request for someone who built his life on water.

THREE

HE'S GONNA CHANGE MY NAME

In the not so distant past, in a very distant city—

I sat on the floor of a broken hotel room while Etienne fucked a girl on the bed next to me (he was doing a real shitty job of it too, if I may add). That's when I knew I needed a change. Love was over. Laika and I were sitting on the floor smoking with our legs stretched while the other two sweated it out. Etienne's the one who had gotten this little party together. That's the kind of guy he was: A clean-cut-*looking* Parisian kid engaged to a cream-faced rich girl he went crazy over. Sadly for him though, she could only be handled in crisp linen sheets. He did her up all nice and vanilla, until those vices built up in him like a boil. Like that day—

We were walking around early afternoon not too far from L—when Etienne announced that he just had to have a woman. Did I want to come along? No. Was I going to go along? There was a place he knew not far and then we were inside, counting our cash, when he winked at me.

–So, what's it going to be, Vivi? One room, or do you want your own?

I shrugged.

–Whatever you normally do.

Etienne smirked and held out his hand, and I put some money into it. But not as much as I should have.

–And? Are we sharing a girl too?

There was a broad-bodied blonde walking down the stairs, looking a little wobbly. Our eyes met.

She waved at me and I flipped him off.

–You wish. Come on.

Two girls were available right then; a smiley older brunette with a nice body, and a surly teen waif. Let's call her Laika. Etienne pounced on the older woman immediately, and then the hag up front gave us a room with two small beds up on the third floor, except that there was only a single sagging bed when we stepped into it. The stairs were rickety and the time was ticking, so I tossed a coin—and got the floor. For the money, we had the ladies for 20 minutes, and that selfish bitch Etienne would use the bed the whole time. One look around: stained sheets, beaten walls, and a window that opened to a chute? It was no courtyard, but a concrete tube painted with the baked-on filth of six other floors.

My cupcake sat on the floor and hated me—I guess in that situation I would've hated me too. I quietly let her be. Then my friend called out a name that made us both cringe, and I realized this poor girl was waiting for me to lay her on the floor, or stand her up, and start something equally bad. Maybe I would have if Etienne was live porn in bed and she looked *at all* into it, but really, he was embarrassing, so the minutes passed. I slumped on the floor and smoked, and my cigarette was halfway gone before she deigned to speak:

–Tu vas pas me baiser? [4]

I bet she was worried that if we didn't start soon, I'd complain about time and try to get my money back or something screwed like that. Her tone, no, this whole thing, amused me. Could this have been any more of a disaster? Lurid roses peeled off all around us on the yellowing wallpaper. I lay my head against the shaking bed and blew smoke at the ceiling.

[4] Aren't you going to fuck me?

–Te baiser? I don't think I could get it up for Mary Magdalena herself in this revolting room. No, it's fine. You can go.

She didn't though; leaned her long back against the bed instead and took a cigarette. Sulky looks aside, once our date was off, she got chatty as hell and two sentences in, I learned we had grown up within 50 kilometers from each other. We switched then to our old language, and it felt good to talk it, though her French wasn't too bad either. Hard tones of grey and wet beton, sounding like back home. A lot of these girls came from back there, speaking three, four languages, looking for papers and paper. (Who wasn't?) Laika was telling me about her girlfriend (she was here too) and how they wanted to leave this place to go work in a bar. But she wasn't sure. The money would be worse, and she didn't mind it here, really. It was safer than the forest, if you could avoid the police raids. I told her, yes, us easterners were meant for nicer things than dodging pigs, and she nodded, smiled like a rogue. A canine was missing on the left side of her smile and the gap was endearing. When she saw me looking at it, she turned her face, neck flushed red (Had I stared too hard?), dragged on the cigarette. And then she said—this was the hour of lonely, upstanding craftsmen and middle-aged sex addicts. Not truant-looking virgins. If I didn't want to, what was I doing here? I was trying to think of a memorable answer when the bed gave a final, magnificent heave, and I knew Etienne was done. His lady was already getting dressed, and I got up.

Laika stood with me right away with an unreadable look I tried to decipher. Sure—in there, I was a cash machine, whether or not we sealed the deal. But still she stayed close, looking at me in this expectant way until I started to regret not having taken her up. Long neck, bruised knees, lips painted redder than red. Weird, but the thought of *wiping her lips clean* turned me on like nothing else, and she would've even let me maybe, but I'd waited too long and now it was time to go.

–Regretting it, aren't you, my baby love?

Laika smiled with my tobacco in her mouth, slipped her hand into my pocket and it was my turn to get red. I was entirely certain she was at least five years younger than me. She said,

–Come back next time, find me. I want to take all your money.

–It's all yours. And who do I ask for?

She told me her name, which wasn't her name, like none of our names were our names, and she kissed me on the cheek. I tipped her well (money flowed good back then) and it was back into daylight, Etienne looking smug as shit—it was his one look those days. He'd had his share of bad times, but with his new girl and flash clothes, he swaggered on the streets, daring his old life to recognize him. I swear though, some of his best times must have passed in a dirty hotel room, the way he kept finding his way back to them.

Stopping to cross, I knew he wanted to bait me.

–How does a girl that young look that fucked up? I don't blame you. You should've kicked her out. Got yourself a better one.

Etienne clapped me around the shoulder, and I pushed him off me, into the street.

–Ta gueule. It wasn't her fault—*you* put me off. Damn. Didn't your mother teach you better than that?

I grinned and Etienne happily told me to go fuck myself and I told him I'd have to now that he'd ruined today's chance. We walked for a while, until we ran into a couple of friends and then sat outside at a café on an alley off the Boulevard de Sébastopol. That's where he ended up joining us, Lero, Leandro; he was a half-Brazilian with a tangled-crazy accent he'd picked up from every place he'd ever been. He ran with Etienne's old gang and was definitely one of the best looking birdies on their strip—the guy rippled like a statue. Connected up and down, but generous too. If he had a good thing, he'd pass it on. And I still remember the conversation that day, maybe because it was the last one I'd have with him, and I'd always liked Lero.

—Ey, Etienne. V.

He turned to me, and we shook hands before he sat down. I passed him some money that I owed from a while back, and Etienne ordered wine and checked out my funds over the table.

—So you still have some cash, V? I thought our pretty ladies had you all cleared out.

Lero raised his eyebrows.

—The cathouse before three; I see it you boys, you are making it, the *boredom*. No work then today?

—I dunno about Etienne, but I'm free.

—And tomorrow?

—Depends. Why, you got something for me?

—Depends.

Lero jerked me around and hung all over the sidewalk. He was as tall as he was big and never properly fit into any public furniture. He also liked to draw out whatever he wanted to say and I tried not to appear too interested, though his offers were usually cream and I had a guess this one would be too. His eyes glinted like two gold coins, and he mussed my hair.

—Depends, little brother, if you still make it the tanned and the blonde your type, eh, V?

I sat up straighter.

−Tell me what you need.

Starting to drink, he smiled at me.

−Two friend, Américaines, they need it the nice boy, show them the town, show them the drugs. Your meeting it tomorrow noon at their hotel; if they like, you make it the guide three days.

−Ok, so what's wrong with them?

−What is your meaning?

−You know, why are you giving this to me?

−Aiya~~, where is it, the *trust?* You think the Lero try to fuck you, but they just two girl and I think it e'special of *you*. You go it to the Mona Lisa, the Montmartre; you show it to them the clubs, and maybe you lucky? ...The boom-boom, but you no want? Is OK; I give it to my Etienne, he takes it, *non?*

But the way he winked at me, he knew I was gone. I'd always liked American girls—they were laid back and easy to please, but they did have a bad habit of wanting to speak a LOT of English.

−And am I using sign language for three days, Leandro?

He slapped me on the back then, flashing the street every straight, white tooth in his head.

−Haha, my V, he think of every *thing!* These girl, they are not so much wanting it to *talk*, but I speak it to them, the French. So they speak it to you. The deal, normal cut for delivery and you make it a round for the Pele. And come by me tomorrow, I have it the shit too, to keep you going. So yes?

−Ok, but I want to see them first.

I smiled at him crooked, and Etienne across from us twisted up in a righteous pout.

−Hey Lero, why you always bring him the good ones?

And that big dude poured the wine and laughed:

−Because I say it to you already, they want it the *nice*

boy. And this V, he looks it le plus innocent, yes? And because everybody knows it you are no wanting it the girls, Etienne. You are wanting it the boys. Like me, you know is better, eh? No worry; I bring you soon, so many nice ones.

Etienne had always insisted he was gay *strictly* for pay, but Lero still pulled him on about it, because he had a crush on him and then, it got the other's black little heart in a fix. That was his contradiction. The way he looked then, you'd think he couldn't count to three.

–You know that's all done, –he said.

–I know it, I know it, baby, is a *joke!* Ok then, I say you wanting it the girls, sure, but you see, the V here, he *enjoying* it, the girls. Besides, I hear you needing it the money not so much nowadays, and (here his voice somehow pantomimed sniffing a line) I no trust you with the shit, hein?

We knew. I also knew that Lero had entered dangerous territory, but Etienne would never take it out on him, because that guy was iced and he took shit from *nobody*. Which left… Having noticed a striped cat on the other side of the street about to get flattened by a car though, I was too busy watching it to really get involved in what they were saying, but then Etienne called me out.

–Fine, then give it to V. I'm sure those chicks will appreciate his sensitivity. Man, you should've seen him half an hour ago, getting all misty-eyed over this dirty little whore.

And he spat on the ground here for emphasis.

With real disgust.

Little whore.

Whore, whore, whore.

A Citroen braked hard, horns blaring. The cat was a fur ball-lightning tearing down the street and I turned.

Don't get me wrong, my problem wasn't with the job.

Or the word. It was how he used it. Etienne was my friend, like a brother, in fact, but he couldn't be honest about one damn thing. He put on these displays around *me*, as if I'd ever cared if he sucked off half of Paris for any reason he pleased. When he condemned whores, I figured it was because he loved and hated himself, but only ever one or the other, and sometimes conveniently forgot that he made his shit decisions for pleasure, not profit. Now he was straight again (on all counts!), but even the new arrogance was fake. He looked me right in the eye then and seeing I had tensed up, went for blood.

    –So haha, you ever take Vivi for a Captain Save-A-Ho? But he pays for this chick, right? And he was so touched by her *vulnerability*, her sweet little track marks, that we were already outside when he realized—he'd forgotten to fuck her!

    I clenched the cigarette tight between my lips and stared at him. My hand started to shake, and Lero reached over and put his on my arm.

    –Cool down, V.

    He liked peace, but the shake wasn't anger. How could it be, when the whole thing was so plastic-wrap? Whenever Etienne got haughty, he'd proceed to systematically abuse your calm until you gave him an excuse to lose it. He wouldn't stop without a reaction.

    And I never liked cutting anyone, even when they asked me to, but he was asking *so nicely*.

    Even Lero leaned in, because I usually talked quiet.

    –What is your difficulty? I mean, what do you want me to say? Yes. She was dirty, I'm a slut and I'd tell *you* you're a cheap ex-whore who needs to get over it, but that jar's already been jizzed in. Nobody cares.

    Lero watched our train-wreck, but I figured if I was going to get stomped, I might as well hit the gas and get there quick. So I unsheathed my best look.

–What? This is what you wanted, isn't it? You wanted a fight and I'm giving you one. I swear to God, if you applied yourself even half this much to a *real* fuck, not this stupid mind shit, maybe Giselle wouldn't have to come crying to me about how...

–Crazy boy, you push too far...

–...crying to me about how you can't get her off! And then I wouldn't have to take her in, whenever you're helping Pele until morning, and console her. Not that I mind, I mean, she is very appreciative... –I pitched my voice high, –'Oh Vivi, I am just not *used* to a boy who lasts longer than five minutes...'

–Va te faire enculer!

That's what tore it. You could call him anything, bring up any past hypocrisies, and probably even piss on his mother's grave before he let you imply that you so much as breathed towards his precious girlfriend with lustful intent. He jumped up, fists drawn, telling me to get up, and Lero started to talk us down while the waiter looked panicky and finally disappeared.

–What's this, Etienne baby, you make it the real clash? Don't piss off so! This V, he fucks with you, but he no *means* it!

–Oh, I meant it. Chaque putain de mot.

It was official. I was leaving in worse shape than when I had come. Fights were Etienne's forte (which is why he liked starting them) and I was thinking there was not much to it if he wanted to take this up and that we'd get kicked out anyway soon enough, once the waiter brought his friends. Ironically, it didn't matter that we all knew I'd never even touched his girl, since besides being rich and flawless, she was also disturbingly faithful to him. What can I say, some people have all the luck.

And I asked the Brazilian who he was putting his

money on and he said, Hah, on the Etienne! Little brother, you think I bet on a crazy Balkan filho da puta? I turned back to my friend while Lero slapped my hand. Him and I were cracking up.

–You hear the names he calls me? *Balkan*, but I'm not losing it. Come on then, either hit me or let me sit back down, but don't wreck my peace any more.

We stood for a second and the color leached out of Etienne's skin. Then it came right back, but he never came closer. I knew we were right again when he started to curse a silver streak (like only he could), softly damning my DNA all the way back to my great-great-grandmother, ending in the miserable pile of genetic spooge that was myself. He finished his torrent by falling back on his chair and slapping his hands palm up against the top of his upper thighs at me in a crude suggestion of what I was welcome to perform. A pretty woman walking by with a kid saw him do it and looked at us hard. So I sucked my cigarette down to the burning end and kissed him on the lips with her still watching.

–Don't worry, I promise you will be the *very first* I let consecrate me in that fashion, should I ever grow wings.

– Little brother, I am thinking he is desiring of that *in the writing!*

Lero was cackling again, Etienne pushed me away, cursed my dirty soul, and I put out my hand and he shook it and had his satisfaction. He may have been a hotheaded prick, but he didn't hold a grudge. Then Lero told us about some party next week, we ordered another carafe of cheap red, and sitting around with them, I knew I'd lived this day many times before.

I looked up at the sky. The bright blue dome was covered by smog. Sleek people were passing by, the sun felt good and I thought, yeah. It doesn't matter who hurt who or how beautiful her dirty face is. Paris and me are done. I knew it when I was sitting back in the hotel room hearing him rail that chick and I knew it now. Leandro paid for us and took off and then Etienne started talking about his plans again. He wanted to fly off to Thailand at the end of the month. It didn't make too much sense to me, because he was finally in a good place and what would happen to the girl he was ready to kill me over, thirty minutes ago? Asking him the logic of his plans was never gratifying though. That is how he moved. Whenever things got going smooth, he did something to tear it all up. Start over. Being comfortable was like a skin rash for him. In no way could I relate. He'd been telling me about this hotel job he'd got in a fancy tourist joint on Koh Samui through some connection he had with his uncle, and he could get me one too. They were always hiring more on and with the money we'd make, life there can be real beautiful.

–We can live like kings.

He kept saying, tracing some structure in the air with his fingers and I had no idea if it was a castle or the contours of a naked girl. Maybe both. Sitting there, I thought of all those gorgeous Thai chicks pressing into him, desperate for his cash, and all the cute Thai dudes he'd fuck, breaking his own back rationalizing it to anyone who'd listen. It made me tired. *I just hope some people out there get rich off of this asshole.* Out loud, I said I'd scrape some money together for the ticket and go after him in a month, but it felt like a lie. I knew somewhere that I'd never see the tropical beaches he kept talking about or those indigo haired babes.

I wouldn't see them and I guess that was all fine.

And then one late morning that next month, he found himself at the river. This is where it started: it all began and ended at the Kamo. Of course, V couldn't know that back then. He was just a blitzed-out 23 year old waiting for his contact to get home so he could drop off his things. Kyoto was alien to him. He knew konnichiwa, sayonara, and that the cigarettes were dirt cheap.

Etienne had set up the logistics as he had promised and had even found V a friend where he could stay for the night of his layover—the only setback being that this apartment was in Kyoto, a two-hour commuter train ride from the Osaka airport.

–You can check out the city before he gets home from work, –Etienne assured him. –It's supposed to be amazing. There's some golden temple there—it's famous.

So V got off at Kyoto's main station and shoved his bag into a locker, then walked straight out into the street. He made a halfhearted stab at finding the temple Etienne had mentioned, but the flight had been very long, and now he was quite lost and uncaring. He wandered around, jet-lagged and listless, not knowing where he went up or down, and then at one point came to a bridge. From there, he saw the expanse of the Kamo for the first time and was taken by the lustrous, silver sound that turned the air. Cicadas. He couldn't remember ever hearing a sound quite like it before, though a picture of summer nights, frogs and buzzing crickets, floated into his brain.

Here, the hot summer air sweat him empty, until he could feel the weariness draining away. The clouds hung low, thick and creamy, heavy with moisture. The water looked clear and shallow and fast, and across the bank a smear of emerald reeds sprang straight from that cracked window—a flock of cranes waded in front of it, plowing the soft mud with their bills, and he was momentarily transfixed. He had never seen cranes outside of a book before. On this side of the river, the shore was pounded to a heavy, red-earth walk that looked like it stretched all along the length of the water. Maybe all the way to the sea. A paved promenade extended below and he made his way down to it—people milled here and there and he moved out of their crowd, to the edge of the water. Every girl caught his eye, they all looked so well dressed to him, but then he saw her.

She was a chubby meganekko with some sort of bizarre- looking food. The girl was sitting alone on the ground, her eyes on the birds across the shore while she ate a skewer of grape-sized balls coated in a ginger-colored, thick, translucent sauce. She nibbled at the stick with an undisguised enjoyment and V watched her eating, thinking he was hungry too. He should've changed some money at the station.

「Doushita no, oniichan? Hoshii?」

Her voice snapped him to attention. It sounded like small waters falling onto rocks. She looked at him and he froze, thinking (not quite appropriately in the moment), *Damn, the girls have nice eyes here. This chick has eyes blacker than ink.* Perhaps she had been telling him to look elsewhere; he was tired enough to only then realize he'd been openly staring. V shook his head slowly, a half-apology and to show that he didn't understand. He would learn that this did not matter.

「Sou nan ya, gaijin-san dakara, nihongo ga wakaranai ne...」

She came over to where he stood and pulling one of the balls off the stick, abruptly put it right in front of his mouth. 「'Ahhhhn' tte yutte.」 Without thinking, he opened his mouth, and she pushed the ball in.

V was genuinely taken aback. For a fraction— The

instant hummed suspended in air with her hand still paused and her eyes on his expression. An amber-colored drip quivered on the very end of her finger, and he impulsively licked it off with just the tip of his tongue. Now the girl was shocked, and she stepped back, pulling her hand away. She started laughing (no offense was taken), but he couldn't have predicted any of this.

From the look of *her*, V had expected someone reserved; from the look of *it*, he had expected something gingery in taste and mealy in texture. This was a peculiar, glutinous and chewy ball that was sticky and sweet—with a salty tang that came from the ball itself? The sauce?

The girl watched his face while he swallowed it. It was... all right and they sat back down together. She gave him another one and then simply began talking to him. The words pattered on him like warm drops of water. He had no clue what she was saying, it could have been her day thus far or an informal lecture on calculus, but he listened with such an innocent rapt attention that she kept on talking. It had been a while since someone had listened to her this intently. And certainly no one had ever looked at her like that for eating kibi dango, of all things.

Eventually, she rose and pulled her bag over her shoulder. She motioned, and V got up as well. Tentatively took a few steps after her once she started walking. He waited for a cue, a headshake, a furrowed brow, signaling she had somewhere to be, a job or a class or a date or an I am done with this, but as she only smiled, waved for him to catch up, he followed her as happily as a stray dog. They walked along the bank of the river. Crossed the bridge. Walked on streets, narrowing into alleys, past high walls swallowing courtyards and flagstone paths cut off by bamboo-woven fences. Past flittering noren covering the entrances to shops and restaurants; earth-toned, humble storefronts selling a hundred things he had never seen before. Doors to unknown places opening directly onto the un-sidewalked tiny streets and vending machines fitted into the façades of residences—shrines, miniature ones in crossroads, under roofs, some with their candles burnt dead, some burning still, with fresh flowers laid before whatever image was housed. The smell of incense blended with unrealized rain. And then Jizou; V saw his divinity as well, guarding the roadsides in clusters of rounded, vaguely humanoid stones—some had aprons, and around them were small piles of neatly stacked rocks.

A strange emotion passed through him at the sight of them, as if looking at something he should not be allowed to see, and the girl turned back. She beckoned and then pointed to the statues, cradled something in her arms, and her look became deeply sad, but then it changed to tranquility—he was still wondering when she moved ahead without him. He would have lost her in all the stoppings, the twists and turns of moss-carpeted alleys, but then a door would swing open: someone wanted to get into their home, or was leaving it. A group of kids passed on the side, or old men with chicken-thin legs scuffled off to get to the bath, and they eyed him, smiling, or curious, or suspicious, until V felt like something he hadn't in any place he'd ever been before. Conspicuous. He hurried along then, caught up to the girl, and she continued to point out things to him. She taught him the names of places. She wasn't satisfied until he pronounced them exactly right.

His head reeled.

They got to Heian Jingu, and she took him into the temple grounds, past the vermillion gate and bright green roof. He was torn by that enormous courtyard. The girl strode across it, leaving him there, and he was a speck out at sea before she came back waving two little envelopes.

She gave one to him, then opened hers: there was a small paper inside and after reading it, she thrust it into her pocket with a frown. Then she took his envelope and opened the omikuji. V watched her read the symbols until she smiled broadly at him, and taking his hand, ran him to a little tree off to the side in that huge square. Its branches bristled with white ciffets he recognized up close as a myriad of these little papers, strung up. She tied her own scrap to an open branch, and then put out her hand until he copied her and put out his as well, and she placed his little paper into his palm, closing his fingers around it and making a grasping motion.

He motioned at her wordlessly for explanation, and she squeezed his lower arm:

「Omikuji da yo.」 She made him say the word o-mi-ku-ji. 「Koko wa ne,」 she reached for his tiny paper and pointed to a specific symbol on it, 「daikichi tte kai-tearu no.」

She said the word daikichi again, and he cocked his head to the side. Her eyes sparkled, she considered a bit and then said what sounded to him like *berry rakkee*. Little did the girl know though that she wasted her breath speaking this English to V. He trawled the fading memories of a middle school education, but nothing presented itself. So he only smiled, imagining that whatever a rakkee was, it could not be anything too bad. Then he followed her to look at the pleasure gardens behind the temple.

The plants were meticulously labeled, and he inspected them all while the girl took out her phone and started taking pictures. Even her phone was enthralling. Back in Paris, he'd used a friend's clunky Nokia now and then; that had been nothing like this. He pointed, and she let him hold it. Flip it, unflip it. She showed him how to take a picture, how you could even reverse the screen to take a picture of yourself. They took one together and he thought—*wild*. Walked on and she kept snapping pictures of the flowers, of him, of everything. Little streams and ponds around them teemed with those gigantic fish. Such aggressive fish! The two stood beside a pond, and the overgrown koi crowded against them, beating against the shore, their greedy mouths opening and closing in a furious beg for food. Livelier than a pack of scaled hyenas. The girl took out the last stick of kibi dango and the fish all but crashed each other to death boiling over it. She threw them two, ate one herself, then offered him the very last one. And they kept walking and she kept chatting to him, and he took more and more covert glances from his side. She seemed tall for a Japanese girl, large, with a dimpled smile, sooty lashes, and an understated (!) that made his palms sweat. How old was she, what was her name? He didn't think French would bring him anywhere closer, but he would have liked to tell her how grateful he was for all that she'd shown him. For keeping him company. Or even, to give her something as a token of his gratitude, but she seemed so complete, so needing nothing from him and as he was contemplating, she leaned towards him and said:

「Sou nan ya. Onamae wo mada kiite nai ne. Onamae wa nan deshou ka?」

His eager, blank face made her laugh with delight.

「Honma ni nannimo shiranai yanke? O-na-ma-e. Ne-mu.」 "What is your ne-mu?" And pointing at herself, she said, 「Araki. Yutte? A-ra-ki.」

He repeated it flawlessly, and this pleased her very much. Then her groomed eyebrows arched expectantly. He got it and pointed to himself.

「V.」

A faint confusion passed her face, but she regained herself quickly and, after a moment of contemplation, delicately disgorged the sound from her mouth, as if spitting out a marble.

「Buwee.」 [5]

He smiled and gently shook his head, making her repeat it until it was right, and then she clapped her hands. He could not remember ever meeting a girl who laughed so much, and then she was giggling again, on a stream of words that flowed from her mouth like loose candy falling into a paper bag.

[5] L versus R, B versus V

「V-chan na no? Nancchuu henna namae, sore?」

He couldn't say, but she got up then and he stood with her, paled at the thought that she would leave him now. In an unusually desperate moment, he wanted to belong to this girl—she knew everything, she was so secure. But she seemed to sense his fear and brushed it away.

「Shinpai shinaide ne, V-chan. Anata wa tottemo un ga ee. Dakara atashi mo shinpai shinai yo.」 Araki grabbed his hands in translation, and he felt a warm strength come from her fingers into his. 「V wa tottemo lucky boy. Jyaa, ganbatte ne.」

Were her last words, and then she waved goodbye and left him there on the bridge. He didn't know what had hit him. From that first Araki, he got 74 minutes, one stick of kibi dango, and seven remembered words. And he sat on the bench over the pond until the garden was deserted, thinking about how he had gotten here, *here*, and what he would do now, to stay. V was a drifter by circumstance, not nature, and he never entered a city with the thought of leaving it quickly. But even settling with the best long-term intentions, he knew his own record. Eventually, the film was ripped away; his expectations were dashed, and the location and he cut ties. Now he had no expectations, not even the faintest glimmer of one, and this was a new thing.

Birds wheeled across the peach-colored sky. They

skimmed the pond and ripped things from the water. His fingers were still sticky, his lips a little too, and he thought of what Araki had said. He knew not her meaning, but the sound of her words was correct. Everything would turn itself if he just let it. Perhaps you could even say that everything was in its exact right place, where it should be, he included. He remembered the plane he would have to board tomorrow afternoon from the Osaka airport, and he smiled in the twilight and leaned back against the bench, taking in the darkening view. It was spectacular, and V thought to himself, Ahh, to hell with the plane tomorrow.

To hell with the plan, to hell with Etienne, and to hell with everything else.

FOUR

ATSUKO ADDS HER 2,000 YEN

On any given day, any of the following odors could be hanging in the air of the common room, licking around the corners:

boiled rice
rusting socks
stunted smoke
korean pickled cabbage
instant coffee
shower mold

and the signature perfume and aftershave of 24 people whose aromas all competed with each other. The boarding house was divided between long-termers, staying on a semi-permanent basis, and transient boarders who swept through the tourist seasons and were quickly gone again. It sagged in Kyoto's northern part, near the Shimogamo shrine, and was just off of the main road, close to the botanical gardens—the Kamo flowed only minutes away. Stay there and open your window and you will smell the river's life. The house itself was a loud and lively place, with a crusted yard and a rotund cat, and the ruler of this filthy little fiefdom was a kanrinin[6] with papery cheeks and a dour expression.

V and Rodrigo were long-termers: They'd shared a room in this particular house for some time. If they happened to be in, they could generally be found in the common room drinking Kirins, chain-smoking, bloviating, and watching yakuza movies, Rice Queen competition still-shots, and manic-ridiculous music videos. The

[6] Landlady

dominating smell of that particular evening was burnt mentaiko spaghetti. Rodrigo slurped an oversized instant ramen hunched over the table, one eye on a variety show. Maury, a middle-aged fellow old-timer of indeterminate origins, was tucked away in the corner, hunting the keys of the communal computer. The paper door struggled, rattled, then finally slid open, and Rodrigo looked up.

「There you are. Did you get the toilet unclogged? And just where the hell *were you* all night?」

V cleaned the empty beer cans from the table, took them to the kitchen—returned. Emptied the ashtray—came back with a wet sponge and started to wipe the table with one hand while he scrolled through programs on the remote with the other. Variety show. Salad dressing advertisement. News. Celeb talk show. *Inuyasha* (he paused). Porn (he paused longer).

A buck-toothed curvy girl cavorted in a bubble bath, giggling and smearing white foam over her brea—Rodrigo grabbed the remote, changed the channel back to variety with one click and slightly adjusted the volume down.

「So, what's the story? I waited until eight and then walked down to Yoshinoya's alone. Couldn't call you, either.」

「My phone was off. Hey so could I borrow money from you?」

Action exploded on the screen; Rodrigo turned to it and V knew he would have to wait at least another 30 seconds for his friend's returned attention and response. He scrubbed vigorously at a badge of fluorescent sauce that had burned itself straight into the surface. The bright sound of commercials blew from the box, and Rodrigo was back.

「Okay, okay. So, you completely blow me off for dinner after we'd agreed to meet, are three hours late, and now you want to BORROW money? Didn't you get paid today? Maury, do you hear this guy?」

「You will make a wonderful stepfather one day. Also, I may have gotten paid and it may be all gone.」

「Nandeyanen.」 Rodrigo's already large brown eyes bulged even more conspicuously from his underfed skull. He was not an unattractive young man (though much too thin and anemically pale), and at this time, his dark unruly hair was threatening to take on mop-like proportions. Now he grasped a handful of it as if to tear it out of his head. 「Do you hear this, Maury-san? Listen, the money is yours if you go do the toilet—and tell me what was important enough to blow me off.」

Rodrigo spoke the best Japanese of them all: After two years, as casually as any man. His grammar was solid; he didn't indulge diphthongs or overt formality, the few pitfalls the foreigners who managed to get ahold of the language inevitably tumbled into. A decidedly un-Japanese bent for crudeness was his only flaw, and all lacking pejoratives he imported from his other languages with startling creativity. His English was passable but deficient, so he spent his days roaming the streets, looking for anyone who might be interested in picking up Spanish or his native Portuguese. The takers were few, as evinced by his threadbare shirts. V's Japanese was much less polished, and his faintly obscene yet feminine style was an endlessly renewable source of hilarity for Rodrigo. His English however was criminal, when it was understood at all. The boarding house had no official language though, so the common room was a New Babel of people speaking broken street Japanese, English, French, Spanish, with the tourists often struggling to understand each other.

V returned the sponge and cleaner to their proper place out in the hall closet, came back in. Sat down.

「Well, you know that one building down past Sanjou, with the dancing girls?—」

「Wait, how literal is the word 'girl' here? Maury,」 Rodrigo waved almost hysterically to the face bathed in the refresh glow of Hotmail, 「you should start listening, this will probably get good. Anyway, what are you doing chasing dancing girls? I thought you were hung up on— don't tell me, I got it...」

「I never told you her name, but no, I haven't heard from her all week.」

「So speak plain, man! You mean you fucked it up!」

「You see though, I don't think I did.」

「Oh, you don't *think*.」 Rodrigo snorted. 「There's your first mistake. And? Your theory is?」

「There is no theory. She got what she wanted out of it and decided she's had enough. And I say: Good for her— I admire a clean break.」

「'She got what she wanted out of it.'」 Rodrigo clutched at his own chest in a theatrical gesture. 「What's frightening is that I think you may actually *believe* yourself. Omee, do you have any idea how girls work? No, don't speak! I don't mean *there*, but here.」 And he tapped his head with his right hand and his heart with his left, but the other only smoked disdainfully.

「I know what I need to know.」

「Yeah—fuck all. Hence the state you're currently in. Have you ever seriously considered getting a *girlfriend?*」

「I've considered getting rid of a few.」

「No, no. You see, Vicchan, this thing I speak of called a 'girlfriend' is a woman who agrees to see you more than once. And sometimes, you may even find yourselves wanting to—*speak*. With your clothes on.」

「Sounds modern.」

「Doesn't it though? But it gets better, because when

you're very lucky, she may even give a flying fuck about your stunning personality— Now,」 his cigarette slashed the air scornfully, 「these girls you are currently seeing, they are not true girlfriends. All they want from you is— 」

The patched door swung open, devouring his words in its creak, and their landlady's parched face appeared through the opening.

「Good evening, Rodrigo-kun. V-kun. I hate to ruin the party, but I'll have to ask you to lower your tone. It's past ten and there are some tired guests who want their rest but don't want to hear your sordid details. I'm sure Maury-san could live without them as well.」 She glanced toward the computer corner and made a pecking bow, and the older man bowed back at her.

「Oh but Sachiko-san,」 Rodrigo protested. 「You interrupt the best part! I was just about to tell this lost soul why he can't get a girlfriend.」

The kanrinin pressed her sunken lips together and smiled, leaned against the door. A bronzy lady who imploded, not expanded, with age, she took in the room with the desiccated glance of one who had seen it all repeatedly and never minded seeing it again. The tenants cycled through her like so many reincarnations, and she watched them year after year, as indifferent as an icon does the pilgrims who march past it. Only rarely did they engage her with their human affairs. Now her heavily penciled brow went up ironically, and her voice was as dry as an oracle's.

「I thought that was obvious. Our V-kun can't get a girlfriend because girls only want his hard—*communism*.」 Snickers all around. 「Boys, you entertain me, as always, but I need your rent under my door by the end of tomorrow. No later than the day after tomorrow. You're late again.」

Rodrigo bowed his head and expelled his excuse somewhere near her sandaled feet. V's apology was as courteous as a college girl's. Sachiko pushed her glasses further up on her face and gave him a full stare before training her eyes back on Rodrigo.

「Rodrigo-kun.」

「Yes ma'am.」

「Please teach this man how to speak like one. Also, did you take a look at the toilet? I don't know how many more laminated signs I could possibly put up there.」

「V's got it. Will get it. You know, I don't quite got his gentle touch...」

「He does have a way with that upstairs toilet. But you both still owe me rent. Don't forget. And keep it down.」

The door closed again, and Rodrigo's grin split his head.

「Toilet, language lesson, you heard the lady. But first, I want to hear more about *your* lady. V, tell me, *tell me*, she was a hot little OL.」 [7]

「She was a hot little OL.」

「You're a terrible liar, so... A co-ed?」

「Well, D— does have a college sector, right?」

Rodrigo sunk into his chair and buried his face in his hands.

「My dear V. I thought you can't even *see* a woman under forty?」

「Generally yes. That is the plan.」

「And it's a good plan, so why the hell are you diverting from it? This isn't the time to rock the boat! An OL would do you fine. A college chick? Ehhh, but a joshikousei? You may as well dig a fucking grave outside of Sachiko-san's window and crawl in. You can kiss your soul and your wallet goodbye. Tomorrow's tabehoudai says she wanted 'dinner, karaoke, and the rabuho.' And then you went into

[7] Office lady

one of those ridiculous picture booths, so she can show her friends in school tomorrow how she nailed her very own bargain-bin Burapi!—」 [8]

「...I need 2,000 yen. Do you have it, yes or no?」

The door opened again. A whoosh of smoke and funk was swept away in the vacuum and replaced by the musty hall air and the clean scent of lightly fruity lotion. A short and shapely girl walked in with it, and she marched over and opened the windows wider, herding the stink of the room out with both hands.

[8] aka Brad Pitt

「Hi everyone.」

「Do you need to use the internet, Acchan?」 Maury turned to her and she waved.

「I wanted to check something, but I can do it tomorrow if you're not done...」

Atsuko, also known as Acchan, was one of the few other long-term boarders. She was a graduate student at Doushisha University and staying at the boarding house to save on rent. Her talk was straight, her skin was glowing, and her—well, it was no house secret that bedding her remained one of V's unattainable dreams.

「No porn running?」 She smiled at them sweetly. 「What's the occasion?」

Rodrigo's mouth bent.

「Too busy discussing V's newest sweetheart.」

「Breaking another poor obasan's heart?」

「More like a joshikousei's.」

Rodrigo leered, V frowned, Atsuko turned to the other boy derisively before throwing herself into a chair by the table. He watched her well-proportioned flesh bounce into place with an unveiled interest.

「I thought you couldn't see a woman under forty?」

「That's exactly what I said!」

「I don't know,」 V said smoothly. 「I'm seeing you just fine.」

「Ugh, don't remind me.」 Acchan paused. 「My sister's in high school. Reminding her tonight to stay away from dirty old men like you.」

He arched an eyebrow, not missing a beat.

「I just hope you're not too late. Because now that you mention it, this girl reminded me of a younger you—but as you know, I'm always about going older so maybe—」 She cut him off with a hard kick under the table, but it was impossible to take him seriously or imagine this was anything more than another round of their blustering. Acchan pointedly took one of his cigarettes and lit it.

「Where's a guillotine when you need one? Isn't that how your people punish those who overreach?」

「It isn't, because I'm not French. But *you* can come cut off my head any day you want...」

「Which head though, huh? Careful Vicchan, she might be reaching for the old girochinchin.」

Across the room, Maury's shoulders betrayed the slightest amused shake and Acchan pinched her lips. Her voice was cheerful and decisive:

「You are an incorrigible pig on a straight road to hell. So don't come crying later when it all falls down on your head, or say that nobody cared enough to warn you.」

Taking the cigarette directly from her mouth, he dragged, then passed it back.

「I don't think that's quite up to you to decide, who is going to hell and who isn't. But your concern is touching. In fact—」 He pretended to think. 「I think *you* may be exactly who I need to get myself off this path of sin. I'd be so good for you, so why don't you come save me?」

Atsuko enunciated each word with relish.

「*Because you're not worth it.* And I have a boyfriend. But even if I didn't, you wouldn't have a snowball's chance. This will come as a shock, but not every girl is dying to go to bed with you. Not by a long shot.」

His half smile was half too much.

「I don't need every. *I get enough.*」

Acchan laughed herself into a coughing fit.

「Seriously, your ego! What on earth have you been feeding it?」

V opened his mouth; Rodrigo was faster.

「Illicit high school poon. Ergo, he's broke. Again.」

「All right. I'll bite. Are you serious?」

「You thought I was kidding, before?」

「Ok.」 Acchan leaned in closer now and rested her cigarette against the table's battered edge. 「I thought this was a bunch of common room bull. You think this is funny, Rodrigo-kun? I don't expect *anything* from V, but you?」

And Rodrigo, who was one of those young men who talked differently when he was only with other men, as opposed to when women were also around (but never consciously THOUGHT of himself as the type of man who talked differently when he was only with other men, as opposed to when women were also around) felt an abrupt swirl of cold air come in around him. Looking now at Acchan's earnest face, a spot of guilt pricked the base of his spine. He glanced over at V, whose face stayed carefully expressionless. His details earlier had been vague—

「You both think this is a joke? Molesting little girls?」

The question made V lower his head, out of contrition or embarrassment, neither could tell, but Rodrigo surged up then.

「Really, Acchan. *Little* girls? Come on now! The high school girls here have grown men eating out of the palms of their hands. They're not kids, they're BRUTAL.」

「I have no idea how high school girls are here as opposed to other places,」 she said frostily. 「But I'm sure they're not much different. And I had zero adults eating out of my palm back then, thank you very much.」

「Now you sound bitter.」

「Why are you defending this, Rodrigo-kun? I've never understood why some men defend *so passionately* their 'right' to slobber over young, immature girls. It's so disgusting. You're not even the one who did it, so why defend it? Or wait, are you wishing it was you?」

「EVERYONE slobbers over these girls! They're goddamn royalty, and they know it, and they eat it up!」

「If they do, it's because they don't know any better.」

「I don't get what you're getting so worked up about. How old do you have to be here? Thirteen? Come on V, she wasn't younger than that, right? Because there is the line where we can't be friends anymore.」

V flicked off the tip of his cigarette and flicked him the bird, and Rodrigo made a sweeping motion.

「See? It's not like he broke the law.」

And now Atsuko slapped the table. Her passion surprised all three of them, herself most of all:

「Nobody is talking about 'the law'! The law was written by sukebe old men too, not to mention, something can still be wrong, even if it's not against the law!」

「But why though? What is so wrong about it? Maybe it was even good for her. Have you considered that?」

「You cannot mean that right now.」

「Listen, Acchan,」 Rodrigo knitted his dense brows and leaned closer over the table. His voice lowered three ticks, from almost shouting, to purely loud. 「When I was fourteen, there was this lady who lived alone in the apartment unit below us. Back in Lisbon. And she looked good, but she was definitely over thirty. Her husband had died years back in some freak accident and she never remarried. So I was looking to make some money during summer break, and the woman told my mother she'd pay me to do odd jobs and errands for her, if that was okay. I'd get called down to her apartment several times a month. She was the one who would call our apartment and tell my mother to send me down, so she always knew exactly when I was going to show up. And I kid you not, every damn time she answered the door, her outfit was like, some intro to a porno. A low cut shirt, with tiny shorts. A bikini. Once, she wore a bathrobe open, with just underwear underneath. She knew that she'd have to be opening the door for me, and she always did it dressed like that. Sometimes, she would invite me in.」

「Maybe that's just how she was. It doesn't have to mean that—」

「Now YOU be serious. Would you be saying that, if it was a girl visiting a grown man's house, and he's answering the door in a thong?」

「...」

「That's what I thought. Once, she even asked if I wanted to have some wine with her. She was wearing a nightgown at three in the afternoon. I wasn't totally clueless. I knew what was going on, but I didn't dare act on any of it. So I always turned her down. She ended up moving suddenly, and it was a while until I told someone about the whole thing and they were like, you idiot, she so very clearly wanted to BANG you. Why didn't you go for it? And I thought, well damn! If I'd played my cards right, I could've lost my virginity!」

「And that would have been important why, exactly?」

「Because my confidence was in the total pits all through school! For years afterwards, I kept thinking, if only I'd done it, I might not have been so awkward. It's not always a bad thing, you know? Having an older person— initiate you in.」

「You can't know that.」 Acchan set her jaw. 「You're thinking back on it as an adult. But since it didn't actually

51

happen, you can't know how you would have reacted— I can't say how it would have affected me either. I was never in such a position. But since you told a story, I'll tell one too. I had a friend back in middle school. Not that you'll meet her anyway, but I'll call her Mio. Mio-chan. She was a sweet, shy girl, but a bit of a shadow. I remember, she had an older brother who was a star athlete. Her parents were preoccupied with him. Meanwhile, Mio-chan was aiming for a prestigious high school, but her grades in math were lacking, so they hired her a private tutor from the university. I saw him a few times at her house after class. He didn't strike me as anything extraordinary, but Mio-chan thought he was the absolute best; insisted he was just her type. Back then, I didn't really get it, but now it makes sense. She was ignored by her parents and he was coming to visit her, and only her, twice a week.

Mio-chan began to tell us that she was sure he liked her too. I remember, it was hard for me to imagine being excited by this. A few of my friends were so into the thought of a guy in high school, or even college, but to my middle-school self, a nineteen or twenty-year-old was ancient. Another friend of ours thought it was glamorous though and kept encouraging her to see if he would go out with her outside of a lesson. Like you, Rodrigo-kun, she said she didn't dare act on it.

Finally, she had her placement test and scored high enough to get into her target school. The tutor treated her to a dinner, to celebrate her progress and acceptance. Afterwards, he gave her a ride home and before she got out of the car, he kissed her—her first kiss. She told us the next day, all flustered and confused. Surely this meant something between them now? But after that, he just disappeared. The job was over, she didn't need more tutoring, but none of this made her more powerful or confident. My

friends told her what you are saying, Rodrigo-kun. That
she should stop moping and see it as a fun memory. A cute,
older guy had liked her enough to kiss! Mio-chan couldn't
see it that way though. She felt cheated and used.

Back then, I didn't know what to say to her and we
ended up losing touch anyway. But now it seems so
obvious that what he did was wrong. And he was old
enough to know.⌋

Rodrigo scoffed, ⌈Acting like he was forty!⌋

⌈Older than fourteen, that's for sure.⌋

⌈Well, once, when I was fourteen, I—⌋ V's soft voice
broke for the first time in ten minutes, and Acchan exas-
peratedly shushed him back to silence.

⌈Nobody cares what *you* did when you were fourteen,
because you? Are not normal. This is a conversation
between *people who are normal!*⌋

The door creaked open once more, she froze mid-
breath, and the kanrinin's ordinarily blank countenance
definitively had an expression etched onto it at that
moment—it was annoyance. She cleared her throat briskly.

⌈Atsuko-san? You too? I already had to tell the boys to
keep it down. We have some tired guests with a small child
in room three; they came to me to complain. If you want
to have a rousing debate, please do us all a favor and take
it to a bar—! You're all adults here. You should know
better. Good NIGHT.⌋

She pulled the door shut with a decisive snap, and for
a few moments, there was no sound at all, save the quiet
click-clack of Maury's mouse and the dull mmmm of the
dim overhead light. Acchan looked over at Rodrigo, V
looked over at Acchan—all three of them hung in the awkward plume, like kids getting reprimanded during a sleep
over. Acchan grabbed the tail-end of their thread one last
time, before it dissipated into nervous laughter.

「Like she said. It doesn't matter. Whatever the girl said or did, *you're the adult,* V. You should know better.」

Rodrigo lit a new cigarette, forgetting he hadn't finished his last one. He was having difficulty containing his mirth.

「But Acchan, can you unironically call V an adult? He's a man-shaped NUMPTY. We can go back and forth about this from dawn to dusk, but some guys are pigs taking what they can get, and some girls are into tempting the devil, and as far as that goes, he's probably the least harmless in that regard. I mean, he's definitely not a devil and more a piglette than a pig. Right, Vicchan? Oi!」

V had started looking icy—and now also, self-righteous.

「I didn't even say how old she was. I didn't even say what we did or did not do. I asked Rodrigo to lend me 2000 yen and it spawns a twenty-minute dissection of all the flaws I have, and all the flaws I don't have, between two people who I thought were my *friends.*」

He sniffled dramatically and Rodrigo snorted.

「Don't you make yourself the victim here when I was on your side! Wasn't I on his side, Acchan?」

「You were. Disappointingly so.」

「So can I borrow the money or not?」

「Kimatten yan! Ttaku. My wallet's back in the room. I'll give it to you before bed.」

「Thank you. That's all that I wanted.」

Acchan got up, brushed crumbs that didn't exist off her lap. Started to pull something from her pants pocket. In the far corner of the room, Maury turned and pinched the glasses on his beaked nose, and she waved at him.

「It's nothing that can't wait. I'll get to it tomorrow, but I need to go to bed now.」

「All right, then. Good night, Acchan.」

「Good night, Maury-san. Good night, Rodrigo-kun. Good night—V—can we break the fourth wall? For one second?」

He looked up with a raised eyebrow. She threw two bank notes at him, and they glanced off of his arm.

「On the off chance that I can appeal to your *decency*. This is my own contribution to your plight. I figure a lot of your act is—an act. But if it's not, buy yourself a mag, let off some steam and stay the hell away from little girls. I mean it. You can pay me back at the end of the week, when you get paid.」

Rodrigo was whooping.

「Dear god, how are you ALWAYS this lucky?! Looks like you're taking ME out for lunch tomorrow. Don't forget who got you this windfall. You owe me, again. And Acchan, you remain an angel too good for this world!」

「Don't I know it.」

Atsuko left the room, closed the door quietly behind her and started to walk down the dark hall, towards the stairs. By the time she reached the second floor, she was shaking her head. Had she really wasted a precious thirty minutes of pre-sleep note-reviewing trying to *morally improve* those nitwits? Though loath to admit it, she genuinely liked V. He was amusing (if exasperating) company, and under that carapace of sarcasm, Rodrigo was sincere and kind. Each nice to look at, in their own way. But still, a silly *yarichin* and a sidekick egging on the worst impulses he didn't dare indulge himself. Beyond a harmless laugh or a pre-sleep chat, best to give them both a wide berth, so what had compelled her to spend this time—trying to ignite a conscience?

Brushing her teeth in the upstairs bathroom, Acchan

met her own eyes in the mirror. Her thoughts went back to Mio-chan. There had never been a Mio. But there had been confusion. Shame. Tears and more tears. Acchan imagined, it wasn't much, so far as heartaches go. She'd had girl friends go through much worse. It barely made for a rowdy common room tale, and it made her wonder, if she simply was more sensitive? For a moment, she was ashamed of having given those two her sincerity, but then she flicked a last minty spray off of her toothbrush with a sharp snap. No. Let them think she was a scold or a bore; she was also *right* and for all his talk, she couldn't imagine that Rodrigo inside was much more different. And V's insides she had no desire to decipher.

It was easy to deflect his ardor towards her as nothing more than his version of a mindless *keitai* game you plugged away at on a long commute. Compulsive addiction to the little burst of endorphins released when you unlocked a new level or uncovered a new prize, yet each level ultimately only ever some version of all the previous ones. She saw that clearly; would she have seen it in high school?— If there really was some young girl out there getting mixed up with V, Atsuko's heart went out to her. But she knew it was not her business and that there was absolutely nothing she could do about it.

...The last thing she did before finally falling asleep was grab her phone and text her little sister.

I moved my schedule around, so it looks like I'm riding the train back for the weekend. I'll make it to your meet. Afterwards, we can get shuu-creams and maybe go on a run? I'll pack my running shoes. ...Oh. You're still awake? I hope I didn't wake you up.

Down in the common room, the variety show continued to flash on screen. A contestant in a counting game had used the wrong counter for 36 baby chicks and a flock of sumo wrestlers charged out from backstage to pound and throw him down in a circle of revving motorcycles. The audience guffawed, the motorcycles kept revving. Rodrigo guffawed along; shoved a dusty rice-cracker into his mouth and, as far as he was concerned, the topic was over. V smoked another cigarette, attended to that upstairs toilet, then went to bed. Only Maury hummed portentously behind the glare of the computer screen.

FIVE
....

THE FIRST POST-OP

V didn't let his friends' conversation disturb him too much. Though it seemed unlikely, he figured if his one evening with Aya *had* sown the future seed of some grave psychic rot in her, there was nothing to be done about it now. And he wasn't overly concerned regards further infractions, being 97.86% certain he wouldn't hear from her again anyway. He'd told himself, she already knew all about him that she had wanted to know.

But as fortune or an impulsive one-line text-message from her would have it, V did see Aya again, and much sooner than he had anticipated. They agreed to meet at the sprawling riverside Sanjou Sutaba five days later. This was the (sometimes) obligatory damage control date whose convention Rodrigo had laughingly styled ⌜the post-op⌟. Shots had been fired across the bow and now came the time for questions. By habit, V generally went for girls who were fast and unapologetic exactly to avoid this embarrassed post-sex eyeballing, but he still occasionally had someone wish to see if her split decision to sleep with him had demonstrated a devastating lack of judgment. He always honored these meetings, but his insolence was meted in direct proportion to his own regret.

When he saw Aya in the window waiting for him, he knew though that there was no regret with this girl and never would be. He squeezed his eyes shut, trying to dredge up Atsuko's disappointment, her bewilderment, her fire, her anger, on behalf of wronged young girls and women everywhere. He wanted to feel regret, shame, hell, even taboo. But then he opened his eyes, and Aya caught his look across the crowd. She seemed so crisp and clear and unregretful too. *Arara,* he thought, happily beaten. He asked her what she wanted (croissant), which she picked at, while he drank black coffee; and he expected awkwardness despite her obvious happiness at meeting again, but other than her dogged insistence on addressing him formally, she drew him right into her life. Aya had no reservations. Now they had stalled on a definite dislike.

「Ugh, I can't stand English sometimes! It's just too horrible! All those phony greetings people use. They're nonsensical. Like... 'What is up?' What do I answer to that? I feel so pressured! And what if I'm not having an interesting day, what if there is nothing that 'is up'? This English speaker would think I was boring, so now I have to lie, just to answer a stupid greeting! Did you have to learn English in your country?」

「Yes. I think you have to learn it everywhere now. But I was very bad at it and never got anywhere.」 Her complaining engaged him; like they were old friends and not two effective strangers in an awkward position.

「Yeah,」 she continued, 「but you would not have to learn it if you came here. Is that why you're here then, to escape English?」

Absently, he unwound a bandage off her abandoned croissant.

「No.」

「Well why then? I want to know. And I want to know why you speak Japanese so well...」

V shrugged. If a foreigner mastered a phrase beyond 「Good morning」 people flattered them as a language prodigy and assumed there was a grand purpose behind this obvious linguistic masochism. But the truth was, it eventually had simply *happened.* Recounting the beds he had hopped through to get to his present level of vocabulary, grammar, and syntax seemed uncouth—

「We're in Japan.」 He nudged her playfully. 「What would you have me speak?」

「But you don't talk like a gaijin.」

「Because I talk like a girl.」

「Yes, but no. I think... you don't talk like anyone I've ever heard before.」 Across from her, he couldn't say if that was good or bad and settled for feeling special. 「But really though, I thought all foreigners speak English.」

「No, not necessarily. But I speak some, or at least as much as you. *I am a pen.*」 [9]

That made her giggle.

「Well, I know a lot more than that. I may hate it, but I'm actually pretty good at English. I need a new tutor though, the one I have now is moving soon. It's really too bad you don't speak it; then I could hire you.」

「Unfortunately, I could teach you a lot of things, but English is not one of them.」

「All right. But if you're not an English teacher, or a student, then what are you doing in Kyoto?」

For as many times as he could remember, V fervently wished that he could exile those last six words from the Japanese language. For in doing so, he was sure he could secure his true and complete happiness: Living in a world that demanded no explanation of his motivations. He looked at Aya's sincere, lightly made-up face (she had worn no makeup when they first met, so V readily and a little presumptuously assumed she was trying for him) and he sparkled:

「I'm living.」

「Yes, but doing what? There must be something you do here, *for* a living. What did you come here to do?」

Ahh yes, he thought, the One Question. Girls always

[9] Urban legend has it that this absurd, iconic sentence used to be the first (and often only) phrase to come to the minds and mouths of locals flustered into speaking English.

seemed curious regarding the trajectory of his life, even if V couldn't make one out. Other people's he could see clearly; flying high or low, striking their aim, or at least attempting before being pushed out of the sky by a gust of wind, or by a stronger projectile hurtling a contradictory way, but to himself, V never seemed to be flying, not even hurtling or falling. Perhaps getting passed from hand to hand? Waiting for the day when he was passed no further.

Thinking on that, he saw Aya's brow furrow across from him and he was suddenly shamed by his refusal to let the topic evolve beyond senseless second-date conversation. She was trying to understand him, really, so he breathed in.

「I'll have to disappoint you, because it's nothing particularly decent or complex. I came to Kyoto by complete accident. I didn't *come here* to do anything, and now I'm just waiting for a beautiful woman to marry me so that I can spend the rest of my life eating Yoshinoya with her.」 Aya's eyebrows ran up and he frowned. 「I'm sorry. I warned you that it was boring. But I'm very simple. We'll live in a haunted, drafty machiya[10] and if I'm very lucky, she's the type who doesn't squeeze too tightly when she sits behind you on a bike.」

「What if she wants to drive and *you* sit in the back?」

「That's fine too. I don't squeeze too tight either.」

She took a sip of his coffee (and grimaced. No sugar). And then her grimace slowly shifted into a smile; small and warm, and a little bit pinched.

「That all sounds very nice I suppose, but what would you do for money? You know, your work?」

「Of course. I have to have money somehow, don't I? You know, Aya-chan, with other girls, I tell them all these lies about what I want to do for work. My *ambitions.*」 He said the word as if it was a particularly pathetic expression.

[10] Traditional Kyoto townhouse.

⌜But I won't lie to you because we won't meet again after this. So it doesn't really matter if you respect me. ...All that noise men make about work, it's a leftover from the times when we were hiding out in caves. The men went hunting and the women stayed home, because the men were more disposable.⌟

⌜Disposable?⌟ she echoed.

⌜Yes. If too many women die, a community cannot go on, right? So women had to stay back from hunting, and war. They were too precious to lose. But after a while, the story twisted to be that they stayed back because they are weaker than men. So it went on and on and by now, men pretend like they forgot how this all started, and still act all important going out to work every morning, but I'll tell you honestly, I hate to go to work. It has never made me feel important. I feel more important cleaning my room than I ever did at any job.⌟

Aya opened her mouth. Her lips twitched, closed again, and he laughed.

⌜You want to tell me that's not very manly.⌟

⌜No, I— ⌟ She blushed.

⌜It's okay. I've heard it often enough. My father always said growing up that I'm like a woman, and what if I am? I figure, if I'm a little more like a woman, there must be a woman out there who's a little more like a man. She wants to have a career. It makes her feel important—that sounds great. I'll keep the home for her. Someone has to do that, no? She'll bring the money, and I'll keep the house clean, and iron her power suits, and massage her feet every night, and give her a houseful of beautiful kids.⌟

His answer left Aya visibly breathless. She sifted through the blasphemies and settled on the last one.

⌜*You*—actually—*want* a lot of kids?⌟

⌜Yes. I always have. As far back as I can remember.

...Don't you think I would have pretty children? I think so. But everything's so expensive. So we'll probably stick to one.⌋

He was rarely serious, with anyone. That was a rule and not an exception, but for this one time, a serene intensity settled on his face, and Aya was jarred by it. His random trust moved her, but gave no clue on how to proceed. She blurted the first thing that came to her head.

⌈I think you're the strangest person I've ever met. ...Or are you normal for your country?⌋

V watched her mouth purse into a bewildered little line, and he didn't want to think in that direction just then, but it was precisely the blatant lack of any sex that made it somehow inversely erotic to him. He could almost see the row of chewed-up pencils in her bag, the victims of her mouth's past consternation. He wanted to hold her close, to kiss that line, but he knew the rules and what was allowed and proper. So he leaned his chair back against the wall, with just one corner of lip curled into a smile.

⌈No. I'm not. That's why I had to run away from there. I've gone all over the world, I couldn't tell you all the places I've been, and here I am now, wanting a beautiful girl as strange as myself. And what about you, Aya-chan?⌋

⌈I'm not sure what I'll want to do once I've finished school, but I'll want something more exciting than a roachy old machiya. Definitely would not have left Paris to move *here*.⌋

⌈There's roaches in Paris too, and the trains smell awful there.⌋

⌈You can't pick a city on how good the trains smell.⌋

⌈I can and I will. The beauty of the people and the smell of the trains, and as far as I'm concerned, Kyoto is as good as it gets, and I'm ready to live here forever.⌋

Aya groaned, the long, drawn-out noise of the victim

of an awful stomach cramp. ⌜That's exactly what I get so sick of! The foreverness of it all. Of course you would say that. You're a foreigner. A man. Everyone treats you different. Even if you decide to come live in a cage, the cage treats you different. And if you ever get tired of it, you can leave.⌋

⌜Yes, you're right. There's an advantage to being me. But there is an advantage to being you.[11] Have you ever considered moving away? Maybe when you're done with school, if you dislike it here so much.⌋

Aya chewed her lip.

⌜But if I ever moved anywhere else, I'd be the foreigner. And I wouldn't want that. I complain about this place, but I also can't imagine living anywhere else. Kind of sad, no? Who knows. Maybe I'll move to Osaka after high school. But I would love to see Paris sometime. Not move there, but see it. You know what's funny though? Ever since I was little and we went to the jinja by our house for New Year's, I never asked for better grades or anything useful, but to go to Paris once. I would've never believed I would meet someone one day who'd run away from the place I want to go to so much. It's so strange to me, to prefer this cage.⌋

⌜Is that wrong?⌋

⌜To like cages?⌋

V shrugged. ⌜*I like them if they're gold.* But it's all relative, don't you think? There's only what we're used to. All I know is, I finally feel like I belong somewhere. It's a start, no?⌋

She played with crumbs in silence. And he fell into quiet as well, feeling he couldn't have explained it satisfactorily anyway. Nor wished to.[12] Drives can be such shadowy, synthetic things. He didn't seek to understand why certain people, places, sounds, smells, could fill you with a yearning for something that couldn't be sated, ever,

[11] Though as far as leaving whenever he wanted was concerned, V had lost his passport two living arrangements back. He preferred to think of this predicament as little as possible.

and the knowledge that it couldn't was what made him desire it. The urge to touch her flared again; it was the purest form of communication he knew, so he immolated himself in smoke instead. Half a minute passed; his phone flashed. V snapped it open.

His eyes flickered over the message, and he stood abruptly.

「You're going,」 she said.

「Yes. I must. My friend is asking me to pick something up for him.」

「Can't you say you're busy?」

「I owe him a favor. Anyway, I have work soon.」

「Aha, so you *do* work.」

「Once in a while, even I can't avoid it.」

「Can I know what you do?」

He sighed.

「I teach French.」

「Oh. ...So then, a French teacher. So fancy!」

「Hardly. I'm just a tutor, really.」

「My mother actually speaks French and English. She's a complete language nerd.」

「She is? But not her daughter?」

「It's kind of funny how opposite she and I are in that respect. Well, a lot of respects. But yeah, she even taught for a while. Before she got married.」

「Well if she's ever looking for a conversation group, please let me know. I never have enough work. And my languages aren't exactly the most popular...」

「She already has one arranged. But if I ever hear her say anything, I'll let you know.」

「That's nice of you, Aya-chan. And now I really should go.」

「But before you do, when will I see you again?」

「Let's not make a date.」

[12] There was only a tenuous connection in V's mind between money and hard work; the partial vestige of growing up in a system where financial success and corruption had tasted exactly the same. There was no connection in his mind between his presence and the course of Aya's life changing irretrievably, but then again, when are we ever aware of how much our insignificant presence has the power to make another life ripple this way or that? In the moment, sitting across from Aya, all her face made him briefly consider was how different their freedoms were, or maybe, that they were both blessed and unfree in a similar way. His relationship to her was already building on a misunderstanding of

65

what he imagined she wanted. An abstraction of foreignity; a door briefly opened to the unknown, and then quickly shut again. This manifested as a single thought in his head: 「She's getting it out of her system.」

And he couldn't say what that meant to him or to her, it only made him imagine that they waited for some form of the same thing:

Conventional, domestic salvation.

「Why not? Don't you like talking to me? I like talking to you.」

「I don't like talking to you.」 He watched her stiffen and his fingertips tingled again. 「I love talking to you, ojousan. But it doesn't matter what I like. I'm broke, you see. I can't take you out. I can't take you to a hotel, or buy you dinner, or clothes or anything else, for that matter.」

「I'm not asking you to buy me things.」

「Maybe not. But a girl like you spending time with a man who doesn't buy you things is plain bad luck. It upsets an important balance in the universe.」

「I don't know why you think you don't give good advice...」

And V lit a cigarette and sat back down despite himself.

「Can I have a drag?」 she asked him.

「No.」

「Please?」

He took the cigarette from his mouth and held it in front of her lips. 「One drag. A small one,」 he commanded and Aya dragged.

He took it back.

「I have a good friend here. He says that when you start seeing a girl with your clothes on, she becomes your girlfriend. What do you think, ojousan?」

「I could be your girlfriend.」

「But you're already taken.」

「A foreigner doesn't count.」

Used to being the resident pisser, it was maddening and a little thrilling to find himself occasionally completely unsure of whether she was taking the piss out of him right back. He frowned.

「That's—*convenient*. But there's an even bigger problem.」

「And what is that?」

「I'm too old for you.」

「Well, how old are you?」

「Hi-mi-tsu.」

「...Do you have a girlfriend right now?」

「One?」 A scoff. 「I have at least six. Possibly more.」

「Honma ni? You know, that is a little bit much.」

「I think so too. You don't want to be Number Seven. Not to mention, there is a girl at my boarding house who would be very disappointed if I saw you again.」

It was Aya's turn to frown.

「I guess she... is interested in you.」

「Haha! She would rather die, honestly, but she wants me to be a better person. And since she's a friend I admire, I've been thinking, maybe she's right.」

「So she's a friend. And you talk with your clothes on. That's another option for us, right? Being friends.」

「But she and I have never.」 He raised an eyebrow, and Aya reddened. 「It works fine enough one way, but it never works going backwards.」

「It could work. Why would it not work? We got that out, so we can do other things now. I'm so busy anyway with school, it wouldn't be often. You don't have to worry about that. But we could meet by the river when I have my lesson down here, or I could come see where you live sometime?」

「Umu, that's starting to sound girlfriend-y again. Anyway, I would hate for you to see where I live. No, no, leaving it at this would be the best. Don't be sad, I'm just trying to do what's best.」

She shrugged her shoulders, stilled her face, and he saw it then again.

The proud countenance of a prince.

Aya painted something with her fingertip through the

crumbs on the table. Concentrating like she was tracing out a love spell. Or a curse. Then she stood.

「Kyoto's small, so we'll probably run into each other anyway. Sooner or later. That's another thing I hate about this city. But if you say you don't want to meet again, suit yourself. I'm certainly not going to beg you. I guess I'll go then. Don't get up.」

He did anyway; she had pushed her chair back so abruptly, it almost fell over, and he grabbed the back of it before it clattered all over the floor. That's when he saw her planner. It had slid off the seat softly and lay on the floor, slightly under the table.

V bent over to pick it up.

He walked towards the front door, but Aya was nowhere to be seen.

SIX

THE WATER TRADE

R odrigo was right. V did owe him, but he the other as well, for that was the symbiosis the two young men lived in—they had nothing in common except trivial likes, but what a cement triviality could be—a love for this land of maid cafés, this home of *Nausicaä*; a city of kinetic-jello unidentifiable cocktails slung in 'American' bars, chatting up doe-eyed Japanese girls in cowboy hats with spray-on jeans tight in all the right places; boot-scootin' boogieing and electric sliding until the wee hours; ringing in the New Year with hot sake; matsuri in the kiln-hot summer with girls paler than orchids in their festive yukata; rambling morning, noon and in the middle of the night through lit up streets; and the frenetic, dead-end window-shopping sprees glitzed with unaffordable and affordable luxuries, in department stores creamed with the best service the world had to offer—the customer is always right, was an idiom Rodrigo had learned once long ago while studying English. Here the smiling girls who served them glided in a different dimension: Okyakusama wa kamisama desu— The customer is God! Even if he only jangled 500 yen in his pocket—and unlike Tokyo, in Kyoto, even the gutters you fell into drunk were clean.

In some ways, such utter opposites in experience— everything about Rodrigo's stay in Kyoto had been completely premeditated. Meticulously plotted, even. He'd never forget—nine years old—his best friend Tomas had brought over a battered VHS tape after school and they'd spent the next two hours frying in his family's fifth-story apartment, their eyes glued to the screen. For years, Rodrigo could recall every single detail about that afternoon. The flickering screen, the sound of violin arpeggios getting crucified in the room next door (his sister, Fia). Princess Nausicaä: a scientist, warrior, and brave explorer of the Sea of Decay; an environmentalist of the future—they watched that tape over and over until they watched a hole in it. When he was ten, his parents asked him what he wanted for his birthday, and kid Rodrigo passed them a scrip of paper with a Japanese name on it and a phone number. One of those slips you tear off of flyers stuck to a pillar, with a fringe of numbers at the bottom. It had been pinned to the community board at his school, along with handwritten advertisements for math tutorage and flyers imploring kids to consider the flute. His parents glanced at each other and shrugged. This had to do with those strange videos their son devoured with the boy from downstairs, but as he was above average at studies and not a troublemaker, there seemed no reasonable reason to dissuade it. For years, Rodrigo commuted across town on metro and tram to Yamaguchi-san's apartment—eventually, he became fixated on the (to them) useless and slightly subversive degree of linguistics, but try as they did to subvert his interest to practical economics or business, their normally dispassionate son would not budge. When he announced he'd been selected to go abroad for his third year of college, what could they do but throw him a bash? Hope he'd go, burn off this strange fuel of fascination, and return with a new appreciation for the familiar.

That, his parents learned, was to be a rocky road. Rodrigo was twenty years old when he graduated his language program in Kyoto—and spontaneously declared his desire to stay on in the city for at least another year. He would support himself by teaching. This torched off a healthy war a few oceans over. His parents had imagined his preoccupation had run its course, but for him, the choice was obvious. Portugal wasn't going anywhere, but his irresponsible days were definitively numbered.

His family wrote him many heated letters; these he ignored with the indignation of emancipated boys everywhere. They told him the city would be much harsher to him once he was stripped of the easy student life, and he knew that. In some respects. Rodrigo made his decision while he looked the wall-eyed truth dead in the face: A dream was nice, but one had to live.

It was around that time that he had agreed one night to meet a school friend of his at a little milk-colored space-café in the east of the city. She was a chemistry student at the university who tutored foreign students in Japanese on the side at his school, and he had secretly hoped the friendly meeting might take on datish overtones. Miho was a real yamato nadeshiko.[13] She had undyed, blue-black hair cut blunt over her eyes and long, long legs graced with miniskirts and calf-skin boots. Smart, stylish, and funny to boot, so Rodrigo was sorely disappointed when she asked if she could bring her boyfriend along. He was ready to hate whomever she walked in the door with that night.

And he did hate V, when he strode into the bar with Miho on his arm. For a moment. He hated his good face and the way the girl was obviously smitten with him. But then they started talking, and Rodrigo found it was impossible to maintain his position for long, because V had a subtle, relaxed urgency, and this was the first time that Rodrigo found himself talking to someone as crazy and as crazy-in-love with the city as he was. Until now, his obsession always suffered in the telling. With each other though, the telling lost nothing.

They were like friends reunited. The two laughed,

[13] A Japanese carnation; a girl considered classically beautiful.

drank, the hours passed, until Miho got up: She had a class the next morning and wanted to get home to rest. V got up to accompany her, but she smiled and told him to stay. So he did and the two talked about everything, from the places they went to drink to the manga they read. Rodrigo told him about his living situation, how his language program would end soon, and then he would have to find another place because his current dorm would be closed to him.

「But even if it wasn't, I'd have to find a new guy to live with. My roommate says he'll shit on me in my sleep if he has to watch the 'Funk Fujiyama' video one more time.」

V smiled faintly.

「Miho hasn't threatened anything... involving excrement. Yet. But her tolerance for my music has pretty much reached its limit.」

「Well, someone told me about a cheap house I could move into in northern Kyoto, up by Kitaouji. Sounds like a real flophouse to be honest, but I'm broke. My parents would pass a brick if they saw me living there, but I'm not picky. If I could find someone to move in with me, it would be even better, because they let you share rooms and split the rent.」

His new companion took a sip of beer.

「Well, depending on when you do it, we could move in together. If you're at all interested.」

Rodrigo raised his eyebrows.

「But I thought you were living with Miho.」

「I am. But not for long.」

And V lit a cigarette, haloed himself in smoke and impassively told him the story of how he had moved in with her almost a year ago. They met, sparks flew, she invited him to stay with her. The catch was that she was engaged to someone who'd been abroad for three years

while finishing his Ph.D. He would be absent for the rest of
the year, but when he got back and she graduated, they
would get married. Until then though, her apartment was
paid for by her parents, and while she lived there, V was
welcome to it and whatever she had. Rodrigo couldn't
believe it.

*So that's where the wind's blowing from. Kac-
chaimashita!* [15] *I guess we're not in Portugal anymore...*

But all he said aloud was, ⌈You're shitting me. Miho?
That nice girl?⌋

The other narrowed his eyes.

⌈Why do you say that? She's not doing anything wrong.
She's twenty-four, been here by herself for a long time, and
then she told me straight up that this fiancé and her are
forever. He's some biochem scientist, and it's more like a
meeting of the souls with those two, or something. Him
and I are night and day—I know that. I could never give
her the things he can in the long run. But she's all alone in
Kyoto. Her people aren't from here. He's coming back at
the end of the month and then she'll go up to Tokyo to be
with him. Anyway, sore wa sore de. So it goes.⌋

Rodrigo was intrigued by this insidiously easy-going
attitude. But that was V's philosophy. All things needed a
beginning, middle, and an end. Miho and him got along
very well and they were pure combustion in bed, but they
knew the limits of this relationship. In the last few months,
both had put their feelings on ice, and now their time
together was drawing to a close. V knew he would soon be
apologetically but unceremoniously turned out of doors.
That was how he liked it though. No betrayal. No lies. He
had no regrets.

Rodrigo listened, steadily drank and was eventually
struck down by the odd, almost lordly apathy V had to
money and his happy-go-lucky approach that somehow

[15] Roughly: Wow...
a real kept boy...!

seemed to always manifest in actual luck. He'd heard of boys like this; he'd read of boys like this, but until that night he'd had no actual confirmation of their existence. Young men with no futures and no pasts—unfettered by histories, mothers, fathers, afflictions, grudges, diseases and financial mirages. And morals. They were cheerful, hearty and never seemed to require medical care (good, as they were in no danger of ever being in a position to receive any). They didn't crawl out of drafty wombs, but warm subway cars—they grew up in cruddy movie theaters with pock-marked silver screens—fed off of unnourishing conversation and unclean habits and had disgustingly short shelf-lives, as friends, lovers, and people—but should one of them enter your life at the right time—say in a smoothly futuristic bar off of Imadegawadouro on a soft Kyoto night, as your own young self paused at the trail head of an ontological cross-roads—they could prove momentously indispensable. As an aspiring runaway in love with all runaways, Rodrigo decided then that V would become his mentor.

Twenty-four days and seven hours later, he was deeply contemplating the sanity of his decision once he'd arrived that fateful afternoon to the boarding house in a taxi, to transport his suitcase and trunk from the university dorms. V showed up on foot. With a backpack. *Fin.* Rodrigo's brain clenched as he watched the long form weaving towards him, wondering, had he lost his mind moving in with Miho's ex kept boy? He didn't know the first thing about him, except that he apparently didn't possess anything that couldn't be fit into a backpack! Once they were shown their room, V mercifully vanished while Rodrigo spent fourteen minutes fretting his clothes into the wall closet and trying not to hyperventilate. Then the other slid back in, looking the inverse of Rodrigo's frazzled mood. ⌈Come on. I found the landlady, she's going to give us a tour.⌋ Rodrigo followed him testily out into the hall. A tour? The last thing he needed was further confirmation that this bister hole had been a fatal miss. The kanrinin herself disquieted him. Pilly bathrobe and chaos eyebrows penciled over the smooth egg of her head. The angle of the brows suggested she wasn't too thrilled with them either. Once Sachiko-san realized she needn't with the English though, she seemed happy enough, leading them around and pointing out the local landmarks. ⌈Long-term renters get the entire top shelf of the fridge. Would you like a pass for the bathhouse around the corner? Oh, that's Maury-san. Konnichiwa! He's a long-term renter too, I'm sure you'll become great friends. The bathroom upstairs is finicky so for a BOWEL MOVEMENT, please make sure to use the toilet downstairs.⌋ Rodrigo's bowels indeed felt loose. Grotty, grit, insect crypts, a pit-stained old foreigner reading in the busted common room. Like a cautionary tale. This wasn't a tour, it was a Hell meguri. Meanwhile, you'd think he was trekking through a five-star suite, not a putrid old inn to get murdered in, the way V glamoured, and tittered, and carried on about who knows what, until he leaned over and whispered, ⌈It's done. We can go now.⌋ What was *done?* Rodrigo felt too raw to even ask. So it was back to their room. Back to the mold blooming virulently out of the top left corner. Wasn't breathing mold poisonous? If V noticed it too, he didn't say. Simply pulled down the zipper of his athletic jacket and threw himself down on the tatami, carefree as a corpse. Lit a cigarette and offered him one too. Across the room, Rodrigo forced himself to step forward and accept it, but even the spit moving down his throat felt painfully neurotic. He'd bragged back in the bar; now, he was ashamed to admit that his first thoughts flew back to his parents. Could he call them still? Extricate himself? Finally, he did it. Pressed the failure out of his body. ⌐Listen... I... This isn't going to work. We can't pay a *man* a week for this shitheap.⌐ And V looked up. Slitted his mouth. Gone was the sweet chip-chirrup of the hallway, he poured it down like concrete. ⌐What the hell are you on about? Of course it'll work. Didn't you hear? Her cleaning person has gone, she can't find a new one. So I offered that we'd do it. Take out the trash, biweekly bathroom cleanup, toilet unclogging— whatever she needs. In return, our rent is half off. Lucky, no? ...You do know how to clean, right?⌐

He didn't really, but he would learn.

And since, right then, Rodrigo needed an older brother more than anything in the world, this dismissive, sovereign tone was actually really comforting.

They worked on settling in and his worries melted rapidly. Yes, yes, if this kid saw a hole, he knew how to flow into it.

Rodrigo determined in the coming weeks that his new roommate was not unlike the Kamo's water: calm, shallow, perpetually restless. He seemed to never sleep. Of his exploits, he rarely bragged (Ok, sometimes, he bragged) but still managed an *almost* entirely unaffected humility that made Rodrigo wonder if he'd spent some time existing as an ugly child. Or an ugly teenager. Not that he ever spoke of growing up. Of the past that didn't exist. Rodrigo himself talked often of his parents, his school and their apartment where he'd grown up, his parents' shop where he and his sister had been impressed into helping out every summer, but the furthest V ever went back to was his life in Paris. Even that, only briefly. Something about a rich kid trying to taboo his socialite parents into an early grave, by mixing with undocumented hustlers and petty drug runners. Of which he had been one. (A hustler or a drug runner? Rodrigo had not had the gall to ask.) But this Parisian boy had taken him under his wing. You know the saying, lie down with the cats and you get fleas. And without that friend, he would have never come to Japan. When he spoke of ex-friends and lovers, it seemed always in a casual appraisal of what they had done for him and what he had done for them, making Rodrigo wonder, was he the next rich kid friend? Hungry for his own corruption? He figured, it made no sense to dissect too deeply. They were in a coalition now. He brought the stability, the background, and the common sense; and V brought an unexpected proclivity for cleanliness—and the confidence that any plan was possible.

Which had its own latent value, because reduced rent or no, the cost of Kyoto living was ferocious. They had no qualifications—their visas lay in various tatters of unsuitability and even with six fluent languages[16] between them, they did not have the golden English goose. So they worked any under-the-table job they could, menial labor when available, and taught anything they could be considered qualified in. Through Rodrigo's university connections, they soon had a small but reliable network of students.

And this is how V's work evolved. For he quickly saw that a *certain* student, inexplicably, came to a language lesson not interested in mastering the perfect, imperfect or future tense. How many AC'd coffee shops did he sit through, how many suburban houses did he visit? (He loved those little, close houses!)[17] The sound of a mauled *Für Elise* tinkling in from a window across the street. Sandwiches offered, pets introduced. Please don't mind him, he barks, but he's got no bite. You're not allergic, are you? He wasn't allergic. Not at all.

Oh, it wasn't a straight trade. He didn't charge by the exchange. His being almost repelled money, as if he could

[16] Japanese, Portuguese, Spanish, French, Ukrainian, Russian.

[17] The windows close enough to pass the Grey Poupon!

not allow himself to ever have more than what he could spend the next day. And it's not as if any of his students felt they were buying him. They may as well have tried to buy the wind. But perhaps there is something about a certain person who seems to want nothing that makes another type of person want to give them whatever they can. Clothes, food, perks, bills. He had a woman for everything.

Rodrigo was cautious; he squirreled money away for the hard days. V spent as if it were water. And why not? His livelihood was set. Women approached him in the supermarket, on the street. They wanted to touch his hair. They wanted to take his picture. It irked him at times to be fetishized, but much more often, it made him hard, and he would flirt back shamelessly.

At first, his enthusiasm was directly proportional to the woman's youth and attractiveness, but as time passed and funds dwindled, Rodrigo (who had a much steadier, if lower, income from steady lessons) urged him to be more sensible. ⌜Look for a provider,⌟ he'd say, ⌜not someone who's looking for a provider. Pretty girls all want a man to buy a bag for them, and a pretty man needs a woman who buys a bag for *him*, not leaves him stranded in the city after he blew even his train fare on taking her to a sushi dinner. Come on. You know that belt is going to die if we put another notch in it.⌟ V's belt was indeed on its last legs—

He moved from the river banks and clubs to his lessons, where the direction of the money flow was guaranteed—the unmarried career women and OLs. Most lived with their parents still and any money not yet taken by Louis Vuitton or the State of Hawaii sat incubating in the bank, waiting to be spent. Perhaps it was the errant pencil sharpening or mashing of elevator buttons, but these girls seemed to all want their dates to stop *hard*. Which is exactly what V wanted. He enjoyed their casual generosity and their youth, and they enjoyed his—but he lacked substantial status and cash. They knew he would never be able to deliver them in the end, which is why he often got the uncomfortable sensation that these ladies were staring at a point just above his head.

Whereas married women stared at him alone. Wives were potentially volatile and had to be handled carefully. Yet they were usually well preserved, and not exclusively looking for sex, but also companionship, the sort that their husbands could not provide them with, being away all day and most weekends on business meetings extending into the night as drunken business meetings. They imagined the extra money their husbands were throwing at cocktail waitresses and hostess girls and maybe even mistresses, and the possibilities fanned six kinds of jealousy. So the bolder ones took up their own afternoon diversions and what better than an innocuous language tutor? Add in that V was undeniably well-mannered and talked the kind of things they liked to hear.

They imagined foreign men didn't grow up soaked in dansonjohi.[18]

He behaved as well as anyone ever asked him to. But his appetite progressed in a chaste line—Rodrigo was always astonished at the ease with which he moved from receiving to giving. His pockets lined from back-pay, V would dish with him in the bathhouse then skip down to the river just in time for the late afternoon. He charmed girls, he took them eating, dancing, to karaoke, whatever they could ever want. He paid like a czar. They drank enough sake to fill a kiddy pool; they sang until they were hoarse; they checked into hotels and fucked away his money hour by hour. And by the morning light, he had

[18] Lit. 'Men above, women below.'

nothing left again. He and his *ike-ike* girls would stagger around to find their clothes, smoke a final stick. And then he would walk home alone.

Now it was early summer. 2003. V was freshly twenty-six. He had no formal education, no family who still admitted his name, no language that still felt entirely correct in his head, but he was most at home on those early mornings in the tiny alleys off the Pontochou when the sweepers came out to tidy the already beautiful little streets and he would walk into a shrine, throw his last 100 yen into the donation box, clang the bell, bow twice, clap twice, and whisper ⌈thank you⌋ to the kami.

Yes, it was so. What he had alluded to with Aya in the coffee shop was the whole and honest truth. Searching the sky, his heart, his soul for Buddha, Allah, Jesus, the Dalai Lama; chasing smack, crack, X, good old Soviet glue; to cure one's nihilism, idealism, consumerism, brutalism, voyeurism, ism, isms; by spending yen, dollars, franks, euros. Security? Longevity? *Things—money—*black hole infinity—nothing—nowhere—never, in this life or out of it had V met a god, an idea, a drug, or a currency that could make him feel as securely, virtuously *complete* as he did in bed with the right girl.

Maybe a good cigarette came close. Other than that, he just wasn't interested, so what more could God or Heaven offer him? Kind of empty, kind of full, it was all here. His life. It was a kind of life.

SEVEN

THE GUCCI BAG

The drink options flash a blue cold cold cold cold cold across the board. Aya pushes the 100 yen coin into the slot and presses the button. A fierce rumble sounds from the bowels of the machine; there is a clang and shuffle, and then a can of Royal Milk Tea is brusquely spit into the slot below. Aya leans over and grabs the can, drawing its coolness against her cheek. A month ago, this same vending machine would have offered the tea hot, which is about when the tourists started coming to see the flowering trees. For her though, beyond the tourists and the crowds, it's the quiet change of the beverage machine options from 'hot' to 'cold' that really marks the turn of the seasons.

She keeps pressing it to her cheek, feeling the chill spread to her jaw, when she hears the sound of her friends approaching from the left. Aya turns, and a chorus of ohayous rings out in their area of the platform. The girls are all wearing identical sweaters with their school's insignia dutifully sewn on, but really, this is the last week for that. Soon it will be too hot even early in the morning, and anyone still wearing loose socks and tights will do it only for show. They crowd closer, their little group fighting for existence amongst the other groups of students, salarymen tapping their feet, craving smoke, and office ladies pursing their lips in the notebook-sized mirrors they carry in their designer reticules.

「Hey Aya, can I have a sip?」a short girl called Yui asks and Aya passes the can.

「So are you coming on Thursday?」

「Were they able to fix the machine?」

「Yeah, I was so stressed out. But it's fixed now. I told my mom we would be using it all day. Maybe you could write Ren and tell her? Or do you want me to?」

「I can do it.」

「Okay. Everything is just like we left it in the work room. If we sew all through Thursday, and then maybe meet one more time on the weekend, we should be able to finish.」

「All right.」

Yui wipes a smudge off of Aya's face, and Aya smiles. Then grabs her bag and pulls out her planner. She has to write it all down, or she will forget. With one hand, she's looking for a pen, with another, she's pressing out a text to Ren. Their event is in two weeks, and they want their booth to be perfect. It will be perfect, but there is that test coming up on Thursday too. This means no time to meet Ren alone this week. *At least I'll see her at Yui's house.* Aya wonders if she's doing something wrong. Stress presses down on her constantly, but if her friends feel it too, they do not say it. She wants to ask Yui a final question about a trip to the fabric store, but her friend's attention is elsewhere.

An excitement buzzes in the air, the source being one particular girl, standing right across from Aya. She's a commuting friend, but not part of the fashion club. The train is still a few minutes coming, enough time for Yumiko (the girl V had dubbed that day in his head as 'the Leader') to draw out her keitai with a flourish. She flips up the rhinestone encrusted top and flurries with her fingers. Less than five seconds and a picture is drawn up from her phone's memory and she turns it around, facing it towards the group with a note of pomp and circumstance. 「Jya... JYAAAAAN!」 she trills, and Aya narrows her eyes to take in the image on the screen. The photo is of a bag. And then everyone's heart sticks in their throat. The little gold embossed Gs. Interlocked, like graceful curved arms, unmistakable. The ultimate in Style. Class. Chic. The girls squeal, and Yumiko is beaming as if she has just won a prize, and she has. She knows that if she brings the bag to school, or walks down the street with it, people will all stare at her. With envy. Like she has always stared, until now.

「I can't believe it!」A girl next to Yui shrieks, and then elbows Yumiko in the side, her eyes as sly as a cat's. 「So, he finally got it for you, huh?」

「Yup.」

「And—did you do it with him?」

「Hi-mi-tsu!」[19] Yumiko drawls in a sing-song voice, which she knows they all take to be a yes, and if they do, she figures, so let them. To an untrained eye, they may have looked like any other group of pretty high school girls, but Yumiko knows that even amongst royalty, not all princes are created equal. She wonders, do any of her friends have what it takes to procure for themselves the very best? The girls are still clamoring when the train slides into the platform, and a troop of immaculately white gloved men materializes to direct the crowds onto the train. Aya and her friends line up at the unisex platform and when the car is to what seems like perfect capacity, everyone gently places their palms on the backs in front of them and pushes, pushes until the entire crowd is in the train, with the white gloved men pushing from the very back. In the car, the girls are pressed tight up against each other and other commuters, so tight that it is impossible to grab onto a handrail and so tight that it is unnecessary to do so.

The train starts after the proper warning announce-

[19] That's a secret!

ments of doors closing, and the whole inside population lurches against each other, hundreds of spontaneous couples doing an awkward cheek to cheek two-step. Aya feels the man next to her getting pressed (pressing into her?) uncomfortably, and the sensation embarrasses her, but they've switched back to the unisex trains after Yui was felt up in the all woman's car last month. Aya remembers the assailant as a tall, shockingly bleached yankee who had leered the entire time. She must have done it for effect, but Yui was traumatized and insisted that if she had to be felt up by someone, she would rather it be a man. The other girls argued for a while over which was worse (Aya thinking all the while that she herself would rather have a woman, but ideally nobody), so now here they are back on the unisex train, with a salaryman's *thing* announcing its presence next to her. Two girls over, Yumiko is still flashing her new bag and venting her new problem, namely, that if her mom finds such an expensive item in her room when she cleans it, she will demand to know where it came from, and some of the girls offer advice, while others keep going back to the papa. What was it like, what was he like again, was it scary, etc. etc. Aya tunes them out and concentrates on the bald spot of the man directly in front of her and tries to plan one of her upcoming outfit patterns out in her head. The man is so short (and she is not tall) that she could rest her chin on that spot. A bony helicopter making a landing.

「Speaking of papas.」 One of the girls turns around now and catches Aya's eyes in the crowd. 「So what happened between you and that *Australian* last Friday? You did talk to him, right?」 The girls snicker, and Aya feels herself blush. The bag was bad enough, but moving the focus to herself is even less desirable.

「He's not Australian, but yeah, I did talk to him.」

She had almost forgotten that they would be expecting some information, and she'd never been a particularly good liar. Her palms moisten with anxiety.

「Talked to him, huh? And? Did he take you somewhere good?」

「Are you serious?」 Another girl cuts in. 「Foreigners are always cheap. And he looked too young anyway.」

「So, who cares? He was probably huge. My sister did it with a gaijin once, and she said he was huge.」

「Yeah, but did she tell you he was floppy?」

「And how would you know this?」 The girl with the internationally inclined sister shoots back, and this sends them all into fresh giggles. Aya wants to sink into the ground. The train clatters on, she clatters with it, closing her eyes and forgetting their faces. She tries so hard to think about *anything* but the few hours they spent together that evening, to keep the red off her face.

What Aya Was Trying To Not Think of On The Train—That Day

Us alone, in a small dark room? Sounds improper.

He'd said, but they'd been sitting in a small dark room alone together for over an hour now, and nothing even remotely improper had happened. They sang. Drank big tall glasses of neongreen melon sodas brought to the room. And didn't talk. He really did have a beautiful voice; she'd said so after the first song, and he beamed at her, 「I told you, I don't lie. But your voice is very pretty too.」 That made her blush. Secretly Aya DID think she was quite a good singer, but she didn't know anybody who liked to go to karaoke. So there had never been anybody to confirm it. Until that evening, her voice had been wasted on her hair brushes and shampoo bottles. Now

Aya watched him from the side while he sang. The song came to the end; as if timed, the phone on the wall jangled too.

She jumped a little, and he put the microphone down. Carefully took a last sip of soda.

「Time's up, ojousan.」

「Yes.」 Aya's tongue felt dried out. Maybe it was all the singing.

「You know.」 He turned to her, running his fingertips along the grooves of his empty glass. 「We never did what we came here to do.」

He will kiss me now.

Her heart was hammering. If she was honest, she had wanted him to since they had first got in here, but had no idea how to make it come about. Should she stare at him, more than she already was? Smile more? But shouldn't being asked out by a girl be enough indication that she desired to be kissed? How could he be so nibui? Or did foreigners operate under different rules? Aya had said earlier *I don't care about any of that, anyway.* And she didn't. Normally. But nothing about the last hour and a half had felt normal to her. This whole time had seemed turned on its head. The phone had rung, but they didn't get up to gather their things. They would be billed for another half hour. He didn't seem concerned though. *We never did what we came here to do.*

「No, we didn't,」 she whispered, and he gave her a look then. Why did she feel like he could read her mind? She wasn't sure if that made it all better, or worse.

「You said you wanted my advice.」

He no longer shimmered as he had back down at the river. Now, it seemed to Aya, he simply glowed, like a bar of precious metal. Or something radioactive. He continued playing with his glass. He was always fidgeting. Chewing his nails. Smoking. Or—

「So, now's the time to talk, no? We won't stay here much longer.」

「Oh.」 Aya looked away, at the TV screen. This wasn't about kissing her. Though of course, why would it be? Why would he even want to? She still didn't know his age, but he was so painfully, firmly in his twenties. And she wasn't advertising hers, but she imagined he could guess. That it was NOT—even close to his. The exact forbidden draw for some, but it didn't seem to draw him. He was right though: once they left, there would be no other chance. He would go his own way and she'd never see him again. Maybe a glimpse now and then at that spot by the river. But she was rarely there. It was another part of today's fluke. And she honestly *did* want to talk— Aya said:

「Yes, I almost forgot. I did want to ask you about something. It seems like it comes easy to you, so I was wondering if you could give me advice on how—to talk to girls.」

「How to talk to girls.」 He seemed genuinely confused. 「What about the five or whatever girls you were dancing with earlier? Your friends? You must talk to them every day, just fine.」

「They're not really my friends,」 she muttered, a little miserably. 「We commute together. One of them goes to my jyuku. And she's my friend. But I don't mean talking like that, anyway. I mean...」 She looked at him and swallowed loudly. 「Talking to a girl... Like this.」

She indicated the two of them.

He said nothing for a moment. Then nodded.

「I see. You want to talk to a girl like *this*. Well, but you seem to be doing fine at that too, no? Do what you did earlier, to me. Go up to her, say something to get her attention. Ask her to do something with you. And then, just see where it takes you...」

「But what do I do if I want to kiss her?」

He laughed softly.

「Baka. Silly. If you want to kiss her, then you kiss her. If she wants to kiss you too, that is.」

「But how will I know if she wants to?」

「You can tell, can't you? A girl who wants to be kissed will act kind of nervous and shy, but keep looking at you in this certain way. You'll know. But if you're not sure, you can always ask.」

Aya shook her head furiously.

「No, no. I'm sure I could never do that. Asking is so embar-rassing. And unromantic.」

He shook his head back.

「You know what's embarrassing and unromantic? Having a girl turn her face away because you misread the signs. So, wait for the right time. Be alone. And if she doesn't want to, don't make it an issue. No problem. But ask.」

「I can't.」

「Of course you can.」

「I really don't think so, V-kun.」

「You can. Try it.」

She stared at him.

「Come on. Try it.」

Aya broke out in a sweat. She rubbed her palms over the top of her uniform's skirt, hoping he didn't see her do that in the dark. She was looking at him. He was looking at her. Finally she whis-pered it, can I? And he leaned down. Nodded the slightest, closed his eyes, drew her into him. The TV blared in the background. Aya was sure that once their lips symbolically touched, he would break off right away, but he didn't. Not at all—he melted into her. Dark water rolled all over her body, under her clothes. *What is this, what is this?* Aya rested her hand behind his neck, hooked one of his vertebrae with a finger. He had a very long neck and on the back of it, she could feel the nubs of his spine. Earlier she had also noticed small bruises along the left side of his throat—*kiss marks.* She'd never gotten or given one. While she ran her fingers along the bones and kissed him, all she could think about was that he would leave soon. It filled her with a determination. Like she had to do something drastic to stop it. He pulled away finally, his face very flushed, and that made her feel a rush. That she had done that to him. *And here I was, thinking he's some kind of **noble adult!*** Yes, it wasn't like any other day ever before. Aya was breathing hard, like she'd been running. She'd already removed her school blazer half an hour ago, it was warm in the room. Now they both stared at each other. He leaned forward, perhaps to kiss her again, and she took his right hand in hers. She would show him instead of asking. Aya planted his hand flat and firm right above her chest and nudged the topmost button of her shirt with one of his fingertips. That made him pull away hard.

「Not here.」

「But then where?」

「Let's go.」

She nodded, put her blazer back on. It felt like she was watching herself, like when you watch yourself in a dream. And they walked out like that; he paid and they moved on. *Now, he'll take me to a—* It all went too fast and surreal for her to feel nervous. Outside, the lit up signs of the big street beyond neontipped the tops of the shorter buildings along the canal. She wanted to put her hand into his, but didn't want to be stared at even more. Aya never had been the type to enjoy drawing attention to herself or being provocative, so she couldn't help but notice—

「Does everyone always stare at you like this when you walk around?」

「How do you know they're looking at me? Maybe they are looking at you, Aya-chan.」

「I really don't think so. Nobody looks at me when I'm walking by myself.」

「I can't imagine nobody looks at you. But sure. People stare.」

「It feels like I'm walking with an idol. I couldn't ever get used to it.」

「I don't really notice. But you said you have jyuku, so what subway station do you need? I'll walk you to it.」

Aya was too struck to even feel stupid. Wait, wait, what? Had she hallucinated the last ten minutes? No. She hadn't. They *had* kissed. She had made what she wanted unmistakably clear. And as far as she could tell, that's exactly what he wanted too.

She made her voice as level as possible.

「But. I thought we are— aren't we going to a—」

「—A what?」

「You really don't know—? I thought we left the karaoke room to go to a—」

She couldn't make herself say it. V obliged.

「A hotel room.」

「...Oh. You do know.」

「I'm not completely dense, you know.」

V kept walking, hands in his pockets, and Aya's confusion continued to mount. *Everything had been going just fine, so can't he follow the signs like a normal person, without DISCUSSING it?*

「So then, if you know—then what is the problem?」

V turned and stopped walking.

「The problem? Is that you met me less than two hours ago. I was serious when I said you shouldn't talk to strangers, and that definitely includes going to a hotel with one. Karaoke was bad enough. Do you have any idea what's going through my head? Nothing decent, I can promise you that, but for all you know, I've been fantasizing this whole time about locking you in my basement or cutting you into eighty-four pieces.」

Aya waved her hand.

「Like you even HAVE a basement. Just stop it.」

「How do you know what I have? Do you know me?」

「I feel like I do. This whole time, I've been having such a strange, good feeling about you. Like I know you.」

「All right then. Where was I born? What's my favorite color? How old am I?」

Here he goes being dense again. She huffed out air.

「I'm not saying I know FACTS about you, but I know that you wouldn't hurt me. I can *feel* that you're good.」

And V leaned down over her, frowning.

「*Bad men feel good, Aya-chan. That's how they get you.*」 *And when they're really good at being bad, they'll make you think everything they wanted was your own idea first.* 「Come on, it's getting late.」

V waited for her to start walking; Aya stood, her feet planted firm. Maybe he truly was concerned, but if he honestly did think of her as some vulnerable young thing, then why had he—? She tossed her hair with an uncharacteristic sharpness, gathered every last drop of Yumiko:

「If you're too broke to get a room, you can say that too, instead of acting all fake-virtuous to save face. Meccha dassa~」

Some expression flitted over his features; Aya's nerves tingled. Did she really say something so abrupt and rude to a stranger? Even if he was a random shady gaijin debating taking her to a hotel room?

The random shady gaijin raised his brows.

「Fake? *Virtuous?*」He didn't contest the broke. 「Ojousan, I don't think you'd have the first clue what to do with me in a hotel room. But okay.」He pulled out his wallet and tossed it to her. Aya fumbled and just managed to grab it. 「Normally, you'd be right, but not today. Open it and look. It's supposed to be my landlady's, but she'll extend. I do hate misunderstandings though. So let's hear what you want first and then we can go.」

She'd only wanted to ding his male pride; now here she was, holding a beat-up leather wallet (it *did* feel thick) while he stood a little over, grinning like an angel. Was something spurring him to make this evening as abnormal as humanly possible? And humiliating as it was to admit defeat, Aya had to concede that whatever she was after, it certainly didn't seem expressible in any unit as prosaic as a *sentence*. She licked her lips, thought of the dark water that had roiled over her skin, but said nothing. He waited for five respectful seconds, then held out his hand, and she silently passed the wallet back with as much dignity as she could muster. He slipped it into his back pocket.

「Yappari. You really expected to do something with me you can't even talk about. How is that supposed to go?」

「But I don't even talk about that with Kiriya— He's my—」

「Your boy. He's real.」

「Of course he's real!」 she grumbled. 「Did you think I made him up?」

「It wouldn't be the first time.」

「Well, I didn't! Or the girl. She's real too.」

「And you've done it with him before.」

「What kind of question is that?」 Her tone stiffened more, and he gave the top of her head a very light, playful flick. Like an older brother would.

「Don't stress it, ojousan. I'm not trying to be a pervert, and I don't need details. It wasn't a question anyway.」

「So you think that I...?」

「Have. Yes.」

「And so what if I have? Are you one of those creeps who only goes for virgins?」

No, I'm one of those creeps who only goes for not-virgins. THE MORE NOT-VIRGIN, THE BETTER.

「Now what would I want with a clueless cherry girl?」 he asked, and Aya stared at him.

「I thought men always want to be a girl's first so bad.」

「Not me.」

The truth flowed effortless.

「Well, I don't get to see him so very often and it's hard to find time to be alone, but we have done—you know. And I like kissing, but I don't really—get the other stuff. It's fine, but I don't really see what the big deal is and—」

「And?」

「And he always... —*Rushes.*」

She blushed deeply and V smiled a little then.

「You're the same age, *deshou*?」

「Yeah. Basically.」

「Sure then, he's going to rush.」

「So you rushed too when you were my age?」

「No. But I've always been a little weird about this kind of thing—」

Aya pursed her lips.

「You seem to be weird about a lot of things.」

「And that's why you're curious. But you don't know what you want, not really. So let's forget it, ojousama.」

V walked faster now, as if to shake her off. He could do it, every stride of his took two steps of hers, and she was almost jogging next to him. On their right was coming up a low stone wall, and Aya hopped neatly onto it. Now she was almost his height, walking along next to him. Her loafers tiptapped on the stones, and he slowed down to make sure she didn't slip trying to keep up.

「I do know what I want,」 she said doggedly.

He ignored that, walking purposefully towards Sanjou. Which happened to be the exact direction she had to go in.

Aya's heart sank. Literally sank.

In the karaoke room it had been so breathless and light, now the organ flopped around in the bottom of her stomach like a fish gasping out its life on a boat's dirty deck. Shinu san byou mae. Three seconds before death. She stopped walking on the stone wall, and when he noticed she had stopped, he did too. Turned to her, and she wanted to say something, something so salient it would show him in a few words how badly he had misread her and this entire thing, but all that came out was a scathing:

「V-san hontou ni —hidoi yo!」

V only smiled again though, and that was awful too.

「I'm horrible because I won't take you to a rabuho?」

「You're horrible because you are playing so hard to get.」

「I'm not *playing* hard to get, I *am* hard to get.」

「Ugh! And so very full of yourself!」

「An absolute beauty is throwing herself at me. You would be too, in my place.」

「Ohhhh.」 Aya stamped her foot. 「Horrible, stuck-up AND impossible! Then why did you even kiss me in the first place?! What for?」 He looked at her then and his expression turned serious for the first time.

「I kissed you *because you asked me to.*」

「What? Because —I asked you—?」

「To. Yes,」 he said quietly. Patiently. 「I'm a vampire, Aya-chan. *You have to invite me in.* In the movies, you silently stare into each other's eyes without saying a word and everything works out. But it's not like that with me.」

「So then... What is it like?」

「You have to tell me what you want.」

「And then?」

「I do it. If I agree to do it.」

They stood saying nothing for some seconds, and he took out a cigarette. Lit it.

「So. What subway station am I taking you to?」

「...By Kawaramachi Sanjou is fine.」

「Let's go then. I don't want to make you late.」

They went another block, saying nothing while she stayed in her thoughts and he stayed in his. The wall had ended a while back; she was walking on the ground again, to his right. V figured she didn't like the looks and stares, but nobody was around right then, and he put out his hand towards her. A gesture of peace. Maybe she would take it. Maybe she was unresolvably disappointed with him.

Aya grabbed it though and started to skip. He gripped her hand, and when he turned to look, she was smiling. Not angry or pouty in the least. He squeezed and she squeezed back, laced her fingers into his, and they kept walking like that. It felt pure. Up ahead, a group started to approach. He was ready for her to let go once they came close enough to see, but she didn't, and he was thinking it had been so long since he'd walked in public *holding someone's hand.* So long, he could not remember when.

The group passed, and Aya tugged at him to stop, so he turned. She touched him on the shoulder.

Red all over. Showed that he should lean down.

No, more. Closer.

「All right. Since you're being so stubborn.」
Aya whispered into his ear—

V listened. He listened.
He came to a conclusion.
Was it the wrong one?
Was it the right one?
Whatever it was,

After that, he took her to a room.

And they stayed until she sighed out his name—
V knelt for the prince until her body fell like rain.

And because her face would be straight fire to remember any of that, Aya dares not even think of it. She pushes it back; the sound of her friends' voices pulls her forward.

「So, did you do anything good with him or not?」

「Shy little Aya-chan? I don't think so...」

「We... talked. A bit. That's it. I didn't even find out where he's really from.」

「Just talked to him, huh? That's too bad. You should've gone for it!」

「Maybe she did and she's scared to say?」another says, and Aya stares out the window, praying for the ride to end.

「Leave her alone, you're embarrassing her.」Yui waves, but the others keep giggling.

「Not that I'd blame her. Tall, blond oujisama. What more can you want?」

Yumiko is not impressed with this sudden reversal of priorities and decides this might be a good time to remind everyone:

「Listen. If I want a good lay, I go to my boyfriend. If I want a nice gift, I go to my papa. A gaijin is good enough for a lay, but a young one is never going to get you this.」She doesn't have to show them the picture again, but they know what she means and nod solemnly. For a certain girl, Yumiko may just have it all. Her boyfriend is an 18-year-old kendo star from the neighboring boys' school, and everyone agrees unanimously that he is a dream. She has shown them other gifts her papa has showered her with, and now she owns the epitome of luxury.

Their stop is here; the girls all pour out of the train, oblivious to the reproving stares of the older passengers around them. They join the exodus of other girls and boys trudging off to their private schools in rivulets of uniform blacks and blues and greens and whites that join branches to form streams, rivers, and finally merge into a sea of school children swinging their bags, giggling, sharing notes, memorizing verbs. The warm morning pulses with their laughter.

「Anyway.」 They round the school gates, and Yumiko can't resist a last jab. 「I wonder what Aya-chan's boyfriend would say if he ever found out about her *kinpatsu sefure?*」 [20] The girls laugh roughly, and Aya is grateful that, unlike Yumiko's and the other girls', her boyfriend is not from the private boys' school down the street. Out of their sight, her boyfriend (usually) stayed off their tongues as well. It's not that she was prudish, but since she did not speak often of her boyfriend even, what could she say about V or being with him that they would understand? She wasn't a fool. Had it been anything but lust, curiosity, a series of strange events and—what? It was this last element that made her stomach ache. Put simply, V'd burned her up. A whole weekend had passed, and she could still feel herself smouldering under her clothes. Phosphorescent, like a star. And she was so certain that he was out there right now, somewhere, burning too. And if she told them any of this, she could imagine them pushing and prodding, pulling and dissecting, then dumping it back into her hands unimpressed, its delicacy crushed and gone forever.

No, let them think what they wanted; she would never say.

「Why don't *you* just make sure,」 Aya's tone is joking, but her eyes bear into Yumiko's with a black intensity 「that your Keita doesn't find out about your papa.」

[20] sex-friend, f))) buddy

EIGHT

The Second Post-Op

D o you know where the Mister Donut is?
    I write her, I'm not so sure.
Well, what about the Sanrio store?
???
Her kaomojis ooze frustration.
Fine, you tell me what place you know and I'll meet you there.
I write, the geesen.
Inside? Outside?
Inside, I write her. Soulcalibur machine. You'll have to find it if you want your book back.
An obasan would find this text brattily endearing. A prince might find it dasai. Aya-chan just writes: See you there soon.

-Hello,
V-san. Are
you busy
right now?
-No,
not busy.
-Did you
bring my
book? Can
you meet me
in the
Teramachi?
-Sure.
Where?

Today, she'd texted me mid afternoon.

I snapped my phone shut. Turned to Rodrigo and told him that I'm sorry, but I wouldn't make the hunt for magical pants that go all the way down to our ankles. Tomorrow maybe? But not today. He dug down forcefully into his murk of curry. Said, I thought your lesson isn't until later, and I said sure, but something came up. What though? Something. What's the big secret? He wanted to know and I grabbed my spoon, bolted the half plate in three bites. I stood and told him I would talk about it later, having no intention of talking about it with him ever. He hollered, you're gonna get ACID REFLUX if you keep eating like that!

And then, wait a minute. Wait a damn minute. You're going to see that joshikousei, aren't you? I'm not. I shoved my phone into my jacket's pocket and he put his spoon down. Are you sure?

I looked straight into his eyes. Big, and dark, amber-flecked, and his eyelashes thick enough to be fake. I always figured, any problems he had with girls must have stemmed from his weird, shifty attitude with strangers. Not his looks. Out loud, I said,

「I am not going to see her.」

「Good boy, Vicchan. We are making progress. Then godspeed and see you when I see you. Later.」

「Later.」

I threw a sen bill on the table and departed.[21]

I reach the geesen, cut through the smoke downstairs, go up the elevator, move through the constellation of kids and haughtyeyed loners, thinking it was easy enough for Rodrigo or Acchan or anyone in the world to say I have no business seeing her, and maybe they are right, but my conscience is clear. I know what I am here to do. Drop off her book and then shove off. I've never been one of those moving heaven and earth for young girls. Give me a middle-aged woman who knows she's lucky to have me over a girl under twenty. Any day. High school girls? Arrogant, vain, and deluded enough to think they're playing the game on your level and no equation needs two of—
「Over here!」 I see Aya-chan waving, over by the Soulcalibur machine. Knee socks, book bag, charms dangling off her strap. Smile, dimples, headcock, wave. 「Hello, V-san.」

Hello, V-san.

Oh hell. She charms me. She guts me. I turn to the

[21] I don't hate peace, so yes, I lied to him.

-You know, we
did 'are'
and I still
don't know
the most
basic things
about you,
like your
age, or your
favorite
color, or I
don't even
know your
blood type!
-Well that's
easy. My
age, I'll
never tell
you. Nothing
personal, I
don't tell
anyone. My
favorite
color is
blue and my
blood type
is B.
-You are
NOT B!
-I am
though...
-Well, my
favorite
color is
green, I'll
be 17 in
September,
and my blood
type is 0.
Did you know
that 0/B
pairings are
supposed to
be really
good?
-No Aya-chan.
I did not
know that.
22

wall, pretend it's allergy season making me dab my nose discreetly, while I'm thinking maybe something seriously *is* wrong with my wiring if two words are getting me eviscerated by a high school girl? Maybe I'm fighting the compatibility of our blood. All around us, flashes, bursts of power ups detonate on screens.

「Here's your book.」

I dig it out of my jacket pocket, lean close to her, to not have to shout in the din bouncing all around. She leans close to me. Tippy toes.

「Thank you, V-san.」

「So formal, stop that. You don't have to get all 'desu' with me.

「But you're my senpai.」

Double deep breath hell, I determine, with a little selfish joy, that Aya looks happy to see me. Happier than she should be. But I'd sussed it from her texts. Her boyfriend is captain of the soccer team and she sees him practically never. Her friends are fake. Her family is busy with their own lives. Seeing her dance by the river that day, you'd have thought she has anyone, everyone in the entire world, but—Aya-chan is lonely. There is that one girl she is trying to get closer to at school, but a crush does complicate things. And I hate being the next disappointment—

「Listen Aya-chan, I've got somewhere to go.」

I hesitate long enough for her to spot the crack. She crumbles her pretty face expertly:

「But you were the one who wanted to meet in the geesen!」

「I didn't think you'd actually agree!」

「Well I did, so now you have to play me. I even know this game! Not the arcade version. But Kyou doesn't have a chance when we play on the console, so come on. One game?」

Kyou must be her brother. Her boyfriend's name is something else. I decide split second: it's okay for us to play this game together. Knowing that's the last thing to worry about, but my sense of honor doesn't always make sense. I forcefeed bills into the change machine. Tokens rain out, and once I gather them, Aya-chan picks them out of my palm like a bird picking seeds. She plinks them into the slot and we step up. Grip the controllers.

I pick Kilik. She picks Taki.

Some girls want you to win; some get a pleasure from teaching you a lesson. Some just want a fair fight. Quick glance. Next to me, Aya-chan's brows are furrowed, slip of tongue out. Today, my sonar can't cut through the noise.

Aya-chan, what do you want?

Something whispers from the shiny dark, I don't give a fuck about your bad intentions.

Back out on the street, she is trying to analyze how I could have possibly been so bad at a game that I picked. Especially when I was good enough at the claw machine to win her a Snoopy charm.

I am trying to analyze what exactly is it about her that is calibrated to melt my brain. It's definitely not the clothes. Forget all that shite about sexy sailor uniforms. Any girl's uniform I'd ever seen, Aya-chan's included, was a dowdy, pleated skirt and a bad-fit boxy blazer. I thought she'd been wearing her seifuku as a fashion statement (I've seen plenty of girls wearing it even on the weekends) but apparently, her summer holiday hasn't started yet. Aya pulls at her shirt's collar like a prisoner on her chains. She's coming from fashion club and going to her English tutor after this. Busy, busy, busy. Looks flash our way as we walk under the sweaty roofs of the Teramachi. Obviously, the

22
V actually didn't know his blood type; B was simply the most popular consensus of his exes. The type B is said to be spontaneous and unpredictable. Tending towards selfishness. The type O is energetic and optimistic. Tending towards insecurity.

An O and B pair is not the best romantically, but they do make great friends. The B keeps things shaking and the O keeps the pair grounded.

two of us do not belong together. Today though, I'm the self-conscious one. I don't normally wash time in the shoutengai—this is a place for people with money. What if Rodrigo circles back to this area? Or one of her friends sees her? It's not like we're holding hands or anything. But we walk close enough that our hands dropped to our sides touch sometimes. Mine cold, like always, and hers hot and a little dewey.

My darling says, 「Really though, how could you be *that bad* at a game you picked yourself? I would be ashamed of myself.」 And I say to her, 「But have you considered that I might have been letting you win?」

「Oh!」

Here comes the footstamp again.

I let each minute of that afternoon peel off into sixty seconds. Let each second flake into shards even smaller than that. When I ask her what's her prize for trouncing me so thoroughly, Aya curves us into purikura and the Book Off and the Lipton Tea House. I buy her koucha and manga and conscientiously burn through my money until the most scandalous thing I could still afford with her is an hour of duets and two glasses of green melon soda. Not that I think she'll ask for a hotel. Today, the winds blow little sisterly. Between shops, Aya tells me about the new outfit she's sewing, how successful their booth was at the cultural fest, how she's *this close* to asking that girl Ren out, and how this is the last afternoon she is letting herself eat cake ever ever again, on account of her phantom daikon ashi. We have fifty minutes left, then 38, then 30, so we start to walk, and on the way to the bus stop, we stop on the Shijou bridge. Look down into the water. The air is wet and full and the clouds smudge down from the sky, scatter

-V-san, iru?
  -Iru yo.
 -I thought
    of you
  today. We
 went to see
  my cousin's
  baby. He's
  five months
   old or so.
  Do you have
 any idea how
 loud he was?
  Oh, and
    meccha
   busaiku
      too.
  -Aya-chan!
   You can't
    call an
   innocent
  little baby
      ugly!
   That's bad
      luck!
    -Relax.
   If you get
  married and
  I ever see
  YOUR baby,
 I'll lie and
   say it's
      cute
    (warai)
    -...

with the green of the reeds. I'm staring at the surface, wondering how we ever decided that water is blue. I could never say what this color is. Along the bank, couples sit discreetly and I watch and chew a piece of nail off my thumb and I don't want to swallow it and have it end up in my appendix, and I don't want to pollute the water, so I try to slip it into my jeans pocket. Aya-chan asks, what? Even though I said nothing. And I'm a little embarrassed that she might have seen me, so I say quick that I was thinking about how the water does not look blue. Just like water in a glass doesn't look blue. Aya-chan says that she is thinking about time. About how sad it is that she will have to leave soon.

We're still on the bridge, Aya-chan asks me how it is that I could stand living so far away from my family: She wouldn't survive even a month abroad, and I tell her, it's easy to survive anywhere when you don't have a family. Aya wrinkles her nose and bumps me with her hip.

「Stop it now, just like your texts. You're not mysterious, answer the question. Everyone has a family.」

I say, Peter Pan didn't. 「Peter who?」 So I explain the story famous in the west, of the boy who spent his whole life flying around, having adventures and fighting his nemesis. A pirate, who had his own nemesis, a ...crocodile who had bitten off one of the pirate's hands and had swallowed a clock. The deeper I go, the more deranged the story sounds, the more Aya's brows crease. 「And Peter had a friend called Wendy-chan who took care of him and all his friends, the Lost Boys, and she wanted to love him, but he couldn't feel anything back for her. Because he was a heartless child.」 Aya listens with her head resting on her two hands, watches the waves. But I can tell she's paying close

-Don't mail me the book. Meet me downtown? It will take five minutes. I have fashion club, tomorrow but it's a quick meeting and then I have two hours until my English. I'll text you around two. You can bring the book with you.
-Sorry I only saw this now. I was sleeping. Sure, I can do that.

attention. When I'm done she says, ⌈I don't know about that story. Sounds pretty awful, not growing up.⌋ I tell her that it was written by a man whose brother had died as a small child. My mother had liked the story, because one of my little brothers had died as a baby too. So I'd heard it as a kid, translated into French. A not-Aya person may have said something here like, a mother and a baby brother is the start of a family! But actual Aya just lowers her head down to the railing and sighs.

⌈Isn't it odd how dying as a baby seems so tragic, but, and don't take this the wrong way, it seems lucky too. I get so anxious thinking about what's going to happen once school is over and having to make all those decisions about growing up. Doesn't help that most adults... don't look like they enjoy being alive. I guess you won't know what I'm talking about. You're an adult who doesn't look like you hate being alive. You don't, right?⌋

⌈I don't.⌋

⌈Maybe you will too, once everything starts to go wrong.⌋

⌈Does everything have to go wrong?⌋

⌈I guess not.⌋

We both keep looking at I don't even know what. My pinky moves out to the left and strokes the side of her hand. Once. Above us, a seagull screams. Aya-chan leans her head against my arm for a moment, there by the rail. A good silence stretches between us, then she says,

⌈You're not much like Peter, by the way. From what you said. More like Wendy-chan, looking after your six girlfriends. I bet they're all so in love with you.⌋

⌈Yeah right. I doubt there's any girl out there right now who feels deeply about me.⌋

⌈I can't believe that is true. But do you feel for any of them? Do you fall in love easily?⌋ 23

One day, no text from her comes at all. By nighttime, he wants to write, even if it's a plain 'good night' but writing her first instead of responding feels like breaking a rule. Which one, V is not sure. He goes back and forth until it annoys him and he tries to casually ask Rodrigo how to wipe a number out of his phone. He never has had cause to before and Rodrigo crows, who has got you so worked up, you have to delete her number? It IS a her, right?

V tells him, forget it.

⌈I suppose that all depends...⌋

⌈Ha! I knew you would slither out of a real answer.⌋

⌈I'm not slithering out of anything at all. I'm just trying to think of what answer would suit you best.⌋

Aya does a schoolmarm tut.

⌈This isn't about what sounds good though, or what *you think I want to hear*, but how you honestly FEEL.⌋

⌈But how I feel depends on all kinds of things, including, what would make *you* most happy to hear.⌋

⌈You are so hopeless.⌋

⌈Fine then, I've got three answers: angel heart, Sparta, and—the truth. Take your pick.⌋

She says, ⌈Jyaa, start with the angel heart answer. Do you fall in love easily?⌋

I pretend to think, wink at her.

⌈I mean, I'm in love three times a week.⌋

⌈You know I'm not talking about *that*.⌋ A deluxe eye roll. ⌈I mean, real love.⌋

⌈Shitsurei! —I'll have you know that it is very much real.⌋

⌈How can it be, when it's just one hour?⌋

I pinch her cheek.

⌈But sometimes, it's two.⌋

⌈You are so very not funny.⌋

⌈Fine then, I'll be serious. Yes, it's an hour, *just* an hour, and for that hour, I'm with a beautiful girl who only wants to be with me. And she is with a, well some have said I'm a handsome? guy who only wants to be with her. For one hour, I forget that I'm broke, and alone, and going nowhere; and she forgets that she has money, and somebody waiting for her, and a home, and a job, and that *none of that* protects her from feeling as alone as a person who is going absolutely nowhere. For an hour, this whole shit world melts away and we want nothing but to make each

[23] Oh, this is where things get slippery with girls. And he knows Aya-chan is a 100% ordinary girl, in her own way— unlike all others.

other feel good. We belong to each other and we are free. Ittai, what is more real than that?」

「I... I don't know.」 She reddens again, so prettily. 「But I'm talking about the forever and ever love. What happens when you fall into that? You said there's a Sparta answer.」

「The Sparta answer is I love. But I don't *fall* in love.」

「So one, you fall in love every day. Two, you've never been in love. And the truth? The very last answer?」

「You want to know about the I would kill for you and I would die for you and I would do anything to have you be mine and only mine type of love.」

「See, you knew all this time exactly what I meant.」

「All right. Well, that kind, I've felt it—twice.」

The din of the crowd behind us gets heavy. A wave of students wells past. Aya glances at the time on her phone, pulls on my arm. We continue down Kawaramachi without a word—reach the other side off the bridge and push by the shops selling postcards and luxury tea. Cross over alleys, filled with shady, pastel-lit bars, but it's still early for patrons and neon. Up ahead, the street widens and we pass over the crowds in front of Yasaka Shrine. I'll walk up by there later, once she's gotten on the bus, but for now we'll wait at the stop. Two obasans sit in the shelter, so I lean against the outside of the waiting area to be out of their earshot. Aya-chan leans with me.

「Two times?」 She picks up the thread effortlessly and her doggedness reminds me a bit of Rodrigo. Maybe that's why her and I got along. 「You've been in real love two whole times. Well, I'm so curious! Who were they? What happened to them?」

「Seriously, Aya-chan? You want to spend your last few minutes with me today talking about *other girls?* And you say I'm strange. Ok. Well. ...One of them I met right after I came to Japan. Tomoe. She was the first girl who started teaching me Japanese, and I was so mecchakucha crazystupid daiai with her.」

「Daiai kka. But then where is she now?」

I point somewhere out beyond the crosswalk. Past the cars, the buildings, the river. The tiled, sloped roofs. The birds. The clouds.

「Over the rainbow. Somewhere in Kyoto. I do not know where. Married, probably. There was someone else she wanted to marry when we were together.」

See-through bus shelter and uptight aunties be damned, Aya-chan squeezes me sympathetically.

「That sounds really sad. Being crazystupid biglove with someone who wants to marry someone else.」

「It was. Incredibly sad. I don't wish it on anyone. We lived together, and that last couple weeks, it was like my heart was getting ground into a powder, a finer and finer dust, every day. I was surprised there was even anything left of it at the end.」

「And the other person you loved?」

「The other person was from back. Way, way back.」

「A French girl? In Paris.」

「Even before that. The place where I grew up.」

「Her name?」

「You are so nosy. Well, in my old country, you almost never call someone by their formal name, but use a sort of nickname. And the name we used for her was—」

「Ksyusha-san.」 She pronounces it carefully and perfectly. 「And what was she like?」

I close my eyes.

「Like the sun at the end of a hard, long winter. It can't burn you, only warm you. She was like that.」

「Jyaa, V-kun mitai.」 Aya smiles. 「You remind me of the sun too.」

「Do I?」 I look out over the road, up the hill. A bus

approaches. 「And you to me are a little like the moon. So bright and charming, but you can never really know it. And Ksyusha was the sun. All around you and beyond untouchable. And Tomoe was a breeze. Feels so good and always slipping away. Which is why the next time I let myself feel dangerous for a woman, she will remind me of *a rock*. Unmysterious, obvious, and going absolutely nowhere.」

「You mean the woman you marry. You won't let yourself love anyone else until you meet her.」

「That is right. Aya-chan, this is your bus, right?」

The two older women fuss their way out of the shelter to the edge of the sidewalk, and I unlean to get behind them, but Aya doesn't even look up.

She says, 「V-kun ppokunain janai no. That's not what I was expecting from you. I mean, a broken ground up heart does sound terrible, but love— true love—it's an emotion. You can't control it!」

I swallow hard.

「You can though. Is what I've learned. I think you're talking about lust. You look at someone, your body reacts a certain way. You can't control that. But choosing to make the feeling grow stronger or to cut it off, that is the part you control, and when I know someone isn't for me and I am not for them, I am not letting it happen anymore.」

「Never?」

「Ever, never.」

The bus pulls away. Aya's eyes cloud and I chuck her on the shoulder.

「See, I wanted to cheer you up before you leave for your lesson. I knew I should've picked different answers.」

「Of course not. You explained it all very well. I told you, I wanted to hear what you really think. And now I feel like I understand your position a little better...」

She sinks to her heels there on the sidewalk, and I sink
with her. Take out a cigarette. Strike the match, the smell
of sulphur hits the air. (*The devil is near.*) Far up on the hill,
a new bus lumbers downwards. Simmers at a red light. We
watch it together, and Aya takes the cigarette from my
mouth. I don't chew her out. When she passes it back, I
take the smoke into me, tilt my head, blow a ring and she
watches it billow up. Breaks it with a clear-laquered nail
and her voice sounds so blue.

⌈I wish I knew how to blow a smoke ring.⌋

I blow her another one.

⌈It's a talent—that took me many years to perfect. I'll
teach you sometime, and by the time you're as old as Uncle
V, you can join the circus as the smoke ring girl.⌋

⌈By the time I'm as old as you, huh?⌋ Her smile is perfectly not-perfect. ⌈So the very last question and then I'll
get on that bus. How long will that take?⌋

I take a long drag, breathe out.

Why not?

⌈One decade, ojousan,⌋ I pause. ⌈Ten years. And I said
I would never tell, so you made me lie. Shame on you.⌋

⌈You're 26.⌋

⌈Awful, I know.⌋

⌈It's okay, I guess. I just didn't think you were so *old*.⌋

Her honesty is like sugar, bad for you but completely
malice free. I ash into a pavement crack. Smile.

⌈Well that's the way it is. I'm old and you're a brat.
Now go, you can't miss this one too.⌋ I shoo her. ⌈Learn.
And don't leave anything behind this time. I wouldn't want
you to have to see me again. But if you finally ask your girl
out, text me. TEXT ME! I want to know.⌋

I stand up to say a proper goodbye. This really is
goodbye, isn't it? Aya steps closer to me, she's got that look
in her eyes. That look I told her that girls get. And I can't

see myself, but I know there is a high chance that I've got that look too. That I'm even debating kissing her means the situation is thoroughly fucked. Aya reaches up, tucks a strand of hair behind my right ear, pickpockets something onto my body. 「Don't forget,」 she tells me, 「you said you'd teach me how to blow a smoke ring! You can give this back then.」 My hand slips into my right jacket pocket. Something slinky. Small. A chain. A necklace. The way it sears in my cold hand, silver-plated for sure. Aya-chan jumps away from me and runs twenty steps up. Crouches down. Behind me, the bus rolls to a stop. Should I follow her? Should I insist she get on this bus? Should I insist she take the necklace back? Should I run down the street and never look back? She calls out 「V-kun, hurry!」 I get it together, run to her. We'd been looking the other way all this time and never saw it until now: A sparrow, lying on the edge of the sidewalk. The bird trembles. Or maybe, that's the summer breeze's ruffle. Behind, people shuffle. Doors close. Bus leaves. And Aya is still crouched. 「He's not dead yet!」 I'm thinking, no, but that letter's in the mail. It's been a stifling last few days. I crouch with her, say we should move it and Aya says she's scared to touch him. I close my eyes. Small kids, dead cats, rabbits, birds, mice, fish. Forehead kisses, no, they're not coming back. Shake my head clear, press money into Aya's hand, I tell her to go get water at the Lawson's. She runs off. My cigarette's clenched in my mouth, I cup the bird in my hands. It jerks. The bird does not like me, but he's too busy dying to do anything about it. I watch him in my palm. Detached, like I figure God would watch us. Bored and sad. Then Aya-chan is back. We walk up a bit from the stop, climb the stairs past the main entrance of Yasaka Shrine. Find a quiet spot under the bushes. I lay the bird down carefully in the shadows, Aya-chan sprinkles some water on it and pours more liquid into a tiny plastic cup. I suppose she got that from the store too. The bird seems disoriented, but then dips a beak in. Drinks a little more. Staggers off into the greenery. Then takes flight. I was not expecting that. We watch it twitch off into the trees. 「There he is!」 She points. Diamonds of light hit her outstretched finger. She's happy again and tells me that the next bus is in five minutes. Wait here with me? I figure we have five minutes left to stand in the breeze resurrect birds miss buses and never grow up.

Our faces gleam with perspiration.

Aya-chan says, 「I've never saved a bird before, V-kun. Have you?」

「No,」 I tell her.

I really haven't.

NINE

THE FOOLISH VIRGIN

H e watched her watching him, trying to figure out if he had home wrecker face. Home wrecker hands. He was thinking, *you never know what gets wrecked until you jump in. That's the light and the dark of it.* When they met here, they always sat in the same spot. The inner left corner table in the back of the T— café not far from Shijou. It was either here, or that tiny fancy French bakery up by Ginkakuji. That's where Miss Chisato lived.

She wasn't here though today, the favorite aunt. Chisato was always a little drunk on life, a little raucous. Prone to be loud and to banter. She made conversation flow. It would have been nice if *she* had been interested, her interest would have been interesting, but one couldn't pick and choose. Next to her, Miss Yuki was the aunt nobody really liked, and nobody could quite say why. It couldn't have been her manners or looks, fault could be found with neither, but she was cold. She couldn't flow. Making him acutely wonder what it would be like, once she finally did.

They had met over a month ago, through a language circle acquaintance. She'd approached him about paid conversation, and he'd told her right away that he was not a native speaker. It seemed fair to reveal that. But it was the first language he'd learned. His mother's family had been French. And he'd lived in Paris for some years. She smiled then and said that for her practice, it was well enough. Native speaker or not, she told him, you speak it *so perfectly*. That 'so' was important.

He knew they would sleep together within the first

five minutes of that first meeting. It wasn't arrogance or wishful thinking; it was acknowledging a fact. Like one who stands on a shore watching a wave come rolling in acknowledges that the wave will eventually wash over them. If they do not move. The thought didn't particularly excite or perturb him. It was simply fate. He could not and should not stop it. And he knew somewhere that while they would become lovers, she would not become important to him, nor he to her. He would merely be a pawn in her life to effect a broader strategy. Such a lowly piece, the pawn. It plays its part, dies without fanfare and is laid down by the board. But once in a great while, instead of simply dying, unmourned and disposable—a pawn might start a revolution. Come reborn as a queen. He couldn't know what exactly he would start for her, only that he'd be a means to her end. And what end would she be a means to, for him? Some pleasant afternoons—and cash. Bills paid. It wasn't romantic, but it could be respectful. Even beautiful. If you played careful and patient and fair. The subtle game required the serenity of a cat waiting endlessly by a hole for the shadow of a whisker. Such patience, he had.

But by now weeks had passed, and she had made no move. And while he expected to be expected to carry out all subsequent moves, the first one HAD to be made by her. It was too risky otherwise. So he waited and began to wonder. These things tended to happen quickly or not at all. He couldn't imagine he had been wrong. (He simply never was. Not about this.) But then, you know what they say. Saru mo ki kara ochiru.

Even the monkey sometimes falls from the tree. Self-importance was ruinous. Conceit—decay. You should never forget your place. He didn't forget his. So he sat, took a sip of his tea. Took out a cigarette. Offered her one. –Miss Chisato isn't here, so you can go ahead, –he joked, but it was an empty gesture. Though she never said it, he was aware she did not like him smoking. Aware that there were many things about him she didn't like. Frankly put, he knew that she found him common and a little stupid. *Beneath her.* But that didn't matter. Fate didn't always pair you with who you *liked*. Fate and his sister Obsession had odd whims. Miss Yuki's onyx eyes were on his face; she was saying something about art. Impressionist painters. She was talking about Van Gogh and the ukiyo-e. The pictures of the floating world. Sometimes, it was tiresome. To mask that these things didn't interest him in the slightest. Some looked at pictures of the floating world—others lived in it. Some people talked of art like it was more real than what was around you, but to him, art seemed made by people unable to live life. Churning out tedious facsimiles of experience which they hung in sterile galleries and museums, where rich people (also removed from reality) strolled and entertained each other with still-born theories on what they were all looking at. He thought he fancied masturbation, yet even to him, this seemed too much.

If he liked art, it was not that type.

The Musée d'Orsay? Miss Yuki was asking now. Oh yes, he had been there multiple times. It was true. Etienne had loved to take girls there, to pose and posture. And tourist girls were always pulling them off to some museum or another—she was talking more about Van Gogh. And Gauguin. Arles, the city where their torrential friendship had gone awry. He nodded, smoked, answered her questions the best he could.

And took her clothes off in his mind.

–You were in a complete daydream, –Miss Yuki said to him and he blinked. *Don't blink. Don't slip.*

–I was listening.

–But with such a smile. –It was the first time she'd allowed herself some intimate observation. Because they were alone? –I've noticed, you don't let yourself a full expression most of the time. You were really smiling though. You must have been thinking about something good.

It was nice to be thrown off. He smiled more.

–*I was*. And you as well? You were smiling too.

–Just something silly. Too silly to say.

–But now I'm curious.

–...I was wondering if anyone's ever told you that you look like Arthur Rimbaud. [24]

He laughed a little then.

–Nobody has. Because I really don't.

–I am surprised you even know what he looks like. I was ready for you to ask who he is. ...Since you're not French, –she added quickly, embarrassed by her condescension. He pretended to not notice.

–I wouldn't know most writers. But I often had to read him out loud growing up. For practice. *Bad Blood, The Foolish Virgin, A Night in Hell.* All of those. Other things too sometimes; Hugo, or Baudelaire, or Shakespeare translated into French. But Rimbaud most of all. I can't remember any of it now, but sometimes, when something particularly poetic comes into my head, I have to imagine it's him talking. Not me.

–Why? You don't fancy yourself capable of poetry?

Her tone wasn't coy by any means, but that feeling surged through him again. That certainty of what must be. He put the cigarette to his lips, narrowed his eyes and gave her a glance as open as he dared.

–I do. But it's a different kind.

Miss Yuki lifted her china teacup to her mouth, stared down into the rich ochre liquid. It seemed to him she was

[24] There is an image from many years back, of a serious-eyed college girl in a tartan skirt, sitting under a flowering quince on Kyoto's Yoshida mountain during a free period, with her scrubbed knees pressed together and her mind wide open (open!), reading a book of poems. It is a volume of French Symbolists. She reads their sweat-stained verses in the original and the words do something to her, as only words ever could. They are like the finest cut jewels, or like the faintly pornographic scent of dreams. Decades later, those old thoughts and images still wander through the halls of her mind, opening and un-opening doors all day like soft, feminine ghosts. Abandoned, but not truly forgotten. I can't say

115

for certain what prompted her to make such a connection that afternoon, because V actually does not look anything like young Arthur Rimbaud, but I am certain this passage had something to do with it:

From my ancestors the Gauls I have pale blue eyes, a narrow brain, and awkwardness in competition. I think my clothes are as barbaric as theirs. But I don't butter my hair. The Gauls were the most stupid hide-flayers and hay-burners of their time. From them I inherit: idolatry and love of sacrilege—oh, all sorts of vice; anger, lechery terrific stuff, lechery—lying, above all and laziness. I have a horror of all trades and crafts. Bosses and workers, all of them peasants, and common.

reading in it the card he had laid down. Chisato had never cancelled before today, and who knew when or if she ever would again. She put the cup down, wiped her mouth. Her features were rather plain, but she had a very full very well shaped mouth. The kind that distracts you constantly while sitting across from it. It made him think of someone, but he could not think who. He said:

–If you are interested in Rimbaud, we could read some of his works when we are done with our current book. I wouldn't mind re-reading it, but I know I never will if it's for myself.

She folded her hands in front of her sadly.

–I doubt Miss Chisato would enjoy it at all. She would find such writing melodramatic and overwrought.

–If you think so. I suppose next time, we'll all have to discuss what to read next anyway. Well, I'm fine staying longer if you wish, but we could also end early? You seem— –The appropriate word eluded him.– —*tired.*

Yuki jumped on the chance.

–Yes please, let's do that. I'm not sure what it is, I'm so preoccupied today. I didn't sleep well last night.

She paid for their teas, and then they were standing outside the door. With any other pupil, it was natural to always speak French, regardless of whether they were actually in a session, but with Yuki-san he found himself switching the moment they were out of it. He knew it didn't matter how well he spoke Japanese, his slight mistakes vexed her. His feminine cadences wrecked her fantasy. If Yuki was king, he'd never be allowed to speak anything but French ever again, which is exactly why he denied her sometimes. Unaware even that he did it. It was a petty, subconscious punishment but—he could be petty too, in his way.

「Then I will text you next week.」

「All right. Thank you. Otsukaresama desu.」

「Otsukaresama desu.」 He bowed, turned to leave, and her voice rang out in the hollow, moist noon.

「Wait. You forgot—I forgot to pay you!」

「Oh.」 He turned back, and she was already searching for her wallet. While she looked, he analyzed her purse. Like her clothes, expensive. But not flashy. Her status symbols were tasteful. Always present and on display though, so anybody could see that—Miss Yuki had money. He imagined her husband made a lot of it and most likely gave her a big sum each month, in exchange for giving him all the things that showed the world he was blessed in more than merely the material. Now she took a neat stack of that money and used both hands to lay it neatly into her lover's hands. He stared at the bills, not needing to count them to know that—

「Yuki-san, this is entirely too much.」

「But today was a private lesson since Chisato-san wasn't here. Aren't those quite a bit more?」

「Still. ...This is enough for the entire next month. In full.」 He frowned. 「What if you can't show up, or I can't show up? I don't want to have to keep track.」

「You don't have to keep track.」 Her voice was, oddly, almost pleading. 「Please take it. I don't really... need it, and there must be something you can use it for. Aren't there... things?」

For food, for cigarettes, for my room. For taking out a girl who makes God swim up my blood.

For life. Oh yes. Lots of things.

She looked at him alarmed. Like it had occurred to her too late that this gesture might gravely insult him. Far from it. Money was a shorthand gift of life. *And it always put him in the mood to please.* He laid the bills in his wallet. Switched back to French without thinking:

The hand that holds the pen is as good as the one that holds the plow. (What a century for hands!)...

From Rimbaud's "A Season in Hell: Bad Blood"

—I very much appreciate it, Miss Yuki. And if there's
anything I can do for you, please let me know. I want to
make you happy. If I can—

He said it with no innuendo. In that moment, he
really didn't care if they fulfilled their prophecy or not. She
was being good to him, and he wanted to be good back.
Nothing less or more. Miss Yuki closed her eyes though.
Took a deep breath.

She switched to French too—
She asked him if he had anywhere to be.
She moved her piece on the board.

They walked not far, and she paid for the room. She wondered if this was what her husband felt like, as they stood
together in the tiny elevator, her face on his fearfully, his
on hers amused, as if certain she would not have the
courage to go through with it. They got into the room, and
he threw off his light coat—she hung up both his and hers
and then sat on the bed. He didn't sit next to her, and she
was grateful. The close presence would have made her feel
pressured or at least obligated. She didn't look at the room,
at any detail—she wouldn't have been able to describe its
most basic features once they left.

—I've never done anything like this before, –she whispered. It really was her first time in such a place, and he sat
sideways in one of the leather chairs and looked out the
window while he smoked. How did he know she preferred
it that way?

—I know you haven't.

—Is that what they all say?

—Yes. But with some people, I know it is actually true.
I've gotten a good sense by now. For who does and who
doesn't.

–Oh.

–I'm sorry. Perhaps I shouldn't tell you that I'm easy?

–It's fine. I don't know what I want to hear. Anyway, I am the one who asked you here.

I am the one being easy. And she tried to go back through their short relationship, through the handful of hours spent and find one time at least when he had allowed an attraction to her. Where he had raised an expectation, or sparked a controversial topic. No, there was none— always, that *professionalism.* She began to wonder if this was all a terrible mistake. If she was forcing herself on him.

–What are you thinking about, Miss Yuki? It can't be anything good. You're not smiling this time.

He played with a lighter, casually running his fingers through the flame he'd flick up, and she gripped the edge of the bed. *What am I thinking about? That I want you, to own you, feel you, be you, not YOU, but what you are, not YOU, but what you represent, your uniqueness, your otherness, your foreignness, your distance, your maleness, your unavailability, unattainability, dissatisfaction, your complete and utter satisfaction at the world, at your place, limitations, strengths. To have a piece of that unreachable still-ness   that   is   y o u r s e l f .*

Her own breath hurt her and she answered, –I don't know.

–I don't believe you. But you don't have to be honest with me. We are no longer in a paid conversation.

–I have to be when we are?

She thought, he didn't smile like people from here. He had the steppes in his smile.

–Most definitely.

–Then I'll remember that for next week.

–I am serious though. Would you like me to leave? I feel like you didn't come with a plan.

–A plan... for?

–My seduction.

She flailed, and he seemed to regret his lightness.

–Really, I was joking! We can talk, if you prefer. Or would you like me to be quiet?

–No. I couldn't bear the silence right now.

–All right. So I will talk. –He kept it in French. –And what can I do to calm you? To make you feel at ease?

The sweat was on her brow. She fretted over her makeup and looked at the shower. He caught her glance.

–Go ahead. Why don't you shower if you like?

–And you too?

–I'll go when you're done. I want you to relax.

–All right, but before that... will you kiss me?

He stood, left his lighter on the chair, the cigarette in the ashtray. Walked to her and placed his hands on her shoulders.

–Right now?

–Yes. And then I will decide.

He nodded and she watched him. He didn't kiss her mouth. He moved on her neck, slowly, and closing her eyes, she imagined she could feel ash on his lips. *It was a strange sensation.* He moved to her shoulders, his hands going down to her waist, her rib cage, and she kept her eyes shut, a picture flashing into her mind. It was her own husband. He would mash his lips against hers roughly, like waves crashing into a shore, then knead her breasts. Always, always, the motion reminded her of baking. Though they slept in one bed still, they made love less than a few times a year, and she was happy with that arrangement. Rather than angering her, the knowledge that he kept a mistress relieved her of any sense of guilt over resisting his advances—the way he cycled around her body, hitting spots as if they were buttons. She fearfully waited for that now, but *he* touched no part of her that could be conceived as sexual—unhurried, from her head, her shoulders, her arms, her upper chest, her face—relaxed, as if he had no need himself and simply wanted nothing more than—to kiss her. Even the tobacco—she was normally put off by the acrid taste of her husband's tongue and disliked smokers in general, yet in this instance, it was somehow different. The smoke belonged to him, unbitter and organic, and no more unpleasant than the smell of a summer bonfire. She enjoyed it, him, the way the elements all fit together and relaxed. Told him that she would go to the bathroom now.

She did, thorough but fast, coming back wrapped in a hotel robe, and then he got up and returned wrapped up as well. When they got into bed, he turned away tactfully while she removed her robe and waited for her to get under the covers before turning back. Yuki wondered if that belonged to some European tradition. She on the other hand had no such reservations and studied him with a thoroughness that bordered on bookish.

–Is something wrong? –He smiled, unconcerned, his head propped on his hand. Miss Yuki wasn't quite sure how to answer. *Wrong?* No, he was very much like she imagined (if she'd been the type to imagine others naked)—broad shouldered, long, consumptive, hairy in the places that men are, unhairy in the places fair, foreign men could be expected to be. It was a splendid body if that was your type and an awful one if it wasn't, nothing wrong or right about it and yet she couldn't help but note that certain parts she'd been anticipating were absent and certain parts she had not been anticipating—were not. The silence stretched until he cleared his throat (something really was caught in it) and Miss Yuki reached out and touched his shoulder.

–I was staring. I'm sorry. I didn't mean to be rude.

–I'm sorry too. I should have said something, but I was so certain that you knew.

–I did, –she lied.

–Well, on the chance that you really didn't and this is not what you want, we can stop right here. It happens sometimes. It won't bother me.

He closed his eyes, removing himself from the decision and Miss Yuki swallowed, surveyed his nudeness stretched out next to her, like a banquet table on which everything was all for her. Carefully, she traced a vein on his forearm and determined from some aloof vantage point that she was actually *more* interested now.

–I already said that I want to. But I... I don't. I'm not sure I'm going to know what... well. What to *do*.

She reddened terribly and he opened his eyes. Crawled forward to her and that tone was back in his voice. A smile, or was it mockery? She never could tell.

–You mean you've never been with a man before?

–Are you making fun of me?

–I would never do that. But then if you have, don't worry, Miss Yuki. –He traced his name on her shoulder with a fingertip—Polite. His quiet, coarse voice bleached her ten shades of white. –I will tell you *exactly* what I like.

She hadn't heard words like that before, nobody had made her want to hear them, and in the language of her heart, no less. –Do this—, or –Yes, *there*—, still, he couldn't make them filthy, and she put herself all over him, observing the uncomplicated way he took pleasure as if conducting an erotic experiment. It was all so surprisingly *easy*. She sunk into a detached absorption, giving him more, more, until he drew his hand along her hair, then gripped her arm, unembarrassed. She watched his face— surprised at her own fascination, but unable to look away.

Then she lay on top of him and his drenched body was still trembling. The heat in the room was almost unbearable. Yuki traced his jutting collarbone.

–You have no idea how long I've wanted to see you like this.

–How long? You've known me for a month.

–Has it only been that long?

–Yes. And I never knew the whole time that you thought anything special of me.

–I was sure it was plainer than day, the way I stared at you in lessons.

–No. –He kissed her on the mouth, pulled back. –Your face is like a beautiful picture. Like a bijin²⁵ in an old movie. It reveals nothing.

Neither does yours. But she no longer had to ask herself if he desired her—he unwrapped, tasted, liquefied her, begged to hear her voice, *I'll do anything you tell me to, anything you ask.* Anything? She found herself speaking, mercifully, before she could think.

²⁵ Lit. beautiful person; a beauty.

–Fais-moi pleurer. –And he gave such a look, that she shrank back. –You... won't?

–If that's what you'd like. But—a little? Or a lot?

–As you think.

–You must tell me though if I do something you don't want. Promise, you'll say.

–I promise, –she said solemnly, and he put his mouth on her neck. A moment later, his hand on that spot. Like he had marked it.

–All right, Miss Yuki. Turn around. Face down.

She put her cheek down into the pillow, and he raised her lower body up towards him. He said and did nothing for some time, and she lay there, listening to the silence of his stare, taking so long like he'd never seen such things before. Like they hadn't been face deep in each other for

the past hour. The sweat dripped backwards off her, spine
to nape, and enough time passed that she opened her
mouth, certain he must be expecting her to say something.
But then she heard him make some sound. The softest
laughter.

–You know, I lied earlier.

–About?

–When I said I couldn't tell how you felt about me. I
knew you wanted me to fuck you from the very first day
we met. Not because of any way you looked at me in lessons, but still. I knew. And now here we are.

Shame squirmed across her profile, but she blushed
too. Making him laugh more.

–It's true. Isn't it?

Yuki bit her lip and nodded, and he gripped the back
of her neck as a mother lynx cuffs its cub. Gently, but with
absolute authority.

–Then say it.

She closed her eyes tight; dredged the obedience from
deep inside. It was liberating to submit to someone she had
no respect for.

–I wanted you—from the day we first met.

He sighed then, like this made him happy and put a
kiss on her lower back. If he didn't do it all soon, she was
sure she would scream, but humiliating her seemed to
excite him as well.

–Did you think of being with me when you were at
home?

She trembled. Squirmed more against his hand.

–Sure.

–Did you think about me doing this to you while you
were with your husband?

Her breath drew in loudly and he asked if he was going
too far.

–Not far enough. –She talked into her pillow and that made him sigh more. Appreciatively.

–Such a good slut for me, Miss Yuki. Your husband is a lucky man to get you every night. Please tell him that I said so.

Hearing him mentioned so insolently felt like swallowing a needle—she almost opened her mouth to tell him to keep him out of his. But absurd as it was, she couldn't help but picture her husband's face if she *were* to ever say it. Imagine! The thought made her glisten, narrow; some unusual sensation welled up—before she could pinpoint exactly what it was or warn him—it all happened so fast. Too paralyzed to even move, Yuki breathed her disgrace into the mattress.

–I am so... *sorry!* I didn't—I didn't realize I had to—

Go to the bathroom? Urinate? What word do you even say at a time like this? She was terrified to look back. Once she did though, she saw that he was utterly unbothered. He kissed the backs of her dripping wet legs; shivering. Like he'd done it.

–I don't care if you pee, but that's not what that was. That's never happened before?

–Not —*that.*

She collapsed back into the sheets, relieved and mortified and...

–You really are the Foolish Virgin. Next time, don't let him stop until you do.

–I'll be waiting a long time. He and I don't...

–You don't—?

–We.

–'We,' what then? –he taunted. –I didn't hear. You and your husband don't, what?

–*We hardly ever have sex and when we do, it's not—*

Right as she said it, he pushed into her again. She

125

cried out, poured out. That he could manipulate her body so easily was its own exquisite embarrassment. He pulled his index finger away; pearl colored strands came with it, and he mocked her more.

–Look how you get while we talk about him. Cheating on him excites you. Does it?

–I don't know. –There was an edge in her voice, as she panted. She resented him cutting so deep. But then, who had asked him to? –Maybe it does. But maybe he deserves it.

–Then he must not appreciate what he has. It's too bad. If you were mine, I would make sure you never wanted anybody else—

It seemed the type of empty boast a man makes when he's with a woman who has broke her vows for him, but she looked back then—Yuki's throat closed. Because she knew. *If he could, he would. He really would.* And yet there was no way to get there. None at all. Never had she been closer, never ever had she been further away. The futility made the tears finally come, and when he saw her eyes shine up, his expression turned immediately. He drew her tight into his arms.

–Here, I did what you asked, let's stop this.

–It's all right. It's what I wanted.

He kissed her forehead. Wiped a tear away.

–But I hate to see you cry. I hate making you cry. Wouldn't you rather I make you forget? Whatever is making you sad.

–You can't—

–I can. You'll see.

He lay her down, so gently then, like she had wanted him to from the start but had been too afraid to ask. (Why was it easier to ask to be defiled than to be loved?) He put his hand over her eyes, drew them shut. Put kisses on her closed eyes, like hers was the precious corpse of someone on a bier. Whispered things to her, whatever came to his mind, to him nonsense making no sense, but maybe it was non-nonsense to her: *La raison m'est née. Le monde est bon. Je bénirai la vie. J'aimerai mes frères. Ce ne sont plus des promesses d'enfance. Ni l'espoir d'échapper à la vieillesse et à la mort. Dieu fait ma force, et je loue Dieu.*[26] Miss Yuki melted, disintegrated (why was listening to him talk better than anything, better than anything); made him talk, made him reach his limit. It wasn't a request: *Je te veux.*[27] More like a brutal wish, and right then, she knew it

he was hers.

Nodding her consent, she was *scared*

don't be, I won't hurt you

and he gave his love slow, with a restrained violence that made him bite his lip bloody while he traced hers with a finger. The sheets were soaked; her mind really did burn to empty cinders. Only the tiniest tarnish—perhaps he had become overwhelmed by her teared face?

「Yuki-san—aishiteiru.」

She had just enough strength left to press a finger against his lips. As if he had uttered an obscenity.

–Do it. *In French.*

Then she lay with him afterwards in the blackened afternoon room, and his body was iridescent and hot. She steeped in his heat, pretending to be asleep, wondering if he was, but not wanting to be spoken to, said nothing. Feeling her own radiance, incandescent, then cooling; instantly, she catalogued it, because it was her nature. The smile of realization was for her alone: *You thought he couldn't, but this is his poetry. Removed from the realm of verse and pens, inscribed on things that die faster than paper.* When she turned to touch him though, she stopped her hand. Stretched on the bed, unaware of her, he stared at

[26] Reason dawns on me. The world is good. I shall bless life. I shall love my neighbor. These are no longer childhood vows. Nor a trick to escape old age and death. God is my strength and God I praise.

[27] I want you.

the ceiling in the melancholic gloom, and she saw his eyes flicker with a thousand thoughts that would never be revealed. He dreamed, belonging only to himself. *Like we all do.* And she was gripped again by that infinite sadness—wondering if he felt it too. Certain that he did.

–Je te comprends.

–What?

He turned to look at her, drugged, and she shrugged her naked shoulders.

–Je te comprends. I understand you.

–You do?

–Yes. So may I ask you a question?

–Go ahead.

–Why did you agree to come here today?

–Because you asked me to bed, and I wanted it too.

Sitting up, he smoked a frightening amount now, one after another, and she pictured him at home. He had a girlfriend, it must be, a childish, sexy gyaru who washed his clothes and licked him in bed.

–So that really is the only reason?

–Miss Yuki, do you wish me to say that I love you? But I already did.

Yes, she said to herself, he is right, and you are being unfair. *You* wanted to see what you were missing and now you know—here was the perfect little sin, the thing you desired no sooner than you were done with it! Candor released some of her sorrow and she turned to look at him. She could do it now, more sure, and her fingers plucked the current cigarette form his mouth lightly, grinding it out in the ashtray on the bedside table next to her.

–You shouldn't smoke so much. –Her hand on his temple was unexpectedly gentle. –It will ruin your face.

If he was surprised by her concern, he didn't show it, but paid her courtesy by not smoking the rest of the time.

They parted two hours after they had come, and he asked
her if she still wanted to meet for conversation next week.
She looked past him and out into the street, while she tried
to gauge the temperature of that one question. Did he think
she was ashamed enough to never want to see him again?
Yuki reflected. In the room, he'd teased her, called her a
virgin, (and what did she know about sex, really?) but now,
with all barriers snapped firmly back in place, she determined he looked young enough to be her son. He could've
been one of her students back at the university. If one of
them had to be in the wrong, surely it was her?

But then, she saw: pale hands, grabbing two swords of
mackerel out of a low cooler in a supermarket. (The fishes
scream silently, lashed against a slate of cobalt-blue styrofoam.) Miss Yuki could imagine his girlfriend as a generally
useless specimen, but the type who would at least have
learned how to properly grill a fish. The meal would be
waiting when he got home, and her mouth would be pursed
with suspicion. They would eat, (fight? watch TV?), bathe
(she'd let him go first), and in bed, he would whisper apologies, and pull her hair hard, and tell her that he loved her.
But unlike Yuki, the girl would be foolish enough to believe
him.

Je te veux.

–So are we still meeting next week?

C'est un Démon, vous savez, ce n'est pas un homme. [28]

A wet, warm relief spread through her and she smiled.

–Of course. Why would we not?

–All right. I just like things to be completely clear.
Then I will write you.

Everything rewound; he bowed at her, she at him, and
then he turned, strode across the street, freer than a flame.
She watched his feet quicken to avoid a scooter curving
around the bend, and for a moment she imagined the

[28] He is a demon, you know, and not a man.

scooter clipping him. Better yet, a car materializing out of nowhere and simply mowing him down. He'd die, but not right away, and she'd walk over slowly, kneel, grip his hand and observe the death leaking out with the same detached interest she'd watched the life seep out of him in their room.

If only she believed in fate or poetic justice!

But she was starting to suspect that she didn't believe. Not like he did.

TEN

Two Procrastinators

This morning rained sheets and sheets, and by noon it all stopped. Now it is the late afternoon time. A hot moistness has come around, and they sit on the river bank, on the far side where nobody goes, stunned in it. Nothing questions their presence, not even the few spiritless ducks that quickly swim away from them. Her bag in the reeds, her umbrella unused, Aya sucks on a lollipop while she tells V about a movie she saw with her boyfriend last week. He lies in the grass next to her and smokes. Although her recap is animated, the actors sound vapid, the plot artificial, and the only interest he can conjure for these pneumatic Hollywood flicks she seems to eat up involves imagining being alone with Aya and her uniformed body for 90 minutes in a matinee dark. The dark and them and all that *possibility.*

⌜Are you even listening to me?⌟

⌜Yes,⌟ he lies.

⌜No, you were *not.*⌟ She pinches him on the arm.

Designated recently as her favorite person to procrastinate with, Aya imagines that V himself is always waiting, postponing. For something. Which is why she called on him today to crush an hour in town. Later, she will have to finish a biology write-up (bovine eye/dissection) with two study partners, but in their lazy moment, that is still three thousand and six hundred seconds away.

⌜Fine, then, if you don't like my movie, why don't you tell me about your day? Did you do anything interesting?⌟

He ashes onto the rich dirt next to them and turns his face to the sun.

⌜I suppose. I had a lesson.⌟

⌜Mmmmmh.⌟ Aya draws the sound out and twirls the candy in her mouth. ⌜And was it with a girl?⌟

⌜No.⌟

⌜So it was with a boy?⌟

He turns to her, his green eyes gleaming.

⌜It was with an angel. They're sexless, you know.⌟

⌜Are you serious?⌟

⌜Not a girl or a boy. She was a woman.⌟

⌜Hmmm.⌟ Her mouth is dubious. ⌜Well, what kind of woman?⌟

⌜A quiet kind. Pretty kind.⌟

⌜Prettier than me?⌟

Now he grins—he never tires of feeding her artless vanity.

⌜Now where,⌟ he reaches out to touch her pout, ⌜am I going to find a girl prettier than you?⌟

⌜Hmph. So are your students always different, pretty women? Like those girls you spend an hour with?⌟

From another, the question would ice his mood, but V knows that her directness is constant—it is herself. She sits next to him, tearing blades of grass out of the earth and scattering them on his jeans, appearing detached, possibly fishing, but more than validation, her posture confirms a pure desire to be trusted with his secrets. He has agreed to try it, he has agreed that they should be friends. And friends tell each other things, though V must confess, the last time he was friends with someone in high school, he was in high school himself. He goes with pure honesty:

⌜*Saa*. Yes, Aya-chan, they are usually women. Not all of them are pretty, but she was. I spent the whole afternoon with her before you called me. Two hours, not one.

Does it matter? Heru mono janai shi.[29] And I still like you more.⌋

He expects her to get grouchy; Aya only glimmers.

「Well if you're going to talk about some woman you were with, guess what happened to me?⌋

He cannot guess.

「I finally asked her. To go to a movie with me.⌋

「Ahh, *her*. And how did that go?⌋

「Better than I thought! I guess approaching you at the river had been like practice. It wasn't nerve-wracking at all. And she was so nice about it. We're aiming for the end of the month. Our holiday will start by then and I'll have a little break.⌋

「See, Aya-chan.⌋ He ruffles her hair. 「I'm proud of you. I knew you could talk to girls.⌋

「You said it was trouble.⌋

「It is, but it's easy trouble. You talk, you smile, you do something together, next thing you know...⌋

She pinches his arm again.

「I'm not *you*.⌋

「Not *yet*. Next time, you can tell me all about it.⌋

「Ok. I probably won't be able to see you until next month though. My supplementary school is starting soon after.⌋

「It's fine, Aya-chan.⌋

「It's too bad though.⌋

She lays her head in his lap and he looks out over the water, thinking. His hands are in her hair, he twists a black strand around his finger, admiring its shiny strength, and she closes her eyes, seeming to sleep. Then her voice rings out, asking for a cigarette.

「No,⌋ he says absently, eyes on the other shore.

「But you promised me before you'd teach me how to blow a smoke ring!⌋

[29] Roughly: It doesn't diminish through use.

133

「Did I? Well, I'm taking it back.」 He takes a drag of his own. 「You're not going to believe this, but I heard these things are *really bad* for you.」

She scowls at him.

「They're really bad for you too. And you're bad for ME. So come on, just one.」

「NO.」

「Onegai!」 Aya turns her eyes up, a glance translated to him as a liquid cuteness. Irradiated, he hands her a stick without further word and fumbles in his pocket looking for matches. He lights it for her and she blows purple smoke at him. All of it skids out around—the smoke, the water, her star eyes, and he is gripped in her look by an unexpected question singed out in his mind—a sudden and twisted prayer sent on to the sun:

God. It's V.

I wanna fuck this little girl and give her more cigarettes. Am I going to Hell?

But as always, God remains silent.

「I forgot your girl's name.」 Something urges him to keep it all moving. Meanwhile, he's trying to show her how to blow the ring. *No, not like that. Put your tongue back. Look. Make a shape like this with your mouth.*

「Her name is Ren.」

「Ren-chan nan ya. So the most important question.」 Her face is serious, until she sees his: 「Is Ren-chan prettier than *me?*」

「Ha ha ha. Why? You want to hear me talk about OTHER people? Okashii!」

「Sure. I'd like to know what turns Aya's head.」

「If you insist. Well, she's so good at school she doesn't

have to go to jyuku, I'm really jealous. She had the second highest grade in class on our last chem test and she's agreed to go over it with me. And she likes crazy movies too, and Miike, and stupid American horror movies. She has legs like Sailor Moon, hair down to here,⌋ Aya draws a pinkie across his jaw, ⌈and we're going to see a scary movie and do purikura. I'm so excited! I'm glad I listened to you and just did it. You're right, I can't wait for us to accidentally kiss, like some anime.⌋

⌈If you want it to happen, you have to make it happen. And.⌋ He hesitates, then figures he may ask. Since they are friends. ⌈Will you tell your boyfriend about her?⌋

Aya turns her face into one of his jeaned knees and sighs.

⌈I should, right? But I don't know what to say. And I don't even want to break up with him! But not telling him is—selfish, isn't it?⌋ She doesn't wait for his answer. ⌈You don't understand. The whole thing is so confusing. Not to mention, I don't even know another girl who likes a girl.⌋

⌈Probably more of your friends do, but they are just as scared to talk about it as you are.⌋

⌈Have you ever loved a boy, V-kun?⌋

⌈Not that I know of. But my best friend in Paris was ryoutouzukai. And my other good friend liked both too. I've had girlfriends too, who were also with women...⌋

⌈I guess that's why you moved to Paris. You wanted to find more people who would understand you...⌋

V tenses, bristles a little over the implication that he is a being who requires a special *understanding*. But then, imagines it is silly to offend himself over the phrasing. His body unclenches and he watches a triad of ducks navigate through the reeds. Since the hotel room, they had not talked about that. Like the conversation regarding his motivations, it is a conversation he never wanted, though he knows it is at times necessary. As Aya-chan will learn those necessary awkward conversations with girls who do not yet have that option on their radar. Knowing when and how to have this talk is similar to knowing when and how to ask for a kiss[30]—one develops a sixth sense, fine-honed by humiliation. He decided that evening to tell Aya-chan before they went into the rabuho, and if that imploded everything, even better. The risk was as always: disgusting her, or *that* becoming the sole reason for her wanting him,[31] but when he told her outside the lobby, she brushed it off so effortlessly. Made him feel so normal. What an addictive feeling.

After love and before sleep, she did start to ask him question upon question, and for once, he answered them all truthfully. Yes, it had been like this as far back as he could remember. As a child, he'd glittered whenever his mother had called him her little man. But it's not as if she'd made him like this. Nobody had made him like this. And he'd had the genetic luck to grow tall and thin. It wasn't so hard to hide, with the right clothes. Also why he always wore an outer coat! No matter how hot. But when he'd lived in Paris, he'd got close to friends who knew how to go about that all without a doctor. Pills and gels, and they couldn't disappear his breasts, but they did deepen his already deepish voice. Tightened his body more. He didn't take those pills now. He didn't know how to get them here. Now that he blended in better (at least in *that* respect), it was harder to meet the right people. Even without it though, his voice stayed gravelled and he still had to shave. Not as often as Rodrigo, but enough. His roommate hadn't even known until the first time they'd gone to the public bath together. They'd soaked in the sentou and V had stretched out his arms, leaned back, closed his eyes. Opened them to find his roommate staring

[30]One day, more people would have this on their radar, but not in the summer of 2003.

[31]And he never wanted 'that' to be the reason for why someone chose him, but he was also a pragmatist at heart; let us leave it at that.

at his chest. Take a picture? he'd asked, body wet and voice dry, and Rodrigo sputtered, turned away. It wasn't mentioned again. Nobody in the bath house ever got on his case either. And women liked being with a man who couldn't knock them up. Not that he didn't think about it. Getting a woman pregnant, a woman getting him pregnant, was his highest fantasy, but if it took him sleeping with a man, he would never do it. And have you ever slept with a man like you? Aya asked. He said, no. No men, period. He told her, it's not that he didn't like men. He liked himself too. But he didn't trust himself. His father had been full of the Bad Blood and so he was too...

Aya-chan put a finger on his cheekbone and played with his hair and made him hard and she said,

I think you're being too harsh on yourself.

Then they both fell asleep.

Now by the river, with a dozing Aya-chan on his lap, he checks his phone. Still some time left. The cramming, the exhaustion, the reports: Aya never really complains about school, only nods off mid-sentence. V is content to not speak. Then she opens her eyes and follows something in the grass near them; grabs it; cups it in her hands, letting the tiny light stream out between her fingers before letting it go. A firefly. V is thinking he never saw one before living here.

He says: 「I want a question now. Why Paris?」

Aya turns her face sideways on his thighs.

「Huh?」

「When we were talking before, on our second not-date, you said you wanted to go to Paris. That you've wanted to go for years and years. But you're not interested in learning French, right?」

「Learning another language would be too hard. I already have enough problems with English!」

「You're young, you'd learn quickly. You're good at singing, that means you have a good ear. I could teach you. But still, why Paris then?」

Her voice is disembodied and muffles into his pants.

「I don't know. It's something I've wanted for a long time. It doesn't really make sense. It's a random thing, really. Like you, I mean, why would you want to have a wife and kids so much?」

「Because I think it would be beautiful.」

Aya sits upright. She wonders what she would call this particular expression of his. Undecided, she puts her head back down on him again.

「You always say the oddest things. Like you're in a dream.」

「Maybe I am. But we were talking about you, ojousan. Paris. Continue.」

「There's not much to tell. I got the idea when my mother went there once when we were little—to visit an old school friend. She was gone for two weeks and it was the first time she had ever gone away from us and I remember being very sad, that she could leave me and my brother like that, but then she sent a postcard. The city on it looked so pretty, and when she came home, she looked so happy. I really wanted to see it with my own eyes. I guess it's a silly, because I'm really not interested in France itself at all—and cheese is awful. But I'd want to go up on the Eiffel Tower.」

He puts his hand over on the top of her head.

「Maybe you could go with your mother, if she liked it so much?」

「No.」

She spits the word so quickly that V tenses—a gull

flies overhead. He watches it, waits for her to gloss over the response, because as open as she is about most aspects of her life, her family she would routinely brush off: Oh, what is there to say about them? A father, a mother and a brother. They're boring.

Now a few seconds pass before she speaks again.

「That sounded kind of harsh, huh?」Aya's voice is small. 「I don't want you to think that I don't like my mother, but being with her is sometimes worse than being alone. My friend Yui is best friends with her mom and they talk about *everything*, but the only thing my mom cares about is if my grades are going up or down. As far she she's concerned, learning is God, and I'm not like that at all. Anyway, if I went with her, the trip wouldn't be romantic, and I think Paris sounds like the most romantic city in the world.」

He lets her have her opinion by not voicing his.

「Well, maybe you could go on your honeymoon then. When you get married.」

「Maybe. So does that mean I should go? Stinky trains and all?」

「Of course. You should see the city at least once in your life.」

「Maybe you and I could go once.」

V's heart thumps.

「What?」

「Paris. We could go together—you speak French. You've lived there. You must know where everything is.」

She says not a word about romance.

Yes, I do know. His mind revolves—

They sit in the vivid, dry sun of the Jardin Luxembourg. Aya wears a summer dress. Girls don't wear white muslin dresses like that anymore, but in his vision she does, and her dark hair is drawn back in a low pony tail.

She wears a straw hat to protect her face. He packed bread and fruit (no cheese), and earlier they walked along the quay, and later they will go have dinner and maybe go to a club and listen to live music, and then stroll along and be meteored in lights, but for now they sit still in front of the palace. They don't talk. She drinks lemonade and passes him the bottle and then they kiss and she's sugary and tart.

They sit there *like a couple.*

Trés romantique.

And trés impossible.

V's involuntary and uncharacteristic fantasy is wrecked by the cry of an alarm—they had set her phone, in case they both fell asleep. Now he sits up, glad for the distraction.

「Time to go.」

Aya's answer is to push him over and lay on top of him in the grass.

「Yes, but can't I stay here with you?」

The feel of her body sinks into his *how can she be so WARM?*, and he breathes out, torn, enduring it—

muslin dresses, straw hats, fluid, lustrous—

「Well, what do you have today? Is it important?」

「Very. Last write up of our bovine eye dissection, which will be worth almost as much as our final exam. But I don't want to go.」

「You never want to go.」

「Well, whose fault is that?」

Mine, mine, mine.

She leans close to him.

「You smell like smoke.」

But she says it like it's a good thing. Contrition and guilt are strains of emotion V's psyche has virulently refused to accept. Still, he blushes. The source of this blood he cannot say, beyond a faint, gnawing sense that he does not deserve such simple adoration, her categorical acceptance of his vices. He brushes his mouth with the back of his hand and lifts her until she is upright.

「Aya-chan, you know I say this with *extreme* regret, but you need to go now.」

「I could skip.」 Starting at his knee, she slowly draws her small hand along his jeaned thigh. 「I could bribe Yui to send over her notes tonight.」

All the weapons are hers, but he stops her hand when it reaches further. With her other hand, Aya runs her fingers along his neck. Her index finger stops here, there; it takes him a moment to figure out that she's resting them on the kiss marks. Next to him, she says quietly:

「I know we're friends now, but still. You always act so cool. Like you never think about that at all. Like you never wonder about doing it again to see if it was as good as you remember.」

No need to wonder, because it was that good, Aya-chan. It was better.

「So, *do* you ever think about it?」

「No,」 he says too quickly and she laughs. Taps a finger on the tip of his nose.

「U-so-tsu-ki.」

Da-i-su-ki.

He turns now, looks at Aya's neck. It rises out of the stiff collar of her school dress shirt like the fresh, firm stalk of a plant. Not a mark on it. He sees her body on that enormous bed after he'd carefully stripped off her clothes. Skin gleaming like a field in August. Running his hands over her, admiring it.

Not a mark on it.

He swallows and his lips move without thinking.

「Of course I think about it.」

Her fingertip presses to a bruise on his neck; she says

into the spot shyly, 「Me too. So can't we go? Just one more time? I want to try to give you a kiss mark.」

And if you did, it would be the only one that counts but
「...or, you don't have any money today—?」

「Today, I have a lot of money and you have a lot of school. Thank God you do because it's the only thing keeping me from blowing a week's rent and slipping a full ten steps back towards Hell.」

Aya turns back to face him, her eyes serious.

「You really believe that?」

「What now?」

「That it's so wrong?」

He looks away sharply.

「You're in high school, Aya-chan. What do you think? Where I'm from, it's against the law.」

「So if you think it's so wrong, why did you do it to begin with?」

「Because I'm weak and stupid! I do all kinds of dumb things all the time, so that's really no good metric.」

「So you are sorry we were together—? Like that?」

「Of course not. That is not what I said.」

「Then I think that means that somewhere, you also believe that it's not really wrong.」

「I don't know, sincerely, I don't. I'm not smart enough to have this conversation. I know two things: That it feels rightwrong, or wrongright. And that you need to go.」

「But I want to finish talking about this.」

「No, we're done here, you're going to be late.」

「Anta no mondai janai. It's not your problem.」

Stripped of her normal polite form, the pronoun has the sting of a mild slap, and he wonders if this is because she's so comfortable with him—or being impertinent. The normally temperate V feels his mood fluctuate in a mildly disturbing way, and he sets his tone into frosty courtesy.

「You're right, ojousan. It isn't my problem. So do as you please.」

「I will, so you don't have to act all high and mighty, like being with you is some dangerous drug. You really are so full of yourself. Yes, I have a crush on you *and* you're a gaijin creep *and* we're not going to end up together and I don't even *want to* end up with some *guy* who wants a bunch of snotty, icky children. So please relax.」

V wants to relax. He is humbled by Aya-chan's ability to corral the situation so cleanly, even as his soul prickles and shrinks. He lies down on the ground, resting his face against the warm dirt, listening to the sound of the earth turning and the moving river. She'll go to her study group now, right? He doesn't even need to say anything more. Later, when his mind is cool, he'll write her a text and apologize. Or what is he even upset about and what will he even apologize for? He pulls himself up and decides, there is no time better than the present.

「I'm sorry, Aya-chan. I didn't want to get in a fight with you. But you said you're struggling with grades and I don't want to be a bad influence.」

「You're the *worst* influence.」 Aya sighs. 「And you're right. I am not doing well enough in biology to skip this. I really should leave. Can I tell you something though? Before I go?」

「You're wearing a new sweater today. It's very nice. I already noticed.」

It's a joke: V has still yet to see Aya in any clothes other than her school uniform—she is not amused.

「Come on! This is important. Lean closer.」

「Just say whatever you want to say.」

「It's embarrassing though. I can't look at you...」

「More embarrassing than admitting you have a crush on me?」

⌈Will you please stop? And close your eyes.⌋

V does it.

The breeze pushes a strand of her hair to his face, and he inadvertently tastes it. A moment later, her lip touches the edge of his ear. The sensation jolts him live-wire, and the sound of his own racing heart sickens him.

So freeze.[32]

---

[32] On Expectation Versus Reality in Love

When listening to women expound on their emotions— he kept his own mind shut. It was better that way. And he wouldn't polarize emotions into male and female. That seemed plain lazy. Perhaps because the contradiction lay latent in himself, but he imagined that for every woman looking for ⌈forever⌋ there were just as many who found the whole idea utterly ridiculous. It was a rather absurd idea, objectively speaking: One person to give the sky above and the ground below; the big beautiful mirror to find, lose, distort oneself in—impregnate the body and mind with every shade of meaning. What a thing to believe! And still—as he was not afraid to be condemned to happiness, he believed in it too.

That afternoon, he knew Aya was not about to ask him to ride her off on a white horse. And she didn't want to only lie with him either, as much as they both would have liked that. No, it was something else. It was the strange way she used her mouth. Not on him, but to get in him, through him, as if his body was a prison she would free his spirit from; as if his flesh had become secondary and, for once, unuseful.

So-called *talking*.

That he was not used to.

And watching her struggle, the awareness that beyond her expectations, his own lay obscured as well, dissolved like an alien berry on the tongue. Fragrant but potentially toxic.

Both of them on their knees, eyes closed, congealed together in that gelatinous evening time, Aya put her hand on his shoulder and gave something of herself before she even spoke. And he gave her something of him. They fused when she let it down, allowing his calm, entropic mind to enter her static world and almost immediately he cut himself on it, as if on the crystal-edge of the sharpest reality.

In that ¼ of a second, she made him feel so godless and *fine*; and he wanted to give it up to her—the whole world and every good thing in it. Everything she desired. However, V didn't have the world.

An incomplete catalogue of the things he actually could offer:

Afternoons like this one, the color of brass; nights the color of glass, naked-warm under futons; mistreated manga and French novels with ash-blistered pages; creatively cheap meals of egg and rice, and pots of borscht (he made an amazing borscht); naps on every bench in Kyoto; lack of discord or explanation; mind-alteringly hot shower-sex; kissing and more kissing (he liked kissing even more than he did smoking); night traipsing; one-sided conversations; uproar; fervid make-ups; empty—fridges, oft empty—wallets; generosity (not) backed up by substance; silences of every hue; joking—music.

Emotional sedition. Ambiguity. Tears.

All thrown together and doused in a love like gasoline —consuming everything; ardent and indifferent.

No mirrors. No illusions. No Paris. No future.

A pile of useless things.

As for his deepest self? It was not a question to be asked. For V, love proffered after sex was just good manners. (It was either that, or an explanation.)

But it stops here. Once long ago he became convinced that thinking too much about oneself was perhaps even more harmful than staring straight into the sun.

He avoided both.

He avoids it now.

....

Aya's body next to his feels subtle and molecular. She shifts, moves in front of him—the wet air is syrupy, but that's not why he is breathing hard. V's abrupt realization that he is veritably dying for a high schooler's (not even certain!) love-confession is the closest to acute abashment he can recall feeling. Still, things are what they are. He figures—this isn't about happily ever after. She just wants to release her feelings—it's harmless.

His eyes are still closed, and she speaks:

「V-kun, I—」

...comme deux bons enfants, libres de se promener dans le Paradis de tristesse...[33]

His eyes open (a hallucination? Or had he said it out loud?)

Her eyes startle open too and—

「Aya, stop.」

「What? What's wrong?」

「Don't say it.」

[33] Like two children, wandering in a Paradise of sadness...

146

「But you don't even know what I'm going to say!」

「Yeah, but whatever it is, it's not for me to hear. Your boyfriend. Or that girl. Ren. Say it to one of them.」

His words fall all around them. Like a rejected present, she holds her hands out—wilts back.

V thinks she may cry and braces himself for it, but he's wrong about her again. She stares at him for a full minute, then stands with an intent composure.

「I... don't... understand you.」

He helps her brush the dirt off her clothes, and they gather her things. He wipes a speck of mud off her face. The super-charge of the moments before lies struck dead in the grass. They both become smooth and calm, and he feels a certain deflated disappointment outlined with relief at the diffused situation. Then she slams her umbrella into her bag. It could be a slip of her hand, but he knows better. *She's hurt.* But will not dignify him with that knowledge. Her back is regal, she starts to walk away, and the part of him that's recessive says: Good.

Tell her you shouldn't meet again, tell her it's over, this is the right time, this is the perfect time. You cannot do right for her, you know that. It's already gone way further than it should.

「Aya-chan, wait!」

Marching purposefully towards the walk, she turns. She's not crying, but her eyes are rimmed in red.

「What?」

He runs to meet her in the middle of the path. Reeds to the right of them and reeds to the left. But although she turned back, her voice is hard:

「What do you want, V? Hurry up, I have to go, remember?」

Say it, say it, say it.

He leans down.

「Aya...」

We won't meet again; we cannot meet again. You're sorry, but you can't. So open your mouth and fucking say it.

She taps her foot, and he bites his lip.

Then breathes out—

「I shouldn't have acted that way.」 He traces a fingertip down her face, and she closes her eyes. 「Let's go do something; karaoke, or I'll take you to dinner. Then we'll get a room. Onegai. Skip the study group. For me.」

There. There.

He knows it. The curse is painted on the wall.

V hangs in limbo waiting for a reaction when a bird flies up and startles Aya. She trips into him. And grabs him around the waist hard. There's his answer. He puts his arms around her, and they stand, without words and— *Oh Aya, I'm terrible at all this, can't you see?*

Finally she speaks, the smile brimming in her voice:

「You could've had me for nothing five minutes ago. But you played too hard to get *again*, so now it's too late. I'll call you next month. I have a free afternoon the beginning of next month. You can wait that long, right?」

But any anger she had is wiped away because now she's sure. Worth more than a kokuhaku,[34] she flies to her studies, and her study mates will spend all night trying to untangle her smile, to no avail.

[34] Confession

V lies back down by the river, and smokes and smokes. When he runs out of tobacco, he chews his nails. At one point, he takes the little necklace out of his wallet. He keeps it in his wallet now and maybe he was supposed to give it back, but now there will be a next time. They didn't have a next time the other times, but now they do. All evening, into the night, *fireflies, starry sky.*

Moonlight mixes with water.

What does his tiny corner of the universe there on the

bank of the Kamo tell him then? That by bolting one door, he has opened a new one that directs him to responsibility? That the burden of conscience is one that chaffs at every step? He doesn't know it, see it, sense it. He can't touch it, hear it, feel it.

He only lays there, thinking or unthinking.

In his mind, he let her say it.

ELEVEN

AYA FALLS OUT OF LOVE

I'm good with numbers. I remember all sorts of random numbers, like how my mother was three weeks and four days shy of her twenty-eighth birthday when she finally gave in and let herself be married. Retaining oddly specific information is something that definitely comes from my dad. I probably asked him at some point, so mom was twenty-eight when you got married, right? And he would've told me no, she was three weeks and four days shy of twenty-eight. She and I both started late. Except for her, late was not even twenty-eight and he was in his forties. We didn't discuss it further, and I didn't think about it any further. Did my mother even want to get married, or have children, or were we her life regrets? She wasn't the type to tell me much anything about herself, regrets or otherwise, and until this day none of it had even crossed my mind.

But my mother isn't like many other adults I know. And that was probably one of my grandmother's life regrets. My grandmother is a true Kyoto lady who has worn a kimono every day of her life. She wanted a girl as soft and pure as could be, which is maybe why she named her only daughter Yukiko:[35] A girl she'd hoped would be as white, and perfect, and cold as snow. And my mother *was* good at all those subtle arts, but she was also drawn to so many things that baffled my grandmother. Like geography and western travel books and languages. She whipped her brothers in any subject. My mother would ask for a light-up globe for her birthday; my grandmother would give her an expensive jeweled pin. That was how they warred.

Once it was settled that she would go study abroad, my

[35] 雪 = yuki (snow)
子 = ko (child)

grandmother worried even more. My grandfather had entirely approved of the idea, but the way she saw it, what would a perfect snow girl do with the knowledge she got from these far away places? They would not teach her what she'd need to lead a good life; only how to unsettle her mind. Men were for having unsettled minds—women were for comforting and smoothing the ripples. And Yukiko still always did what she wanted.

But then my grandfather died, and my mother rejected any suitor that came for her, until she got a letter in my grandmother's beautiful script saying that she would do well to remember an only parent's sorrow. Would she have her mother grow old without seeing her only daughter settled in her own rightful kingdom, with her own rightful heirs?

Yukiko was busy though. She taught as an assistant teacher at the university. She spoke three languages and they crowded her head too much for romance. Dating exhausted her. But then my mother gave in and her two requests were that her future husband be intelligent and have a full head of hair. The omiais slid through and my grandmother championed a certain Dr. Okada. He was sixteen years older than my mother and had a bald pate. He was also a successful orthopedist with a modern house in suburban Kyoto, just waiting for a bride to move into. Who cares about a man's hair anyway, you're not twenty-two, my grandmother said in that voice, soft as ripping paper, and she had the last laugh. You can stop the university work now. It would never do for a doctor's wife to be working, and so the unwilling snow princess was married off on a cloud of Parisian tulle and Kyoto silk, where she has languished ever since. If she did languish.

My mother was smart as a whip but she could bend like one too. Nine months and two weeks after her marriage day, she gave birth to me, Ayami. Thirteen months after that, she gave birth to my brother Kyousuke. And every spring, we'd drive down to visit my father's favorite brother in Shimonoseki, and every winter, we'd all go skiing. Back before school got so hectic, I was even on a junior softball league with Kyou. I'd grown up cheering for the Hanshin Tigers with my dad, and some Sundays all three of us would go lob the ball around in the neighborhood park up the street. He was gone so often for conferences and talks and busy with his practice, but ironically it was my mother who was much harder to reach.

Growing up, I didn't wonder if she was happy, but I suspected there was a part of my mother we were not allowed to reach. Locked deep and maybe superior to anything we could offer. These were the languages she kept hallowed, polishing her English and French like rare gems that shine for her alone—she's fluent in both. There is no opportunity to speak them anymore though, except with language partners or in circles once a week. This she does like others go to temple, and when she reads in these foreign words, her face is beautiful. They are her passion.

But I suppose now you can picture me sitting there on that afternoon, seventeen and a half years after my mother's marriage day. I'm on my bed (it's high, western style, cream bedspread) and I know I shouldn't have skipped my afternoon session, but lately I've been so good, and it's rare to have the house to myself. At home, all of us have our routine. My mother does housekeeping in the morning, shopping and errands in the afternoon. Breakfast at 6:50, lunch packed for all three of us, dinner at seven sharp (my father's dinner and ours after jyuku, heated again). Bath at eleven. Racquetball on Mondays, hair salon on Fridays. Sundays for the family. Right now though, my dad is gone for a three day convention; my brother is away on an overnight school trip. She wrote me ten minutes ago, asking if I was at school and I told her I was, and that I won't be home until much later. She said she would see me tonight then. She's about to drive my grandmother home from an appointment and she'll stay and have tea. I write her, All right. See you tonight.

So I'm sitting on my bed, enjoying the empty house, eating Apollos[36] and listening to American music. It's sort of fun to pick out the English words I don't know—I write them in silver ink in my notebook to ask my English tutor, but there are so many after even a few lines that I stop writing them down and lay back to enjoy the music. I love R&B—it sounds like cinnamon candy. As I sit and listen, I take out my keitai, write Kiriya a quick message (he's in practice right now, so he won't respond until the evening). I answer a message from Yui (tomorrow she'll need her math textbook that I'd borrowed); and then randomly flip through messages. I stop on the last one from Ren. She wrote me earlier, and I'm still trying to think what to text back. We're in that new phase where I still worry about writing back too fast or being annoying.

After Ren, I stop on V's address.

I stare at the blank field and tap something to him. Unlike Ren, I never worry about what to write or stress about it. I can write him something that happened that day, or share a picture, or just ask a silly question. Girls with long hair or short? (His answer: middle.) Summer or winter? (His answer: fall.) Maybe I shouldn't write him so much, or think about him so much, but that only makes me want to do it more. I can't imagine ever running out of things to talk about—funny because with Kiriya, we rode together for a whole year in Aoki-san's car, to and from jyuku, barely exchanging a word. He and my friend Aoki Yui and I all live fairly near each other, which is why her

[36] Chocolate-strawberry candies shaped like the Apollo space-craft!

mother usually gives us a ride home. Kiriya is one of the only two people in our jyuku not from my school or the boys' school next to ours, so he kept to himself at first. He was quiet, well-prepared, and his face was burnt bronze from daily soccer practice. Yui would pester me sometimes because she likes these still-water types, asking me if he had a girlfriend. But sitting with him in the car twice a week for thirty minutes while she talked with her mother in the front seat didn't mean anything, so I told her to ask him if she wanted to know so badly, but she never had the nerve. And then one day, she and her mother were still inside talking with our sensei about the red mark Yui had got on her last chem test, and Kiriya and I sat in the car waiting for them. We didn't speak, just waited in the darkness until I became conscious of his breathing—it was like a living heartbeat, and I looked over at him then, because it seemed louder than normal, but he said nothing.

Then I remembered. Maybe it was easier to talk because I couldn't make out his face, but I told him Yui wanted to know if he had a girlfriend. That made him laugh, but not in a nasty way— only friendly, as he was. He confessed that he actually did not, and I nodded, thinking I would report via text once I got home. But then he leaned over. Even under the dark-copper sunburn of his face, I could see the color of a sunrise. He told me then that he didn't have a girlfriend, but there was a girl he liked—

He kissed me then, easy as that. And his kiss was warm and safe, not too wet, nor like the back of a hand. A few minutes later, Yui and her mother came back out and got into the car. They drove us home and we sat quietly as the streets swished by, watching the shadows of telephone poles black out each other's faces. Smiling.

I became Kiriya's girlfriend because he asked me to and nobody had ever asked before. At the time, it didn't occur to me to wonder if I 'liked' or 'did not like' him. Maybe this is how I thought these things go. If a boy asks to go out with you, and they're good looking and get good grades and they're nice, you say yes, unless you have some huge objection (I did not). Yui was so understanding too. So Kiriya and I went to movies and jyuku together, kissed only at first, then eventually did everything else, but nothing about what he did pushed or pulled in one manner or another. No matter what, I was always still me, and he was always still him. I don't know when I started to believe I love him. Maybe again, that is what I thought love is. Your circumstances line up. It all passively falls into place.

But when I first met Ren after she transferred to our school, nothing about liking her felt passive. I had such a strong urge to talk to her, to try to get close. At first, I thought it must be me wanting to be her friend. But I kept imagining things like holding her hand. And making her laugh felt so good. I admitted after a while, that I wanted to kiss her. And this didn't make me feel weird or bad or anything, but I didn't know how to go about it. You might be thinking that it's easy to ask a classmate to do something with you, especially if they're new, but I wanted her to understand how I meant it and not feel like I was taking advantage of her trying to find a new friend.

And this is where V comes in. Because the first time I saw him, I really wanted to talk to him too. Except unlike Ren, I knew that it would be easy. I could tell, the way he was looking at us, he was looking for an excuse. So I gave him one. And gave myself one too. At first I really did strike up a conversation only to see if I could do it. Be the one who makes the first move. It felt like practice. Or research. I told myself, even if I fell on my face, it wouldn't matter at all. He is a total stranger, a foreigner. But sometime around in the karaoke room, my feeling for Ren started to overlay my feeling for his situation. Or the other way around. It felt good and easy being around him. Not because we necessarily have so much in common. (Though finally having a friend who also loves karaoke and actually has free time is amazing.) But we could joke around and I could say things to him I wouldn't normally say to anyone. It didn't feel so serious, so formal, so you are the guy so you have to do this and I am the girl and so I have to do that. Maybe that was another connection I'd drawn to the Ren question. I mean, if you're with another girl, neither of you is the guy or the girl anymore. You're two people. I got the weird feeling that I was simply another person with V, too. He's a guy and yet the whole balance felt different. Good different.

And like with Ren, I kept wondering what it would be like to kiss him. To do more. I wanted to. I don't know why—I liked how he looked, but not more or less than anyone else. The urge didn't seem tied to that. When he said, you don't know what you want, at first, he was right. And then it clicked. [37]

So all of that made me wonder—I know there's different love for friends, or for family, but can Love have different kinds? Can you have Love that is quiet and safe; Love that is sharp and hot? (Love that is warm and soft?) Can you feel all of them at the same time, but for different people? I don't know. I don't have anyone I could ask, but when I see V again, well I guess I could ask him. He would know. He would honestly tell me. I think that's what I wanted to say too the other day by the river. That he doesn't have to be scared. When I think of our evening together, my whole body still gets red. When I look up at the sun, I smile. When I see a message from him my heart squeezes, and maybe it's a little too mechakucha, but I know nothing will happen between us, nothing really can,

[37]
....

and it doesn't make me care about him any less. And I can feel that he feels it for me too, and is afraid that if he says anything, it will make me confused. That I can't understand, but if that's what he thinks, then he's wrong. How could I not understand when I know I have feelings for Kiriya *and* for Ren? And if I try to imagine running into him on the street somewhere in a few years, with his own family, in my mind I'm always happy for him. Not upset or jealous. That is love, right?—

Bzzzz.

My phone lights up and my stomach flips. Did he write me back? But no. It's Yui. She needs her book sooner than tomorrow. I write to her, is tonight okay? Outside, our neighbor's dog barks and barks. And keeps barking. A car door slams. Yabai.

I sit up and tear the headphones off.

The heavy front door swings open, and all this wooshes right out of my head. Since my dad and brother are both out of town, there's only one person who could possibly be coming home right now and if my mother finds me here, she'll be *angry*. I wasn't joking when I said that to her, learning is God. Hooky is not something she tolerates. But I calm down because she tidies my room in the morning. She has no reason to come in here. I guess this means she brought my grandmother here instead? If I'm lucky she just came to pick something up. At any rate, she'll either leave again soon to drive my grandmother home, or go read in the living room, if she's alone. That will be my chance to sneak out.

Downstairs, I hear her in the kitchen talking to someone. Probably making tea. No matter, if they go into the living room to talk, it will be even easier to slip out the back door. Then I hear her coming upstairs. She's not talking anymore, but I hear another pair of footsteps coming up as well. My heart pounds as I slowly creep to my door. Why would they come up here?—Unless. Yui's mother wrote her and asked to come pick up the book herself. Seems unlikely, but if they come in my room and see me in here... My heart skips three beats. I go over to my closet and open the door to step into it. Blood pounds in my throat like a girl in a horror movie about to be murdered. My hand is on the knob; I'm trying to be as quiet as possible and feeling so silly too and then, coming from down the other end of the hall, near her bedroom, I hear my mother laugh.

It's so unlike her that for a few seconds, I forget to even be scared. Never have I heard her laugh like that in my life. What is she saying? Now I realize why I can't understand— Her voice flows in the rich tones I associate with her speaking French. I calm down. So this is a language friend. They won't come in my room. My body starts to relax, but then I feel my throat close up in a different, much worse way. Her voice sounds like hot honey. I have no idea what the words mean, but they give me the chills.

—Alors, tu viens?

And then a voice answers her in fluid French.

—Que faisons-nous ici?

It's a... male voice.

One I'd recognize anywhere. In any language.

I do not hear the bedroom door close. Why would it? My mother thinks nobody is home. That I won't be home for hours. I never lie to her about where I am, mostly because until very recently, I had no reason to. She has no reason to check the rest of the house and make sure they are alone.

Water starts running. This is my only chance.

My room is around the bend of the hallway, so if I run

out now, they won't hear it. I have to cry, I have to throw up, I have to scream, but most important, I have to run away from here.

Next thing I know, I'm at the downstairs door, pulling it open. *Open it carefully, she'll hear it, he'll hear it,* goes through my head, but I'm in such a hurry, I can't be quiet. The door is wrenched open, hot daylight cuts my face. The neighbor's dog starts to wag his tail. I always spend a few seconds at the fence before I go anywhere, giving him a pat—now I'm simply bolting.

Is this because I was thinking about him? Is this because I was thinking too much about him? Why would you do this to me?

Can't see straight, can't feel straight; I dash into the street without looking. A car screeches. The driver stares through the tinted window, her mouth twisted in fear, and my body is still hurtling forward. I can't stop and my fingertips touch the hood of her car. *I'm sorry, I'm sorry.* I bow at her concerned face beyond the windshield. She looks my mother's age, like someone who might even open her door and step out to start lecturing me: Why would you do this? Do you know how reckless it is to rush forward without looking? I could have killed you! I almost wish she would open her door, because then I could tell this woman—I'm really sorry for frightening you, but there are just so many things running through my mind right now. So many things I hadn't even considered, until this very moment. Like Yukiko hating it here. Like her being someone beyond my mother. Like us being her life regret. Like her needing to forget us for an hour.

Like letting the vampire in.

TWELVE

THE WOMAN FROM HEAVEN AND HELL

Un soir, j'ai assis la Beauté sur mes genoux. - Et je l'ai trouvée amère. - Et je l'ai injuriée. Je me suis armé contre la justice.

One night, I sat Beauty on my knees—and I found her bitter—and I insulted her. I steeled myself for justice.

—Arthur Rimbaud

Ako's an attractive, deep, and totally unnatural brown. I see her face in the car window, and she rolls it down, calling out to me:

「Are you going to get in?」

I do, but as soon as I do, she cuts the engine. She turns to me, and I see she's made up right this side of kebai. Her thin wrist, weighed down with a massive rhinestone Dior bracelet, rests on the shift, and she smiles at me, her teeth perfectly straight, china-colored, and glinting in her tanned face. Her lips are shinier than candy.

「Are you hungry? We could go eat,」 she says.

One of my long standing suspicions: Ako lives off of cigarettes, champagne, bottled oolong tea, and Calorie Mate. Going out to eat is for my benefit alone.

「Let's do that later,」 I say.

She seems surprised but shrugs.

I can see the wheels turning in her mind to come to the next activity of our togetherness, so I quickly intercept her. I want to draw it out. Ako's a rusher. I like it slow.

「The weather's nice. Let's go on a drive.」

「A drive?」 She looks skeptical. 「I've had a long day

today. I thought that last meeting would never end.⌋ But she wants to please me. ⌈I guess. You drive though.⌋

⌈Me? I don't have insurance. Or a Japanese license.⌋

⌈Don't worry about it. Just drive. I'm sick of driving.⌋

We get out of the car to switch seats and like always, her figure blows my mind. I look her up and down, slowly, and whistle. She slaps my face but drinks in the attention. Ako's ass was sent by an angel and her voracity was sent by Satan himself. She wears five *man* ripped jeans that grab her slim hips, a thin snakeskin belt, stilettos, and a shoulder-less white cashmere shirt that shows her off to perfection. Her pants alone could pay my rent for months; her shoes could buy our house. All of her is long and sleek and slightly sinuous, and while I peg her to be in her mid-forties (of course I've never asked her and of course she's never told me), she could easily shave two decades off. Only the lines around her mouth betray her, but it's getting darker fast. Next to her, I'm looking a little under-dressed, and we're back in the car when she asks:

⌈You really don't want dinner?⌋

I shake my head, adjusting the seat back and the rear-view mirror. She looks at me then.

⌈Suit yourself. Ugh, not that ugly old coat even in the middle of the summer! Here, let me look at you. What are you *wearing?*⌋

⌈This? Is the height of American 80s fashion.⌋

Otherwise known as I've run out of clean clothes, leaving only this shirt from Rodrigo and my last pair of decent jeans. The few bracelets I always wear and that's it. But I spent a good hour at the sentou before I came here, scrubbing every pore, so she can complain about my dress, but *no one* can complain about my cleanliness.

Ako manhandles me into a turn and reads the writing off my shirt, her pretty mouth tripping over the sound.

「Ee-ghee... Poh-ppu. What does that mean?」

I have no idea how close her pronunciation is. I'm pretty sure whatever I say isn't too much better.

「He's a singer. From the United States.」

「Like Elvis Presley?」

「Yeah, he's his brother.」

I smirk, and Ako looks at me.

「What is so funny?[38]」

39 It's all Greek.

「Nothing. Anyway, I think Iggy is a little too—angry to be Elvis's brother.」

「Sure, whatever. It's all chinpunkanpun[39] anyway.」

---

[38] Have you ever tried to pronounce unpronounceable words in a foreign language while drunk? It puts me straight into a fit. The room was pitching, and the moths were coming down to land on the tatami around us. I watched the moths worship the light while I turned my head towards the crappy stereo. "Search and Destroy". Rodrigo lay on the ground next to me, pouring himself another shot. We rarely spent on booze, but a student of his had gifted him a bottle of sake. I turned to him while music crashed over our heads.

「Somadi ghanna seh mah sewh. Any idea what that means?」

「A person is coming and then. Shiranee yo. Not a damn clue. This last year, my English has gone completely down the toilet... cockroach!」

Rodrigo grabbed his slipper to stun a big one about to run into my arm. I cleaned our room daily, but the house in general was rambly and dirty, so we still got them sometimes. He tossed its body out the window while I frowned, thinking we'd come far from the kid who'd almost shat himself the first time he'd stepped inside this room. A little too far.

「I told you to not eat in here. That's the second one tonight.」

「I haven't; that roach probably got lost on his way to the kitchen,」 he grumbled at me.

「No, I saw the onigiri wrapper this morning. Even the smell of food brings them, so don't eat in here. Ii no?」

Rodrigo sat up next to me and clapped his hands to my cheeks.

「Daww, my stepdad sounding so cute...」

I shook him off.

「U-ru-sa-i.」

「See, there you go! No and no. Repeat after me, uruSEE.」

「U-ru-SA-I.」

「Yeh, yeh. Anyway, I eat in here. You steal my shirts.」 He waved at the stereo. 「Don't think I didn't notice you take my Iggy Pop shirt yesterday.」

「...I'm doing laundry tomorrow, so you'll have it back soon...」

He shrugged.

「Fuck it, I'm drunk, so keep it. You're always taking it anyway, so might as well give it to you at this point.」
「Maji de? Really?」
「No, not really.」 He pushed me. 「I said it was yours, didn't I?」
「You want something for it?...」
「Forget it, V. Take it and wear it in good health.」
I threw my arm around Rodrigo then, which I think surprised him. He was casually touchy as far as Mediterranean guys go, but me, not so much. I said:
「You know... you're... a good friend. I think you're my best friend.」
「Of course I'm your best friend! This is up for fucking debate?」
「No, I mean... like... a brother.」
Chords sawed the air. (Quiet sawing. The walls were paper, so you go careful with the volume.) I lay there with my arm around him for a minute maybe, both of us tipsy and comfortable. Then he carefully peeled my hand off of him and put it back to my side. He was smiling.
「And *you*, my dear best friend brother, are fucking drunk. ...But yeah, talking of shirts, that's a nice one you're wearing right now.」 He sat up, checked the label and whistled. 「Since when are proles like you wearing D and G? Where the hell did you even get this?」
「It was a present. From Ako.」
His eyebrows rose.
「Quite the present. You must have made her—happy.」
「Well, she didn't ask for a refund, if that's what you mean.」
「Hmm, details?」
「Stepdad doesn't share H details.」
He poured me another shot.
「Let's change that.」
I could've motioned towards the robust stack of skin mags we kept under the desk, and asked about his details, fully aware he'd been faithful to the same gravure model for at least four months. But I wasn't going to be a dick.
「Anyway, if you like my shirt, why don't you take it? For the Iggy Pop shirt.」
「Are you crazy? This is an expensive shirt.」
「Whatever. If you like it, take it.」
「Won't she expect to see you wearing it though?」
「I can always borrow it back from you.」
Rodrigo turned over to pour himself another shot to toast his new shirt—and promptly spilled the bottle of sticky pearl sake all over me. So I took it to the laundry room the next day, hung it up outside, and someone from our house (a tourist, I'm sure), nabbed it...
We never saw that shirt again.

. . . .

I futz with the AC; Ako draws one of her fingers over my knee, and I feel her fingertip find a tear and touch my bare skin. She looks at me slyly.

「Your pants have a rip. I could sew that for you.」

And that'll be a fine day in Hell, when a girl like Ako's darning my clothes!

「Hey, so do yours.」 I look over at her shredded designer jeans and she laughs.

「Yes, but that is *on purpose*. It's called fashion!」

「So are mine. I just didn't have to pay—to get torn pants.」 I let the silence fill in whatever arienai price she paid for them, though I have to say, on her, they were worth every last yen.

She sighs.

「I want to take you out and show you off and you dress like *this*. Honestly, do you have to wear that ugly jacket everywhere?」

「Yes. I get cold.」

「No, you get *paranoid*. But even in a T-shirt, you can't see anything. ...Why don't I take you shopping the next time I come over? I'll drive you over to Osaka and buy you an outfit—」

I make a face and she makes one back.

「Fine then, if that's how you feel. Thinking about it, maybe I shouldn't bother. I bet you never wear the shirt we got that other time.」

「Yes, because it got stolen the first time I washed it. Probably because it was the nicest item washed in that house. Ever. Anyway, what is wrong with my clothes?」

Of course I know what's wrong with them. Even at her age, Ako's into too many idols who look like they need more time to leave their house than five women—but there's no way I'm spending more than the bare minimum in our pit of a toilet. And I will *not* primp in a public bath.

「You are such a *boy*.」 Ako shakes her head. 「You won't even wear nice clothes for *me*.」

「For nobody. But I thought that's why you like me.」

「No-o, I like that you're cocky and dumb.」

「Shh, Ako-san. That's not nice.」 I try to touch her thigh through one of the rips, and she flicks my hand away, telling me to behave myself. But we know I'm right. When Ako wants to go out with an overstyled bishounen[41] plastered in labels, I'm sure she has plenty to choose from and doesn't call me. But she did, which means that today, anyway, this is what she's in the mood for—

I get a feel for the wheel and controls before I rev the engine.

「You know.」 I put the car into first. 「I've never driven on the left side of the road before.」

Ako is unfazed.

「You'll do fine. ...You do know how to drive?」

「We'll see, no?」

I haven't been behind the wheel of a car since Paris, and I only now realize how much I've missed it. Her sleek Nissan has great response and I drive fast, enjoying it. Ako's right: after five minutes, I feel like I've been on this side of the road my whole life. She rolls down her window, blasts the Spitz song and leans her elbow out. *Stargazer.*

「I want you to sing me this song next time we go to karaoke. Will you?」

「You know I'll sing you whatever you want.」

She looks happy then—not that Ako's the kind who goes to karaoke booths to sing. Her own voice is pretty unsteady so she rarely joins in, but she likes to sit next to me, thumbing through the big listing book, punching in song after song. I usually won't go with a girl who won't get into it, but with Ako I don't mind, because music puts her in the best perverse mood—I still remember. It was our first date, second drink, seventh song, dark room; neither of us could wait anymore, which is when I knew we'd be good for each other.

「So how have you been? How are Ako's other boys?」

[41] Pretty boy

Ako's unmarried with a little girl and lives with her mother and father down in Fukuoka. She works for an advertising agency and travels relatively often for them (their main office is over in Osaka), but I haven't seen her in three months. You could say we're sporadic. She has many casual boyfriends, and I know I'm not her Kyoto only. Still, if she asks for me, I never turn her down: Ako's fun, raunchy, and shrewd. And then, while she's getting on in years, she has clothed, dyed, massaged, and mortified her body to absolute excellence. Our dates follow an unstated, clean itinerary each time: we go out. We do something insignificant. We go back to her hotel room. I fuck her senseless. Food, drink, karaoke, room—they're all on her. And before I leave the next morning, she gives me a nice wad of cash. Says, be good and buy some decent clothes before I see you next. Knowing that I'll be spending the money on any old thing but that. And not to mix business with pleasure, but I can't say that wasn't a big factor in me returning her text the other day, because I am broke and not a little. Ako smiles her model teeth at me.

「You're a beast today. It's not the you I know.」 She puts her manicured hand on mine. I shift the car into third and it surges forward.

「So where are you taking me?」

「To Fushimi Inari.」

「What? I thought we were going somewhere else! Why? It's going to be dark soon!」

「That's exactly why. Haven't you always wanted to see it in the dark?」

「I don't even care to see it in the light. It's in the middle of nowhere.」

Ako has a casual disregard for all holy spots, but hey, nobody is perfect.

「I bet you've never even been there before! And if

you're scared of the nurikabe,[40] don't worry; I'll protect you. Hey, will you pass me a cigarette?⌋

She does and gives me a light as well. Ahh yes, she has the good ones. Not those thin, minty abominations or the cheap crap Rodrigo inhales. I feel kissed.

Ako puts her hand on my shoulder.

⌈I think I'm getting a nicotine high just looking at you. You could sell tobacco to a lung doctor.⌋

⌈Makes sense. Smoking and sex are in the same part of my brain.⌋

⌈You don't say.⌋

⌈Mmm. Started both when I was ten.⌋

⌈Is that when you started lying too?⌋

I lean over and give her a kiss.

⌈I've never been a liar. Not when it mattered.⌋

⌈Keep your eyes on the road.⌋

Good call. The road is insanely narrow, curvy, and a car is coming straight towards us. I don't drop speed, just grin as I make eye-contact with the other driver. Ako grips my shift hand white as our vehicles whip past one another with two centimeters clearance, and I hit the curve fast, wrench the wheel in the opposite direction.

⌈Watch out!⌋ she hisses.

We drift. Low evening sun sprays past us outside in slow motion. It's gorgeous and I'm thinking yes, I have missed this.

⌈You weren't sure if I could drive. So I wanted to show you...⌋

I drift through the next curve too and Ako laughs. Puts her needle-heeled feet up on the dash.

⌈You're crazy. You know you're my slave for life if you wreck this car.⌋

⌈Unless we die.⌋

⌈Then we'll die together. So careful, unless I'm the last

[40] An invisible moving wall that has no end and traps night travelers.

167

person you want to see on earth. Your mama would have to go down to the underworld just to kill you again.⌋

「I don't have one right now.⌋

「Uh-huh. Then you should move down to Kyushu.⌋

One of our standard flirting tropes is me becoming her live-in man, though we both know this will never happen. I can't move in with her elderly parents, and then the thought of leaving Kyoto always makes me nervous. I say:

「Why don't I get a steady job before we move in together? You know, 'When poverty comes in the door, love flies out the window.'⌋

She gives me an odd look, then sniggers.

「Where do you get this melodramatic crap from, anyway?⌋

I bring the car to a halt. We're in the parking lot of Fushimi Inari, and for once, it's even almost empty. Maybe it's the hour—close to dinner. I squint at the grand torii leading up.[41] The ripe summer air turns with the cicadas. Ako looks less than impressed as she comes out of her side and peers into the darkening mountain.

「I don't know why I let you talk me into your goofy ideas. Why did you want to come here again?⌋

「I want to walk to the double torii tunnel. Come on.⌋

「But I'm in heels.⌋

Ako's lighter than air, I know this from her dynamite mannequin proportions. I swing her over my shoulder, and she laughs and pounds on my back to put her down. I do it only when we get to the top of the first set of stairs, and we start walking up and she's asking me why I even like it here when it's spooky. I can't explain to her that it feels like a place you need to go to sometimes. Ako stops at one of the booths still at the base, in one of the main courtyards. I wait for her off to the side, and when she's

[41] Miho was the only girl V'd been with also drawn to all holy spots, rivers, forests, mountains, graveyards, and temples. As a Kamakura native, she'd never seen Kyoto's famous temples with her own eyes and so they visited many of them together for the first time. Fushimi Inari's mountain especially made a deep impression on him …

done, she comes to me, slips one hand around my neck, a small paper sack into my pocket. ⌈It's Inari-san's mountain, so I got you a money charm.⌋ I thank her, tell her money luck I definitely need, but I need a walk even more, though I know there's no way she'll walk up with me all the way to the Lost Lake, so we go up to the Alice in Wonderland tunnel instead. The torii gates gleam all over this area, but here specifically they're put one after another, hundreds and hundreds, making two orange-red corridors with darkness flashing through. The scene strikes me unreal, and I want to pass through them, but Ako doesn't want to go a step further. She's tapping her foot.

⌈Let's get out of here before a kappa[42] gets us!⌋

Ignoring her, I walk around, then duck in a gate behind her. She starts turning around in the darkening half-light, her long bleached hair whipping like a cyclone.

⌈You better not leave me alone here! V?!⌋

I let her turn around in circles for another five seconds, her voice getting more anxious, until her back is to me and then I jump out and grab her around her waist. Ako screams and the sound makes the dark eerily turn in. The altars around us are like sepulchers.

⌈You ass! I could kill you for that.⌋ But she's laughing. ⌈We're leaving right now. This place freaks me out.⌋

It's a weird mood, for sure. The wet air's narcotic; I'm dazed, like in a hot, pretty dream. I don't want to go anywhere else, just tramp all over the mountain with her, take her to the three altars on the very top and kiss her on the 1000 stairs, but I know we'll never make it, so instead, I pull her into me exactly where we are. I put my hand under her face.

⌈You don't think it's beautiful?⌋

⌈I think you're nuts.⌋

She's not angry though.

[42] A water sprite that causes mischief—but occasionally also eats people by sucking their innards out through the anus.

「Tell me a ghost story, Ako-san. A real Japanese ghost story.」

「In this dark? No way.」

「I'll give you a cigarette if you tell me a story.」

「We can't smoke here anyway, but sure. I haven't told a good one in years. Give me one of yours then.」

I give her one and she puts it into her bag. We walk a way up, beyond the torii corridor, to an open, empty space filled with altars. She paints her lips while I read the inscriptions (or try to, at least), and then we both sit on a bench under the darkening trees, and she starts in with her husky voice.

Intermission
Ako Tells the Tale of O-Yasu

Once, many hundreds of years ago, in a tiny village of the province of Gifu, there lived a peasant boy called Shinjiro, who was betrothed from birth to a village girl called O-Yasu. She was beautiful and kind, and he was a hard worker, so they were both very happy with this arrangement and grew up waiting for the day when they could live together in marriage. However, O-Yasu suffered from poor health, and she was very delicate. When she turned sixteen, she became deathly ill with the consumption and finally, everyone in the village saw that she would die. Shinjiro was especially despondent, but nothing could be done, so he went to visit at her death-bed, promising that he would never forget her.

Oh, but Shinjiro, the dying girl said to him. Do not despair. We will meet again.

Yes, he agreed, wanting very much to comfort her. I know we'll meet again in the Pure Land.

But she smiled weakly and waved him away.

No, no, I don't mean the Pure Land. We will meet again in this life. I will be reborn, and we will be able to marry at last. I'm sorry for you, because you'll have to wait 15 or 16 years for me to grow up again, but you're not even twenty yet, so you won't be that old then.

But..., he could not imagine how this would be possible. How will I know itis you? Will you look like you?

No, I will neither look nor sound like me, but you must trust that I will send you a sign, and then you will know.

Shinjiro looked at her wan face and knew immediately that he would do it.

To wait for you is a joy, not a duty, he said, clasping her hand with emotion. I will wait until we can meet again. This I promise.

But my love. Her eyes were dreamy, yet severe. Do not promise unless you can truly bear it. For if you were to break your promise, you would do me and yourself a grievous wrong.

No, no, he insisted, sure in his devotion. I will not be content until we meet again in this life and are married, as we were meant to be.

Then I can die in peace. The girl smiled at him, and with that, she closed her eyes and was dead.

* * * * *

Shinjiro had been very in love with O-Yasu and, when she died, he had a mortuary tablet inscribed with her death-name on it, which he placed on his family's butsudan, and left offerings in front of every day. He prayed that he would be strong enough to wait for her all the coming years, and he did face many hardships. His parents ailed and died, and he lost the small money and land that they had left him. He

took up his few remaining possessions and
started to wander all around Japan, dedicated
completely now to finding the girl of his childhood again. He wandered high and low, seeking
but never finding her likeness, until sixteen
years later, when he came to a remote mountain
village called Ikao, still famed today for its
hot springs. As he was resting in the thermal
bath at the inn one day, he was waited on by a
girl who struck him immediately as O-Yasu. True,
she did not sound nor look like her, but she was
sixteen years old and had the same gentle, pure
soul the other girl had had. Shinjiro became
obsessed with the girl, more certain each day
that she was his lost love, and because he was
still rather young, and a very sympathetic man,
the girl fell in love with him as well. He
settled down in the village to work and proposed
to her, she accepted, and they waited for their
marriage day in complete happiness. He was
convinced that this girl was his O-Yasu and that
her affection and gentle love was the sign he
had been waiting for all those long years. The
night before his marriage, he lay down in a
perfect anticipation of the coming day.

There's a sound behind us, and Ako and I both jump. A late
pilgrim coming down from the mountain noiselessly
stopped at one of the shrines, and the monotone as they
keep muttering the nenbutsu prayer drifts over. The
person lights a candle, and it makes me want to light something too. So I take my lighter out, flick it. In the dark,
Ako's eyes are colorless holes, and she grins at me wolfishly.
It's close to 30 degrees still, but I shudder.

That night, Shinjiro saw a very strange dream.
In the dream, he was also in bed, but he woke up
in the middle of the night and started walking
around, until he got to the bathhouse where he
had met his bride-to-be. Being night, it was
deserted, and yet he walked into the bathhouse
and there, scrawled in blood above the entrance
where he had first seen her, were the words,
Remember your promise.

Shinjiro woke up with a start; he was covered in
sweat, but he could not remember his dream in
the morning, only that he had seen something
profoundly disturbing.
　　So happy was he for the wedding though, that
he shook off the vague feeling of dread, and
that next night, he lay in wedded harmony with
his young bride, certain that he was finally
reunited with his girl O-Yasu. He was just on the
brink of sleep when he heard a noise from the
door...
　　Shinjiro sat up. His bride was asleep beside
him, and yet there in the doorway, coming from
the darkness, was the form of a young woman.

　「It's her, isn't it?」
　She swallows and puts a finger to my lips.
　「Shhhh...」

　　Standing there in the door was the ghost of
the girl who had died of consumption years and
years ago and she looked as she had that final
day, beautiful and white as a lily. Her eyes were
closed, and she came at him like a sleepwalker.
His heart cut a knife in his throat as she
approached the bed, slowly, slowly, one step,

another. When she was standing directly above him, she stopped, her face as peaceful as if in a dream, but then her eyelids pried themselves open: Nothing remained of her gentle gaze but two eyeless, bloody holes. The girl was dead, every part of her was dead except the depth of those eyeholes, which he could see were filled with life, glistening white things squirming and chittering. When she stopped at the bed with a lurch, a few of them fell from the eyeholes and squittered away on the floor. Shinjiro was too horrified to speak, and she started tearing at her brittle hair and wailing.

Why did you promise you would wait if you could not keep your promise? Oh, you have ruined us! And we could have had such happiness!

But, Shinjiro's voice was cut, yet he managed at last to speak. But… I thought… He waved at the girl lying next to him, still asleep, and the corpse hissed.

I gave you a sign, but you chose to forget it by morning. Now see what you make me suffer!

And with that, she took a rusted dagger from her faded kimono and plunged it into her own neck. Shinjiro screamed and clawed at his face and the next morning, when his young bride woke for the first day of the rest of their life together, she found her husband struck next to her, bled to death with a dagger in his throat.

And that is the story of the man who could not wait for his reincarnated bride.

THIRTEEN

V Gets Fucked

We sit in the tar-hot August night and Ako reaches out and absently pulls a strand of my hair down to my cheek.

「What, no applause? You didn't like my story?」

I don't really know what to say about it, but she's waiting for an answer, so I say:

「Maybe I should have asked for a love story.」

「Come on, V-chan. That *was* a love story.」

I pull her to her feet and we start to walk back down. Now I'm the one spooked—I stare at the ground, concentrating hard on making no eye contact with the candles flickering here and there while Ako's almost running ahead. Now and then she turns back to laugh at me, beckoning. Her teeth glint glassy in the moonlight. I'm sorry I asked for the story; my mood has got all twisted and now I need to be alone. No talking, we walk back to the car. She silently hands me the keys again and I drive, as furiously as my foot can compel the machine—I dare myself to keep going faster. I keep thinking she'll tell me to slow down, but the speed seems to excites her, and I feel her hand on my thigh, the nails turned in. Her breath quickening. My heart starts pounding, but not from the excitement of her. If anything, I want to get back to downtown Kyoto and out of her company as soon as possible. I'll go down by the river and sit and watch the water and feel fine again. *And what about the money?* I tell myself, that doesn't matter. I'll make some excuse to Ako, and Rodrigo will be pissed 'cause rent is due, and tomorrow will be another day.

The road is dark out of Fushimi Inari and we're on a lonely stretch when Ako squeezes my knee.

「Do that thing again. In the turn. With the steering.」

「Drift? I probably shouldn't. It's not great for the...」 I don't finish, because right then the car jars and there's an ominous give. I break.

「What was that?」 Ako pulls her hand from my leg. I slowly drive the car over to a little side road, turn onto it and get on the shoulder. Turn off the engine and get out of the car. The night air is molten, heavy, and rotten. The smell of the country road mixes with the dull metal glare of the cicada cry, and the noise and heat are making me sick. I look at the tire and get back in.

「The wheel's getting flat. Maybe I hit something earlier. I don't know. I'm sorry. It's not gone yet, but I should probably change the tire. I hope you have a spare?」

「There's a spare in the trunk, sure.」

I put my hand on the door to get out again when she grabs me.

「The flat can wait.」

Her nails dig into my arm harder than I would like. Ako's fast and insatiable and on most days that's exactly what I want, but right now I want to get the hell out of this car because I know what's coming, and I don't want it to. My script is on the windshield though.

I just need to read it.

From far away, I see the pinpoint of headlights, and my voice is edged.

「This is a pretty busy road.」

「The main road, yes. But not this side-road. Shh, I've always wanted to do this.」

No preamble, Ako just unzips my fly and slips off her shirt. Her collarbones are two horizontal slashes across the top of her chest, but I'm not looking at her body. I look into her eyes, which are enormous and so black, they make me dizzy, like being on a very high ledge. I think of the ghost girl again—Ako's mascara-crusted lashes remind me of broken spider legs. This is our first opportunity in three months, and normally by this point, I'd want her up against a wall. There is no reason not to now, what an inexplicable mood.

I want to stop, but I don't have the resolve to make her hate me.[43]

....

[43] I COME FROM A LAND OF FOOLS AND SLAVES

(an arguably relevant interlude of some length)

Every playboy in a sticky spot has been a kid once, upon a time, and V was no exception. He'd been the oldest of five, and his mother Oksana (a woman with hair the color of ingots) grew vegetables and kept chickens and rabbits in their tiny yard to supplement the table. They lived in a falldown house on the rural brink of a big city and poverty, somewhere deep behind the iron curtain of a kingdom called the USSR.

When he was around 12 years old, his mother made a special surprise for him. It was her rabbit stew, a recipe passed down from her own French mother. It was his favorite dish in the whole world, and that afternoon, she had slaughtered enough rabbits for the entire family. She was generally too ill to cook, so his father grumbled. (So much work! So much meat! On a weekday! Such extravagance and whatever for?) But the rabbits were already dead; he accepted it grudgingly, and once the table had been set, the two adults and five children settled down to eat.

She served them all, his father muttered a prayer, and the boy picked up his spoon to dip into the broth. However, at that exact moment, something in him recoiled and his stomach turned so thoroughly upside down, he knew that he would not be able to eat. Not a plate and not a bite. He laid the spoon down.

His father, Ilya, noticed and asked him what was wrong.

« I'm not hungry, » he said and the whole table stared then, for he was and always had been the hungriest, thirstiest of them all. He could never have enough of anything.

177

« You know your mother made this especially for you. The least you can do is honor her by having some. You don't have to eat it all. »

No explanation came forward and no eating either. The silence stretched to the limit. As their oldest brother, V was adored by the younger kids, and when they saw his refusal to eat, they promptly put down their spoons and said they didn't want the stew either. His mother was frantic, his father livid. He stood up menacingly, yet the boy kept his composure, and *that* is what itched him to reconfigure his face. Not the waste. But that illegible air of entitlement he wore; which, for his father, completely marred an otherwise complaisant disposition. Standing directly behind him, his hand was poised over the kid's head, as if deliberating whether to force it face-first into the plate.

« I'd start eating right now, boy. »

« I can't! »

« You see? Here's your problem! You think you are above everyone else! You think the rules don't apply to you! »

« What rules? » he said desperately. « I just... I just don't want any! »

« But why? »

« I don't know why. If you leave me alone, it'll pass! »

At this time (and perhaps he never would), the kid did not have the proper words or thoughts to express what he nevertheless felt, more instinct than concept, to be indelibly true: That to force a pleasure polluted all good and beautiful enjoyments in a potentially irreversible way. He couldn't say it—only feel it moving in his spine and bowels, until he stopped and froze.

If they had dared, the younger kids would have risen and left. What is more dreadful than when parents fight? And Ilya was always fighting. If he wasn't fighting with their mother, he was fighting with their father.

Ilya made to strike him; his mother jumped up to soothe her husband and cajole the younger children. The kid sat rigid, his eyes jade-pale and burning. They all started in, ignoring him, and the stew was eaten, and the table was cleared, except for his place. « No, he can sit there until it's all gone. » They prepared for sleep, the younger kids went to bed early and Ilya had to go to work. And the kid sat in the darkened kitchen staring and once his father was gone, his mother lowered down on the bench, to sit with him. She said in French:

–He's gone now. I'll put it back in the pot, if you won't have it.

–He'll kill you. Please leave it.

–Eat some. Half of it. Can't you try?

No he would not, so she turned off the lights and left him in the dark.

It was right before dawn when his father came back from his shift. He would have a cup of coffee (it didn't affect his sleep) and go straight to bed. Oksana stumbled behind, brushing tiredness out of her eyes. And the kid was still sitting at the table, his face ashen and asleep.

The stew was congealed. The spoon had not moved in the last eight hours. Drunk with exhaustion, Oksana started to pull her husband away, but the expression he turned on her made her back off, as if from a provoked bear. Fully enraged, he slapped the boy to wake, dragged him to his feet, hauled him out into the cold dawn and drove him down the whipping of his life. When it was over, the kid lay over the stacked wood pile. Ilya himself was panting, worn out and strangely thrilled. He snapped the belt a final time.

« You know, there are times in your life when you just o b e y. It makes everything easier, for you and her and everyone around. Do you get it now? Of course you don't. Stubborn as a mule and twice as stupid. ...Clean yourself up already and go get them ready for school. »

The boy turned around from the wood pile and pulled his shirt over his back. He didn't cry, shudder or curse; he did give his father a single iced-green glance of the purest, unadulterated white hatred. The type of look that made the other dread every centimeter his boy grew taller and every week he turned older. The kid let that look burn into his father's impression, stiffwalked back into the kitchen, and the incident was not mentioned again.

Never in a thousand years could Ilya Petrovich have imagined that 14 years later, that prodigal son of his (loved most by his wife, understood least by himself) WOULD subconsciously remember that lesson in a parked car a third of the way around the world, on a sultry late-August night, sweating under a woman twenty years his senior.

Never, never, never.

....

「Lower your seat,」 Ako orders me—even though she usually likes me to take the lead. I tell myself to do as I'm told. She kicks off her heels and slithers out of her jeans, but as she gets naked, my desire sinks even lower. Her body, ecstasy when clad, is all gaunt angles and it was a non-issue the other times, but now, there's something grotesque about her in the dark car. Like a warning. I close my eyes as she pulls off my shirt and try to flow with it.

Ako may sense something's wrong, but she says nothing. Or maybe the *do-S* in her likes this even better.

Either way, her tongue is in my mouth and she straddles my seat. At least the weather works with me, my skin is hot and wet. Autopilot kicks in and I strain against her. Oh, so this is your conviction?

I murmur:

「I thought we'd go to a hotel. I don't have a condom with me.」 This is a final and weak excuse, but Ako laughs it off. Mock-pouts and hums into my mouth:

「Pfff, V-chan doesn't want to give me my next abortion?」

Priez pour lui.[44] 51/49, I want to rail her into the dust or open my door and not stop running until I'm back in the city. For a heathen, I'm thinking on God, she wants the heavenly shit, the fuck you descend into Hell for. *So let's go.* Resigned, I put my hands around her slick, tiny waist, but she grabs my wrists and thrusts them down by my sides. Her eyes strike mine.

[44]Pray for him.

「Sawarantoite.」 Her mouth is rough against my ear, and I know now beyond a doubt that she wants to push me around. Which is fine. I can't recall Ako ever going for this angle—normal Ako wants to shower, and lotion, and lay her fancy little ass into a bed (preferably across a big, tacky mirror) and admire herself getting systematically destroyed. Normal Ako is a lazy, selfish fuck, which is exactly what turns me on about her, but I imagine now I'll have to get turned on by something else.

I keep my hands to myself. Ako sighs, grinds against my knee, and the way she kisses, almost drinking me with this weird aching anger makes me wonder what is going on with her. I couldn't say, but this neesan is *in heat*. Omoikkiri. I pray she doesn't want a marathon in here because my legs are already cramped, but then she sits up and her voice is bloody.

「Shikkusu nain wo yarou.」

I look at her and right as I'm about to say something, she clasps her hand over my mouth. 「Who said to talk? Just be good for me and do it.」 *Uh-huh.* So she wants her obedience *silent.* I nod faintly and lower my seat all the way. She turns around (I marvel at her agility in this box) and settles over me. Pulls my pants down, I peel her wet panties off over her ass and obey.

I'd forgotten how good Ako tastes. Like eating cherries by a gas station. Salty, dirty, benzene—*sweet.* No shame, two seconds in and I'm gone from apprehensive to licking all 23 letters of my full name into her. Then again, this chick does have two decades of practice on me and she is *unbelievable.* The turn would come for a corpse and I grip her thighs rough, bruising her, hoping the malaise is gone, knowing it should be, because Ako was engineered to turn men on. And I was engineered to get her off. A flick of her nail on my neck is enough to make me sweat, and now she's actually *trying,* so hard, and I'm so easy, so let her, don't think, no thinking, *damn she's good,* yes thinking—*concentrate.* I can't let myself go because tonight, V's definitely a one shot deal, and she will want it all. So I focus and hold back while the air, the car, our clothes, our bodies. Everything. Gets. *Drenched.* She can tell I'm struggling, stops to laugh against my inner thigh. 「So close already? V-chan, *what a good boy for Ako.*」 I say nothing, press my mouth into her, press my thumb up her—deny her until she gasps—let's not forget who's good for who—until she commands me to. Hot spit spreads on my upper leg as she groans against me, comes hard against my hand. Her body bucks, drips out and she turns around slowly, carefully, blushed up neck and chest *yes or no, make up your mind.* Ako massages me between her wet, bare thighs until my jaw clenches: 「Hoshii yo, V.」 Oh lady, I think, I want you too, or at least some part of me does, but not the *right* one. She hauls herself up, her long, muscular torso is poised—I think of a soldier sheathing a blade after decapitating someone—

The sensation rips my breath away. I was so close a second ago, but the way she looks at me now—God leaves my veins and he's not coming back. Je suis perdue. Je suis saoûle. Je suis impure. Quelle vie! [45] You'd think something was whipping Ako though, so I wrap my hands around her throat and be the dildo she wants while I try to make the long climb back up. I imagine my very fourth girlfriend (Ah yes, *her*), the second runner up to the 2003 Rice Queen competition, the centerfold from last week's Young JUMP I used this afternoon after Rodrigo left. Aya. *Aya.* Her rounded body protects me against these sharp angles. I picture her clearly, her face, her voice, my breath quickens. *No, don't bring her into this.* I sigh hard for plain sadness; Ako thinks it's a warning and digs her nails into my neck, drawing blood. 「Don't you *dare*,」 she snarls, and I don't have the guts to tell her to not flatter herself. At this rate, asa made demo ii yo—you could ride me until dawn. I am so bored and hopeless.

This angle. This *position.* Ever fuck a girl and start feeling like you're swishing your dick in the Pacific Ocean? It's beyond mortifying, so I hope you never do. Slowly, so slowly, Ako pushes me to the brink once more and she comes, again, again, but it's not the One, so I keep taking myself off-edge waiting, until my dick is duller than my mind, and the accommodating sex-toy has reached a certain dreary limit. I debate risking her anger by opening my mouth and suggesting a position switch when she lifts herself off of me. Panting and desperate, Ako grabs me on the shoulder, lacerating me under the collarbones, and I look to see what she wants—she tells me that she wants me to come. Normally code for you're boring you're chafing

[45] I am lost
I am drunk.
I am impure.
What a life!

you're off of your game—and all I am thinking is thank God and Jesus and every weeping Saint up in the sky—she finally wants me to come.

「Where?」I gasp. 「Chest? Face?」

「Naka ni dashite,」she growls and I'm turned on and off and press myself down over her.

「You know I want to *and* that's a very bad idea.」

「I just had my period, nothing is going to happen. But you know, if it was yours, I might even keep it.」 And I didn't think I could dishonor myself more, but hearing that makes me groan against her wet neck. Even in the dense H-fog, Ako misses nothing. She laughs, comes down on me, my teeth grind hard enough to crack and she wrings me *out*. 「Look at you. V-chan wants me to call him in two months? Call him crying? Tell him Ako's getting fat for him?」「*Yes*,」I whisper. *Yes, yes. No,* what the hell is this night, when I've never told Ako about that, like I've never told her about any sixteen year old girl, like I've never wanted anything to be over faster, but she starts to make these weird, high-pitched yips, and if she made them before, I never noticed, but as we are now, extremely detrimental, so I stop her mouth with my hand to shut her up. Ako sucks on my fingers; the two seconds of silence is enough to break me above ground. I smell cool night air. Moonlight. I'm breathing again, everything feels good again, 「*ahh, that's so good, don't stop Ako-san, don't stop Ako san don't stop ako don't don't.*」 She keeps sucking; likes me talking, likes me begging, likes her own taste; my fingers go down, further, I fuck her throat—deeper—*I'm going to*—her throat contracts, fights back— *I'm going*—Royal Milk tea and something else spills back up out of her. Ako's couture puke washes over me. Nothing matters anymore.

The spill makes us both cross; it's an exorcism. I turn

away, muttering curses while I jerk out of her not entirely in time, add an unholy amount to the black mass mess already all over. Not that she's paying attention to what I'm doing. Ako is busy. Coming out brains, body, and soul. Then at least it wasn't a total waste, I think, and sink back onto my own side, trying to force sullenness off my face. Things I want now: A cigarette and a stiff drink. I pick my shirt out from behind the steering wheel, wipe my hands with it, and once she finally subsides, offer her a pack of tissues from the glove compartment. The car's interior is trashed into next Tuesday. *You know you're my slave for life if you wreck this car.* Ako's rage has evaporated who knows where, and she's laughing softly while she draws two fingers through some condensed milk pooled on the soaked upholstery. She uses the whole pack to wipe her face and neck clean, checks what's left of her desecrated eye makeup in the rearview mirror, then starts to look me over with this ironic concern, like she only now remembers I'm not made of plastic or rubber.

「My poor V-chan looks so banged up, I hope I didn't hurt him. But he was so good at playing he doesn't want to. It turned me on *too much*,」 she purrs, then looks up. 「You know, your eyes are the prettiest.」

Oh Christ—I want to open the window and release the stench or simply roll out of the door. This is where I've got to flatter her back. No, *you're* the hottest, the sickest, the thisest, the thatest.

「Your bracelet's the prettiest,」 is the best I can do and Ako laughs. Tries to slip it over my wrist as a joke, but it won't fit. That's when I remember the tire. I put on my clothes, get out without a word and change it in fifteen minutes. When I sit back in, she thanks me exuberantly. My answer is a curt nod and slamming the gears, I race back downtown faster than I think I've ever driven. The pressure point has reached a deadened low. Ako no longer looks thrilled; she looks terrified, but unable to say anything to me. I do not give a single, solitary fuck. Don't ask where to next, just screech to a stop in front of Kyoto Eki and she turns her cheek to me and I perfunctorily kiss it. Thirty minutes ago I was icing her like a cake, now she plays the auntie. Go figure that.

「So, meet next time I'm in Kyoto?」 she asks.

「When are you here?」

「I'll be over in Osaka next month for a wedding. I can drive over then and pick you up. We'll be staying at the Osaka InterContinental, with my friend Risa-chan. She really wants to meet you.」

「And do I want to meet her?」

Her smile is slick.

「You tell me. Twenty-four, crazy girl, *dynamite* body. And if you're too wrecked for the buffet the next morning, Risa and Ako win.」

Ako extends the luxus 3P like a lollipop to a cranky kid. We did one once before; and when she comes with a girl as wild as her it's a night you don't forget. She's trying to smooth this, her way, and I know I need to cool it and let her. She's got no patience for the moody shit, and for that matter, neither do I. But I can't.

Ako pouts.

「This isn't my V-chan. Is he worried we did it without a rubber? I was teasing. Nothing is going to happen, and if it did, it's not like I'd call you.」

But you should call me. There is a time and place to say something like that, and with Ako, that time is never. And that place is nowhere. But if I stick around, I will say it. So I exit the car. Ako's hard, and I can guess what's made her hard, and I don't want to blame her when technically she's done nothing wrong, but I can't stop it.

She shrugs, gets in the driver's seat, and I'm on the curb when she calls me back.

「V-san?」

「Yeah?」

「Aren't you forgetting something?」

She raises one hand up through the window. Between her French-tipped forefinger and thumb are two crisp man[46] bills she flicks in my direction. The amount itself is a deliberate challenge—too much money to reasonably turn down. Take it, don't take it. Ahh. Some misplaced and particularly resilient shred wins out. I shake my head at her.

「Come on,」 she goads me. 「It's not like *that*, but I know you need the money. Don't be a fool and tell me you don't.」

「Iru kedo saa. Hoshii janai. I need it, sure. But I don't want it.」

I turn, but she calls me back again.

「V.」

Don't turn around, don't turn around, fuck me, I turn. I know I shouldn't look at her again, but I do, at her face, beautifully kept, but fighting so fiercely the battle against time. I'm staring at her and Ako's laugh is its normal, superior self. A raspy chuckle. She's back on top.

「You've been living here so long, but you still make the most basic mistakes. It's hoshi KU nai, you know? Anyway, you're sweet—but a kaishounashi[47] who needs to grow up. You're not going to be young and pretty forever. I know, I've been there. Think about it.」

She looks at me heavy, still smiling and drops the money from her fingers. The two bills flitter to the ground. Her car peels out of the station.

[46] 20,000 yen (roughly 200 dollars).

[47] A good-for-nothing, useless man.

Oh V. He roams around the bowels of Kyoto Eki, clenching
and opening his fist for a good ten minutes. He's not even
sure what angers him—his metaphorical impotence, Ako's
patronizing, his lack of cool, or that this whole affair has
now, in some way, tainted the sacred Fushimi mountain.
Completing his loop downstairs, he passes back up to the
lot where she dropped him off. The air is dark, heavy,
windless. He tells himself he doesn't care, he's not looking
for it, but of course his eyes trawl the spot where he got out
of her car almost ten minutes ago. Miraculously, they are
still there. Two earth-toned crisp bills, next to a trash can.
A man typing into his phone walks by them, never looking
down. A taxi shudders past. The notes flutter, drift dangerously towards a storm drain. *Good. Fall in. Good riddance.*
Then the edge of the top note touches the grate. *Rent.* His
lungs squeeze a bit. V walks over. Picks the paper up. He
stares at the money in his palm. Fukuzawa Yukichi's warm,
mellow gaze stares back off the front of the bill, right over
his left shoulder. *Why so upset?* his eyes ask. *Sulking, what
a luxury! Help yourself and Heaven will help you.* Before he
can think about it more, his keitai pulses against his thigh.
Bzzz. He takes out his phone, flips it open. One of his
friends, Akira, is drinking with Rodrigo in a cheap
nomiya[48] up towards Shimabara. Won't he come join? V
vacillates for a few moments, go don't go, then shrugs and
decides that getting plastered is better than steaming alone
over things that can't be fixed. He starts to walk over, figuring he'll indulge this rotten mood for ten more minutes.
But then no more.

[48] Lit. drink store

The nomiya itself is an unremarkable little hole in the
wall, crowded and hectic. V steps in, and from the far side,
his roommate's voice booms out.

　「Hey! Over here!」Rodrigo's volume is a good ten deci-
bels louder than usual; the sure sign that he is no longer

thirsty. ⌜I told Akira here that you're busy tonight, but he insisted on writing you— Glad I was wrong! We're fresh back from Taka's, thought we'd have a last drink...⌟ Both his friends seem genuinely happy to see him, and V is honestly glad to see them back, so why the trepidation furling out in the pit of his stomach, some clammy distant cousin of nausea?

Impulsively, he flashes his money, slaps it on the table, then sinks the bills back into his pocket.

⌜I got this, so get another round.⌟

⌜*Mate, mate, mate, mate*, rent is due, but he's got money to spare? Is this—evolution? It's shouchuu, by the way. Want some?⌟ V nods, takes the tumbler he's offered and Rodrigo inspects him.

⌜So were you out fucking? Or fighting? You look like a goddamn MESS.⌟

⌜Sometimes, those two overlap.⌟

⌜And you smell really—*weird*.⌟

V swallows more drink.

⌜I don't want to talk about it.⌟

Rodrigo's slightly bulging eyes start positively glowing for information.

⌜He's paying and he doesn't want to talk about it. Well, this is all ayashii, little brother, very fishy indeed!⌟

Akira has already flagged their waitress and she stops briefly now to pass out new drinks. V picks his up and gulps quickly. His friends joke and laugh and he wants to join them as fast as he can, but whatever place they're in seems so unreachably far. A needle's thin proboscis probes the base of his skull.

⌜Nothing ayashii at all. And I'm older than you.⌟

⌜Older, yes, but nobody can say he's wiser. Proving that age, like money, is but a game, my good V. Now let's see. I was expecting your keitai to be off all night; weren't you supposed to be out with, hmm, what's her name again? Don't tell me, I got it... Akemi? Akami? Akuma?」

「Ako.」

His friend gives the table's surface a spank so hearty, their glasses jump.

「Ako! Ako, oh yes, how is she doing? You know, I'll never forget the first time V went out with her, Kira-chan. I'll never forget it and I wasn't even there. Gone for 48 hours straight and he could barely walk when he got back. That obasan truly is from heaven and hell.」

Akira is a nonchalantly fine boy with a night-black shag of hair and well-picked clothes. He grins next to V, and uses his oshibori to wipe lipstick, blood, and a small spot of vomit off of V's neck.

「I'll bet she is. So how obasan is obasan?」

Rodrigo smiles like a jackal.

「Ako is deep in obasan territory, but she may have single-handedly coined the term 'old is gold.' I met her once, hmm? Six months ago? Blonde hair down to her ass and legs down into next month. Am I right, V?」 He turns to his roommate, eyes catching on his neck. 「Oof, and by the looks of you, she must've really fucked you sideways, but what are you even doing here? None of this adds up. No, no. Don't tell me she took you to her Four Seasons or her Hilton and turned you out after round one? That doesn't sound like her at all. Or you, for that matter. And V, my dear V, are you *thirsty*? She couldn't even bother to give you a glass of water? Drink some WATER; you finished my drink, you finished your drink, and now you're drinking Akira's and you've been here less than ten minutes! We'll be pulling you home at this rate. Sumimasen!」 He bawls into the roiling bar. 「Omizu wo moraemasen ka? OMIZU KUDASAI!」

「HAIII!」 Their waitress hollers back with a cheery

anguish. She returns quickly with a carafe, eyeing the table of boys nervously while she smiles and pours them all water. Strange, because they haven't been here long, but she knows this look. The noxious sheen on the eyes, the howling laughter. The blond one in particular looks grey in the face. She hopes they'll leave before they cause a scene—or get sick in the bathroom. She bustles, wipes at their table; her eyes meet V's for a shard of a second; both of them hang together in a sticky despair. For a moment, he is desperate to grab her hand, to beg her to stay at the table. It would force the others to behave. Everything seems so shouty and foul. Before he can make any such request though, she rushes away and, at Akira's urging, V drinks half a glass of water. The liquids slosh sourly inside him; the water fights the shouchuu, and both fight the walls of his empty stomach. Not unlike when he was in the car with Ako, he is famished for air.

「Let's go,」 he mutters.

「Go?! But you just got here! And you haven't even told us what happened. Don't think we're letting you leave until you do!」

Is that what it takes?

It's his turn to grin like an animal.

「You want a story, but there really isn't one. I drove her to Fushimi Inari, the mountain put her in some mood and I fucked the puke out of her in her car. Then we split. Everyone happy? ...Also, will you ask for the bill, please? You know I hate to shout.」

His friends look one part revolted, one part intrigued.

「Well, that explains why you reek, I guess. Anyway, anything for you, dear brother.」 Rodrigo turns his head. 「KAIKEI ONEGAISHIMASU!」 he calls into the alcoholic gloom and the waitress's voice calls back.

「HAI! KASHIKOMARIMASHITA!」

While they wait for her to return, they finish their drinks, and Rodrigo turns back to him.

「So there's really no reason for why you're drinking like a broom maker?」

「Drinking like a what now?」

「Like a fish. A lord. A priest. A fucking BROOM MAKER! You NEVER drink to get drunk. Your father drank and you hated it. So you don't drink to get trashed, ever. That's what you told me once.」

「You're confusing me with someone else. I said I don't drink because I can't hold it.」

「You *are* a notoriously bad drinker, but it was definitely you who had said that. So I figure you must be upset. But why? A beautiful older woman paid you for a nasty fuck and *you are upset about it.* When the rest of us are out here having boring screws, with ugly girls, for free? Kira-kira-chan, is this copacetic?」

「Rodrigo, will you shut up? I'm tired is all, and as far as the date goes, Ako can get fucked and her money too.」

「Ako can get fucked, you say? Yeah, you already took care of that, Vicchan...」

He crackles lewdly, they all look up: the waitress is standing by their table, their bill in her hand. Her pursed lips hint that she has heard more of their conversation than she ever wanted to. V reddens lethally—the other two slide off their stools and are swimming towards the outside world without a care.

「We're gonna have a smoke and start walking, you said you got this? It shouldn't be too much...」

They are gone, and it's just her and him.

The waitress is waiting, he is the reason she is waiting; V clambers to his feet. Suddenly, the bar seems even more cramped. The walls slide close and she seems so small, looking up at him. He can see the deep shadows etched under her cheeks. She's tired after a long shift. The fourth wall quivers, but they both hold it. A shine is mustered into her eyes, her mouth contracts into a smile, she announces the total, and the urge is so instant and unexpected. To fall to his knees. To clasp her around her knees. To tell her, she can be as openly tired around him as she wants. As tired as she WANTS. It takes a sickening amount of willpower to not do it.

⌜You don't have to smile for me,⌟ he murmurs, allowing himself that much and the unexpected sentence disorients her.

The girl freezes—he's intense and he stinks and she wants him to pay already and leave.

He is about to do that. V peels one bill away from the other, then thrusts both into her hands. ⌜I don't need the change, please keep it.⌟ His urgent, polite voice flusters her further and the waitress breaks away from him. Keep it? But why? She has heard that foreigners insist on 'tipping' sometimes, when they have drunk to generosity, but he seems distraught, far from a cheery, tippy tourist. The whole situation is unsettling.

"Please, take back," she babbles in English. Like him, the girl barely speaks it, but she needs the distance right then—he says nothing more though, turns and bolts into the hot night. The waitress stays in the epicenter of the bar, staring down at the two *man* bills in her hand.

Outside, V jogs until he catches up with the others. Hearing the trot, Rodrigo swivels around.

⌜There you are! You were taking so long, I was sure you must be on your knees in front of that poor waitress, proposing to her, or making some kind of ass of yourself. We were ready to go back and fetch you.⌟

「Hardly.」 The money off his body, he feels immediate relief. *I should've never taken it. I would've felt fine this whole time.* Before him, Rodrigo and Akira continue a heated discussion. Akira insists that Rodrigo still has his volume eleven and twelve of *Judo-bu Monogatari*, and Rodrigo insists that he does not. Straight ahead and almost above them, the marshmallow tip of Kyoto Tower broils in the night sky. They stumble towards it. It's close to midnight by now, but the streets are still seething with walkers, diners, drinkers, and partyers. And there they are, moving forward like three ghosts on the wide side-walk when they pass the Higashi Hongan-ji. The night air sears them, and the compound doors to the temple are open. As V goes by those massive wooden doors, his eye catches on the ocean of gravel refracting the court's moonlight—it is a snow-field equally hot and cold.

To him, the sight is out of this world beautiful. Mad to touch it, he drifts in through the gates and kneels down. Above him, the immense temple roof cuts a silhouette against the black-blue sky. The other two don't follow him in, they just wait and catcall from the entrance. 「Nani yatten da yo? Zakkena, jikan nee yan! What the hell are you doing? Come on, we don't have time for this!」 They do not want to miss the last train home. V stays crouched in that lonely courtyard, so big and empty, until he can't hear them or anything anymore. He may as well be on Venus. He captures four chalk-colored rocks, warm in his hand, and as he gets up, his face bleached bone-white as the rocks below and the moon above, he knows with a sudden realization that, no matter what has happened, the city bears him no grudge. Or he imagines he knows, but can't be sure. Does she love him still? As he loves her? *Oh, I could never be mad at you, Aya, where are you?* he thinks, muddled and strange, and then falls back out to the street, more stunned than when he walked in, and almost collapses against Akira, who holds him up and finds this a great comedy. They are soon swept back into the crowds that move. As a single living, breathing body. Kyoto Eki and its shining tiers are alive as well, and the boys descend on it, flicking boozy sweat out of their faces, flushed from the swollen night air.

In V's increasingly blottoed state, the situation back in the car starts to take on proportions of an exponentially sublime hilarity, and he can no longer remember any reasonable causes for his squeamishness. What an amateur! He's practically skipping, whistling with vibrato and Rodrigo is pushing him and laughing.

⌜Nandeyanen? First, gloomier than Hell, now this Peer Gynt shit, hey! Good thing I remembered. Gimme whatever was left over from the bar. I promised Sachiko-san no later than tomorrow, so I'll slip it under her door when we get in, before we pass out and forget. She was already bent out of shape, so I *promised*.⌟

Deep down under the leaden blanket of his intoxication, something bristles ominously in the colorful refuse littering V's mind. *The rent.* Wasn't that why he had picked up the money in the first place? In the chaos of the nomiya, that tenet had utterly melted away and now, it seems there's no way to blunder out of this fatal blunder. He must give himself up to it. V stops at the bottom of the stairs by the station and reaches into his jacket's pocket. Finds his packet of cigarettes. There's only one left, but he lights it like it's the first in a full pack. They have less than five minutes to catch the last train, but he strolls like they have twenty.

Rodrigo turns.

⌜Oi. Did you hear? Give me the money while it's still on my mind. Whatever you have left from the bar.⌟

「It's gone,」 V says simply. He's still smiling, it feels too good to even lie about it. His levity pulls a blade. So does impending doom. Rodrigo's jaw tightens.

「Well damn it all, what are you standing there, grinning about? Did you drop it? You must've still had it in the bar. You DID pay, right? Or are you so fucking blotted, you left without even paying her?」

「Of course I paid.」

「Then you should have a good 15,000 left. I need to give it, with my portion, to Sachiko-san.」

「It's fine. Calm down.」

Not defense, nofence. He stands and smokes, as tranquil as a fluffy cloud drifting through a Sunday afternoon. Next to him, Rodrigo paints an interesting contrast— approaching apoplexy.

「Instead of me calming down, you could try getting worked up? Just a little? When was the last time you remember having the money? Do you even care? Or wait. Did you lie about having money AND skip the bill?」

V exhales silver and his eyes narrow the slightest.

「Did you drink yourself out of your head? Since when do I lie about money? The first thing I did when I came in was put two *man* bills on the table. You both saw them.」

「No, the first thing you did was announce you were paying! Always the grand gestures, huh? But we never actually saw the money! Did you see it, Kira-chan?」

Woozy himself, Akira is nonplussed by the sudden tension spike. He mumbles:

「I don't know. I feel like I saw the bills, but maybe you're right, Rodrigo. Maybe...」

「Of course I'm right!」 Rodrigo shouts. 「I KNEW he was acting shady as hell. His night with Ako went to shit, he fucked up and didn't get paid—or worse, blew the rent on some—」

Akira tries the path of placation.

「I'm sure there's a good explanation, so there is no need to—」

「No need?!」 Rodrigo bellows. 「NO NEED? The need is that I'm goddamn done with this garbage. You know what living with him is like?」

「Living with me?」 V cuts him off. Turns to Akira like a tarnished groom to the judge in a shabby settlement court. 「I'll tell you what it's like, it's *peaceful!* I do his laundry, air out the room each morning. I certainly never yell like a deranged person, and if it wasn't for me, that whole damn place would be a dump, overrun by bugs.」

「It'll be for you if we won't HAVE that dump, if you don't tell me what the fuck happened to that money you claim you had.」

「You didn't even think you'd see me until tomorrow, so what is this? Manufactured, bullshit outrage! Sachiko-san won't care, we're always late.」

「*You* are always late, I like to be on time!」

「Money is a game, who said that, 30 minutes ago?」

Akira steps between them.

「Oi, oi! I've got some cash on me and I'll lend you what you need. The train's about to leave and you're both carrying on like some old married...」

Rodrigo almost chokes on his own spittle.

「Married...? You have full permission to shoot me *point-blank in the face* if I ever marry such an irresponsible, pus-brained twat! And you are too good to offer, but this isn't about that anymore. It's the principle of the thing. I already told him to unshit himself. He said tonight was good, sure money and now he's shifty and lying and...」

「I didn't lie!」 Yelling is not in the repertoire of sounds V makes, but his face has whitened too.

「Then where the hell is the money?」

「I—」

「You—?」

There is no where else to run.

「I gave it away.」

Both Rodrigo and Akira stare. Twenty seconds pass. Rodrigo opens his mouth finally.

「Aho yanee ka? You fucking... To *who?*」

「To—the —the waitress. At the bar.」

「All of it?」

「All of it.」

「For Christ's sakes. ...I thought you worked smoother than throwing cash in a girl's face.」

「Come on, like I remember what she looked like!」

「Then why?」

「I don't know why.」

「YOU ARE BROKE AND WE NEED TO MAKE RENT AND YOU GAVE ALL YOUR MONEY AWAY TO A WAITRESS AND YOU DON'T EVEN KNOW WHY? YOU WHISPERY FUCK?」

「Because it wasn't good, okay? It was... tainted.」

「Tainted? Did you say tainted? A thousand apologies, V-sama, but I regret to inform you that you do not possess the financial LIBERTY to declare *any money tainted!* What's next? You will be declaring our rent bourgeoisie nonsense? Levas um estalo e nem sabes de que terra és!」 [50]

As sometimes (rarely) happens under emotional duress, Rodrigo's speech will revert back to his native Portuguese and V isn't sure what has been thrown at his head, but he doesn't like the sound of it. His whisper is savage:

「Lower your voice already. If you want to fight over this, say less, but if you want to keep yelling, I'm getting on the train.」

「Good luck even catching a train when you *made us miss the last one!*」

[50] I'm gonna slap you so hard, you're not even gonna know what country you came from!

They all look up at the big station clock. It's true.

It left three minutes ago.

A thick two seconds slide by.

V crosses his arms and sighs.

⌜See, this is why I hate drinking too much. You lose track of time and even your best friend degrades into an uncivil troll...⌟

Rodrigo froths:

⌜Lofty dipshit, talking about *civility*, while he stinks like a failed Calvin Klein fragrance, 'Upchuck'! I won't talk for Akira, but I was ashamed to be sitting with you in the bar!⌟

And V sighs more.

⌜I know what you want. You want me to be as upset as you are, but I can't. I'm too sleepy. So I'm walking home. There's nothing else I can do. You can shoot *me* if I ever act this disgraceful over fucking two *man*.⌟

He spits roughly. A slight breeze blows past. From the far north side of Kyoto Eki's main building, a night watchman eyes them, trying to determine if this affair warrants his involvement. They stand on the stairs, facing each other, bodies tensed, Akira a little off to the side. Rodrigo relaxes his frame first.

⌜You're right. You know? You're right. I'm standing here, yelling like a cretin. I'm not going to yell anymore. I'm not going to fight you, I'm going to go back with you to that bar. I'll explain to the waitress that it was terrible mistake; that you are drunk, were drunk, and she'll give the money back. Minus what we actually owe. She was a nice sort, I remember her well, even if you say you don't. She seemed like that direct, honest type. The type who would feel uncomfortable, having money thrust on her like that.⌟

⌜It was incredibly awkward,⌟ V confirms.

「Exactly. So she'll be happy to see that it wasn't some clumsy nanpa, just a drunken, weird impulse. She'll give it back and feel better about herself. I can pay Sachiko, we won't have to borrow money from Akira; rent will be taken care of and I can feel good too. Everyone wins. All right. Akira-kun, I understand if you have to go, but V-chan and I have to get going and...」

「I'm not going with you,」 V says.

「...Pardon?」

「I said. I don't want that money. I don't want it. I should've never taken it to begin with. And you're right; the whole exchange with her was terrible. The bar girl, I mean. I never want to set foot in that place again. I never want to see that girl again.」

Rodrigo's craggy features redden and swell. The last minute of cease-fire may as well have never happened.

「Are you REFUSING to rectify your fuck up by coming back to the bar with me? I'm not the one who paid, she probably doesn't even remember me! You HAVE to come!」

「I won't.」

「You don't even have to talk! I'll explain, you smile. Act drunk! Not that you have to act, tonight you are worse than a—」

V's head hangs with a solemn, leaden drama.

「I will die before I go back there.」

「You will what? Well, I can arrange for that. Kira-chan, grab him! I don't care if we have to drag your deadbeat ass all the way back up to Shimabara—!」

「Don't touch me, Rodrigo. I sincerely mean it. I'm not going with you.」

「You're laughing? LAUGHING? You think I'm joking? Get him, Kira-Kira! Grab his ankles!」

「Don't... not the ankles... I'm very ticklish...」 V is kicking with laughter; he almost rolls down the stairs.

Almost kicks poor Akira down with him. The watchman has thankfully wandered off to attend to a more pressing issue on the east side of the building.

「Get UP, goddamn it, V,」 Rodrigo curses. 「You are worse than ever tonight. Do you know what you are?」

「I know exactly. I'm drunk, exhausted, and needing my bed. ...So were you serious when you said you would rather get shot in the face than live with me?」

「THAT'S what you're concerned with at this critical hour, you vain, flea-bitten fool?」

「Stop pulling on me, you're shaking everything up. And that's not an answer.」

「I said, I don't want to marry you. But I would continue living with you if you could hold your shit together. Now are you going to come help me or not? Get up!」

V wants to, he does. But his eyeballs feel soused. His skin crawls, so pickled and toxic. He stays where he fell down, watching a candy wrapper flutter by the stairs. In his state, it morphs into two crisp-folded bills, making him wonder, maybe he didn't give the money to the waitress after all?

Maybe he never took it.

Like he didn't want to.

Maybe he is a better person than he even remembers. A stronger one. Imbued with more dignity. (Why does dignity have to be so damn expensive?)

Or is it?

Maybe like money, dignity too is but a game.

Maybe the money blew over from where Ako had dropped it. It would be a miracle if nobody had picked it up after all this time in such a busy spot, but maybe his luck hadn't abandoned him.

For a moment, he's earnestly sure. Of all of it.

It's going to be okay.

Everything's going to be purely okay.

「I see it!」 he chirps.

「The money?」

「It's by the bottom of the stairs!」

Rodrigo breathes in sharp. Squints. His hopeful inhale deflates into hysterical, tired howling.

「That's a piece of trash, you absolute dolt!」

V's face falls, like a kid's.

「Really? I could've sworn it was the money. I could've bet two *man* it was...」

Akira hahas weakly; even Rodrigo can't help but crack a sodden smile; V pulls himself to his feet. He leans over as far as he can, confirms for himself that the flutter is nothing more than a husk of candy wrapper not yet quarantined by the street cleaners, and as he turns to the others, straightens his back, the walls of his stomach constrict violently. Foul, hot liquid arcs out of him without warning, hits the stairs and he's laughing, even as his friends scramble away from the splash, disgusted. Cursing. Screaming in glee.

At the randomness that made this all happen.

FOURTEEN

THE CROSSING OF THE LION CUBS

「So this is it.」
「So *this* is it.」
「So this *is it*.」
「Yare yare...」

V and Rodrigo sat on the viewing deck of Shodenji, trying not to think about that last and final cigarette they had bummed off of a girl. The autumn air ran crisply through their thin jackets. This little temple was a favorite spot of theirs; it was quiet, being a bit removed from the city and tucked away in the surrounding hills. Unlike the most famous rock garden in the entire country,[51] only minutes away by car, this garden remained untouched by tourists. The mountains were usually visible over the wall behind the garden, including the one with the character *dai* carved in, left from the Obon festival, but the day was hazy, and the peaks remained outside of their eyes' grasp. The garden was a white landing of spotless gravel, raked beautifully around not mounds of rock, but neatly groomed bushes that appeared to be animals converging in two groups.

In the past they had come here on bikes, by bus, even by taxi once in a fit of extravagance, always unplanned, but after hearing the news that morning, V had suggested they walk up, in light of their limited funds. Lately, they avoided any strenuous output of energy due to a lack of spare calories, but today not even practical Rodrigo had complained. They made the one and a half hour walk in silence. Once they arrived, they were greeted by a monk.

[51] In the temple of Ryouanji.

He was a trim, pleasant man who kept the temple with his wife and two little sons, and he'd had several conversations with the two boys in the various seasons they'd come to visit. Today, he was surprised to see how much thinner they had become. He'd last seen them in May, after the cherry blossom season, when both had been blooming with what may have been called a late seishun. This day however, their clothes looked worn, and Rodrigo's face especially was alarmingly thin. The priest made them a gift of some persimmons and rice balls, which they accepted and devoured greedily, and then he was off on his business.

Now they sat on the deck, their legs drawn out in front of them. Pinned to the wooden floor by their stretched legs was the four page letter Rodrigo had gotten the other day. They stared alternately at the thin aeropostal paper[52] and then at the garden, as if the two arrangements of things were koans to be reflected on together for their ultimate understanding.

The garden was called *Shishi no Ko no Watari* or 'The Crossing of the Lion Cubs', and they contemplated it and then the pages, Rodrigo knowing the contents of each page by heart. What did the garden mean? What did the letter mean? The rocks and gravel, the mountains, the congregating bushes had infinite solutions, but the letter pointed to but one.

「So you're leaving.」

V breathed out and curled deeper into his jacket. He was aware that in the last couple of weeks, at most only half of his consciousness was ever fully invested in a conversation. The other half was deep in a food-fantasy because eating always came last. After rent, cigarettes, commuter fares, everything. Without Rodrigo's influence, he may well have tried to live beyond his means, wheedle

[52] To Rodrigo's greatest chagrin, his parents refused to enter the new century and learn how to use email, so their letters continued on regular paper.

extensions out of their landlady and quickly dig himself into a dire mire of debt, but as it was, their bills were always paid. Not riding high, hardly breaking even, but they were surviving. And now this.

They stared out into the garden, their heads dizzy. It was unusually cold. The rice balls and fruit had been their first meal that day, and while both of them were waiting for back pay from students to come at the end of the week, they knew the money would be gone. Fast. Rodrigo's students had drifted away one by one as the summer neared its end. Two remained, of which one would leave for New Zealand at the end of the next week. They had both braced for another bumpy stretch of the water life, so V had been happy (and only extremely privately envious) when Rodrigo had told him about the position he'd found through his old school. He'd gone through the interview process a while ago, not daring to hope: a liaison program between a Brazilian and a local university. Portuguese and Japanese speaking instructors needed. Steady money. And the platinum circle reward: a work visa. Hope dies last and now—they wanted him. All he would have to do was hang on until the spring semester. It seemed easy as kasutera, after all they'd been through. He wrote his parents, so proud to be delivering them good news for once! Not another missile covertly (worse, directly) squeezing them for money. And while he knew better than to expect praise, even prepared himself for a fight, this felt plain dirty.

Their response had come a week ago and how Rodrigo had blustered! How he had ranted, walking up one bank of the Kamo and back another, for kilometers and kilometers. Rage-walking until the sun came up. V had gone with him. They can't do this! He'd never asked for a plane ticket home for the end of November. Certainly not a one-way. He understood that it was a milestone birthday (his favorite grandfather, throat cancer survivor, 90). He understood that he could go back to the University of Lisbon next semester, if he wanted. Make nice side money in his family's prosperous downtown shop (textiles), if he wanted. But he didn't want any of it. Hadn't they digested that by now? He would write them back (no, expensive as it was, this warranted a phone call). He would tell them that he was rejecting the ticket, and if that money went down the pipes, it wasn't his fault. They'd never asked. They shouldn't bother showing up at the airport with the whole extended family—no balloons, no welcome home banner—he would not be there. And he knew the limits of his parents' patience. It had been stretching for years and years and now it would break. So be it. If they wanted to brand him with the scarlet 'I' of 'ingrate,' so be it! If they wanted to disown him, he would accept it readily! All of this, he told to V, and after they'd discussed everything his family could do to checkmate him, they walked back to the boarding house, split an oversized instant ramen. Fell into their futons and he slept the best five hours of sleep since he'd been living in Kyoto.

That had been six days ago.

And for almost six enchanted days, Rodrigo wholly believed that he too was finally ready to be one of those young men. With no... well, maybe he'd have a future with this new job. But no more past. No more ties. No more obligations. And no guilt over it either. The resolve to announce it felt so solid. Unshakable. And yet somehow, each day, a fresh reason would conveniently present itself for why the next day would be more suitable for making that fateful call. And the next. And the next. Hour by hour the sword to slice the Gordian knot grew heavier in his hands. Until on the dawn of day seven, in the four a.m. dark of their room, listening to V's slight snore and watching through their dingy curtain the subtle pinks start bleaching the bottom of Kyoto's indigo sky—Rodrigo knew.

Now, they sat on the viewing deck of Shodenji, and he kept compulsively folding the letter and unfolding it. Again and again. The thin paper of the envelope was pinned under his left thigh. Next to him, V fidgeted slightly, but not consciously needing to smoke. Strangely, in the yards of temples and when he held someone were the only times when the urge completely vanished. Just as temples were the only places where Rodrigo ever seemed able to rein in the dimensions of his voice. He said quietly:

「I'm sorry.」

And V turned to him, surprised.

「But for what?」

Their breath hovered in the darkening air. It would soon be a razor sharp fall dusk.

「I really had myself convinced. I must've had you convinced too.」

「You gave it more thought, is all. It's how things go.」

「I figured you'd say that. It's so... Damn it, why now, of all times? When things are finally looking up?」

V glanced at the sky.

「Because, you said it. Things are finally looking up. You know what that means. You're not in Germany or France, a short plane ride away. This year, you write that you have a steady job lined up. Next year? You write that you're moving in with someone. After that, it's only a matter of time before you tell them, you're never going back.」

Rodrigo's somber expression cracked the slightest.

「I already had that convo with them about moving in with someone when I met you a year ago. Come to think of it, they didn't like that either.」

「See? They want you back before they get the next installment, announcing that I've knocked you up and we're getting married.」

「Goddamn, why do I have to be the one to get knocked up? But if you could grow a decent pair of tits and make an egg tart like my avozinha, I might consider it, too.」

「So glad to see I've moved up from 'shoot me in the face' to 'I might consider it.'」

「Pfffft, really, V. You don't have enough girls blowing smoke up your ass? I got to do it too?」

「Sure. Who doesn't want to be a. What was it? ...A pus-brained twat?」

「Ahahaha, I can do without the pus for brains, but if I could not give a fuck as expertly as you, we'd go buy a phone card on the way home and I'd make that call tonight, no problem. Isn't that what you'd do?」

「Well...」

A bat screeched, squealed. V's voice cut and they watched it snap an insect out of the air, hardly a meter above their heads. Far out over the mountains, a pale, pale moon was starting to shine in the darkening sky. Stars lit up around it; mint and blood and rose-quartz colored stars. The bat circled, winged off to the left through a fringe of pine, and they sat for another quarter minute of silence before V continued:

「It is what I'd do, because I'd do what's best for me. And going back is what's best for you. So that's what you have to do.」

「Yeah.」 Rodrigo nodded. 「I didn't want to admit it last week, but I can only solve a problem my way. Not your way or anybody else's. Omae... I hope you know that whatever I said that night by Kyoto Eki, this past year has probably been the best year of my entire life. You do know that, right? It was terrible and it was stressful and it was crazy and it was amazing and a part of me wants it to never end. But if I'm totally honest, when I try to picture living here long term, I'm always stuck on the outside. I love this place but I won't ever... fit in here. You won't ever either, but you also have in your own weird way, as well as you can fit anywhere. Or maybe that's it. You don't have anywhere to belong to, but I do. So I've been asking myself, why am I wanting to throw that all away? And I was making excuses, telling myself I couldn't go back because I would be disappointing myself and letting you down. But I did what I came to do and I have to accept that it's over now. And you'll find your own way too.⌋

Of course. What else could one do? V nodded, but his insides chilled. *You don't have anywhere to belong to.* Surely his friend had not meant that in any disparaging way? He herded his mind from it, thought about something easy instead. Where had it gone to, all the money he once had? It went to the skies, to the stars—it went any old place. *Easy come, easy go.* V smiled wanly.

⌈Sure. I'll figure something out.⌋

⌈I do feel bad though. It's all really sudden and you won't have time to find a new roommate. You know, my dad will be so happy once I confirm I'm coming back for good, he'll be ready to pay for pretty much anything I ask. I could tell him I owe you money, or rent...⌋

Take it, a voice hissed. *Doesn't his family have all that they need? More than what they need. And you heard him: the best year of his life! It's not a handout. It's a tip.*

Suddenly embarrassed and not even sure why, V wrapped his arms around his own knees and stared out into the garden.

⌈Thanks. But I'll be fine. ...It really is cold, huh? Wouldn't expect it, this time of year.⌋

⌈Yeah, you wouldn't.⌋ Rodrigo folded the letter one

final time, put it back into its envelope, then tucked it into his jacket's pocket. 「And fuck! I'm starving. I think that fruit made it worse. But yeah, I know I shouldn't worry about you. Jikan no mondai before you find a new sucker.」 He had enough energy left for a raucous cackle. 「So there's no 'student' around you could move in with?」

V shrugged.

「They're gone. Most of them.」

And they were. In the spring, in the summer, in the hot, wet season of tsuyu, everyone seemed more eager for everything. But now it was fall, and he had let those contacts drop away, for foolish reasons, serious reasons— Not long ago, a huge financial blow had been struck when his most lucrative lady had gotten *compromised*, as he phrased it. She wanted to rent a permanent room for him, where they could have privacy. Of course, V was tempted, but reluctant. If he were to accept, he would be at the complete mercy of *one* mistress. A misstep could leave him stripped. And he didn't trust himself, he knew he was a prince of missteps. He longed for monogamy, yes, but in *marriage*, with all of the glorious status changes that would bring regarding his visa. No more scrounging, no more worrying that any involved ID check would reveal his illegal status. His dream girl was youngish, beautiful, *unattached*, somewhat traditional, but not so much that she couldn't be drawn to a foreign man, to him, unexpectedly. She would risk it all to marry him, break her parents' hearts (they'd forgive her in the end), run away with him to Hokkaido, where they would marry. They would come back to Kyoto to live in perfect happiness. He would never want to leave her and he would never have to leave. But that was the world of the yume.[53] In this world, all he had were women looking for some salty afternoon fare, but nothing too spicy. Reputations. Families, had to be protected at all

[53] Dream 夢

costs. Of course. After several days of balking, he told the woman he could not accept her offer. She cried a bit, V must understand that she could not continue to support him if he wouldn't give her the signs of fidelity she needed. Thus it had ended and at the moment, he had only one serious pupil, but not nearly as generous as that other lady had been. And she was showing signs of the crack.

「Oh?」

Rodrigo cocked an eyebrow as they stood up to walk off the viewing deck. The air was getting colder and they wanted to get moving.

「Yeah.」 They bowed to the monk who had started to rake the gravel in the garden below. He bowed back. Strange, skinny foreign boys. But nice. 「She—well, she's starting to get indiscreet. I worry she's going to do something stupid and blow her cover.」

「And yours?」

「I can safely say I have way less to lose than she does.」

「Cool as always, I see.」

V's voice drenched with uncharacteristic acid. 「Any reason not to be? Did *I* make a promise to God and the world to have and to hold her husband or family, or whoever she has, for the rest of *my* life?」

Rodrigo whistled low. 「No you did not. ...Any kids?」

「Not this one, actually. Just a dusty old husband she's bored to death of. Anyway, what goes around comes back around—she says he fucks around on her all the time. I'm not saying that justifies either of us...」

「Attarimae. You're a mere cog in the giant, spinning wheel of Japanese passive aggression. Were it to stop spinning, who knows what would happen to any of us.」

V glanced at his twinkling eyes, not sure if he wanted to laugh with them or bruise them, but he understood Rodrigo as much as he did himself—and that any barbs he dealt were said in the spirit of truth. One arguably did not always have an appetite for truth though, so temple or not, V wished for a hundred cigarettes and roughly bit his nails.

⌈*Please*. I draw the line at serious conversations regarding sex and fidelity. You'll only bore the shit out of us both.⌋

Jovial mockery. Ridicule. Beaming scoffery. These were Rodrigo's standard expressions, but V caught a glimpse of his friend's face in the gloaming and was surprised to see it looking unusually grave.

⌈Now you see why I worry about leaving? Look, I am the last person who would force anyone to be *serious*. But maybe you should think about the contempt you have for this guy—for all these guys, when you're going *to be one of them* one day. Doesn't that concern you? Or are you seriously naive enough to think a wedding band can change that?⌋

The question froze in the air. He was free to answer or not, and Rodrigo was sure he had taken the latter by the sheer volume of silence, but V was in fact considering. It was a query he was forced to turn in his mind more and more of late. In the coldest corners of his soul, predators had begun to whisper that the sanctuary of his dreams was no haven at all—and that in it, he would never find peace. The price of wanting something for forever was too high. No mortal could pay it. And while at times it was as if the gross disproportion between actuality and the pictures in his head would rent him in two—

He simply wasn't fashioned for cynicism.

And rationality he found undeniable, as necessary as shitting, but inevitably lifeless. With no soul, no smell, no touch. Life was somewhere else—everywhere else—in the air, the melting snow, the cold, the spring. The smell of incense at temples. Picnics under the trees. Long dinners with the extended family. Fights—impetuous, loud, tear-filled. Soft, murmured reconciliations. Peace, the color of silence. A room—it was cold. Austere, as rooms here will be. The opaque eggshell of the shouji surrounds them, bedding spread on the floor. A man, arms wrapped around a woman. Between them, a child, a little older than a baby. And he wakes up to their breathing and the overwhelming knowledge that *it is arrived*. Who were these people? He wanted to meet them both, so badly—and the whole world resonated with a possibility to be realized—when?

He looked down in his contemplation and noticed his nail bitten to the quick.

A bead of blood gleamed in the dark like an ominous ruby and he gingerly licked it off. As he did, the maddening look came into his eyes. Rodrigo sighed—the argument was lost again, as it always would be.

「Yes,」 V spoke evenly. His words cut clean. 「It would change, because then we would belong to each other. I would be someone better. I would try.」

「People don't change, V.」

「I wouldn't be changing. *I'd be going back to the person I used to be.*」

Rodrigo's exhale shivered in front of them like a specter.

「Then I give up. It's good to see you living up to your reputation though. A pus-brained twatty romantic.」

「A romantic? No. A realist.」

「A wanker.」

「A compromise then.」

He reached out his frozen hand, and Rodrigo clasped him strongly, his grip warm and true. *Always the hellos, always the goodbyes.* They finally left the temple, bumped down the hill, seeing the lights in the distance of the city flick on one by one. At one point, they broke into a run and could almost hear the bones grinding in their bodies. *Bones, meat, muscle, sweat.* Tearing the last scraps of energy out of themselves. The boys ran until they reached the pebbly banks of the river's delta and collapsed on it, wiping their mouths. Their laughter was not entirely sane. By now it was dark and V went to the water's edge. He lowered his body, sank back on his ankles. First he looked out at all that flickered on the other shore. Street lights, and dining room lights, and headlights bobbing on bicycles and cars. All pointed home. Then he looked down. The river's surface was still enough that he could see his reflection and the rising moon in it, and he put his hand out, palm first. Lowered it. Water slicked under his fingers, shimmering and cooler than B-flat minor. His best friend was leaving, but the Blue Dragon was always here. It had been here long, long before he was born; it would be here long after he died, and knowing that, how could he feel lonely? How could he worry? *If I'm not married by this time next year, I'm going to marry this river.* Two meters over, Rodrigo started skimming pebbles out over the water, picking up the conversation as if they'd never stopped talking.

⌜You know, there is something you could maybe try, once I'm gone. Have you ever considered a host gig? Dress nice, schmooze with the ladies, say what they want to hear. Get one to make her your pet. Come on, it's perfect!⌟

V picked up a stone too.

⌜This *stone* is perfect. Look at it. Not too big, not too small, flat with just the right amount of—⌟

⌜Let's not stray from the topic here.⌟

⌜I'm not. And believe it or not, I did have an offer to set me up with that, years ago. Remember Masao? He told me once that he could get my foot into the door. Don't need papers or anything. But I would have to move to Osaka. Somewhere with more nightlife.⌋

⌈See, hit the big city, be some bar's token patsukin. And you already have a weird porny name.⌋

⌈Nah, I'd take a stage name. Like hmm, how are we feeling about—Rodrigo? He's a white Brazilian who moved to Japan for love but she broke his heart and now he's...⌋

Rodrigo snorted.

⌈Possibly the worst hustler name I've ever heard, but I'm proud to be a part of the backstory. I could even give you a crash course in spicy Portuguese before I leave. You'd make a killing; the job really would be brilliant!⌋

V gripped his stone loosely, flicked his wrist and watched the flat disk skim out over the water. One, two, three, four—finally sinking away after the fifth plink. Such a satisfying sight, until he remembered that he was hardly more secure than the little stone he'd just hurtled into the wet darkness. He backed away from the silver edge uneasily.

⌈It's a brilliant job, except that I don't want it.⌋

⌈Why am I not surprised, you stubborn piece of— Well, why the hell not? Give me FIVE GOOD REASONS!⌋

⌈Five? I'll give you six. I have no nice clothes; I despise drinking; I loathe Osaka; I need one woman who wants to be with me, not 36 who don't; I'm on the wrong side of 25, and that's even if they'd allow a new half in their bar.⌋

⌈*Omee*, I can lend you the money, you don't look a day over 24 and a half, and girly talk or no, I had to sit with you ass naked in a bathhouse before I figured out what's up. And even then, I wasn't sure. If anyone doubts you, drag them to some water and make them watch you skip a stone! Females can't skip past two, everyone knows that.⌋

⌈I can't leave my girl.⌋ V gestured out to the river.

⌈*Boke*, there's water there too.⌋

「Not this water.」

「*Six* skips hah, so beat *that*. Well,」 Rodrigo combed the ground with his eyes. 「Mind you, I'm only prying for your own good, but are you sure this isn't about something else? Say like that sweetie you were all wrecked up about a few weeks ago?」

「...Who?」

「Let's not play stupid now. Little Miss 16-gets-you-20. What was her name again?」

「I didn't say.」

「But you did. This one, you did. I'll remember it in a second. You thought I hadn't noticed you covertly mooning all summer, but the last time you mentioned her was, hmmm. Hina-chan's party, does that ring a bell?」

「Not really.」

「Yeah, I'm not surprised. You'd gotten yourself shit-faced on her good booze. You sure you hate drinking? And then that fine girl Hina, man, she had it for you *bad*, she was petting you hard. Goes to show she was shitfaced too.」

「God, you're an ass.」

「So I told her to definitely take a rain check, because in your condition, you couldn't even raise a smile.」

「Did I mention that you are an ass?」

「And then you sat up all of the sudden and started raving about this girl, you even showed us her picture on your keitai—meccha kawaikko datta yo, she was a major cutie. I was wondering how such an innocent looking thing had gotten tangled up with our resident angel of lust—」

「Are we going to get to a point? Tonight?」

「—But even more surprised at your level of attach-ment. I think we all were. You waxed sentimental about how considerate she was, how she cared about you, *really cared,* and you really cared too, but now she was gone and it was so sad. It was really something.⌋

⌈Like you said, I was shitfaced.⌋

⌈Like someone else said, 'a cat chasing his own dick gets his head chopped off by the streetcar.'⌋

⌈...Is that ...a real Portuguese saying?⌋

⌈No, but it fits. So where'd that girl go? Did you ever find out? Or what, she wasn't good enough for a follow up, only to corrupt and throw away? Another nubile virgin sacrificed on your altar as a human tissue...⌋

⌈Off. This. Now.⌋

He started to stalk away, but Rodrigo followed him.

⌈Ho, ho, ho, has evoking her actually rendered you incoherent? Just as I suspected: Minasama—Ladies and Gentlemen!⌋ He turned to address the river, and his cry was swallowed in the Kamo's muted night. ⌈A sign of the apocalypse, or has it really happened? I think it has: Our V is in love!⌋

⌈I am *not.*⌋

⌈My god, he's blushing! Is he blushing? Vicchan, trust me, 'tis no shame! It's a bitch that gnaws us all every once in a while, and why should you be exempt? Now arguably, you could've picked a better candidate than someone who still sleeps with teddy bears, but baby steps, pun semi intended. What's her number? I'm going to text her right now and ask her to check in on you once in a while once I'm gone, because, and I do say this as a brother—⌋

He started to reach for V's pocket.

⌈Stop! She doesn't want to talk. I've been texting her and she never writes back.⌋

⌈Well, what'd you do? Try to hide the fact that you've banged half of female Kyoto? Hey, we've all got baggage. Tell her you're sorry and all will be well.⌋

⌈No, it won't. She doesn't care about who I am with,

and I swear I didn't do anything this time, but it's complicated. She has a boyfriend and a...」

「I don't know. You've moved your rivals from husbands to a puny high school boyfriend! Sounds like it's getting simpler, to me.」

「Joudan janai wa—It's not funny. She always texted before, so she must have her reasons if she doesn't want to see me anymore and I will respect that. I mean, I knew getting involved with her wasn't necessarily the right thing to do in the first place...」

「'Getting involved' and 'not necessarily right'—man, you've really got to wean yourself from these euphemisms. I mean, fucking her was wrong. Amen. Loving her and letting her love you? Even worse, but then your modus operandi always has been in another moral dimension. That's just you and I like that. Maybe it's what she likes about you too.」

「Can you just drop it? Look, I don't give two screws about what *moral dimension* I'm operating in: I liked being with her, I'm not sorry it happened, but I knew from the first moment I saw her how it would end. Something like this. And she's obviously over it and so am I. So, the end.」

「Are you convincing me or you?」

But he walked off. Cutting a lone figure against the dark shore, Rodrigo watched him for a moment, then cried out.

「V! Oi, V! You think it's bullshit, but I'm being serious now—so listen up! Maybe the host thing isn't for you, but at some point, you need to fight for something. Or someone. Maybe this girl even. There is such a thing as being too Zen! Are you listening?」

It was close to eight o'clock by the time they finally reached the downtown area, stooping their shoulders against the wind. In the middle of the river, the Kamo was so shallow that one could cross and not get their calves wet. Near the bridge, a crane stood in the water picking at a piece of garbage and the two of them looked at the bird, and the bird looked at them, its eyes radiating frighteningly whenever a car passed overhead. V wondered deliriously if they could catch the bird if they waded out to it.

Catch it and roast it.

Further up the bank towards the streets, two boys were sitting on some stairs leading down to the river. One was strumming a guitar in the blistering wind, the other was singing in a high, clear voice. Clearer than the wind. Under the bridge, a group had built a little compound with a fire, and they twirled around it, swaying their bodies to the music. They had long, dangling necklaces made of bottle caps, and their hair hung down to their waists. Black, coarse, straight hair on everyone. They called out to the two boys and Rodrigo laughed.

「Toshi-san, is that you? Mie-san?」

「Rodrigo-san!」 An older woman in a patchwork skirt and several layered thermal shirts waded out of the circle towards them. River mud crept up her clothes and her smile was broad and rotten. 「You got something for us?」

The group called themselves the Immortals and they wandered about the city, slept under bridges and swayed on the banks. They claimed to live off starlight and firelight and dancing through the night, but they would accept change, bottled green tea, sparklers, or tobacco.

「Well, we got ONE cigarette. Everyone share it?」

The woman ambled over to them with interest. V got the cigarette out of his pocket. Rodrigo lit it and passed it to her. She inhaled gratefully, passed it to a woman on her left, who passed it on. That little light made its way all around. The boys caught the hippies' laugh like a cold, and though in the past they'd politely refuse to join, it was a night where you could do nothing but dance. High on iced wind and two puffs of nicotine, they shook their bodies in the circle of fire while the two boys on the stairs kept singing and playing. Toshi sashayed forward, put one of his necklaces over Rodrigo's neck and another around V's, and Rodrigo thanked him, then went on:

「Listen Toshi-san, me and Vicchan here are down and *out*. Know any place where we could get some food? Not all of us are immortals, you know.」

「You hungry, man? 'No problem,' dayo. You know the MOS Burger in the Teramachi?」

「Near the geesen, right?」

「There's a café next to it. The bakery in the café has the best throwaways on Tuesdays and Thursdays. Bread, pastries, they got it. Today's Monday? You can have food tomorrow night. Even a dier like you can wait a day for food, can't you?」

Rodrigo nodded and thanked him again, then they walked up to the stairs with the singing boy and guitar player, who scooted to let them pass. Down under the bridge the Immortals took out sparklers and lit them, drawing lazy circles in the dark, and crackling stars.

「It must be nice to live forever. Not have to eat.」

V set his ragged shoes on Sanjou Douro, and they were off to the glitter and bustle of the night-time Teramachi. Rodrigo glinted at him.

「Even if you no longer know what day it is?」

「Sure. It is Tuesday, right?」

「You bet your ass.」

Two girls walked in front of them, hair dyed the color of honey, thighs pulsing briskly beneath their short skirts. The seasons were of little concern to the skirt lengths in the city—only shoes reflected the cold days. On the trains and streets everywhere, boots had nosed out the pumps and delicate sandals. V stared at those thighs until his lungs went numb and Rodrigo nudged him roughly in the side.

⌈Hey, why don't you spare your blood flow for keeping yourself warm?⌋

One of the girls turned around and caught him staring. V blew her a kiss. She winked back and flashed him a victory sign, before Rodrigo pulled him away. His head swam, with exhaustion, hunger, joy, despair.

⌈Let's get married! Let's get married and fly away to heaven on love's white wings! You angel, I love you!⌋ She laughed at his lunacy, and Rodrigo pulled harder.

⌈Come on, you fucking fool. Unbelievable, koitsu.⌋

He pulled V towards the Teramachi, off to the center of the city.

Once, Mibu's wolves ran freely here. They'd cut their enemies in the streets until the pounded earth ran crimson with their traitor blood. The City of Peace and Tranquility, the Son of Heaven's old capital. Where was that blood now? Trapped under a layer of concrete, forgotten by a synthesis of streaming neon light. But yet it flowed, back and forth to the river; it was there that night too, under their feet, and he loved the feeling of it, the fusion of the pulsing newness and oldness. Rodrigo rambled on to him about the Shinsengumi, the signs fried his eyes, and his friend fried images into his brain with that endless talk. They both ran laughing, until his head was about to pop.

FIFTEEN

THE INFERNAL BRIDEGROOM

Il vient de recevoir la croix d'honneur…

T hose are the final words. Miss Yuki closes her book,
sweeps her eyes around. She knows she has a habit of
moving her lips when she reads, especially in French. Had
she been doing that now? No, it does not seem so. The
man at the table to the right ruffles his *Yomiuri,* looks up
and does not see her, as she does not see him. They see
past and through each other and then Miss Yuki glances
at her watch. Five minutes still. The waitress comes and
brings her a black tea and asks if she is ready to order. She
is. Two plates of sandwiches, a salad and a soup, and the
waitress jots it all. I'm waiting for somebody, this isn't all
for me, Yuki explains and the waitress nods. Yes, what
will happen now is that he will come, and he will be
hungry, and have none of his own money and be too
proud to order on hers, and the food will arrive, and Yuki
will tell him to eat, and he will refuse politely. Once, twice.
And the third time, finish everything on the table. Once
his stomach is full, she will say it. A full stomach might
soften the blow. The door opens on the far side of the café,
but she does not need to turn her head. The air is too still.
Another glance at her watch. Three minutes. And then
Miss Yuki takes out her book, opens it to this particular
passage she had highlighted:

Elle se répétait: «J'ai un amant! un amant!» se délectant à
cette idée comme à celle d'une autre puberté qui lui serait

[54] She repeated, 'I have a lover! A lover!' delighting at the idea as if a second puberty had come to her. So at last she was to know those joys of love, that fever of happiness of which she had despaired! She was entering upon marvels where all would be passion, ecstasy, delirium.

from 'Madame Bovary' by Gustave Flaubert.

[55] Keats' 'Ode to a Nightingale' was the only English Saito Takamitsu ever felt comfortable speaking out loud. He had the entire poem memorized and later, his one daughter would have it memorized too. They could spend hours in his study, reading together in silence, or eating

survenue. Elle allait donc posséder enfin ces joies de l'amour, cette fièvre du bonheur dont elle avait désespéré. Elle entrait dans quelque chose de merveilleux où tout serait passion, extase, délire.[54]

Passion, ecstasy, delirium.

She taps her pencil tip on the period after *délire* and tells herself that once he is finished eating, she will tell him that he is a wonderful tutor and she has enjoyed their time together, but she would have to find another. This wasn't for her. This *wasn't her.* Perhaps it wasn't him either. Never one to hurry and yet these days, he has a harried air that makes her suspect he is in some trouble. With his health or his woman or his finances but she can never find it in herself to ask. In that respect, they are much the same. Only in the written word can she find a real friend, [55] like only horizontally can he ever speak. And how can she even explain it to him, truly? The way Miss Yuki sees it, men are useful but fundamentally unfascinating creatures, and women even more inscrutable. And as he is both and neither, she let herself be miraged into thinking this could all be something different. Oh, to go back! To the first day they'd met, could she ever forget it? That demeanor of his, like a glass of water she couldn't wait to spill. That satisfaction when she finally got to scratch through his unruly hair. But by now, she'd scratched herself raw.

The door swings open again; the curtains blow, the china rattles on the table—her poltergeist sweeps over, stops at the table, and her neighbor looks up again. This time, he does see something—not just sees, but registers him, moves his gaze over, registers her too, then back to him, as if summing an equation—yes, take a long look, you *hage*,[56] it's exactly what you think, and it's this spitefulness that frightens her. *He* notices nothing though;

pulls a chair over, apologizes and asks if he may sit close next to her. He is not prepared today, he has not brought his book, though he did finish the reading. Miss Yuki looks up to greet him. Takes him in.

–You are... so dressed up! You must have an engagement after this?

–An appointment, yes, –he amends slightly and doesn't offer more. –It's so dark in this corner, Miss Yuki. Are you sure you are all right with this spot? And where is Miss Chisato?

–She didn't write to you? She wrote me earlier that she won't make it today.

He frowns, checks his phone.

–No, I don't have anything from her. I hope it's not too serious?

–A stomach flu, I think.

–Hmm, I hope she is better soon.

–I'm sure, she said she was almost over it.

Next week they will meet again, or he will write Chisato before then, and her lies won't fit. By then however, it won't matter. Perhaps, she wonders, he has his own lies; as they start talking about Flaubert, he is checking his phone every other sentence until he notices that she notices his constant checking. Banishes the phone to his pocket, reaches for a cigarette, stops—reaches his thumbnail to his mouth and then stops that too. Puts his long hands down and domesticates them flat against the table. It seems wherever he is going after this, ragged nails will not do.

–I'm sorry, Miss Yuki. What was that? I didn't catch it.

She looks up too abruptly and stares right into him. His hair, always chaotic, has been cut. Even styled. His suit is immaculate and the shirt underneath fresh and sharply

---

tangerines, or she would read out loud to him in English, or French (her personal favorite), or poems from his beloved Bashou. He was the one to encourage her to study further; the only one who encouraged her to go abroad, despite the illness that had started to haunt his body sometime in her late high school years. Saito Takamitsu died not long after his only daughter had returned from her studies in France and it is possible that he was the only person Miss Yuki had ever considered a true Friend.

[56] A disparaging term for a bald/balding man

ironed. And if they were in a hotel room right now and he would ask her, as he sometimes still did, what she wants from him, she would tell him to stand in the middle of the room in all his clothes, for the full hour. Yuki swallows.

–I said that to me this book is exploring the theme of the eighth sin. Curiosity. I don't think that's how I would have read it when I was younger, but this second reading, it all seemed so clear. In this story, Flaubert was able to explore the themes and tropes of a woman in love he did not dare examine in his more 'serious' writing. And hasn't a man exploring the feminine position always been considered subversive? The serious male writer sates his curiosity for writing feminine melodrama. The virtuous reader sates their curiosity regarding adultery.

She imagines he knows little about Flaubert, literature, or virtue, but he does know something about—

–...Curiosity is one of the deadly sins? And aren't there only seven? La colère. La Gourmandise. Hmm. L'Avarice. L'Envie. L'Orgueil. La Paresse.

–La Luxure. [57] –Yuki looks up at him. –And Curiosity.

–Do you think it is sinful to be curious, Miss Yuki?

The waitress comes back, mosaics their table with the order and Miss Yuki notices her for the first time. A waifish praying mantis, a vile little doll, *an exactly his type*, but he's occupied with the text and the girl lingers infuriatingly, seeming eager for at least a superficial exchange. Next to them, the man has put down his paper; Miss Yuki thanks the waitress, *he* stares at the book. The pageant is set, everybody knows their lines, only Yuki breaks character. She reaches over the table and slips her hand over his—sure, possessive—he finally looks up, notices the dishes, notices her hand on him. He is so startled, he thanks the waitress in the wrong language—Merci, he sighs it. The girl titters like an idiot—*The dog had risen on*

[57] Lust

its hind legs. And spoke! Their neighbor lays his paper to the side, watching them openly now, truly as if he were at the theatre and Miss Yuki says:

–You can tell me if you are going to meet some other woman after this. You certainly didn't dress up like this for me.

Ten minutes later, Miss Yuki is walking up the road going east. The person she follows walks almost a block ahead, but she can still make out the figure. The fall air is brassy, almost hot, but she does not want to spend the 15 seconds to stop and undo her light trench coat. Nor does she want to walk too fast; her pace is set somewhere between never losing him and never catching up. She squares her shoulders and grips the handle of her reticule tightly. Her low heels click on the walk, click click, but she can't hear that. Why, she wonders, had she not noticed? Or perhaps she had? Yes, of course.

That afternoon. She'd agreed to drive her mother home. The procedure had been nothing too involved; still, Miss Yuki offered to spend the rest of the afternoon there. They could have tea together, or dinner later? Let's not, her mother had said, why don't you go home? She said she would prefer to be alone and sleep. Afterwards, Miss Yuki had sat two streets down from her mother's house, in her parked car. A mysterious fluid had gathered in her throat and before she even knew it, she had written him. Told him she could pick him up in her car, if he wanted. Oh yes, he wanted. Assumed no doubt that she would drive them to a hotel. It was what she had assumed as well, so they were both surprised when the car stopped where it did. Where are we? he asked once she turned the engine off and she noted with satisfaction his fingertips drumming a little faster once she said, my home. She told him that she would go in for a minute, to pick something up. And that he should come in too. She told him not to worry. Her husband was away at a doctor's convention. (That is what they always told the children too. He is away at *a doctor's convention*.) And what if one of the neighbors sees me? he asked. I don't exactly blend in. Shh, she chided, did he think she was a prisoner? Spied upon? Of course if anybody asked, she would simply say that she had invited her tutor to conduct their hour here. It wasn't a crime. He finally entered.

Her house is narrow, two-storied, always ready for visitors—shoes and jackets and house-slippers meticulously locked away in wall closets. Her son's room can especially get disordered, but she knew the children's doors were closed and out of sight beyond the bend of the upper hall. Not that she imagined him the type to go door-opening anyway.

She showed him the first floor first. The living room, kitchen, verandah. You have an exquisite home, he said in French, and she remembers breathing in his envy. Here, she had everything that he wanted. He asked to open the tatami room and she watched him pull the fusuma aside, breathless, like a child peeking behind an altar to catch God. Step in, she said, so graciously. She felt grateful to her husband that day.

Then she took him upstairs.

On the second floor, he admired the polished floors and the newly redone bathroom, but when she started to pull at his coat in front of the bedroom, he paled. Here? He could be so laughably prudish sometimes. She teased him, did he not know how many times she'd been with him in this room already? Each time her husband touched her, she'd closed her eyes and imagined Rimbaud. As Verlaine had done. He said okay, but then take off your wedding ring. She extended her finger and he pulled it off, peeled off their clothes next. She could tell he was incredibly excited too. Once his airs slipped away, he adored all taboo. They showered together, then he took her to bed in his arms. She really did feel like his bride, and his eyes above her glittered as pale and terrifying as an infernal groom's. But he wasn't hers and she wasn't his and she wondered if this had been Verlaine's lot as well. To think of his wife when he was with Rimbaud and to think of Rimbaud when he was with his wife. It struck her then, as if she'd been defeated by some ancient, petty curse. When he saw her stiffen, he stopped, carefully laid her down. What's wrong, Miss Yuki? But she could say nothing. Only cry. He held her, went to the bathroom, held her more, smoked, finally dressed himself. She was still crying. She watched his concern decay into irritation. Where is the nearest train station? he asked. That was her cue, to gather herself together. She could not. Yuki waved out the window. He waited a moment. Raised his voice so slightly. Where, Miss Yuki? I don't know where we are. She said nothing. Okay, he said. And left. Four hours later, her daughter came home. She was composed by then, but when Miss Yuki saw her girl's face, the silence of an evening alone together stretched out between them, as lonesome as a night sea. Cautiously, Yuki asked if they should order delivery and watch a movie. Since her father and brother were gone. She wanted to sound like a normal mother. Not someone begging for mercy. Her daughter shrugged, seemed surprised by the offer. They never did such things together. Yuki didn't know why, but she seemed in a dismal mood too.

    The delivery arrived and when she tried to pay is when Yuki discovered that he had harvested every last yen from her wallet before he'd left, except for a single solitary *sen* bill. Now she did not have enough to pay for the food. Luckily, her daughter had cash on her, but it was so humiliating.

She wasn't angry at him though.

–Miss Yuki, –he says once she taps him on the shoulder.

　　–How did you know it was me?

　　–Who else would follow me for this long?

　　–Don't say that, please. I feel so pathetic.

　　–Don't. Just imagine that any pathetic thing you've done, I've done nine times worse.

How unpredictable this fall weather is! The wind blowing so cold before, and now it seems warm to her. Almost playful. She frowns.

　　–Did you really have to leave like that? You dashed out so suddenly, I could barely flag down the waitress. And all that food! I ended up leaving it. It was so embarrassing.

　　–*You* were the one acting so strangely, the man next to us could hardly keep his eyes away. Then you grabbed my hand! Then you wanted to know where I was going later, when normally you couldn't care less. You asked to end the lesson early, so I did. Now you are following me.

　　–Yes, because. –Yuki breathes deep. –I don't understand. You've never talked about leaving Kyoto before. Why didn't you tell me you need money?

　　–I always need it.

　　–But you must need more? I could help.

　　–How? When you have your own family and your own problems. I need to take care of myself.

And she knows it is wicked of her, but she can't help it. Rarely one for mirth, now her laughter peals out over the street. –But you can't. You know that, right? You are like a cat, you want to roam free, but you need a place to go back to. You will never know how to take care of your-self.

–Then Miss Yuki. –He stops and turns, waits for her to stop too. Points his gaze at her smart new fall coat, designer pumps, and his smile is guilelessly brutal. –You understand my position *exactly.*

But she isn't offended. As he seems not offended; he trails after her a little dejectedly, like running away from her was too hard and now he had given up the desire to. They've reached the Philosopher's Walk and it's as crowded as anyone could expect on such a lovely fall afternoon. They break into the merry wave of people streaming up towards the Silver Temple. Like two contradictory birds, they fly stubbornly against the grain of the crowd.

He was right though. After her accusation in the café, she had pressed until everything came tumbling out. It all fit then. The nerves. The strange over-polish. So flashed up, as if he were auditioning for a host bar, not a teaching posi-tion at a language school, and when she had said the words 'host bar,' his ice cracked and he reddened terribly. And she did too. After that, she knew she would not be able to keep talking about Flaubert, or literature, or art, or any of the things they regularly conversed about that seemed so important, and instantly, were not. She was afraid that if they stayed in the café, she would begin to cry and his face would take on a certain arrogant, loathsome expression. As for the topic she'd wanted to broach, it dissolved like a fist of cotton candy tossed into a warm puddle. She can't even recall now what it was.

Here on the path, they pass packs of school kids scouting for somewhere to have a sweet and old women craning their necks for a suitable spot to have tea. The trees, the birds darting through the bushes, the ribbon of green water winding along the bottom of the canal. Miss

Yuki longs to hook her arm into his and admire it together as innocently as with her girlfriends back when she was a student. Or with her father, when he was still well. Impossible, as the two of them are already too conspicuous. A bench opens, and she steers them towards it. Trembling, fluttering, her hands won't stop moving, reminding her again of her father. His hands had been so restless that final year. Yuki says,

–Where did you even get that suit? Or did you have it tailored?

–I did. It cost me all the money I didn't have so I really hope this all works out. Do you like it? Does it look good?

–No, –she pauses. Lowers her head. –Yes. Your tailor did a wonderful job. And your hair is cut too. You look spectacular.

He smiles then, as if only her saying it makes it true. As if her approval truly matters to him. The air, her hope lightens. Next to her, he takes out his phone, checks it again and tells her that he plans to leave around four in the afternoon. She says:

–Then let's go somewhere before then. There's still some time.

–We would have to rush and I'd have to take the suit off. The shirt is freshly ironed, I don't want anything to wrinkle.

–Nonsense. I'll hang it up in the bathroom and the steam will keep it from creasing.

He frowns. –Miss Yuki, what is this? I'm going two hours away, not to the moon. This is not a good time.

And just like that, the direction of the wind turns back to arctic. Icy. She is bathed again in the pure shame of the café, of feeling like she needs everything while he requires such an infuriating nothing. She pushes her hands into her purse, opens her wallet. Knows it is the wrongest thing to do in the moment, which is perhaps exactly why she does it. *Go ahead then and pretend that you do not require this.* Yuki thrusts the bills at him.

–Your mood really is atrocious lately. I hope this can fix it.

She watches the hand closer to her grip the bench, long fingers tighten to the bone, knuckles whiten and she imagines him grabbing or striking her. As if he ever would! Unless she asked. *You have to ask to be hurt by him.* He says:

–Thank you, but I won't be taking it.

–Why not? You always wanted it before.

–Today, I don't. I'm not a vending machine, Miss Yuki. Shove in the money and punch in what you want.

–J'aurais pas cru. You could have fooled me.

Why is she trying to hurt him so hard? He doesn't look hurt though, merely tired. Like he has heard these words, or similar ones, too often and they cannot injure anymore. Only exhaust. She says softly,

–I know you think I look down on you and perhaps I have been unfair at times, but you can be so smug too. How nice if you never compromise yourself, but not all of us have that luxury. Sometimes, we get on our knees not because we are too weak to keep standing, but because we simply *have no other choice.*

It's a quarter second too late to realize the unfortunate choice of phrase. He jeers more.

–Who is on their knees more than me?

–Oh, shut up. I'm not talking about when you want to be. I'm talking about going on when you've given up your dignity. Not lost it, but handed it over. Not even compromising but debasing yourself. Day. After month. After year. But you still have to go on because there is nothing else you can do. Do you know anything about that? I doubt it, *men never do.* So spare me your pride.

He seems to be considering, actually weighing what she has said. It occurs to her then. Yuki couldn't help but wonder—they'd spent so many hours. Feeling the other's heart beating, lying on each other both too weak to move. Like God had struck them dead together. *Like two children trapped in the same paradise of sadness.* They'd done things to each other to make angels blush and fiends weep, and still managed to come all the way to this point without a single conversation of any significant personal depth. Until right now.

The urge wells up, she cannot stop it.

—May I please have a cigarette?

Yuki braces herself for some joke after the many times she'd harped on him; worse, an acidic comment regarding a woman with a lover almost half her age she plies with money, lecturing *him* on male vanity—he really has a knack for catching any dagger you throw his way and flinging it back triple strength. He says nothing though, passes her a cigarette. Lights it gracefully. His hands are so close to her mouth. As if his hands could say it:

Maybe I know a lot about debasing myself, or maybe I know nothing. Maybe like men do it or maybe like women. Do you know anything about it, Miss Yuki? You act like you do, but in the end, aren't we looking at each other in a mirror? You lost yourself to have everything. And I lost everything to have only myself. Each one has its price.

Tiny leaves, like schools of fish, hurricane near their feet. Dash themselves to death against a rock by their bench. The canal water flows underneath them, cool and indifferent. The world passes by. It's usually she who sits primly while he's lighting up, but life is upside down today. He sits with his big hands resting on his knees and Yuki smokes. The last she'd had a cigarette was in university and they taste just as horrible as she remembers. Even worse. She waits for him to light his own, but maybe he has no more. Maybe she's taken his last cigarette. She's about to ask him, when he says:

—I don't think we should see each other anymore.

The cigarette burns her throat from the inside and Yuki swallows her cough.

—Is this about you moving to Osaka?

—It has nothing to do with Osaka. I've been thinking about it for a while. It's not good for you. Maybe it was, maybe back in the beginning, but not anymore.

—How presumptuous of you to assume what is good for me.

—Am I wrong? You've gotten reckless, you don't care who finds out. I shouldn't have to say this, but it's become too risky.

Yuki inhales hard, watches the rippling tops of the trees. *And what if there was no more risk? What if I told you I'm leaving my husband?* The idea only just now occurs to her, but she itches to say it, to make up her mind right here, rip her whole life apart on a whim and see this one's face change. But then, what reaction could she even hope for? Gilded diplomacy if she is lucky. Brutish callousness if she is not. And of course, what could he even do or offer? Promise to sweep her off her feet, become stepfather to her teenaged children? Yuki presses her fingertips into her eyes. She is alone alone alone.

But at least now, he has said it for her. She will not have to pull it out of herself, show him those passages she'd outlined and circled, gripping her pencil's neck as if to strangle it. She thinks of Flaubert again, of that second puberty. Is this even her first? Her teenage years had passed with no bluster or fire. And hadn't she always felt safe, so long as she had her words and studies? That she did not love her husband could not bother her. That she bent to her mother's will could not make her resentful. It seemed childish to Yuki to wring her hands over moldering dreams. She could leave the university and her students, they were not what gave her purpose. Her purpose had burned, self-sustaining and eternal, enshrined within her own self—so what has changed? Well, perhaps that she has met someone who made her curious as to what lay beyond the veil (beyond the pale?) If we elect to have an eighth deadly sin, may I propose Curiosity? *And there sat the platinum haired Devil, come to make a deal with Faust.* You've read all those books, but what do any of those things you adore to read about actually *feel* like? What does it feel like to want to scream at someone? To want them to beat you? To have them backhand your face until your makeup distorts and your eyes roll back into your head? To be drained so hard, you need their help to get back to the next subway station? So you can get home in time to cook dinner for your family. What does it feel like to live week to week, for only one day a week? To drug yourself on someone's hands, their voice, the way they hold their cigarette, because there is so precious *little else* to hang on to? Because you don't even know their name? You don't dare know it. Finally to fantasize, about opening the door. And stepping through it. Never looking back. Is she allowed to do that? Is she ready to throw herself away for a cliche, like a heroine throws herself down? He is right, she hasn't the first idea what debasing herself really is. She's been falling for months now, and has yet to reach the bottom of this pit. Maybe she will never reach it. The tears come down her face, one, another. Stinging, hot.

The first time they went to bed, he said he hated seeing her cry. Now he only shakes his head.

—What a scene, hey. I will let you be alone.

—Tu es brutal. I'm crying for myself, not for you.

–So then that means I may go.

–You really are a bastard. Did you know it?

–What do you want from me, Miss Yuki?

She tells him and he frowns. –I've said it so many times before.

–Say it here. Not in a hotel.

–Even if I did, you wouldn't believe me.

–I would now. Because I... well. I've realized that I also... Well, that I also love...

What she has never said to her children, or her beloved father, or her husband, or herself, she says it now to this unworthy, wretched creature. But gilded diplomacy? Brutish callousness? He starts *laughing*. His shoulders shake with the pure amusement of a heartless child. Yuki hisses.

–Tell me please, what about any of this is funny to you?

–All of it. Everything. You don't love me, Miss Yuki. You don't. You don't. I wouldn't even say that you *like* me. You love me talking dirty French and that is that. Go home please and rest. I know you are in hell right now, but tomorrow, or the day after, you'll already feel much better. You'll see for yourself. And it'll get better each day after this, and it was good while it was good between us, so why do all this? Why ask me to say things you don't want to hear? Why say things yourself that you don't feel? So ugly and sticky and what for?

Because if there's even a shard of beauty left in it, it hurts too much to let it go. But Yuki imagines his was a rhetorical question. So she says nothing.

He stands and she expects he will leave now, and she will not reach after him, and she will not even raise her face for a final look, but then he reaches down. Stretches out his arm. Puts his hand under her chin.

Yuki cannot help it. She looks up and his eyes are the color this canal will be come winter.

Frozen neon pond scum.

Lépoux infernal—The infernal bridegroom! *Cést bien ce demon-la.*

He wipes one of her tears away and the last she hears from him is in the clearest, most beautiful French:

–I'm sorry for all of this, Miss Yuki. Really, it wasn't my intention.

And walking south down along the canal, he disappears.

SIXTEEN

EVERYBODY HATES V

You won't find a prettier fall anywhere in the world. Even I say so, and I don't love this city. People don't even know where to look, it's so wonderful.

Summer or winter? Was one of the questions and you said fall. That is the correct answer.

The hills blaze copper until you are sure you can smell the burning, and they singe your eyes like the sun. Then the leaves come down—the fire is gone, and only small ones stay, smoking through the high, walled gardens. Old men burn the gathered leaves. The air is the color of grayness, rising up from the smoke and the mist and the old men; from the dying.

That is the reason I also hate fall—do you agree that it's just about dying?

So why then, I wonder, is it so beautiful?

I suppose this will take as long as it takes. I don't think about it much, not anymore. Nobody says I've changed—and I don't feel particularly different. What hurts the most is that I can't tell this to anyone. Not a single person comes to mind who would understand. Except—you. So there's nothing to do.

I've stopped skipping school. That was something we did together. Now I don't come home unexpectedly, nor do I wonder about where my mother goes or who she sees. I tell myself I simply don't care. Then I see her face. Yukiko's face is like a frosted-glass mask, and I can't tell what's behind it. Most of the time, I don't want to know, unless I see her in her secret world, when she's reading with her feet drawn up under her on the sofa. Yukiko sits like someone is always watching her. She won't change her eyes, they still scan the pages, but then she starts to hum. That's when I almost can't stop myself from asking her: What does the humming mean? Are you happy? Are you nervous? Are you meeting him later? *Do you want to compare notes?* Because we could, you know.

Then I feel so sick, I go to the bathroom to throw up. I come back out and she looks at me.

「Are you all right? You look ill.」

But she's still humming. She's only asking to be polite. It's a role for her, like it was for you.

You said it's like having your heart ground into a fine powder, and I agree. My heart gets ground to dust and dust until my chest cavity feels so tight and full, I have to go throw that awful powder up.

But back then, I floated in a daze for weeks. I didn't want to see anyone. I avoided Ren. I made excuses to Kiriya, saying I couldn't meet because my grades were awful, and my mother was furious. I actually *was* failing chem, so my mother told me I couldn't go out at all until my grades improved. I didn't mind. Most of the fashion club members were gone right then, and I didn't feel like drawing or planning patterns anyway. The next month, all I did was study, write in my diary.

And see many dreams.

Dreams where I started getting sick all the time, and not only from seeing Yukiko's face. Even boiling water for tea would make me sick. The smells of things especially. And in the morning especially. I walked around, perpetually nauseated, until I got scared. I called you, and you believed me right away. We moved away from here. I don't know where to. We lived in a small apartment and we both worked. I went to a language school, and I actually knew what it felt like to be you. To be a foreigner. And when I'd wake up, I'd think, what a waste of a good dream. But there were other dreams. Like the one where Yukiko told me and Kyousuke that she had remarried and wanted to introduce us to her new husband. He's a bit young, she said nervously, please keep an open mind. You walked up in a new suit she had bought for you and my brother looked perplexed, and I had to shake your hand. You smiled at me, and pretended you had no idea who I was—

You know, my cousin Hana from Okayama came to visit us for the weekend not long ago. You would like her. She's three years older than me, with a neck like a ballerina and the biggest manga collection *ever*. When I was smaller, I used to wish she was my sister. Like an older best friend who lived with you. I used to think if Hana-chan was my sister I'd tell her everything.

That weekend of her visit, we went into the city to go shopping and we were riding home on the train afterwards, when she brought it up. Out of the blue:

「My mom told me what's happening with...」

She squeezed my hand and I frowned. I was sure my mother would never tell anyone until after the fact, but Hana-chan was my cousin from my father's side. His younger sister's, my Aunt Chihiro's, daughter. So my dad must have told his sister. It made sense; they were fairly close and called each other regularly.

I wasn't sure what to say.

「I'm fine. Don't worry. I mean, of course, I was shocked too when they told me, but I'm staying in the same school. I'm staying in the same house.」

「You're not moving out with Aunt Yuki?」

「It's easier to stay, with exams coming up.」

「I guess that makes sense. I don't know what I'd do in

your place. I'd miss my mom so much...」 Hana-chan squeezed my hand tighter, and I felt awful then. Like she was already too far away for me to be honest with her. Like she already had to lie to me and act like Yukiko is a person people miss. She isn't. I'm going to miss my room being cleaned, and my bath being drawn, and my dinner being made. And missing your mother should mean more than that, but it looks like to me, it won't. How could I tell my cousin that I felt terrible for being a terrible daughter? For never imagining my mother having a life beyond those things? The woman leaving our house is a stranger. I never knew her, will never get to know her, *and I was still glad she was leaving.* None of these things could I say.

So I smiled at Hana and took out my keitai and started showing her pics from our school trip last spring. To make myself think of something else. The train was pretty much empty by then, just an obaasan sitting on a bench across the way. Nobody else. Hana-chan asked if we could look at each other's albums, so we traded phones. She loudly approved of my food pictures; I fake-gagged when I got to a photo of a gigantic spider she had found nested up in their yard. *But Aya-chan, if you zoom in, you can even see the hairs on its legs!* I remembered that Hana was a nature nerd; she'd even had a spider terrarium for a while. I scrolled past the spider. The light in our car dimmed. Outside, it looked like it would start to rain. I was wondering if we would get caught in the rain on the way home and was checking my bag for my folded umbrella when Hana-chan tapped my shoulder and turned my phone's screen to me.

「*Dare?* Who is this?」

I looked at the picture longer than a second, as if I really couldn't remember. *Why hadn't I deleted that? Great. More lies.* It was hard to keep my face in order.

「Oh. Him. Nobody. Just a gaijin I met once, downtown.」

「Bidan yan.」

The way she said it embarrassed me and my blah shrug was real.

「I think it's just the picture. I didn't think that when I saw him in real life.」

「Well, you both look super happy and he has his arm around you. Doesn't look like a nobody, to me.」

I almost choked and turned it into a cough.

「Are you serious? He was like... old.」

Hana-chan narrowed her eyes at the picture.

「Really? He looks my age. But I guess with foreigners, it's hard to tell. ...So this wasn't a date?」

More coughing. I explained something had gone into the wrong pipe.

「It wasn't. He needed directions to the subway, and then we ended up talking a little, so I took a picture with him. You know, for no reason. For fun.」

「I see. So what was his name?」

「...Tomu.」

It was the first western name I could think of, provided by a billboard outside the train window, advertising the newest Tom Cruise movie. Looking down at my keitai, I don't think Hana-chan noticed.

「Tomu? He doesn't look like a Tomu. Oh well, I guess his parents couldn't know that. Does he work in Kyoto?」

「No. He was visiting. A tourist. He must have gone home by now.」

「To?」

「America.」

「Oh, an American. Neat! Did he say what city?」

「New York City.」

「Maji de? Sugo~i! Wow! I've always wanted to see New

York. I wonder which part he lives in. I bet in, what's the famous part called? Man Something. Somewhere fancy.」

Yeah, right.

「I don't know where he lives, but he said it's great there, and he can't wait to go back. He never wants to live anywhere else. Apparently, there are a lot of good-looking people and the trains all smell wonderful.」

「That's funny. I've always heard that New York is dirty and unsafe? He must really live in a nice area then.」

「Maybe. He said he had graduated dental school and was traveling to relax before he started working.」

「A dentist called Tomu. You should've gotten his address, so you could visit him in his New York penthouse! I'd have gone with you. So, you spoke in English?」

「Yeah, but it was really hard to understand him—I felt like he had to repeat everything. You know how fast Americans talk.」

「And they slur so badly! 'Eye ahmu Tomu. Naws too meecha!'」

Hana started to stream off some garbled American-style English and we were both laughing. Which is nice, because when she first showed me the picture, I got so tense, I was worried she would know something was wrong. I'd never been a good liar but somehow this time, once I started, the lies came out naturally, each one giving birth to the next. Maybe that's how liars are born—out of easy lies. I don't know what made me reinvent everything like that, but it felt good. I said to her:

「You can erase that picture. My memory's getting full, and I need to get rid of the older ones anyway.」

「But you shouldn't delete that one. You look so cute together. Just don't show Kiriya. Delete these instead?」

She scrolled to the next few, which were blurry shots of our neighbor's dog. I took the phone from her and started deleting, and then I got back to that picture with you. Hana-chan's phone buzzed and while she was preoccupied, I wondered what I should do with it, and my fingers moved independently. They brought me to your last message. The only one I'd kept.

```
Aya-chan,
Mada ikiteiru no?
Are you still alive?
We were supposed
to meet this month, but
you never write back.
I figure you must
be busy with school.
I hope you don't
think I'm stalking
you. I was just worried.
If you don't write
back to this, I'll
take it to mean you
don't want to talk
to me and I'll
leave you alone. No
explanation needed.
I want you to do
what's best for you
so, in that case,
good luck with
school and life. Be
good, ok? V yori.
```

It was a two month old message I'd gotten in the beginning of August. I hit *reply*, then stared at the empty box on the screen. It's like it was waiting for me to feed it. I didn't know what to put in though. Finally, I wrote:

```
Hello.
```

(In English.) That's all. For weeks and weeks, I hadn't even thought about writing you. I never wanted to. I felt like I still didn't want to, so I don't know what made me push the *send* button. Maybe it was my fanciful lie about Tomu in New York City that made me remember our actual conversation about going to Paris together...

「Aya-chan, are you okay?」

「Un.」

I put the phone into my pocket quickly, and Hana's eyes were suspicious.

「Kao iro ga warui yo. You don't look good. Is everything all right? I was watching you read your phone, and your face got white as a ghost!」

「No really. I'm fine.」

She looked so concerned that, for a moment, I wanted to tell her. I thought of making her swear that she would never tell anyone, and then I could release it to one person, pour out my heart and finally be free, but I couldn't risk it. If something ever got back to my father or Yukiko, I would die. Simply die. And a minute ago, we had been laughing, I had felt so good—now my mood was wrung out. The phone buzzed in my pocket, and I almost jumped in the air. Hana pretended like she didn't see me grabbing at it like a maniac. I froze every muscle in my face while I flipped it open. You responded! So quickly!

> The address you entered
> is no longer available.

My eyeballs were paralyzed. We got off the train. Hana-chan didn't say anything to me as we walked back to my house, just took my hand. I could tell she felt sorry for me. Of course I was moody, who wouldn't be? My mother was moving out, my family was falling apart. Things would be different from here out. Hana wanted to be there for me, but I couldn't talk about what really hurt: Growing up. In only the bad ways, it seemed. It wasn't only the divorce; I was upset about feeling myself turning into a twisted adult. Feeling myself becoming angry and secretive. Feeling myself getting good at pulling on the mask. Pretending like it wasn't so bad, when really, I despise my father for lying to my mother. Despise my mother for being so cold and lying to us all. I know why she is really leaving, even if my dad and brother do not. I despise adults in general for being cruel, and selfish, and hurting people weaker than themselves out of nothing but boredom and resentment at having to be adults. As if it were children and teenagers who had put them on this earth, not the other way around! I'm not a hypocrite, though. I'm on that list too. A liar, a cheat. I didn't used to be. But let's not forget the person I hate last, most, and highest of all.

I've thought a lot about what I would say to you if we ever met again. If I would yell and curse, like a jilted, desperate obasan. Or act all composed. Like you do. Ask pointblank whether you knew. Watch you slither and lie, because of course you did, how could you have not? (Then again, you are so dense sometimes. And she and I look nothing alike.) Some days it seems to me like it doesn't matter. Whatever you knew or didn't, it's all poison now. Other days, it feels like if I can't see you one last time I will go out of my mind. I'll pass by that spot where we first met, telling myself that I'm only walking. And every time I picture you actually there, it loops back to the beginning. Would I have the guts to walk up and say it to your face? Or would I turn and run?

Looks like I'll never find out though because you just left. Why else would you cancel your phone plan? Unless you went back to your country, like Tomu? Maybe you got deported (serves you right). Maybe you're in a splashy penthouse right now? In Paris, or New York, or whatever the hell city you came from, with some beautiful lady who's agreed to marry you, sipping champagne, and joking with her, and staring into her eyes, and hoping she never finds out what a viper you are. Good luck.

I cannot believe I used to think you were so special. A daiai, like you said. No, you're just the person who taught me how to be a sick adult. The person who makes me puke. I said I hate you, but it's worse than that. I think: [58]

....

[58]   « You are worthless. »

He said it not as an opinion, but as a fact, a banal fact like, "You have brown pants" or "Today is Wednesday," all the while wondering if his words would have the proper impact. Actually, they had no impact, no more than announcing the particular day of the week, or the color of one's pants, but then again, that was expected under the circumstances. They sat at the kitchen table and he pushed the plate away from himself. The food was good, and he would have liked to have eaten more, but his appetite was spoiled. *It tastes exactly like hers; it's not right.*

The boy sat across from him, silent, his plate even more full than his father's. Neither of them could eat. He started to get up and clear the table, and this annoyed Ilya, but he said nothing about it. As much as he avoided it, the topic had to be broached.

« You don't want to talk to me and I don't want to talk to you, so let's make it quick. Things are changing and you'll be learning how to work, not coasting by anymore. God knows you're old enough. »

« I know how to work. »

His voice wasn't defensive, it wasn't anything. He washed the plates, laying them on the drain board with care, and then came and sat back down.

Ilya grimaced.

« Oh yes, I'm sorry, I forgot. You've always been outstanding when it came to women's work. »

« Work is work. Somebody has to do it. »

How sure he is! How nice it must be, to not have to prove anything to anyone.

« Hoho, she did a good number on you, but I won't get into this argument again. » Ilya cleared his throat. « I talked to Petra and she said she would start coming in regularly to help around the house, with the kids and the cooking. She may even move in. »

« I can do a better job than Petra. »

« And I don't doubt that—nobody can deny your talents with an iron. But I've also arranged something with Mitya down on the line, and you'll be coming with me starting next week. The pay is low, but I'm vouching for you, and they'll push you up fast if you work hard. We can really use any extra money right now. And I want to keep an eye on you. »

« What about school? »

« What about it? You'll quit. I already explained to the headmaster that this is the only possible solution. And then, you were never the big brain, but with the way Sasha is going, who knows? Maybe he'll make it to university, if he gets a scholarship. He could use an education... »

« If I finished school though, I could become a teacher, » the boy said hopefully.

« Sure. » His father sneered. « A language teacher. And by the time you are qualified to do that, I'll be in the poor house for shelling out who knows how much on tuition and abortions—unless you get yourself tied even faster to some unlucky girl you knock up in the next year. No better than a dog, and at your age! Not that you'll listen, until it's too late. »

« Good thing I'm more careful than you ever were with my mother. »

......

Ilya thought about hitting him. He wanted to, but talked himself out of it. It would be unsatisfying.

Yes, God tell me, what am I going to do with you? At times, he wanted to rationalize his eldest as a bastard; then at least he could savor the luxury of uninhibited hatred, but alas. The kid was a foreigner in all ways but genetics. Ilya could still see exactly how his mother had looked on that ill-fated night. Too beautiful for words. How bewitched he'd been by her. Three months later, all sixteen years of her coming to find him, eyes cast down and fingers resting shyly on her already thickening hips. He had no intention to marry, but called on by her family and his own to do the right thing, it didn't seem such a terrible idea. She was so gentle, so pliant. Too young to be a wife to a too-young morose husband, and that misplaced affection she poured into her firstborn. Until the others came, she could pet and sing and read to him all day. He was her baby doll. The kid shot up in her wet love like a weed in warm rain. Eventually, he grew big enough to cast a shadow, growing, spreading, watching his father through slitted eyes like he'd swallowed a secret. Ilya had scoffed often enough at the kid's prowess in the kitchen and with a cleaning rag, but he himself had to admit: *That* was no girl. And underneath his skin ran something wild.

So Ilya set out to purify him, but not even a steady diet of brimstone could wear the kid down. He liked church. He spent all mass sniffing incense, memorizing hymns, amusing his siblings with dirty epigrams he composed in his head, and once the organ stopped and the priest started dispensing the wrath of God from the pulpit, he would stare at the plaster statues, wondering what it might be like to kiss the stark white lips of the Virgin.

In school, the teachers complained. Well-behaved, but a terrible student, a compulsive thief, a dirty fighter, and if the schoolyard rumors held any truth— Another scene Ilya couldn't erase—the house was empty, the air kinetic—he'd passed the shed while returning to work after an unusually late lunch-break when he saw a strange flash, beyond the shed's open door. Stopping, he looked, then stepped back, frozen with the embarrassment of a child who stumbles onto his parents' love. A neighborhood girl, no more than 14, her shirt off and against the wall. His oldest boy, a good year younger than that, his shirt off as well. The wind gleamed the color of diamonds. The girl was trembling and the way the boy—that pale kid! Held her, whispering, as if to a skittish horse, until she threw her arms around his neck and let him. Ilya watched their childish lovemaking with a fascinated torpor until he remembered himself. After some deliberation, he brought it up the next evening, while the boy tinkered with Yevgeniy out by the garage. The two of them both worked on the old bike together religiously.

« Get lost, » the father told the younger son, not wanting him to hear, but even after he disappeared into the house, the other wouldn't stop fiddling with the suspension.

« Are you paying attention? » Each lazy turn of the screwdriver drove Ilya mad. He wanted to shake him. « I don't want you talking with Shymko's girl again. »

« Why not? »

« I saw her here. »

« Yeah, she dropped off some tools this morning. So what? »

« I mean I saw you. » He breathed out. « Do I have to say it? Out in the shed. »

Kid's back still to him, he saw the shoulders tense, but only momentarily.

« So you were *watching* us? »

Ilya's ears turned scarlet. He cleared his throat.

« Just stay the hell away from her! ...Did you hear me? »

« I did. »

« Then say something when you're spoken to! Look at me! »

He turned slowly and did as told. It helped nothing—His father felt himself fill with lava, from the feet first, like a hollow man.

« On the Sweet Virgin and all her Weeping Saints, I swear to Christ, just the *sight of your damn face* is enough to flick the switchblade open in my pocket! »

The boy's voice fell like a gentle night breeze.

« *Then perhaps you shouldn't carry a blade.* »

« Come here! Now! »

The kid tossed the tool carelessly to the side and stood up, then walked to his father—Ilya stared down at his head. *It's a poisoned relationship, father to son*, he thought, despairing. He knew he needed to release, punish, or absolve him, and didn't know how. He'd never planned to be a bad father; he'd never planned to be any father at all. This wasn't the life he wanted. And the years ran out of his hands.

Sitting at the kitchen table that last afternoon, the feeling brewing in his chest was identical to all those times. That shameful fear. How could he be *scared* of him? But he was. Those mornings before Mass had begun, their two shining heads resting, nestling against each other's, whispering in French and joking with the smaller kids. Prettier than a family of angels! Happier than doves in a tree. Ilya always one row behind, or to the far side; brooding, hungover and unnecessary. The things he thought in his blackest moments! A true wonder lightning didn't strike to purify him right there, in the Holy House.

I'm more careful than you ever were with my mother.

Ilya's fist was still clenched. He was standing, and the boy remained sitting at the table, expressionless. Hotcolored afternoon light filtered in through the window and tinted his eyes a dazey topaz. The vapid yellow stare of a feral cat. Or a reptile.

He started to bite his nails; one stick in a pack of gruesome habits his father loathed, but neither threats nor physical harm could make the boy give it up.

Ilya let his fingers relax.

« *Your mother.* Yes. She never wanted a man. No surprise you were the light of her eye. »

The kid still looked out into the yard. Talked to something out beyond.

« On God, but what does this have to do with 'being a man'? She wanted someone who didn't treat her like shit. That person wasn't you. Nothing deeper than that. »

Ilya's heart started to pound.

« Nothing deeper. I've watched you two playing at it all these years. And I can't pretend it's never crossed my mind. Ksyusha and her precious V--------. So tell me. Your mother. I know she was always yours, but...»

The boy looked up.

« ...did she ever make you hers? »

Smoky blood spread through Ilya's mouth from biting deep his own tongue. *Christ, did you really just say that?* The iron taste was almost immediately quenched by the flavor of triumph. The kid's face blackened dangerously. *Finally. For himself, he won't. But for her...*

Moments scraped by. The other opened his mouth. Breathed in. Swallowed. Mastered his face. Mastered his voice. Said in his coldblood voice.

« Really, father. I haven't heard such filth since the fourth grade. »

Ilya was instantly, thoroughly exhausted.

« Let's forget it. All of it. Tie up whatever loose ends you have at school, and then you're coming with me, starting on Monday. You'll have to get fitted for a uniform »

« As you say. »

The boy got up and left the kitchen. A thousand unsaid grievances he took with him and just once, Ilya needed his son to lash out and rain down his resentment, to engage, to accuse him back, because maybe then all of this could be drained and they could begin to live with each other, but he wouldn't. *A martyr, like his mother,* his father thought bitterly, knowing it wasn't true.

« I can't do this. »

« Give it to me. » She did. « Did you try this? »

« No. »

« See this here? If this line crosses here, then this one can't possibly be what you have. » He rubbed her answer out with the eraser. « Do you see what you did wrong? »

« Yes. » She lay sprawled on his bed and was doing her math homework when she looked up again. « What are you doing, anyway? »

« I'm packing. »

« Why? »

« Because I'm leaving. »

He heard her school book fall to the floor with a tremendous thud. The walls lightly shook with it. The soccer stars kicking on the walls fluttered in the breeze of it.

« What do you mean, leaving? Going where? »

« I'm going to live with Uncle Leo until I can figure out what I'm going to do. I'm using the money Mom gave me to buy a train ticket. »

« But why? Did you get into a fight with Papa? »

The younger kids all spoke with some sprinkling of French mixed in, learned from their mother. Their grandmother had been a Frenchwoman who had taught her daughter well, and she in turn had tried to teach all her children the language, but only her eldest had ever gotten really fluent, perfected once he started learning it in school— Between his mother and him, it was their private language. He associated it with affection, and his father associated it with another aspect that locked him out of their circle. Yet while he would have liked to, he knew better than to forbid the kids from speaking it.

« No. But one of these days I will, a big one, and then I'm going to kill *Papa*, and I don't want to do that, because I think you need him still. »

« But we need you more! »

« Don't talk stupid, Tati. He works hard, and until you're old enough to move out too, you'll be fine here and he'll watch out for you. Petra will come and take care of the house and Nana will come too. »

« I don't like Petra. »

« Then you don't have to marry her, but someone has to run the house, and he won't let me do it anymore. »

« And when will you be back from Uncle Leo's? »

He breathed in hard.

« I'm not coming back. »

Threw three shirts into a duffle bag, and he heard his sister's body jerk on the bed. She jumped up and latched onto him.

« What? But you have to! You shouldn't even go in the first place! What about us... what about me? Don't you love me anymore? »

She looked up at him, her big green eyes shining like pools of disturbed water, and he sat down next to her, devastated.

« I love you more than anyone in the world. You're my favorite and best girl, you know that. »

« But then why would you go? We can't lose you too! We can't.... »

« If I stay, you'll lose me harder than if I leave. After everything else, I couldn't stand it. »

« That doesn't make any sense! »

« I mean, Tati, he won't leave me alone until I hate everything here. And I don't want to hate anything here, ever. If I go, it'll stay clean. At least the parts that can. »

« Why can't he leave you alone? I don't understand... »

« It's complicated. I thought I could stay out of his way until we're all older, but he'll never be happy. Not until I'm as miserable as he is. »

« And what about us? »

« You'll be fine. No matter how he feels about me, he'll never treat you badly, and you'll be so busy with school, you'll forget about me. And when you're older and a famous actress (she had just been awarded a main speaking role in the primary school's next play, unheard of for a third grader), I'll come see your shows and fill your dressing room with roses. We'll be with each other again. But until then, you'll have to grow up and be good and listen to Sasha, because he'll be the oldest now. »

« Sasha only cares about his marks though—and he gives me arm burns all the time! »

« Then I'll talk to him before I go and make him promise he'll never do it again. »

« You really are going, aren't you? »

She started to cry.

« I am. »

« But what about Sveta? Weren't you going to marry her? »

« Where did you get that idea? Tati, I just turned sixteen, she's fifteen. I'm not going to marry anyone right now. »

« Don't you have to marry her if you make her a baby? That's what Papa said you were going to do. »

« Did he? Well he lied. And don't say 'make a baby,' it's so crass. You *have* a baby, or you *make* love, but she's not having one right now, definitely not mine, and we're not getting married. »

His sister dabbed her nose on his sleeve, and he felt the moistness soak through to his skin but said nothing.

« So, » she sniffled. « Then you and I could still get married? »

He smiled weakly.

« But I've heard you say you want to marry Nana? And Yura? You're not faithful. »

« If we did though, then at least you wouldn't go! »

« Not joking anymore, Tati, you better not marry anyone like me ever, you hear? »

She pressed her teary face against him.

« What's wrong with someone like you? You do housework... » She was crying hard now, in earnest. « And you help me with my homework. »

« And I'm your brother. And I'm leaving. I want you with someone who will never leave you. Blow. Harder. » He wiped her nose. « Yura and Zhenya have that handball meet today, right? I'll need to talk to them too. I'm leaving in the middle of the night, so I'll need Zhenya to pick up the bike from the station tomorrow. »

« He'll tell on you. Zhenya will tell him that you're leaving. »

« No he won't. None of you will. »

He rushed around the room, throwing things into the bag more chaotically now. She watched him, finally gathered her courage to interrupt.

« V-----? »

« What? »

« I won't say anything to Papa. But... »

« What? »

« A song. Please? »

His tone softened.

« Which one? »

« About the soldier. »

It was something he had done for her since she was a tiny girl. All the way back to when she'd been a newborn baby. He had been eight years old when his last (living) sibling and only sister was born, and the infant could cry unbelievably at times—as hardy as she was now, Tati had been a sickly, fretful baby. That pregnancy had really worn his mother out, and she lay in bed exhausted most of the time, and his father was exhausted as well; the sound of the steady wailing quickly driving him to the brink of rage. It would wake the younger kids. Yevgeniy would start whining, so he would crawl over to his sister's crib and take her around the house, singing to her in the dark, rocking her until she fell asleep. Many nights, he was unable to put her back in the crib once she was quiet again, it seemed so lonely, and brought her instead into the bed he shared with Aleksandr. Her first word was at ten months, *mama*—blurted at three in the morning, to V. He thought his heart would burst. Until she was five, Tati slept next to her brothers almost every night, and though she earned the privilege of a single bed in a semi-private alcove after that as the lone girl, this she voluntarily forfeited whenever she was cold, had nightmares, or was scared for any reason. At the age of 16, in their tiny house, V had never slept in a bed without at least one other person present. Now she lay against him on the one he shared with Aleksandr, and he started singing in the dark room, his voice low and clear in its timbre—

The slain soldier sings to his girl at home, who forgets him quickly once the news of his death comes to their village. She gets married to another man who raises their child as his own, even as the soldier lies dead and longing for her in an unmarked mass grave. It was a morbid theme, to a melancholic tune that had captured Tati at an age before she could comprehend the words, before he even fully understood them. He himself had learned it, along with many others, from his mother. The end of the song came, and they sat in the silence, his cheek against the top of her head.

« V-----? »

« What, my life? »

« Who will sing that song to me if you go? »

« You can sing it to yourself. I've heard you do it before and very well. It's not the same as being sung to, but if you remember it and I remember it, then we won't ever be far. »

She sighed deeply.

« So there's nothing that would make you stay here with us? »

He shook his head, and she stood up abruptly then. Looking at him with all the deadly seriousness of an eight-year-old:

« Ok. Go then. But if you leave, you should know you're not my favorite brother anymore. Yura is. And I won't remember you. I won't burn candles for you. And I'll hate you for leaving us. I'll hate you, for as long as I live. »

« Oh Tati. » He was trying to joke with her, but his voice sounded how she thought of voices sounding right before their owners burst into tears.

« Take that back, or I'll give you an arm burn ten times worse than Sasha's. You know I taught him how to do it. You don't want a burn from me. »

« I take it back. »

She still did hate him, but she lied. Not to comfort him, but for her own sake. The burn she could have lived with, but V crying simply did not and could not exist. She had never seen him do it before. None of them had. Happy he was often —on rare occasion, sad —but crying—?

Not when he had gotten into a motorbike crash two years ago and had come home with the bone of his left arm broken right through the skin.

Not when he'd gotten a piece of glass wedged under his fingernail while helping in the garden, and Nana had pulled it out with pliers, making it bleed like a fountain.

Not from any beating administered by any boy at school or by their father.

Not on the day they had all stood together in the L— cemetery last February, five kids, and watched their mother's coffin get lowered into the frozen ground.

There was only one phone in the boardinghouse and using it meant one of two things: The user was a transient in the city, a tourist, a passerby. Or the user was too poor to afford their own phone. Ellen Kingsley was a transient. She had been in this city for one month, in this miserable house, and would have to spend one more week before she was due to continue on to Korea and finally home. She was fresh off the phone with her fiancé (attending a conference in Tokyo) and was now trying to call her mother. The line was breaking up though, and her mother had agreed to call her back in a few minutes, so Ellen stood around in the dismal kitchen, brushing some fallen, hardened rice sullenly with her flip-flop's toe.

What a shithole, she thought darkly, glaring at the surroundings while she waited. Ellen couldn't picture anyone preparing something destined for consumption in that kitchen, though the landlady was notorious for grabbing unwashed glasses and even individual spoons and knocking door to door to find the culprit who had left the offending item on the counter. As far as Ellen was concerned, she could give up the lost battle; it seemed like sticking a band-aid on a gunshot wound. The only thing that could improve this place was a flamethrower. At least Ellen could be thankful that it was late fall and not summer, when the lively flies would have been performing their St. Vitus' dance over everything and all.

Even stranger, Ellen could've sworn the house was getting *worse*. It had been homely since the day she'd reluctantly moved in, but the first few weeks, she distinctly remembered the kitchen's surfaces, visible and clean. The bathrooms tidy and smelling neutral. Now, garbage littered the countertops. Cockroaches scuttled from the trash. The toilet on the second floor right by her room was chronically blocked. Only this morning, Ellen had complained to the landlady and after an eon of miscommunication, was reassured that toilet complaints could be taken to— Ellen's smile flatlined while she internally weighed another night of sharing a wall with a festering BM with seeking that idiot out.

...Another night of smelling the BM was winning.

Speak of the devil.

From down the hall, she heard the creak of a door rattle open, followed by footsteps. Ellen wrinkled her nose as he made it to the kitchen and passed by. The guy smelled like trash and batteries and moved with a strange lethargy. A defeated lope. It seemed in the past weeks, life had come to take him down a peg or two, and if nothing else, this at least gave her an immensely satisfying satisfaction. Few things did she hate more than the man who couldn't even see you once he determined he wasn't interested in fucking you.

They had spoken maybe once or twice in the common room when she'd first arrived, and Ellen instantly wrote him off as another white himbo looking for a brainless Japanese schoolgirl sexbot to fetishize. She still fumed when she remembered that night in the house when this guy had been hanging out with his friend (Spanish? Italian?) in the common room (she hadn't seen that other person around for a while and recalled some going-away party). That day, those two had kept up an endless parade of lewd shots scrolling on the common room computer screen, with the older bloke occasionally fondling a choice favorite or two until Ellen could take it no longer and mentioned that she found their actions offensive and could they please stop objectifying women in front of her? The blondhair looked at her blankly (he had a hard time with British accents, or perhaps, as Ellen suspected, with big words altogether), and so the other guy translated patiently for him. Comprehension crossed his face, and he glanced over at Ellen, at her sweatpants, her no-nonsense bun, her upturned nose and glasses; a long, lazy glance that made her feel positively naked. ⌜What?⌟ he drawled in that peculiar voice he had. ⌜You think only ugly girls can be feminist?⌟ The Spanish kid guffawed, and Ellen jumped up and left the room in a huff. She didn't speak a word of Japanese, but based on the two-dimensional women they ogled, she could piece it together. His tone alone was enough to add another shovelful to the mounting pile of (guilty) feminine inadequacy she felt when assaulted in the streets by the inexhaustible waves of devastatingly fashionable, rail-thin Japanese women. Anything she was ashamed to admit to herself she draped in contempt for a female population that refused liberation, and now this stranger dared deride her for being comfortable. As if she had nothing better to do than slut up for a night of lonely emails in a sordid common room with two underfed bums!

Ever since that night, the sight of the guy was but one more thorn in her side regarding this place. This city. This country. Bogged here by a hideous stroke of misluck, she was supposed to have met her fiancé in Korea over two weeks ago. But she'd be damned if she understood why her friends were so mad to visit. Damned if she'd ever come here again. Claustrophobic, hectic, confusing. The taste of fish in everything. Squat toilets. Public baths. Shopkeepers wide-eyed terrified the moment her white, broad face popped over a counter. *Exorbitant.* If only her mother would call her, if only she could get their plans finalized!

The phone rang as the guy was coming out of the bathroom (the only place to wash one's hands was at the kitchen sink), and Ellen shot him a scornful glare before she snatched the ancient, stained receiver off its hook.

"Hello. Mummy?"

Silence on the other end. Then a voice, shaking, asked in fluent, somewhat accented English:

"Excuse me, may I speak to V please?"

Ellen rolled her eyes. Of course some tart was calling him now, when she was expecting an important call. Why couldn't he have a bloody mobile if he was living in this bloody-shagging country? She turned around, tapped him on the shoulder as he was drying his hands on a questionable tea-towel. Motioned with the receiver. He looked at her blankly, and she waved it at him again, almost threateningly, so he took it and spoke into the phone:

「Moshimoshi?」

"Are you going to be long?" Ellen mouthed to him in English, making a little phone motion with her hands. Looking momentarily confused, he proceeded to ignore her completely by turning to the wall. She felt like putting her strong hands over his skinny dirty neck and *wringing* it, but instead hung out in the kitchen, purposefully rude and close, in the hopes that he would get the hint and finish his conversation quickly. He spoke in Japanese, softly, then louder. At one point, he raised his voice slightly and gesticulated. Ellen perked up her ears, not even pretending to act like she wasn't listening (not that she could hear the woman's end, not that she could understand either end). Next, the woman yelled so loudly, the guy winced and held the phone away from his ear. She continued to yell, in French if Ellen wasn't mistaken, and this was one of the only times she found herself wishing she'd applied herself more back in Mlle. Bisset's class. Not that straight marks are needed to decipher when someone is being called a bastard and a cunt. She could only hope the woman was also threatening to call the Office of Foreign Affairs to get him deported.

The woman yelled one more thing, presumably hung up, and the bloke stood there in the kitchen, staring at the dead phone in his hand like it was a spent grenade. He finally hung it up, not even turning to apologize for bogeying it. Well, I hope his slut *does* call the Foreign Office, Ellen was thinking when she remembered. "Hey. Hello?" She called out. He was almost out of the kitchen and it took three seconds, but his feet paused and ground to a halt. He gripped the edge of a counter like he would topple or vomit, but then steadied. Encouraged, Ellen continued. "You need to do something about the toilet upstairs. I won't sleep another night by that filth."

He paused another moment, turned to look at her. The blank stare was definitely sapping her optimism. "Toilet. WC." Ellen outlined an air-toilet with her right index finger, then jabbed the finger in the direction of the upstairs. "It's clogged. It's your job, the landlady said, so fix it. TOILET." She knew he didn't speak English, but surely whatever God-whipped backwater he'd crawled from had taught him that at least? But he continued to not move. To stare at her, his stupid face static and bovine. A powerful wrath coursed through her body. She couldn't stand it anymore. She just couldn't stand it. "FIX IT!" Ellen shrieked. The bloke shivered like a flame on the end of a match. Blinked. Then disappeared into his room.

If an angel had come down from Heaven right then and given Ellen the power to kill the dirty young man with a thought—she would have refused this gift. Would have opted instead to have him tied to a kitchen chair, old-fashioned pulled out his fingernails with pliers, and poured molten lead down his throat until he was—

Brrrrrrring!

Breath ragged, she almost tore the receiver off the hook.

"Mother, I'm so sorry. This absolute arsehole..."

"Hello?"

This wasn't her mother's brisk tone. It wasn't the woman from earlier, either. This caller's English was broken, hesitant. She sounded young. *If you're calling for that prick again.* But all she wanted to know was the nearest subway stop to the boarding house. This happened sometimes. Potential guests would ring the common phone by mistake. The girl was interested in renting a room, but she wanted to come see the place in person. Ellen took another deep breath. Something about the girl's tone drained out all her anger. "You need to go up at the northern exit. Keep walking past the botanical gardens. If you reached the Circle K, you've walked too far..."

SEVENTEEN

DOWN AND OUT IN KYOTO

The room was completely darkened, except for a shaft of light that cut from between the blinds onto the floor. V stared at that shaft from his futon, mesmerized by the particles that danced in it. Particles of his scalp, particles of his sweat, particles of his new inane roommate. Who wasn't here. It was something he could recall doing as a kid, getting lost in dust dancing in a single ray as the motes fell to the ground in gold, then silver, then copper: every color of a metallic rainbow. The room around him didn't reek so much as steep in an almost touchable fug of closed in air and he lay on top of his duvet in a T-shirt three days running, and two-week dirty, torn jeans. Oblivious to the filth inside his room. Outside his room. The entire house was gently unravelling now that he'd stopped cleaning and regularly emptying the garbages. Sachiko-san had tried to approach him about it. Told him that she could get her sister from the bathhouse to try to send someone over to clean, if he was ill. Was he ill? V wasn't quite sure. He had been hungry. He'd been hungry for days, and that ache in him had sharpened until it had felt difficult to keep his eyes open or a single thought in his head. But by now, that blade had dulled. He never thought about food anymore. He didn't think about the new suit in his wall closet either. He'd spent the last of his money on getting a quality secondhand suit and getting it altered so that it fit beautifully. He'd polished himself like never before. Tick tock tick tock. He wasn't twenty-one anymore. And the day had come and he'd put the suit on, and he'd gone to Kyoto Eki and bought a train ticket to get to Osaka. And the train had arrived and the train had left, and V had not put himself on it. Nor on the next one. Or the next. Why? He didn't know. All he knew was that he went home, hung up the suit carefully, changed into a T-shirt and jeans and lay himself into bed. His contact Masao texted him multiple times. V did not reply. Masao stopped texting him.

He tried to think about nothing at all. Not Rodrigo, who had sent him multiple emails since his return to Lisbon. V had left these unanswered. Rather than comfort, the emails only served to remind him that his best friend was now back in whatever constituted the normal life of a, well, a young man from an affluent family. V was not bitter, (knowing there was nothing to be bitter about) but he also accepted fate's decree. That they officially had nothing more to do with each other. Rodrigo was mending the frayed ties of the last few years, wearing clean shirts, sorting undergrad credits at his prestigious university, and that was an existence so incredibly removed from V's situation that he could barely comprehend it.

Meanwhile, his own body was starting to feel like a totalitarian demesne, of which he was both the despotic ruler and the downtrodden hero trying in vain to make a new sense of things—except V wasn't sure he was looking for a way out. It didn't feel like it.

For the last four days, he'd crawled out of his room once in the morning, to fill a large jug with water in the kitchen and bring it back to his bedside, and then several times to go to the bathroom. There was no further urge for movement. He had no TV or computer in his room. The first day, he tried reading books, then magazines, then manga, but nothing could hold his attention. Elastic and scattered by hunger, his brain spread out, so he let himself lie back and see things in his mind, which did not feel the same as thinking, as they were involuntary snatches and pieces of events that had transpired. To pass time, sometimes he masturbated while he watched them, until eventually he rubbed himself sore and the room started to smell of his tranquil frustration.

Strangest was that he didn't mind—and was never bored.

The intangible, the fleeting, he let the memory slip over him and then tried slowly to release it. Erase it. Let himself be ruled through rhythms. The room darkened, lightened, darkened again. Sometimes, he whispered to himself.

Il faut être absolument moderne.

Who had said that?

A far off room, a far off time; a frayed Persian rug nailed to the wall. Sitting back to it, reading French out loud. *Very good, my life, you read it so very good.* Made to read thirty minutes a day out loud, to improve his pronunciation. Il faut être absolument moderne. The words wrapped around him, binding in infinite repetitions, comforting and post-mortem, like a bandage.

One must be...

Absolutely.

He tried not to think about death. Recalled that slop of conversation from long ago, when they had both been crushed deep down in their cups.

Who had they been 'both'? Rodrigo? Yes, he was there, but V himself had been talking to Ranko. She called herself Ranko, Child of Disorder, though her real name was something much more floral—not that he remembered it—she herself was as floral as an electrified orchid ripped out of a well-behaved marshland and thrown into a bar. She was one of his trampled friends from way-way back when he'd first come to Kyoto, moved in with a soapland girl (the infamous Tomoe), and then was passed around her circle like an affable and fashionable disease. Ranko herself had never been interested—No, no, no, people with pale eyes don't have a soul—but he did become her confidant—

They'd meet in bars, where she'd bare to him her wet and wounded life.

「Oh Buwee.」 Ranko hated pressing her incisors into her lower lip and would do it for no man. 「Buy me this next drink. I'm pregnant again.」

She laid her heavy head against his by the bar and dutifully cried ten tears out of each eye—

「Is it Hiro's?」 he asked.

「Not sure. Maybe. I think so. I'm fairly certain. I'm calling him tomorrow to get money for... you know. Do I sound heartbroken?」

「No. And I thought you said it was a maybe on Hiro.」

「It doesn't matter. It may as well be. After all I've put up with from him, he can pay. Hiro has enough money anyway.」 Their drinks came, and she openly stared into his wallet while he paid. 「You certainly don't. Good thing it's not yours. Can you even eat tomorrow if you pay for this round?」

The truth was that he couldn't, but he was in no mood.

She saw his face, poured the cocktail down her throat and scowled at him—mostly in jest.

「There there, don't be so sensitive.」

He sighed and put his arm around her.

「Have you thought of keeping it? You're going to... hurt yourself if you keep doing those so many times.」

「Don't you worry about me. Worry about all the girls who are getting themselves cut because of *you*.」

「I take care.」 His hand stiffened on her shoulder.

「It's good, if you're taking care. But it's also luck, and you, oniisan, used up all your luck years ago. I'd start looking hard when I cross the street, if I were you.」

「Nobody's come complaining to me yet,」 he said testily, and Ranko donated him a look usually reserved for the posse of men she tried to shanghai.

「Oh Buwee—sometimes, right when I think you might be the man to actually understand the soul of a woman, you say something so touchingly *ignorant*. Just because nobody's ever come complaining to you that you've knocked them up doesn't mean that you've never done it—it means you're so broke or so hopelessly irresponsible, *they don't even try.*」

He could not argue with that logic, only sit, smoking himself ill. Half an hour later, they'd moved out of the bar to sit by the dark night water of the Kamo while Ranko sobbed for real against his shoulder. Two more drinks had stripped her of her irony and control, and she was going to die alone, she was sure of it. Her funeral would have no one. *Just—all those little—ghosts!* She cried while he rubbed her shoulder, hush, hush, hush—he tried not to think about that or extrapolate it to his own self—But maybe she was right? Did he have his own army of little...?

Ghosts. Who knew where they went now? He had no way to contact them anymore, and he couldn't imagine they had any need of him. Shadows filed through his brain. Yevgeniy. His favorite brother and assistant mechanic. Yuriy. A solemn, good kid. Not quite twins, though both had an identical thyroid problem (you could thank Chernobyl for that). The second oldest, Aleksandr. The family's star, the most like their father in looks, but V never held that against him. Tatiana. His baby, raised truly, like she'd been his own. Hadn't he shared everything with her? Down to his face, because they said she looked the most like their mother, which is what they also said of him. All of them grown now, though it was impossible to see them as anything other than the kids he'd left behind 1,000 doors ago. He pushed past their forms quickly. Ilya? He moved past the fastest, throwing no more thought towards him than a fleeting prayer that he'd drunk himself to death. Oksana. She stayed the longest, though her image had faded, frighteningly, the most, and for a brief moment, V let himself bathe in the pure feeling of loving her with that hot ferocious love only small children are capable of. *One day, I'll kill him for you. Shh, you must not say such things. Don't make trouble with him, my soul. It only makes trouble for you—and me. He makes trouble for you every day. He works, he brings the money. You must give him respect. I will, when he gives it to you. It's not how it works, my life. You must accept it. No, I won't. I won't. I won't.* SUCH A MAZACON, DARLING. NOT WHAT I EXPECTED AT ALL. He tried to grip the eternal loss of her tight, and despair. But his heart was empty. His eyes were empty. How could he feel fresh pain, hitting at a thickened scar a decade old? And if he couldn't even be sad for her or imagine she'd be sad for him, who else was there? The road was drab, and the glory hole of self-pity so warm and beckoning, yet before he chucked himself into it completely, V smirked. Even when he tried, he could never properly upset himself over his own meaninglessness. All was not lost.

Surely his landlady would shed a silver tear for a lost toilet genius.

The fusuma started to open slowly, and in his debilitated brain, the creak instantaneously killed all thought processes but for a single one. No, no, no. His new roommate was home. Born-again Christian, white French-Canadian, with a pumpkin head and pockmarked face, barging in with yet another ridiculous camera phone picture of some poor girl's legs on the train: –Dude, check out this sweet babe's legs, she never even saw it coming! As if they were goddamn blood brothers in perving. Sachiko-san had randomly assigned him a new roommate some weeks back (diplomatically not mentioning that even with his discount, he could no longer afford a single) and though V didn't imagine anyone could take Rodrigo's place, any hope he'd had at even a casual camaraderie sunk away the moment the new roommate shook his hand.

Matt had the sort of insipid personality V detested, with just enough intelligence to be aware of his own benignity. His attempts to add complexity to his blandness via overt shows of contrasting spirituality and lasciviousness resulted in nothing but a thorough failing at both. So there he stood: A flaccid Christian. And a garden-variety creep. To someone who considered himself a true libertine, this falseness was a direct affront, and it made V's hair stand on end to think that people such as that dowdy Brit twit down the hall probably lumped two individuals as diverse as Matt and himself into the same generic category of perversity. Of course, he did not harbor the slightest illusion that he himself did not flagrantly sexualize women, he only hoped others acknowledged that he did it with commendably more panache. And now this Matt was about to burst into their room, braying in his ugly French about something or another. He closed his eyes, praying that, this once, his roommate would actually mercifully ignore him if he feigned sleep.

「V-san?」 The voice was not Matt's. It was a girl. She pronounced his name like a short attack. His eyes opened painfully. A white, round face floated in the dark, near the opening in the fusuma.

「Ojyamashimasu.」

She was already coming in, Aya was coming into his

room. Had he been more lucid, he would have jumped to his feet. He would have told her: 「Wait for me outside. Don't come in here. It's disgusting.」

As it was though, he stayed silent, and still, and tremendously happy.

Though V wondered at first if she was possibly a hallucination. After all the things he'd seen—she could've very well been a shard of his lonely imagination sent by some bored oni to confound him, so he stared at her speechless, with the awe reserved for supernatural phenomena—ghosts— or an angel of death.

Aya's hair was shorter, her plumpish frame thinner, the school uniform blazer perched like a garment on a child-mannequin, those narrow shoulders. Her makeup was different, heavy and dark. Meat-red knees from the late November cold. Though they had stopped meeting long before, he still saw her often enough in his mind, during the night or (he wouldn't have admitted it) in moments of sexual ennui, and the person standing in his door no longer fit at all the image he was accustomed to carrying. He wondered if he would have even recognized her if they'd randomly passed on the street. In his memory, she remained resplendent, her eyes gleaming with mischief, whereas this girl looked unwell, but even more alien was the expression on her face. He couldn't classify it.

「Aya-chan? What... what are you doing here?」

Her already wide eyes widened more in the grimy darkness. 「This is your room? I thought you were supposed to be—clean!」

「I was. I changed.」

「This whole house is awful. I think I saw a mouse when I walked through the kitchen.」

「It's not Miko-chan's fault, he's a good mouser. The guests cook and they don't take out the garbage. The house is full right now and I haven't... the toilet... the English busu...」

「You sound delirious. I think you need some air in here.」

「No, please,」 he croaked as she stepped towards the window. 「I can't stand the light right now.」

「Are you sick?」 She stepped closer, peered at him in the half-dark. 「What *happened* to you?」

She seemed worried enough, so he tried to stay cheerful in her presence.

「Well, we hit a rough patch here, that's for sure, but it's nothing I can't handle. I just need a bath, a meal, a smoke, and a screw. The order is totally negotiable.」

「...Is this you being funny? Foreign humor? You should become a comedian then, instead of wasting your talents here.」

Aya dashed out the door, and V wondered if he looked so grungy she had run out, never to come back again, but she did come back about fifteen minutes later, with a shopping bag. She spread out the contents: instant ramens, a yogurt, a small carton of milk, a tangerine. Two rice balls. 「So, what looks good to you?」 She held instant noodles in one hand and a rice ball in the other. He poked at the noodles warily, and she put some water on in the kettle. They sat saying absolutely nothing, listening to the water heating—boiling—then she started to open the packages.

「Maybe you should wash your hands before you eat?」

Aya's first sentence once he reached for the chopsticks was vacant and tactful, and his face blazed. Nodding, he shuffled out to the bathroom to thoroughly wash his face, brush his hair, and teeth. When he got back into the room, the food was on the table, and she pushed his portion

towards him, then looked him over. Nodded, then took up
her own plastic bowl.

「That's better. Now eat slowly. I don't want you to get
sick.」 He slowly slurped the soup, the first hot food to enter
his body in he could not remember how long. His stomach
lurched at the solidity, left, then right, and fighting the
wave of nausea, he forced himself to eat a little more, then
finally spoke.

「How did you find me?」

She shrugged.

「I told you there was no way to be a stranger in this
city. Everyone finds everyone sooner or later. I hadn't
heard from you in a long time and tried texting your
phone. The number was dead.」

「Yeah, I ran out of money for it. I had to start using
the house phone.」

「I see. I was worried you'd left the country or something, and that's why your plan was cancelled.」

「You really think I'd leave forever and not even try to
say goodbye?」

She said nothing to that, only stared ahead, and he
was about to ask where she had been all the weeks *before*
his phone had died, when Aya put her styrofoam bowl
down with such a look, he almost scalded himself.

「*You have something that is mine.*」

The way she said it gave him a thrill, as if she had
uttered something brilliantly and ominously profound
and his mind ran torpid circles trying to unlock this
cryptic remark before he realized. Her silver necklace. Aya
had given it to him back in the middle of last summer—
and he'd never given it back.

Having it still gave him comfort after she had disappeared, because while of course he would not contact a girl
who no longer wanted anything to do with him—he fig-

ured that keeping the necklace in his wallet would give him a reason to talk to her, should he and Aya ever randomly meet again. He had imagined their reunion a few times. It was always in a public place—perhaps a temple, during a matsuri—he would look up and see her across the crowd, make eye contact—Aya would be with a friend, or maybe her boyfriend, or maybe that girl she liked, but she wouldn't pretend like she hadn't seen him. She'd find her way over. Then they'd stand behind a booth selling yakisoba or kakigouri, under a linden tree and a little out of the way, and she'd say I can't talk right now, and he'd say I know, I only wanted to give this back, and she'd take it, and they wouldn't kiss, but she'd put her small hand on his arm and squeeze it—thank you, V-kun—my pleasure, ojousan—make him high for the rest of the week.

Now here they were, the exchange was happening, but without any meaningful looks, words, or linden trees. What an easy disappointment it was to fixate on and V frowned.

「You came all the way here... for that?」

「It's important to me. I'd like it back.」

V stood up. He walked to the small desk by the window. Opened the lone drawer where he kept the CD Rodrigo had left him and a few other mementos. And his wallet. He knew exactly where the necklace was. In the change compartment, curled up like a dormant, little snake. He fleetingly considered closing the drawer, looking for a few more minutes and then telling her he couldn't find it, but not wanting to reach the new low of stealing a cheap silver-plated necklace from a high school girl made him reach in, take it out of his wallet and give it to her. Or rather, put it on the table, because even when he stood next to her, Aya didn't put out her hand, as if physical contact with him was most undesirable. Not that V could blame her. His earlier stint in the bathroom had confirmed his suspicion that he did, indeed, look like an unwashed wraith. He sat back down and she waited a few moments before she reached out and unceremoniously jammed the necklace into her blazer's pocket.

「Thanks. And I know I'm the one who stopped writing you back first. Things just got... so hard. I got grounded since my grades were so bad and well. My parents are getting a divorce.」

「Oh.」 A jumbled thought-process unfolded in him. A partial, guilty relief. *So this is why she disappeared last summer. For once, it wasn't you.* He picked up his bowl, tried to eat more. 「I'm really sorry to hear that.」

Aya shrugged.

「I guess my mom found out about some longtime affair my dad's been having. My grandmother is on a rampage. She says she won't be able to hold up her head in public after this, that my mom will never be able to remarry, what's going to happen to us kids and so on. She thinks my mother is being immature and hysterical and that she should just let him have his... mistress, and ignore it.」

「And what do you think?」

「What do you mean? She *should* ignore it, of course. I mean, she's destroying our family.」

「I thought your father's infidelity is what's destroying your family.」

He was sorry the moment the sentence left his lips.

Aya's eyes flashed dangerously. 「Until this happened, we were all fine! So I'd say the real person at fault *is the person breaking up their marriage.*」

「I'm sorry. I shouldn't have said anything. I don't know anything about your family...」

「Well, I never hid anything about them, if that's what

you're implying. I just didn't know there was anything wrong—I thought I had a normal, boring family.⌋

There is no such thing, he thought, but kept his mouth shut on that.

⌈Aya-chan—I don't know what the situation is exactly. I don't know your father or your mother, but from this little bit you've told me, you seem madder at her than him. But he's the one who cheated, so... don't you think she has a right to try to find some happiness?⌋

⌈If she was a better mother, keeping us happy *would be her happiness,*⌋ Aya spat. Recoiled, like a rattlesnake encountering herself in the grass. Quickly recomposed and settled for glaring out the window. V leaned into his chair and breathed in heavily. He was sure it was the wafting scent of hot broth causing his stomach to turn. He looked out to where Aya-chan was staring. The sky looked doomed. Aya sat and sat, her fists balled up on her lap. Purple waves rolled off of her and he couldn't shake the impression that she was both waiting for him to say more and waiting to use whatever he said to get exponentially angrier. A wave of frustration broiled him. Fuck this, the last thing he needed right now was a girl selling a fight in his room. He was sorry to hear her bad news, but how was that any of his problem? V would wait another minute, thank her for the food, and tell her he needed to sleep.

The guilt was instant. A 'girl in his room,' this was Aya-chan, and she'd always been a cipher; wasn't that one of her charm points? So she was angry. Expected when life came tumbling down and one was sensitive. But she'd taken the trouble to come find him and shown more concern than any person he lived with. She'd been a friend to him and wasn't she waiting for him to be a friend back? Someone on the outside who'd listen and let her cry. Not inject his unwanted opinion. And V was capable of doing that; he wanted to do that. So he slipped his hand over the table, placed it over hers and gently pressed, without saying a word.

For once, her hand was so much colder than his.

Aya pulled away pointedly, met his eyes over the table, and in that one gesture, V finally saw what was different. Once he did, he could hardly believe that it had taken him so long to identify, because it was all so laughably standard. Whatever storms she was weathering back home, Aya still had the Look. [59]

And now, having identified that he was in that intimately familiar situation yet again—he realized that it was nothing like the other times he'd gone through it—was that even what was happening here? A kid was mystifying him. He fidgeted in the rickety chair and was still trying to make some whole of these broken pieces when Aya stood up, leaned over to his side of the table and—kissed him.

There were few things she could have done right then to confuse him more. Aya came over, twined her arms around his neck—and V was immediately and strangely hot. And it felt good that she wanted him, and it was wrong. He asked:

「What are you doing?」

「What does it look like?」

He stood up and gently pulled away from her.

「I know what it *looks* like, but *why* are you doing it?」

「Because I want to.」

「Aya-chan, I don't know what's going on or what exactly has happened, but I do know that you wouldn't normally act like this.」

「How smart you are suddenly! Tell me, what else do you know? About me?」 Her voice was stone quiet and sharper than a saber. 「I don't think you know anything, V.

[59] He knew the Look well, he'd seen it often enough (more often lately, actually). It was the way women looked at him when he stood stripped of the ideals they'd had— and they saw that they had wasted their time, their energy, their love, their words, their bodies, their emotions, on someone utterly unworthy. The ones who didn't disappear without a trace came back with faces like subpoenas to tell him his presence had changed their life for the worse. They would demand remuneration, and V, who did not believe in emotional shoplifting, always paid. He paid in whatever tender the situation demanded, harsh, soft, pleading, a brutal sending away, being fully aware himself how the relationship had gone wrong and what exactly he (or the other) had done to come to this point. He knew the full dimension of their lies and what he owed her and what she owed him, and once the score was settled and the bodies counted, he walked out the door intact and happy to never have to see her again. As he presumed she was happy to never have to see him. It was a mutual, understandable, painless, and perpetual process.

275

You're clueless, and I suspect more than slightly stupid, and you always will be.⌋

He bowed under the words, closed his eyes.

When he opened them again, she was unbuttoning her shirt.

⌈Aya, please, this isn't a private room! I have a room-mate! He could come home any minute—I can't even lock the door.⌋

⌈I don't care.⌋

⌈But I do!⌋

⌈Oh, so now he's a gentleman! Then get us a room.⌋

⌈Remember how you brought me food ten minutes ago? I don't have two yen in the world! I would love to get you a room, I would love nothing more than to get you whatever you want, but I can't.⌋

⌈Then let me do it. I have enough money.⌋

She started to take out her wallet. He tore his hands through his hair.

⌈Come on, put that away. ...A friend of mine in the house owes me money, I'll see if I can get it. Just stay here and wait for me, okay? With your clothes *on?*⌋

⌈Fine.⌋

She sat back down and began to stare out the window again, as if he had ceased to exist. V found his cleanest shirt, changed quickly and ran out of the room. His body felt rusty and sore, though the food had spread some energy into him. Already, he could feel himself getting hungry again, the movements of his bowels resuming, even as his mind turned slowly. What was he going to do, what was he going to do? On top of everything else, that silly proud lie earlier; he should be so lucky to have anyone owe him even a 100 yen coin. But what was the alternative? He pulled himself up the stairs, past the slimy upstairs kitchen, through the festering air on the second floor, not that he even registered that. All he could see was doors. A whole corridor of them, but those two in particularly beckoned, as doors to people who knew and (at least vaguely) liked him. Chikushou! [60] V could've fallen on his knees for a sign. Atsuko or Maury, at whose mercy should he throw himself? His brain sludged through snippets of a conversation he'd had with Atsuko and Rodrigo months and months ago. *You are an incorrigible pig on a straight road to hell, so don't come crying when...*

So he avoided her door and charged into the one at the end of the long hall instead. [61]

[60] Damn it!

[61] And this was a sound decision, because Atsuko was actually not in right then, and all knocking at her door would have achieved is waking and annoying her roommate.

EIGHTEEN

THE ROUGH TRADE

Maury's room was the shabby single of a perennial bachelor. The tatami was stained and warped, covered in a futon riddled with unhealthy looking lumps. A dim light buzzed overhead, but the window lay open to let in the crisp, early winter breeze, which he enjoyed, in a pilled-out sweater and faded slacks. When his door opened, Maury happened to be reading a paperback in English with a blanket on his knees and a mug of green tea perched on the window sill, getting colder by the minute. I realize you may not remember who he is. Understandably. He was not important to any of this until now, but Maury was the boarding house's official longest tenant and had been a quiet background presence at the computer for countless common room talks between V and Rodrigo. As it is, while he and V were not truly friends, his omnipresence in the common room had always given the other a feeling of particular kinship. Whether Maury agreed with this sentiment would have to be seen, but now he looked up at V's form in the door as if he had been expecting him all day.

—Raised back from the dead, I see. Hello, Lazarus!

His address was in French, one of the half-dozen languages he spoke proficiently. Removing his reading spectacles, Maury closed the book to give the visitor his full attention. His face was quizzical, rouged with a faint tinge of amusement, as if he couldn't wait to see what antics V would come up with next. The other went straight to the point.

—Maury. J'ai besoin d'une grande faveur.

–I know. You need money.

The words flowed forward, smooth and surreal and V wondered if he could have caught a break. If this would be easier than he had imagined.

–You are correct. That's exactly what I need. Can you help me? I can pay you back.

The older man got up with a groan and shuffled to his desk, where he opened a drawer with a small key from his pocket and took out an envelope full of cash.

–Ahh, my back. I am not in the age to be sleeping on the floor anymore. And did you know, the toilet down the hall...

–Yes. I know. I will get to it. I swear, I could die tomorrow, and the only thing anyone in this house would miss is their unclogged toilet...

So bitter! The sentence rushed out before V could stop himself and he bit his mouth, but Maury seemed merely amused by the outburst.

–Oh, I'm sure you would be missed for more than that, boy. –He rubbed his lower back with one hand, groaned and started to sift through the envelope. –You were looking so down in the mouth this week, I was waiting for our comely V to come up here to panhandle. And lo! Here you are.

V didn't know what to say. He had never borrowed money from the other before, and the open gloating made him apprehensive. Still, he figured, Maury thoroughly relishing his fall from grace *and* lending him money needn't be mutually exclusive. Didn't he already have the envelope in hand? If his read was correct, Maury would savor his shame for a bit, but he'd come through. And V wanted to get out of this room and back to Aya as soon as possible, but every movement the older man made seemed to require a deep slew of thought. Maury extracted some bills.

–So how much is the prince needing today?

–One *man*.

The other clucked his tongue.

–One *man*, one *man*. That is a lot of money.

It's really not, V thought, fully irritated again, also fully aware he was in absolutely no position to bargain. He checked himself and went on.

–Maury, come on—can we skip all this? I'm desperate. Just help me out, please. I'll agree to any terms you got, but I've got to get out of here right away. With a *man*.

–Impatient *and* a beggar? That's a hell of a combination, my lad. But all right, all right. You mentioned paying me back. When can I expect that, exactly?

It was a good question.

–Well, I'm really broke right now, but...

V riveted on the money and trembled. The other's laugh was dry and his hand paused.

–So, I can translate that as you requesting a loan to be paid back at some unspecified point in the future? I believe in the common parlance, that means 'give me money—for free'.

The voice was peevish, and his hand stubbornly pushed the notes back into the envelope. Maury started to move back to the drawer, fishing for the key in his pocket to lock it all back up.

No no no.

V licked his cracked lips—the sum lay etched into his irises. He thought of Aya's burnt-out face downstairs. He could not know where the day would lead them, but he knew it had to lead them somewhere together. And he had to spare Aya a plunge into further degradation, because she would not leave him today without whatever it is she had come for. The only question was where and on whose bill. And that was something he refused to let her do.

Well, he'd made it on his instincts so far.

What did he have if not those? And what did they say the road leading to a certain somewhere was paved with again?

Oh, fuck it all to hell, he thought, wanting suddenly to laugh, and he jumped into the pool like a blindfolded man.

Who has no idea if he was to hit water or concrete.

—Not for free.

His smile was slight, and when the older man absently looked up, V connected squarely with his gaze and scorched him.

The look was transparent, amateurish, and completely confident.

Tick.

Tick.

Tick.

He wanted to howl. *Was I wrong? Please, please, do not tell me that I've bitched this gamble up!*

His fall was right around the corner and then—click.

The older man's cheeks tinged, he fumbled the envelope, and V could've danced for joy. It took a super-human self-control to not break into a visible form of jubilation, but though the money now lay in the realm of possibility— it wasn't in his hand. Yet. Pin pricks dropped behind his eyelids and when Maury spoke again, it was in another register.

—My boy, I must confess, even from you. I wasn't expecting this. But you have my attention. What exactly are we proposing now?

—One afternoon.

—With...?

Maury held the envelope just out of reach, as if the other were an untamed dog to be tempted in out of the cold with a tidbit. Annoyed to fury, V's voice flat-lined and he stifled a curse. Things he normally associated with subtlety, innuendo, *effortlessness*—delicacy. He swallowed and set the curve of his mouth:

–Tout ce que tu veux. Listen, for that money, you can strip me, touch me, fuck me, or me you, whatever and anything you want, I'll do it, tomorrow, whenever, but right now, I gotta go. So please, is it a deal?

The room's oily cold lay still and then—

–Ok.

Done. Maury gingerly extracted a one *man* note and tucked it into the young man's palm with a twitch, and V pocketed the money without compunction. He was about to leave, when emboldened, the other reached out and ran a light finger over a cord in his neck. Motioned for him to wait, took another bill from his envelope and extended it.

–I do not mean to cause offense, but I would ask you to do me one very important favor, before we meet again.

–Sure. What is it?

–Use some of your newfound funds to patronize a bathhouse.

He nodded dully and backed up against the door. *A cheap, dirty whore.* The words didn't occur to V. The cash finally his, he could've kissed the patron saint of whores everywhere.

–Then I'll be back here tomorrow. No later than two.

–All right. I'll be waiting.

And the sweltering in the older man's eyes flickered out. For a moment he smiled at V, such a strange smile that it struck him. What was it? *I hate you, but we are in this together.* V could not help but smile too.

Tomorrow, he'd be back, but not tomorrow nor ever again did he think they would understand each other as they did right now.

Maury put the envelope back into the drawer, locked

it with the tiny key and put it back into his pocket, then lay
on the futon again and picked up his paperback. He looked
as if he would stay in that position until the promised time,
and V was already out the door.

–You've saved my life. Thanks.

–Harumph. I suspect it won't be the last time, either.
One must be. Absolutely.

–Maury?

He turned before pulling the fusuma shut.

–Yes?

–Who said 'Il faut être absolument moderne'?

The other laughed.

–A poet, my boy! A soul not unlike yourself!
Modern.

Outside the door, V let himself a deep breath, then
slid down the stairs and shoved open the door to his room.
Aya was still looking out the window as if she had not
moved a muscle in the last ten minutes. She turned as he
entered, frowning at him like a brooding teenager. *Which
she is*, he thought uneasily.

「Omataseshimashita.」 He grabbed her coat from the
back of the chair and started to help it on her. 「I got the
money, let's go.」

「I could've just paid, you know.」

「Come on.」

They walked out of the boarding house and her dour,
raw face frightened him, but the money felt exhilarating in
his pocket; a belated symbol of competence and hope, so
he let himself hope.

「Aya-chan—where are we going?」

「A hotel. Where else?」

Where else? Was there anywhere else? Movies—darkness—karaoke—food—river—talking—talking—finding
out—Kamo—blankets—*sleep*. He was so sleepy.

⌜There's a lot of other places. Wouldn't you rather do something else—?⌟

⌜No.⌟

V was certain this is what it felt like, to be dead.

The early winter air slashed him, and he looked over to see how she was taking it, but Aya had wrapped the bottom half of her face in a thick, checkered scarf. Only her eyes shone out of it, and her hair, tossed by the wind, and she seemed to be walking with a strange, singular purpose.

⌜Aya, slow down. I'm exhausted,⌟ he groaned and she turned to look at him. ⌜I haven't moved in a week. Please give me a couple seconds.⌟ She waited for him patiently, and then started walking slower, even offered her hand. He took it, bewildered by her sudden concern. Out of breath.

⌜There's a place down the street from here. Do you want to go there?⌟

⌜No.⌟ Her answer was monotone and almost leaden. Hearing it sunk him. ⌜I want to go downtown.⌟

⌜All right.⌟

They got on a train, he paid for the fares, and they lurched along until the city center. He knew many spots in this area, but he let her lead and Aya finally took them to a love hotel close to Kyoto Eki, merely indicating it with a bick of her head. He had no idea why she chose this place or if there was any significance at all, but he went in with her. He couldn't find a tactful way to ask her how long she wanted to stay and ended up paying for the entire night.

The concierge passed him the key with a slight raised eyebrow.

V glowered at him. Then they walked up.

NINETEEN

BEAUTIFUL WORLD

R oom 457 had no extra amenities. It had been created for function alone. In the center was a very large bed that ran almost to the walls, with only enough space on the sides for a slim body to stand. A bathroom the size of a broom closet off of it (no claw-footed tub this time) and a single chair. A homely night stand, with a lamp and a small plate of wrapped prophylactics. The sight of them was vaguely lewd in the otherwise conspicuously barren surroundings. The window was tiny and so high, it would never offer a view, and the bedside lamp illuminated the whole space with a limp, butter-colored light.

Nothing more than absolutely necessary.

V stood at the foot of this big bed and watched Aya as she removed her coat and shawl and carefully folded them with precise movements.

「Do you have to be somewhere later today?」

「No.」 Aya's voice was steady, and she didn't turn to face him. 「My mom thinks I'm staying the night with a study friend.」

He was glad to hear that; it would be the first time ever that they had no time constraints, but then she turned, and he saw that her eyes were brimming with acrid tears. Grey from the makeup, they stayed barricaded behind her lower lashes. As afraid as he had been of touching her before, he ran to her then.

「Aya, what's wrong?」 V held her to him and felt her body momentarily stiffen, then relax. 「You've been acting so weird this whole afternoon, and I can't figure out if you like me still, or if you want my head on a stick.⌋

「Maybe it's both.⌋ She buried her face into his side.

「Come on, let's get out of here. You're in a bad state. This isn't what you need right now.⌋

「We can't just leave—you already paid for the room.⌋

「So what? I'll get the money back and if I can't, okane wa dou demo ii!—I don't care! I don't need it; I need you to tell me what's going on...⌋

She shrugged, started to remove her shirt. Robotically.

「Aya, stop! This isn't right; I can't help you if you don't...⌋

Aya hurled her cast-off shirt against the wall and whirled so abruptly that he bumped into the chair behind him. He was certain that, had she been taller, she would have struck him. His tone and his patience both snapped:

「What the hell has gotten into you?⌋

「You, okay?!⌋ She turned, shouted at him. 「*You* are what's gotten into me! I need to get this over with. You don't care anyway, right? You do it with anything that moves! *What difference does it make to you?*⌋

Shivers pulsed up his arms, tiny electric charges. He asked himself, what difference *did* it make? She was right; wasn't he used to perpetually being treated as something more *and* less than what he could be? But Aya had never treated him like that, so what was this, what was it? V grasped at anything he could say or do to calm her.

「Aya, please. Please. Just sit down. Listen... I don't feel well. I can't think straight. I don't know... why you're so... I always knew you had a boyfriend... you always knew that I'm... but that doesn't mean that I don't care for you... and whatever it is that's wrong or if I hurt you or made you confused, I am so...⌋ He tried to touch her again, but she put her hands straight out, as if she couldn't bear it.

「You're what? Were you going to say 'sorry'? 'I'm so *sorry*?!'」 Aya mocked him, her bitterness heartrendingly adult. 「Don't even bother saying it, when I bet someone like you *doesn't even know how to feel sorry* at all!」

She threw herself on the bed, face down, and a minute ticked by, washed in the sound of her quiet heartache. *This is a young girl, this is a young girl, this is a very young girl.* He crouched next to her, trying to think over the voice drumming in his mind.

「All right. You're not going to tell me what's really wrong, I can see that. And I can't read your mind, as much as I would like to. So please, what can I do?」

She talked into the sheet folded tight over the bed.

「I want an hour. You said that's what you're good at. Remember? Making people forget for one hour that everything's wrong. So for one hour, I want you to make me feel good, and I want you to make me forget everything and I don't want to talk about anything or do anything else, and then if you want to go, you can leave. Or if you want to go now, you can do that too. But if you're staying, that is all that I want from you.」

Tick tock tick tock tick. The bedside clock.

V swallowed.

He walked into the bathroom and wet a washcloth with hot water. When he came back out, she was still sitting shirtless, with all her other clothes on, and he quietly sat down next to her, turned her around and wiped her face. Tried to rid it of as much makeup as he could. Right then, he wanted to see her the way she had looked the first day they'd met, when she'd worn nothing on her face at all. He gently took off her shoes, then socks. Her skirt and his own clothes. Their underclothes. Slowly peeled off their layers, one by one, while she sat saying nothing. Neither resisting, nor helping.

He picked her up and carried her into the bathroom, where he ran a hot shower, as hot as he could stand it. Aya sat on the toilet, lost in the steam, looking down morosely as they waited for the water to heat and then he put her into the shower and stepped in behind, and they stood in the tiny cubicle, pressed against each other with the hot water raining down. She was completely silent now. The moisture made her hair blacker than black. V washed her hair carefully, his own, their bodies; pulled her out of the shower and dried her in a wooly hotel towel. He bundled her into one and sat her on the toilet—he blew her hair dry.

Picking her up again, he determined: The girl weighed nothing. He laid Aya into the huge bed and started to crawl in next to her, then froze in that motion, one knee on the covers, a foot on the floor still. Eyes on her. Half in and half out. He suspected but couldn't ask if this was their last night, knowing full well that a melodramatic question couldn't save him from what would now transpire, another familiar phenomenon. That craving some had when intimacy had gone sour for complete devolution, what baser types called a pity fuck, or a hate fuck, or a revenge fuck, he wasn't sure which and it didn't matter, only that now, once he crawled into bed next to Aya, their relationship would be reduced to a trope fuck. And he desperately searched his psyche for the appropriate shards of guilt; he wanted so much to *not want* Aya right then, because in that moment, physically being unable to comply would demonstrate beyond anything that came out of his mouth, that... well, what exactly?

「Are you coming?」 Her voice broke into him. He looked down.

「Aya-chan, tell me first why you're so angry at me.」

She laughed dryly. 「No.」

「Don't I have the right to know?」

「No.」

「Please, if you won't say, then let's sleep. It would be better.」

「I said you can go. So do you want to go?」

「Of course not.」

「Then what?」

And she reached out of bed and pulled him to her. Aya's face was flushed; her eyes still lightly rimmed with a ring of smoke. Hard, toughened eyes, dry of tears, and the way she looked at him, he could feel the woman rising in her, not the girl any more.

Something had happened to make her hate him, and she was still pretending to want him, pushing herself to. No, he revised, she did want him and this disgusted her, and made her loathe him even more. He was teaching her that sometimes, you could desire and despise the same person; you could love someone's body and hate their soul, or hate and crave some part of their soul and body to a measure that sickened you, and he didn't want to be the person to teach her this lesson. However, what he wanted ran inchoate through him, below his mind, below his veins; the desire to burn himself down, clean both of them with fire until they were two naked, shivering, hopeless things and perhaps then he could say to her: See, Aya-chan. Don't hate me or the world for being what it is. There are vampires and there are virgins and the virgins will always be pure and desirable and the vampires will always be depraved and desiring. Virgins are there to be beautiful and young and vampires are there to tear them up and throw their petals into the wind, but that is their job, until the earth stops turning, and one day every virgin, without even knowing the exact time they do it, will cross over and become a vampire, but that time for us isn't yet. We're still pure.

He wanted to be pure for her.

To still be on the same side.

His body felt heavy and clean, and he lay it into bed next to hers.

Eyes closed shut, the room was entirely cold and silent, like she was hot and silent; opposite silences sucking away all sound and feeling until he was conscious only of the blood pounding in his head and of a monstrous thirst. The dim awareness that right then, he desired a glass of water perhaps more than he had ever wanted anything in his entire life.

Aya crawled over his body and looked down on him.

「You're just lying there. Do you even want to?」 She crawled over, reached behind and started to grope him. He coughed delicately.

「You're over me naked, ojousan. Is it a time to ask, do I want to, do I not want to?」

「Your body, fine. But I'm asking about you. Do *you* want to?」

Aya looked down at him then; his hair was in his face. He was already sweating, as if they were in it. She put a hand on the base of his throat, pushed his hair to the side with the other. His eyes connected with hers to ask a question, if she really was ready, and that's when the storm broke. And she looked just as shocked as he did. Like this was the last thing she had expected herself to do. Water crashed over V's head while he held her shuddering body to his, cautiously at first, then clasping her to him as hard as she allowed, blinking at the slow, rhythmic childish grief pounding out of her, against him like a sea's surf. He'd held another girl sobbing this purely ten lifetimes ago, but his mind no longer remembered it.

「I thought I'd never see you again,」 she heaved, 「and I had so much to say. So much to talk about, to *you*.」

「Then why on earth did you not call me? My phone was dead these last weeks, but it was fine for so long. You disappeared first!」

「It wasn't about your phone. I didn't call because *you* weren't there. I always thought you were, but you weren't.」

His confusion reached its absolute summit, but he knew there was no sense to ask.

If she decided to, she would tell him, but.

He stopped wanting to know.

A night passed. They stayed wrapped in each other, passing in and out of talk and lucid sleep. And nothing more. Whatever had been spurring Aya before seemed quenched, like fire drowned to death with an entire bucket, and V was incredibly grateful. It was right this way, he thought. He was tired, drained, happy, sad—V couldn't sleep. When she talked, he listened; when she slept, he studied her, thinking she had grown. Her limbs seemed longer, and she had lost her baby fat. Perhaps she'd even been sick. She was seventeen now. Are you twenty-seven yet? Aya asked him sometime later, stretched over his body, her fingers in his hair—they did nothing, but didn't bother to get dressed either. He wondered, if a girl who wanted to talk to you with your clothes on was a girlfriend—what was a girl who wanted to talk to you with your clothes *off*, but expected nothing else either? Her voice snapped him back. I asked about your birthday, and he shook his head. No, his birthday wasn't until April. He was still twenty-six. Then until April, you're only nine years older than me.

Aya smiled at him, as if it even mattered.

He listened to her life of late, and she told him she had missed their talks. He was the only adult interested in these boring details. Aya gave him updates about her school, and how, as bad as she was still in chem, she had top marks in math. She might even become a math teacher, if fashion doesn't work out. He told her he had also wanted to be a teacher when he was still in high school. Why didn't you? she asked and V shrugged. He had quit school. He never thought about it anymore. Maybe, if he ever became legal, he could pursue it again. Aya talked about fashion club. Her first date out with Ren. Yes, it had happened, though Aya had put it off for so long. And it had been so wonderful. They'd even kissed. *Now I see why you're so crazy about kissing girls, V-kun. Is there anything better than kissing a girl?* He nodded. *I can't think of a single better thing.* Of her parents' divorce she said no more, only mentioning that she would rather keep living with her father than move out with her mother; and V, not wanting to disturb the delicate peace of the last few hours, did not ask her to elucidate.

「And how is your boyfriend?」 he did ask though, biting his lip to mask his anxiousness.

「He's fine. He's always fine. I put a deadline for myself, to tell him about Ren by the end of the year. With everything else, I can't take any more serious conversations right now. But I will tell him...」 He was relieved to hear all that was intact in her life still. She even showed V a picture of him on her keitai (she never had before). Once she drew it up, he squinted at it, shocked at the young kid beaming out at him, with his perfectly angled hair and high-boned, tanned face—did Aya look this young and he didn't see it anymore?

「Kao ga ii deshou?」 she pressed him.

「Ultra good.」

「Are you just saying that? Or do you mean it?」

「Of course I mean it,」 he smirked. 「I want to steal him from you and make him my first boy.」

She snatched the phone away from him, frowning.

「Kimoi. Don't be gross. Anyway, you're totally not his type.」

「Hmm, a challenge then. Even better. Maybe I could. Does he play around as much as you do?」

「I've never *really* cheated on him.」

V laughed out loud. 「Is that so, ojousan?」

Even naked in bed with him, she had a prince's dignity.

「Her and I just kissed. And I told you,」 she proclaimed, her voice suddenly cold, 「a foreigner doesn't count.」

This time, he was 100% certain she was not joking, and perhaps it was a mockery he had earned entirely, but it felt strange to be so far above (so far below?) her normal experience as to not count.

Then around dawn, Aya stopped talking mid-sentence while relating the complex plot of a manga series she had finished not long ago. V pulled on his clothes and got two bottles of juice from the hallway vending machine. He came back, drank from one of the bottles. Stripped. Crawled back into bed.

By then, enough light had come through their postage stamp window for him to actually see her face.

Aya was not asleep.

「Aya-chan. Are you thirsty?」

「Yes. ...You know what I realized? I don't know your family name.」 She reached for his bottle.

「And I don't know yours.」

「I must have told you though.」

「No. You said your name was Ayami, and to call you Aya, and that was it.」

She gave him a look, as if doing a mental calculation, but then seemed satisfied.

「Maybe you're right. I honestly don't remember now. But I don't even know your given name. Unless it really is only one letter. Is there more?」

「There is.」 He looked almost shy.

「Can I know it?」

「If you want.」

「I don't know. Maybe after all this time, it would be weird. ...I'd try to guess it, but I can't think of any western name that start with a v.」

「You would never guess it anyway.」

「So it's unusual?」

「Not in my country, but I doubt you'd have ever heard it.」 He smoothed the sheet by his thigh and traced his name with a finger. Aya stared at the lines.

「The first letter doesn't even look like a v.」

「Yes. Our language has its own alphabet.」

「Would you do me a favor?」

Aya got up, went to her bag, searched for a moment. Came back to the bed, and handed him a notebook and a silver gel pen.

「Write your name for me. In your alphabet and romaji. It's my English notebook, so on the inside cover is fine. In the back.」

He turned away from her and wrote. It seemed to her he was writing a long time. Then he blew on the ink to dry it. While he was doing this, Aya opened the night stand's drawer. There was a directory in it. More condoms. A pen. A pad of hotel stationary.

She took the pad and wrote in the middle of the page, then ripped it off. Stood up, took something from her blazer's pocket, and then folded the paper into a hexagon. Back in middle-school, her friends were always trying to one-up each other with complicated folded notes. Aya was surprised she could still remember how to do it. She wrote

'V-さん〜' on the front, right as he was putting her book and pen back in her bag. She asked, 「Did you write your full name?」

「First, last, and everything. Look at it after you go home. Then you alone will know all my dirty secrets.」

「And I wrote you something too. For later.」

She passed him the tiny note-packet and he slipped it into his jacket pocket.

「I'll look at it after I go home too. But now, you should sleep...」

「But I don't want to sleep. I want to talk.」

「We've been talking all night. Wouldn't you rather sleep?」

He smiled and Aya smiled back.

「No. Is that strange? I find it so much easier to talk to you than to Kiriya. It's easier to talk to Ren, too. I guess that should have been my tip that I don't love him.」

「It doesn't have to mean that. Some people, you love for what they do, not what they say.」

She pulled close to him.

「So do you think you can love more than one person... like *that*... at a time?」

「Of course. Why would you not be able to?」

「I really do care about him, but I don't think he would understand me wanting to be with someone else too. I will be honest with him and apologize, but I'm so scared he's going to hate me.」

「He might. But that's how it is. Be sincere with him and go on. He'll be hurt for a while, but he'll go on too.」

「See. You always understand these things right away. You know, I'm embarrassed now, for how I acted before. Last night... I said some awful things to you...」

「It's fine, Aya-chan. I'm sure whatever you were so angry about, you were right.」 For a split second, he wanted to take it back, but she only shrugged.

「I don't even want to think about it. ...There was one
other thing I wanted to ask you about though.」

「Then now is probably the best time.」

She lay on her back, stared at the ceiling.

「You have relationships with so many women.」

She was telling, not asking. His voice turned, uneasy.

「That's true.」

「Does it feel good? To be loved by so many people?」

「It has nothing to do with love, Aya.」

「Before you said it was love. So if it's not, what is it?」

His head was spinning.

「Maybe it's like what you said about me. That they
don't count.」

「You sound sleepy.」

「I'm very tired.」

「You can go to sleep. I'll stop talking to you.」

But when he closed his eyes, he knew that she wasn't
going to go to sleep. She was sitting next to him, watching
him, and V wanted to drown in unconsciousness, but he
could feel his own breath, rising and falling a little too
sharply, from feeling her eyes on his naked body. Then she
said quietly, can I touch you? And he nodded, whispered,
you don't have to. But I want to, eyes still closed, feeling
her light hand run down his side, and up again. Her fingers passed over his face—in the cold room, her skin
smelled like summer, like the first and last day of school,
like every well-scrubbed boy and girl he'd ever met. The
passing minutes created an incredible crawling tension
under his skin that he wasn't used to, and he wondered if
it was the unfamiliar sensation? The fact of not having
been with another for so long? Or if it was Aya, the way she
did nothing more than simply pet, pet, pet, turning him
into a bowl of warm milk on the brink of, but never quite

spilling. She added drop after drop after drop until spilling seemed catastrophic and irreversible. His right hand moved to his face, finger wandered to his mouth; spit from the cuticle streaked the sheets. Aya watched, moving her lips. The way she moved her mouth reminded him vaguely of someone, but he could not say who, and he closed his eyes again, wanting to focus only on sleep, not the bad blood pounding through his body, but had he fallen asleep for a second?

「V-kun.」

「Yes. No. What?」

His mind felt so slack.

「I was asking you a question.」

「Ask me again?」

「I was asking about those women. The ones you said that don't count.」

「Okay. What about them?」

「Was I one of them? ...Or did I ever count? To you?」

He was amazed that he could still follow. With one hand, she gripped his upper thigh a little too tightly.

He gasped, 「I don't count to you. You said so. But you still want you to count to me?」

「V-kun. You're never serious.」

「How can you expect me to be, when you...?」

「You're changing the subject. You didn't let me tell you how I feel about you that other time. Remember, the last time we met? By the river. I wanted to tell you, but you didn't want to hear it. I'm not stupid. I knew I wouldn't be someone you loved, you said you make sure that doesn't happen, but after... that... I started thinking, maybe I didn't even mean anything to you. *Nothing at all.*」

The tops of her cheeks reddened, and she stared down at him and right then, her hand settled in a place that made him bite his nail so hard, it began bleeding. Blood flowed down the cuticle, and he watched it, feeling like he should get up and not smear it on the sheets. Then the blood was on the sheets, more of it and more of it. Lemon, he thought dully. I need a lemon, to get this out. Where had he learned that? The pond of his memory disturbed, and he lay down in the water of it, staring at the blood coming out of his finger.

Where had he learned that?

When?
Could anybody tell him?

Je suis perdue. Je suis saoûle. Je suis impure. Quelle vie!

I am   lost. i am drunk i am impure what a life!
Il faut être absolutement moderne   Il faut être absolutement moderne Il faut être,
he is a demon , you kno w, and not a man
c'est un Démon, vous savez, ce n'est pas un homme.
C'est bien ce démon-la then I'll see you tomor   row youread it
s o   g o o d ,   s o   v e r y   g o o d ,

where do you want me to be from **what** would you do for money **when** will I see
y o u   a g a i n ?   l e t ' s   n o t   m a k e   a   d a t e
doesn't buy you things is plain bad luck bad luck
prey on them? as in eat their hearts   you have to accept
it, my V▮▮▮. I won't I won't
accept it. V▮▮. I need a song you meant nothing to me nothing at all
worthless
kimoi
k i m o i

                                        Ksyusha and her precious

                        V▮▮ if we got married then you wouldn't go get one
room or do you want your own. Vivi. vivi vivi? Oi Vicchan
you are an incorrigable pig on a straight road to Hell come save me y o u a re n o
t w o r t h i t

                              tu est brutal tu est brutal I said i loved you and? you
don't. do it in French you have to fight for something I say this like a brother
                didn't your mother teach you to fuck better thanthat depends
l i t t l e   b r o t h e r
don't we can't lose you too meccha kawaikko datta
v-chan looking so banged up so hopelessly irrespon sible
how much is the prince needing today? i need it but i don't want it iru kedo saa
hoshii janai hoshikunai just say hoshikunai hoshii janai yanai? janai yanaijanaiya
h e f o r g o t t o f u c k h e r doushita n o o n i i c h a n
she never wanted a man   you were the light of her eye. You look like a liar

aya-chan seriously she was like the sun she was like the moon she was like the wind she was like an ordinary girl, in her own way, unlike all others she was like the i'll hate you for as long as I live we need you go get the others ready for school. My Liar. Do you ever think about it **NO** u-so-tsu-ki-da-i-su-ki of course i think about it Go get the others ready for school. a debt so deep so good so wrong when it comes time to pay it

Ever want to see if it was as good as you remember? No because I know
It was. Even better.

My Soul.
My Heart.
My Joy.
My Light.
My Love.
My Life.
My Everything.

Get them ready for school.

My Light. My Life.
My Aya-chan. You're going to be late for school.

「Aya-chan, you're going to be late for school.」

Behind him, Aya shook his shoulder gently, but he did not respond, so she got out of bed, naked and a little cold, and crouched on his side, resting her chin against the mattress.

「But... I don't have school today.」

「All right. Then why don't you go to sleep.」

「V-kun.」

「What, my darling?」

「Are you okay?」

「Of course. I'm about to sleep too.」

「But...」 She turned her face, wincing. Like she was pointing out something really rather compromising. An unzipped fly. A black sesame seed in the teeth. 「You're... crying.」

「Baka. Don't be stupid.」

「What's wrong?」

「Does something have to be wrong? It's just water. There's too much water in me.」 *Always has been.* He closed his eyes, pushing more tears out.

「Still though. You were fine a moment ago. I must've upset you. With my question. I didn't mean to, honestly. I only wanted to know—」

「—if you ever meant anything to me. I know. I've been thinking. And I wasn't fine a moment ago. Or all night. Or all week. Or for... a while, if I honestly think about it. I've been thinking about how to answer your question. I won't slither out of it. I promise.」

「You don't have to answer it. I didn't mean to make you so upset. If my question is what upset you. ...I've never seen a grown man crying before. Not in real life.」

「I haven't seen myself cry either, Aya-chan. I cried so long ago, I must have been a little kid the last time. Or when I was a baby. But not since then. Not even when—— It feels so strange. It feels really good. When I think about you, I'll say, she was the first girl who ever made me cry and even that felt so good.」 He turned and wept, and his shoulders shook, and Aya rattled.

「V, shikkari shite yo!」

「I'm sorry Aya-chan, but I will not be able to be shikkari. Not this time. You'll have to forgive me.」

「But please, just tell me what's wrong? I can help.」

「You didn't tell me what was wrong either, last night. And you worked it out yourself. I have to work it out too.」

「But I could see how much you wanted to help me last night. You did everything you could— You tried to fix it for me, and I want to help fix it for you—」

「Oh Aya-chan.」 He cried harder. 「But I fixed nothing. Not even what I broke. And nothing is wrong. Nothing can be fixed. God himself couldn't. You see, I've been wondering for hours and hours why you showed up out of nowhere. Why now? I've been wondering all this time, what you wanted. What I could give you. It's usually so easy to figure it out. What someone wants, what they want to buy, what they want to sell. And you decide if that price is worth it. To pay it. Or not. But this time, this whole last night, I couldn't figure it out. And I think I get it now, Aya-chan.」

「V-kun, I...」

「No. Please. Be quiet. You must be quiet. I won't be able to think in five more minutes. I won't be able to say a single word. And I won't see you again after tonight, will I? I won't. So listen to me, Aya. I need to tell you a story. I used to tell stories all the time, to the kids. They were my siblings, but they were also my own kids. I know that sounds strange, but that's how it was. I was so proud of them. I never told you about them, there's so many things I haven't told you about. I'm going off track. The story.

Don't worry, you'll like it. You liked so much to hear me
talking about the girls I loved. It's a continuation of that.
So you know about the girl like the sun. (Ksyusha-san, she
whispered and he smiled. Heaved. More tears fell.) Oh see.
You remembered. The sun. And she burned out. And there
was the girl like the wind. (Tomoe-san.) Yes. She blew away.
But then, there was a girl like the moon. She's the point
here. This girl, she was so bright and lovely. And charming.
And so so far. And she would shine on you even in the
night, when you were alone. You could think about her,
and she would shine. And she was friendly, and she was
honest, and she was short, and she made jokes in bed, and
she was smart, but she said fuck you to school. I respected
that, because I always said fuck you to school too. Last but
not least, she was beautiful; so much that even sitting next
to her in her shapeless ugly school uniform made your skin
burn. And besides all the people who already love the
moon, she had a boy who loved her and a girl who loved
her. Made sense, because she was the type of person
anyone could not help but love. This moongirl came and
asked me for a cigarette once. No, that's not what happened. She warned me. About smoking. She told me,
everything that's good kills you. I was standing in my
favorite city on this whole fucking stupid planet, in my
favorite spot. Of that favorite city. I think you know this
spot too. It feels holy. And if you stand there, good things
happen to you. Well something very good happened to me;
the moongirl came over, and I lit her a cigarette, and the
first thing I saw was her eyes. Like the fairy tales. Eyes
blacker than gold. Skin golder than wheat. And I got to
strike her a match. Put yourself in my place. Imagine, you
were standing in front of a prince who had the world at her
feet, and you. Were a nobody. And a nothing. But somehow,
she noticed you. And you knew what's for you and what's

not allowed, but you thought—(V's voice broke, he sobbed here and the sound jarred Aya. It was so *loud*. She tentatively put two fingers on his bare shoulder, and he heaved for a good four seconds.) —You know what he used to always say? ('He'? she wondered, but didn't dare interrupt.) He used to say *stubborn as a mule and twice as stupid*. God, how I hated him, but goddamn if he wasn't right. About that at least. Some people never learn, Aya-chan. They never fucking learn.

So you knew you could never have the moon, and you couldn't marry the prince either, because once she grew up, she would pick her boy or her girl. Which was right and what should happen. Someone *her age*. She wasn't for you, plain and simple. But you started to think, maybe, you could love her. You couldn't have her. But you could love her. Quietly. In the background. Maybe, you could be good for her, talk to her when she needed advice, because besides being a prince and a heavenly body, she was also a normal ordinary girl. And sometimes, she needed advice. Your task, if you choose to accept it. Give her advice. Be a friend, a true friend. And avoid fate. Fate is to hurt each other. So you never admitted nothing. This was your second mistake. You wouldn't paint the devil on the wall. You wouldn't let her paint it either. She tried to say it out loud once and you didn't let her. And then one day, she disappeared, and you were sad, but you thought, okay. Come and go is what the moon does. You told yourself, she has to shine over so many places, you must understand if she can no longer come personally visit you. So you tried to imagine she was happy. That not coming around was best for her. You went about your business and tried not to think hard on it.

But then you had some bad days, bad weeks. One day you fell into a darkest hour. Everyone gone. Your best friend who lived with you, like a little brother and an older brother, rolled into one. He was gone. The sky was cold and empty. No sun, no wind, no moon. Not a single star up in the sky. You were thinking of the things you never think of. Never let yourself think of. Every person you wouldn't see again. Every person you had hurt. Left behind. Lied to. You wanted to cry, except it was useless. You couldn't feel anything. You'd lost so many people, your entire body and heart ached like a tough old scar. And who to blame, but yourself? You never did things the way people told you to. So you thought you deserved it, and it was all for the best. But then, in that fukai hour, there she was. Shining again. Except you realized—the two things were connected. You were in this low hour, *because of what you had done.* Because you had wanted her, and loved being with her, and being in bed with her, and kissing her, and talking to her, listening to her, and teasing her, and you wanted to protect her—when the person you should've been protecting her from was you. And people like you. That's what you had done wrong. *You had failed to protect her.* That must've been it, because nothing else made sense. You had no fucking clue. But you didn't even want to know anymore, whatever heinous thing you had done. She was kind, and sweet, and honest, and beautiful, and you had messed her up. And you knew, she didn't love you anymore. Though she had once. Even that was special, because girls said they loved you all the time. But it always meant I love to fuck you. I love how you make me forget. Which was fine, it was a form of love too, but she loved the real you. Not the part people swallowed and woke up next morning, feeling hungover and like they have to throw up. She loved *you.* But she didn't anymore. You could tell, you could always tell. And your heart being broke here isn't what mattered, what mattered was that you had taught *her* the powder. That awful, fucking low feeling. That total emptiness. Of your heart grinding to bits and falling out of you. Ashes. Like sand out of a cracked hourglass. You hadn't been a good influence; not even a good H memory. You were an infected scar. All your fault. And do you know what the worst is, Aya-chan? The absolute fucking worst? (She had no idea what the worst was, and so she gently shook her head, waiting for him to continue.) The worst is that, you were right earlier. Remember? You said you didn't think I was sorry at all. That a person like me doesn't know *how* to feel sorry. And I said girls are trouble, but men are one thousand times more so. Because they will lie, and they will cheat, and they will say anything at all to get their one hour or eight minutes, in the dark. And as soon as they're upright again, they'll wring their hands and say they didn't mean it, and say they didn't want it, and say they are so sorry. So they can look themselves in the mirror and do it all over. But I guess I must be even worse, some kind of devil, since if I was a man, this would be when to say that part. Tears and everything, so you'd believe me if I told you right now that I'm so sorry. Right? I know I would believe me. But I'll tell the truth. Which is why I'm even crying. The truth is I'm not sorry for being how I am. I'm not sorry for you being how you are. I'm not sorry for being with you. I don't regret anything what happened between us. I fucking *refuse*. And if I say I would not change a single thing, that even if this is the most I can ever have of you, knowing all that, *I'd do it all over again*, how can I say I am sorry? I could not, Aya-chan. That's my one, only, and final disgusting answer.

So that's the end of the story. You see where I am right now. Broker than broke. Loster than lost. Mechakucha boroboro third time in my life crazystupid in love with a girl I'll never see after this night. A sweet girl I had no business looking at, five minutes before I ever first saw her. Crying like a four year old because I never learn a single thing. How stupid am I? Which is why I can't—I can't...⌋

V turned away from her, and he made no more sound, but then his body started to lightly convulse and being at a total loss, she did the only thing she could think to do.

Aya wrapped her arms around him and after a brief hesitation, started to sing a song. It doesn't matter what it was, maybe it wasn't even a proper song at all, but she sang it to him softly and she moved on to another when it was over—a song right off of the top 50 hit charts, humming it under her breath, gliding over the lyrics she didn't know, then another, and another, all through every tune she could think of, until she felt his body slacken. She finished what she was singing and he was asleep. In a deadened and comalike sleep, but also peaceful and she stared at his tear-stained face then, lightly touching his hair to see if it stirred him, but it didn't. And then Aya started kissing V; as odd as it was, she wanted him then, as much as she ever had. She touched his body in a relieved fever; she thought his sleeping, calm form was so lovely, but not wanting to wake him, she put her arm around his back instead and pulling the covers over, Aya put her cheek against one of his sharp shoulder blades and consumed herself in dreams.

They woke right before eleven and checked out of the room. V asked if she wanted to get something to eat, but Aya said she had to go, so they parted in front of the hotel. The wind that day was surprisingly mild. Yellow clouds covered a soft, hemorrhaging sun.

It was odd weather, the type that makes pupils humble their masters and monkeys slip out of trees. When it seemed to him they had not even a minute left, he leaned over Aya and the tip of his nose had just brushed past her cheek when she turned away from him at the slightest, sharpest angle. He stopped as if pricked by a conscience.

Her voice was crisp:

「You didn't ask.」

V stammered. Flushed.
And the silence on the street roared.
「You're r-right. ...May I?」
「Hmm.」

She considered for three seconds. Looked up. Shook her head. Then gave him the faintest smile.

「Sorry, but I really do have to go now.」

There was no kiss, no hug.
No peck on the cheek. No handshake.

They stood for one more moment.

—And then she went left and he went right.

TWENTY

La Vierge Folle Reprise

The sun walked him home. And the moon. And the wind. He had enough money left to take the chikatetsu up to the botanical gardens, but he thought the air might clear his head, so he moved along the river, on the left side. A glance at his keitai revealed that it was past noon. In the sky, the sun bled softly still; and a pale and peculiarly pink disk floated far off from it, to the right. He imagined it was the moon, and wondered if Aya had already made it home. It occurred to him then that he never had asked her about the finer details. Not like all those times she had texted him. Those quick, desperate little questions that had charmed him so much. He had such questions too now, like where is your house exactly? In Kyoto proper or out a bit in the suburbs? Is it a modern house, and if you don't have tatami, do you have those fancy heated floors? As he walked, the blood roared louder and louder in his skull, the rushing up that accompanies extended hunger, yet despite the money in his pocket, he had no urge to veer off and wander into the streets to look for food. And no urge to smoke.

Past Nijou and before the river forks comes a place where one can cross the Kamo on large man-made stones dropped into the water, like the abandoned dominos of forgetful, giant children. On impulse, he walked out on the stones. Smelled the perfumed, red wind and crouched down in the middle of the river. The shadows of water rushed under his shoes and he was thinking, it wasn't even deep enough to drown yourself in. Remembering, he pulled the note from his pocket and inspected the expert fold. Opened it. Her message was short, written smack in the middle of the page, and she had included the little heart pendant in the parcel.

Please keep this.
岡田文美
おかだ

His kanji knowledge never had progressed above the bare minimum encountered on a regular basis, and names, with their various readings, were particularly capricious. Anticipating this, Aya-chan had included a tiny subscript for the reading of her family name. 岡Oka 田Da. He didn't have to think long on why the name was familiar; one of his students had been an Okada. But which one? Not Miss Sayuri, her family name was Oota. And not Miss Akame, her family name was Okura. So who...? *Sitting in a compact Suzuki, zipping along a narrow street. Once, she had come to the lesson by car and offered to drop him off at his next appointment afterward. Do you have any children, Miss Yuki? he had asked that day. Why do you ask? Just to ask. He looked over at her driving. She wore glasses, but only when she drove. She swallowed and the movement rippled down her long white throat. No, she said. It's just my husband and I. The way she looked made him wonder if perhaps the question had been tactless. He avoided the topic after that.*

His hand trembled; the necklace slished off the paper, hit his shoe. Tumbled into the water. V stared at it stupidly for almost a minute, his head rushing harder than the liquid under his feet. Perhaps he should leave it. Perhaps it belonged there, hidden under the water. A part of him wished to leave it there, to never think about it ever again. He got up to go, walked three stones away, changed his mind. No, he could not leave such a thing in the river. If Aya-chan had wanted it buried, she wouldn't have come back for him. She wouldn't have given it to him. He got on his knees and fished for it. It wasn't easy—the Kamo was never so deep, but it had risen from the recent rains. On the bank, two older people stopped to watch, trying to figure out what on God's Green Earth he was doing. When he drew back up, they turned around, clipped away quickly. The chain was in his hand. Cold mud clung to it, and the little stone on the front was dirtied too. He rinsed it off in the water, dried it on his jacket. Put the necklace in his pocket, then folded the note back, advanced north and finally bore off the banks, onto the streets. He was almost home when he remembered and made a detour to the bathhouse. Soaked himself into a further stupor.

By the time he reached the boarding house and was back in his own room, he really wanted nothing more than to crawl into his bed, but there was that last thing. That very last loose end and then all ends would be tied and he could sleep through the rest of his life and think about nothing. But for that—V looked around, his roommate was gone again. He went to the wall closet and impudently grabbed one of his roommate's shirts and a pair of his briefs and socks. (Pants he left, for they were not even close to the same height.) He changed, laying his own dirty items by his rumpled futon, figuring, was there any sense to bringing a clean body if you presented it in dirty clothes? He would try to wash and return the items quickly, without the other noticing.

The common room and halls were empty. The college students went home on the weekends and the tourists were already out pounding holes in their shoes. Not even

Sachiko-san sleuthed around in the kitchen, and he climbed the stairs, grateful for the silence. Had he met anyone and started to sweat, the trip to the bathhouse would have been a waste. At the top of the stairs, he peeked into the toilet on the right. It smelled fusty, but not offensively so. The bowl was clean. He internally thanked whoever had done that, then walked to the end of the hall.

Yesterday, he had barged in like a madman; today, he knocked politely, and waited until he heard the voice in French imploring him to enter. So he did. V rubbed his eyes: the window was open again. The room, as bare and austere, as shabby but as tidy, as yesterday. The mug of tea was on the sill. (Was it the same mug? Or a different one?) Maury sat in his futon reading, with his reading spectacles perched on his nose, and perhaps even the time was identical (hadn't he come in here sometime in the afternoon?). The older man looked up and put his paperback to the side.

–Raised back from the dead, I see. Hello, Lazarus!

–You said the same thing yesterday. Don't mess with me too much. I already feel like I'm about to lose my mind.

–How was your night? It must have been nice to have money again? –Maury pointedly ignored the other's first statement and didn't wait for an answer either. –I'll be honest with you, my boy, I wasn't expecting to see you here today. Or tomorrow, for that matter. I was expecting you to avert your eyes in the common room after this, and pretend you don't know me and I would have forgiven that too. But it's nice to see that you're a man of honor.

–If I make a promise, I keep it, sure.

–As one should! And yet, many don't, so I told myself that money had swam. But you were so harried yesterday. I don't think I'd ever seen anything quite like it! That alone was worth the two *man*. To see that even angels must pray sometimes, and who do they call on when they do?

–Maury, for fuck's sake.

–You're right, my boy. We both know that me enjoying you *not enjoying this* is part of it all, but I shouldn't abuse that too much. And I won't. But you're practically shaking! Don't tell me you're nervous? The blushing virgin—!

He stood up. Amused sarcasm spiced his tone again and V bristled.

–I'm tired. It's been an incredibly long night. ...Not for the reasons you think.

–I do not think anything about you. I do not dare to presume. But you really do look exhausted. Clean, but exhausted.

–I am, and I could drop dead any moment, so let's begin.

Not quite sure if he was supposed to approach Maury, or wait for Maury to approach him, he paused a beat, but instead of coming closer, the older man groaned. Dramatically rubbed his lower back and patted the duvet next to him.

–Drop dead? I could not have the death of you on my hands. If you are exhausted, my dearest, then sleep. You can sleep right here.

V couldn't pinpoint if the older man's tone was patronizing or sincerely doting and either possibility supremely irked him. A cord jumped in his neck.

–If I sleep, I may as well go down to my own room.

–I have never seen the inside of your room, but I can only imagine it is absolutely hideous. No no, how can you ever get good rest in there? Just sleep here. ...Don't be nervous, I happen to be picky regarding sheets and I pay Sachiko-san extra to have them laundered twice a week. They are cleaner than anything you've slept in lately. Unless you spent the night in a hotel.

He cackled here and V stared at him.

–Sleep? Now?

–It's what I said. I am paying for your time, and if I want, I will pay for you to sleep.

–But if I sleep, the time will pass, –he said stubbornly. It was the most courteous way he could indicate that his desperate moment had waned. Another hour, another minute, and he might change his mind altogether. Hadn't Maury himself said that he hadn't expected him back at all? Goes to show what being a man of honor brings you. The other seemed unperturbed:

–And if it passes, it passes. But I insist. Sleep. Sleep! Don't keep standing like that. Take off your shirt if you like, it's always too warm in this room. It's why I keep the window open. Do make yourself comfortable.

–And you? –V was suspicious. Did Maury intend to stay in the futon, and read and sip tea next to his passed-out body? It would be the absolute tiara to crown this chain of absurd 24 hours. Seeming to anticipate this complaint, the other was already crawling out from the covers.

–So suspicious, my boy. Honorable, but full of suspicion. I will sit next to the wall and read. Now come. I insist. Clean sheets, fresh air, not a cockroach to be seen. Nothing like what the commoners are used to on the first floor. Am I not right? Please. Sleep.

V hesitated one more moment and then he could not any longer. He slipped the wallet and keitai out of his pockets, lay them on the tatami next to the futon. Slipped off his shirt (Matt's shirt if we are being pedantic) and lay himself down as well. As Maury had said, the sheets smelled recently laundered with only the slightest prick of cologne to them. That old man cologne. Next to him, Maury sat up against the wall, pointedly out of reach from the other. He adjusted his glasses and picked up his paperback, giving a final concerned glance before he resumed his reading. The way he looked reminded V of a father. Not his, mind you. But still. A father. Yesterday's gloating, mercenary gleam had faded from Maury's eyes (but weren't fathers also gloating and mercenary?), and V actually relaxed. Perhaps he had been wrong about Maury. Perhaps he had been the mercenary one? And the contempt he had read in the other was merely the reflection of his own.

There was no more time to think of it though, for once his head was on the pillow, it took him less than 20 seconds.

The world blacked. It whited. And he slept.

When V woke again, it was dark. *Aya-chan*. No, she was gone. This wasn't the hotel. Clean sheets. This wasn't his futon either. He sat up bolt, stared into the darkness. Maury's room. But Maury was gone as well. His phone still had enough charge to show him it was two in the morning. *Two*. The time had passed, Maury hadn't woken him and he had slept longer than he had in weeks. And now, the room was empty. Where would the other go at this hour? He pulled his shirt on, thinking, it wasn't his concern. He'd fulfilled his end of the deal, and if he left now, it was with a clear conscience. He was gathering his wallet when the fusuma pushed open and Maury entered. V didn't even bother to mask his disappointment.

–Don't be so happy to see me, dear boy. I was starting to wonder if you really had died, as you had threatened.

–You didn't wake me.

–Wake you? God would've smote me had I disturbed you, never did I see anyone sleep so soundly. I have hellish insomnia so it was a pleasure to watch you sleep. I only now stepped out to get something to drink. And now it's time for you to go. Is it not?

He is letting me go. He is making it easy.

–Sure.

V grabbed his things lightly, jammed them into his pockets, too surprised to even feel grateful. He felt around. Aya's note was still in there and the necklace. The trick was to, well, he knew the trick.

–Good night then, Maury.

–A good night to you too, dear boy. And if you ever need a restful night, you know where to come.

He did not seem disappointed in the slightest. V wondered if perhaps he really was satisfied; if he had some kind of peculiar fetish. Watching people sleep. Wasn't that a thing? He wandered towards the door, behind him, Maury motioned for him to wait. He opened his magic drawer again, and the envelope was out. What had V done, but come back at the time they had agreed on? Nothing more than that; he had not even been charming or courteous. But here the other was, pressing another *man* bill into his hand. This was easier than he ever imagined. Etienne had bragged about desperate old men, but this was the top. He wondered if politeness dictated that he refuse the money, but his instincts kicked in again. Sleep had cleared his head. He took the bill, smiled gallantly, bowed at the older man, and was out the door, before the other could change his mind or get any ideas.

The corridors were empty, and he drifted down them, and it was a shock, after Maury's cultured, slightly cardamomed French to hear his roommate's acerbic French-Canadian twang:

–Whoa, where'd you go?

–Nowhere.

V hoped to be curt enough to throttle mindless chit-chat, but experience had taught him this was a fruitless endeavour.

–Haha, you okay, man? You just been lying here, day after day, and then you disappeared. Even Miss Sachiko was asking me if you were sick or something. At least that's what I think what she was asking. So, I was thinking...

–I have to go. I just came to pick something up.

–Going back out, man? Haha, two modes huh? Vegetating or beast. Hey, isn't that my shirt?

–No. I bought it today, –V lied lightly. Absurdly. Anyway, later.

–...

He pulled the door shut, walked out into the kitchen. Paused for a moment by the grimy fridge. He was almost expecting Matt to follow him out here and apprehend him about the business of the shirt, but their door stayed closed. The boarding house was too quiet, until he remembered. It was two in the morning. He walked out to the street, bought himself a drink from the vending machine. Went back. Considered. Walked up the stairs. Sachiko-san had trouble sleeping too and sometimes she roamed the halls at night with her cat perched on her shoulder, but she was nowhere to be seen now. V wondered what he would say if she asked him what he was doing upstairs at this hour.

This third time, he didn't barge, or knock. Simply slipped the door open.[62] Maury didn't even look up from his book.

[62] Tourists locked their doors with tiny padlocks assigned temporarily by Sachiko-san. Longtermers kept their doors lockless and hoped for the best.

–You're still awake, –V said.

The other shrugged.

–I told you. I have the worst insomnia. Did you leave something here?

–No.

–Then what do you want? More money, is it?

Now he did look up and that voracious, hollow glow came into his face again. Seeing it made V imagine, perhaps Maury didn't want anything like *that* at all; perhaps the fetish really did oscillate between watching him sleep and watching him squirm.

It was a mistake to have come back up here.

–I don't need more money. Never mind.

He started to turn. Maury croaked.

–Stop, boy.

V stared at the square of dark in front of him. The opening in the fusuma back to the hall. Back to the hall which would lead back to his room. Back to his room which would lead back to his own bed. He took one more step forward. Waited a second. Lowered his shoulders. Exhaled. He was not moving. The other said behind him:

–Step in. Close the door.

Not used to being commanded made it intriguing. V obeyed and turned around. Put his back to the wall. In front of him, the room shimmered, perhaps the lack of food was starting to push him into an even newer state of delirium. And nerves. Maury walked up, the room was quite dark, though the overhead light was on. That sickly, greenish glow from the old traditional lights, and under the lights, the Rubicon rippled softly. When he stopped in front of him, V looked at the other man, really looked at him, for perhaps the first time thus far. Where had Maury come from? He did not know, though he'd had a few friends back in Paris who'd echoed his accent and patterns. His skin was darker. His features blurred. A sagging body, an insignificant head. Thinning hair that curled without conviction. Eyes that were neither brown, nor blue, nor grey. With a woman, even if she was not particularly beautiful to him, there was still always something about the appearance, a facet he could fixate and obsess about. Now, it was odd to be unable to find a single sexually fascinating feature. Like trying to light a fire with no fuel. He remembered Maury offering him sleep though. Offering him peace and a clean bed when he had been more weary than he could ever recall. Something stirred in him. He wondered if this was how women fucked. Based on abstractions and rewards for random acts of kindness.

–I have no idea what you want, –he muttered. –So you'll have to tell me.

He worried that Maury might want to kiss him now (was he expected to kiss?) but the other kept a good meter distance.

–What I want... is probably much simpler than what anyone else wants from you. So just keep standing there against the wall.

No standard order. This could be some test, but he complied and Maury went on.

–Yes, like that. Make yourself comfortable. You'll be standing like that, well—it all depends on you, but for a good five, ten minutes.

Maury laughed a little here and the other's whole frame stiffened. Then V figured, why tense up? It would do nothing good to go into it kicking and screaming. If he was sitting, he may as well eat. And if he ate crow, it may as well be fat. He leaned his length against the wooden slat, between the two stretches of fusuma and relaxed himself the best he could.

–Good. That's good. Now what I want you to do, is to think about something.

–You want me to think? –His voice dulled.

–Yes, my lord. I want you to think. ...Do you know how to think?

V narrowed his eyes. Matched his tone.

–You've paid enough. I suppose I could try it.

–Excellent. I know you take... pride, –he laughed a little again, –and I know you will do your best. Even if I'm not your preferred *arrangement*. Now, I want you to close your eyes and think of your first sexual encounter. Not anything bad or forced. The first time you *enjoyed yourself.*

–...You want me to think about someone else?

Maury eased off his own belt.

–Unless you'd rather stare into my eyes and think about me. In which case I would be most flattered.

V swallowed, thinking: yes, this Maury was wise. Looking at him was already producing a certain stage fright, so he took the advice and closed his eyes. It was not an easy thing to remember. The first time. To find it under the mulch of a thousand times. Or to recall even, what exactly the first time had *been.* But then, he knew it was simply a matter of getting himself excited one way or the other. He could think about the first time or the last time or linoleum, if that did the trick—Aya-chan—no time at all. Behind his closed eyes, he shook her image out roughly. No. Not that.

–Whatever you are thinking about, picture it. Every aspect of it. How the person looked. What kind of day it was. Where you were. How old you were. What you did. What it felt like.

His eyes stayed closed. Shoulders relaxed. Maury's voice hitched, he filled the room with the sound of his white breathing. The floor creaked, Maury was coming over to him. V drove the sound away. His irrational state already whirled with a mess of images; he tried to sort them. Direct them. Images piled. Images upon images. Truly the first days. Before he'd met Etienne. The first. The first. Smells rippled through. First room he'd rented. The first train station he had rode into. The stink of the Gare du Nord, until he moved again. Maury stepped up to him, put his hands on him. You don't have to open your eyes, the older man said, and V thought, good. He really didn't want to. First few weeks. Learning the lay of the city. It was one of those hot fetid nights. Only a Parisian will know it. His first summer. The Seine in the dark. Color of the Seine at eleven at night. (That river never had been his. Not like this one.) Skin so dark, it had the most delicate sheen of indigo. Highlighted on her cheekbone, when they stood in the window. And on her delicate wrists, she wore two slim bands of gold. They'd been talking in her room. She had a nice place, if very small. Just one room. The ceiling was high, window was high. If you squinted, from her window you could see the curve of the Sacré-Cœur. Sitting on the sill, smoking cigarettes together. She'd lived in Paris her whole life. Asked him, where are you from? You have such a charming accent. And he laughed. I don't though. It's slight, but you do. I don't want to have one, he said to her. She smiled. Don't worry. In two months, you will sound like any other irritated Parisian without a charming accent. You will lose it, and nobody will know. *That you are not from here.* At that point, he had been prepared. To one day become absorbed into the city. The girl turned off the lights, lit a candle. Such a small room really. But carefully decorated. Peonies on her table. In a wide mouth jar. Perhaps it had held sour cherry jam before. Or pickles. No fancy vase, nothing fancy. But it was pretty. And in her hair too, a flower. A bone white camellia. It made him think. Already he was thinking. He must find someone to live with. Women knew secrets he didn't. He could be clean, but such touches he didn't know. He hated to live alone. Until now, he had lived with relatives. A month at a distant cousin of his mother's, near Lyon. This was his first time ever truly alone. It was forbidding. He missed his siblings horribly. He missed his little sister. He could not bear to call them though. To hear them, in a cracked phone booth. To put his mouth to the receiver reeking of 250,394 strangers' spit. To hear her cry out, Where are you?

You need to come home! He couldn't bear to lie to her. Next month, Tati. Soon. To hear Ilya shouting in the background. *Tell him he can* die *wherever he is because he is never setting foot in this house again!* They were looking at the lights, down on the street. Out over the city and she said, what are you thinking about? He didn't want to say, that I'm scared. Of living alone. So he said, that I want to kiss you. He braced for it. Get out. Leave. But all she said was, Alors, fais-le. Watching the lights on the streets. She was the same height as him. A body long and beautiful as a sword. They didn't move to the bed. Stayed, standing. Looking. Out the window, they watched couples walking deep below and small cars struggling to parallel park. While he did everything to her. And she did everything to him. But when it came at last to that. He stood behind, hands rested on her waist, go on, she breathed into the window frame. You can't stop now. But he did, because— She turned, her eyes level with his. What's wrong? A shard of pink neon seared in his dilated pupil. Closest to the window. He told her—well. He was the first born of a viciously fecund family. Feracious blood ran down in him. Both sides. Which is why he had never— Her laugh was most beguiling. She kissed the tops of his breasts, whispered. I don't think you need to worry about that. And he turned. Held her tight from the back. Fitting the blade of his body to the blade of hers. Still, he said into her hair. She had the thickest waves of dark sepia hair. And the girl arched against him, her tone subtle. You are a strange one. The first time I am with someone more worried about that than me—and my first vierge. Is that what the 'V' stands for? She directed him to her dresser. She had things to prevent that. Top drawer. He left her by the window then. Walked to the dresser, thinking. *A virgin?* Oh no. He may have never done *that*, it's true. *But he had lots of experience.*

His eyelashes tremored. Against the wall, he sighed, the slightest. He remembered Maury, forgot him again. His head buzzed. It ached, the color of piercing sunlight. The girl was gone. Light in patches over his skin. Watching the dust. Molecules shifting. You rarely had the room to yourself. The bed to yourself. When you did, you had to take advantage. Coarse hands easing his pants down. Bunched, below the knees. Five, six. Breath on the inside of his leg. The first time his mother had said: Oh! She never got mad at him. She never yelled. It was one of the reasons he loved her so much. He loved her as much as he despised loud noises. And she never made any. From her, he had learned. The art of talking so quiet, people leaned close. But her pretty face looked almost scared that day. You do that alone. When you are alone. So you too, mama? You do that when you're alone? She reddened, with that scared look again. Oh! That had been the first time, really. Hadn't it? In that sun-drenched room. Hands feeling, running up and down his legs. Knuckles knobbed, big. And this was the first time a man had ever touched his skin. That wasn't a handshake. A blow. Or the touch of a doctor. Though he could not remember when he had last seen a doctor. Thank god, he never needed one. Insane, how rough men's skin was. Did his skin feel this rough? To others? His eyes still closed, running his fingers down his own side, almost carefully. Like he would be scared to find another's body. His own skin didn't feel rough to him though. He reached out; a fingertip belonging to him brushed hair. Coarse, greying hair. He shook. Put his hands back, against the wall. Maury made a noise. The sound dove him back into his own head. And then he found it. Like finding the book you were looking for in a whole heap of mishmash books when you could not remember its name. Here it was. Not Paris, not that lovely girl, not her lovely room, not in his

room either, rubbing on his bed, barely old enough to go
to school, and his mother's shocked face. It was here. Hazy,
rushed, flashes, they slowed. When he was ten. Crystalled.
It was summer. She was older than him. Not so much
though. Then do it, she had dared. In ten years she would
be. Someone's Standard state-issue wife. But that day she
was sugarstained thin lips stringy dirtblond unwashed
hair and black eyes; a pale flesh ball of bruised elbows and
infected mosquito bites. That first girl in Paris had superb
dark eyes, but this scrubby goblin was the original. After
her, he would chase dark eyed girls for the rest of his life. A
fancy boy! She took him to her room. On the bed, he
kissed her. And she said, That's all wrong, moron. Then
how? You be the girl, and I kiss you. He closed his eyes. For
all her grubby fingers. She was patient. Soft. 17 times. She
showed him. As for the thing she asked for next. The next
lesson. He knew, had known since he was six. He'd seen
his mother gestating his whole short life. Held his hands
against her stomach, feeling the life slithering inside.
When was *he* going to be pregnant? And she had smiled.
You won't, my life. But when you are grown up, you will
make someone pregnant one day. A lucky one. How? ...
How do *you* get pregnant? The red dots back on the tops of
her cheekbones. Like when she had found him in the room,
in the patch of sunlight. Well... He'd listened, heart sunk.
Not his Ksyusha with Ilya. That loping, stinky *wolf!* But at
least now he knew. What NOT to do. The very idea was
monstrous. He was preemptively paranoid. The goblin
child from the house across just laughed at him more. You
really are a moron. A kid can't get anyone pregnant. I will
if that stuff gets in you. No, that's pee. No, it is *not*. No, it
has to come from an adult. He would not be swayed
though. Well then, there's other stuff, she said. Secretively.
Like what? It wasn't excitement. Mere curiosity. Like what?

Show me. ...I will, she said. But only if you do exactly what
I say. I will. I will! And you can't tell anyone we did it! I
won't. I won't! Maury was on his knees, gripping his knees
from behind. Talking into him. V's eyes stayed very shut.
Candy, powder, fruit, plastic. Girl smell. Tea, cologne, the
slight rottey smell of the old tatami. Nobody will know.
Don't worry. Nobody will know. Don't worry. Wax camel-
lias, flecks of dustgold, rubbing himself, Ksyusha's shocked
face, her eyes, which were not like his. The color yes, but
not the shape— the black eyed Parisian girl urging him,
you can't stop now, the neons, when he finally did it, that
wet gasp when you finally, he reached down, gripped the
other's hair, pressed his face deeper against him. The other
groaned, Ksyusha's eyes were not like his, they were round
and big and the color of sun in a forest, framed all around
by very long very thin eyelashes, and it made him shudder
violently, without warning. Maury murmured on his
knees, V pressed back, released, it went on—the other
waited. It went on, a good seven seconds. The older man
wiped sweat from his forehead, V pulled his hips back, and
the other pulled his face away. Cold hit his body on the
places that were wet and Maury put his cheek against the
younger man's thigh, muttering a language the other
didn't recognize. It had all happened so quickly. Maury
switched back to French.

 —I knew a good memory would do it.

 —I should've thought of something else.

 V stood still slouched against the wall, pants still
down, wondering, what now? Should he pull them up? It
was awkward. But not as much as he had expected. Normally, aloofness, assertiveness, tenderness, when it was
over, when it was not over, instinctively, one act segued
into the next, yet here, he was confused, nor did Maury
raise himself from in front of him.

Embarrassment spiked, a self-disgust, the cold fact of it was—

–You're not done.

Maury seemed amused, unable to hide his pleasure, and the other said tightly:

–My body's all haywire right now. It happens sometimes. It'll go away.

–Will it? J'aiderai.

–Aide-toi, le ciel t'aidera.[63] –Ksyusha had used to say that. V started to laugh, softly and almost hysterically.

He didn't want to stay and he didn't want to leave. His system felt full and achingly tired again—the sleep from before had not been enough. The other watched him, as if to decipher what he wanted, impossible to do, as V himself had no idea. And then suddenly, as if on a whim, he stripped off Matt's shirt, stepped out of his pants. Laid the full length of his form down into the cool clean futon on the ground in front of him.

[63]Help yourself and Heaven will help you.

–Alors, fais-le, –he said and Maury stepped behind him, wiping his own mouth and grinning. His tone seemed a pendulum rocking constantly between quiet mockery and genuine appreciation.

–See, my boy. This is why I said you're like a poet. You don't overthink, you go with what you see. Most people are concerned forever with that which is not concerning, but a poet sees only what needs to be seen. What is there.

He pulled off his own pants and V shivered.

–Stop lecturing, Maury. Is that—will that be all right?

He hoped what he meant was obvious, but the other only laughed crudely.

–You haven't eaten for a week, no? It will be fine. –He carefully got to his knees again. –So is that what you wish?

–Anything. Just put me to sleep. I need to sleep.

–As you like. But this isn't a fancy love hotel, boy.

Behind his back, Maury glanced at the flimsy wall separating them from the next room.

–Keep quiet if you want nobody to know.

V rested his face in the inverted triangle of his own arms, wondering, what was there for nobody to know? Only what everyone already knew or wanted to know. Hadn't he often watched a woman's face while she was in ecstasy, wondering what exactly it was she could be feeling? No mistake, he had been in ecstasies too, but he knew they were not the same kind. Now maybe, he would know. Maury muttered, sat next to him, running his hands over him for a long time, until he was entirely keyed. He could want to admit it or not—ugly or not—the older man was skilled. V told himself he would keep quiet, so every time he found himself making a noise, it surprised him, like one of those dogs that never barks becoming uneased by the sound coming out of its own throat. Eventually, he forgot that too. Forgot himself. Maury then used some-thing slick on him— A thick, iridescent sweat broke out over his skin the moment the older man entered him and they were both surprised when he came again only min-utes into it. –I can see why you used to be concerned for making girls pregnant, –the other murmured behind him and he said nothing, nodded, sighed. Grabbed the other's wrist and held it hard to him, ne t'arrête pas. And the older man obliged and kept going. Ten minutes more, and he did again and he could sense the other's momentary wane (was he finally getting more in tune with him?) but he nodded *keep going*, until they came to the very end, final, slow, mined out of him precisely; his muscles peaked, clenched, as if he had come to the end of a skittering, mir-rored corridor he had been falling, falling down and reaching the end of—he bit his own arm and the other pushed down on his wet shoulder blades. *Valerchik you*

were worth every yen of that three man. And more besides.
Something raw burst and spread up through his insides, as
sticky and mysterious as the first Two Beings who had met
over on the stalk and fucked the islands they now lived on
into existence. As hot and clean as Creation itself.

His skin heaved. His eyelids flickered. And though it
seemed ill-mannered, he could not even turn around to
say a single word. Instead, V fell face forward. His head
tumbled onto the pillow and he hurtled into the deepest,
longest unconsciousness.

He swooned.

Marid 'Maury' Hamou was faded now, but in his youth he
had been handsome; he'd known lovers in his native
Algiers, in France, Canada, Vietnam and Japan. In his day,
he'd been courted and courting, men and women and
others, but never in all his experiences had he ever been
put into or put anyone into a faint as deep as the one V had
fallen into. It worried him considerably. The young man
lay in his room, unconscious and delirious, run with fever,
for three days and three nights. His sweat wasn't that
pretty, house-of-pearl liquid of the night before either, it
smelled chemical and anxious. The futon was wrecked.
Maury wet an oshibori in the upstairs bathroom and
would occasionally mop the other's brow, wondering if he
should call for a doctor. However, something kept urging
him not to. Instead, he stayed close by, periodically wiped
the other off, cleaned his body when it got soiled the best
he could, and sometimes spooned weak sugared black tea
into the unconscious man's mouth.

Though he was worried, he wasn't entirely surprised
it had come to this, considering the condition the other
had arrived in the afternoon before (and the afternoon

before that). Already teetering on some unseen, precarious ledge and thinner than an alley cat. Maury wondered if this was not brought on by some emotional breakdown compounded by physical weakness and their night together, but when he checked through the other's pockets for something like a clue, he found nothing except a folded note, the type school girls pass each other under desks. And a silver locket. *Some girl trouble.* He looked at the trinket and note warily, and decided he should not unfold and read it.

On the third day right after dusk, his visitor sat upright, as suddenly as Our Lord Herself, and pulled himself up. He asked nothing and said nothing, but crawled to his feet and went off to the door (Maury imagined, to the bathrooms). When five minutes passed and he did not return, the other assumed that he was gone for good, but thirty minutes later, the fusuma gently slid open and he was back. Freshly showered, shaved, with the filth of three days of illness removed. Figuring it best to assume his regular amused indifference, Maury sat in his spot by the wall, pretending to read and only glanced at the low table to show the things he had brought up from the convenience store—a katsu bento. Bottled green tea. A pack of Marlboros. A matchbook. The younger man fell on the spread, ate ten bites of rice and five bites of meat, drank six sips of green tea, then stood in the window smoking, holding the burning tip of his cigarette against the black-velour sky. Staring at the sizzling end in wonder, like he could not believe what burned in his hands was the same stuff burning out in the stars. Maury was of a mind to tell him to go outside, that he would not have his room smelling like a pachinko parlor, but he held his tongue.

Once the other finished his cigarette, he cleaned up the food he had not eaten then left again, though not before Maury stopped him in the door to give him two more *man* bills. The young man looked at the notes with open skepticism, asking what they were for when he'd already been paid? And Maury reminded him that after his performance five days ago that would have put a Phaedra to shame, had he not yet learned to toss his airs out the window and wordlessly take them? Or he could not, and eat his pride. For Maury, it was all and any the same. After two seconds, V plucked the bills from his hand with a certain polish. *Pride?* the gesture said. *I never knew her.*

After that, though they would not sleep together again for a while, the young man developed a habit of coming into his room and they would talk. Concerned at first that he would no doubt fitter away the money he'd been given on women he was trying to bed and impress, Maury was happy to see the other invest sensibly. He reinstated his phone plan, bought himself some new clothes. Got himself a haircut and some decent looking shoes. Made a reconnaissance out to the international house and at the local colleges, scouting for new students. He spoke French and Japanese well (of his other languages, Maury could not judge) and had a certain presence which Maury thought might help him make connections—but he remained muted, his face pallid and thin, and the older man would sometimes slip him a one thousand yen bill, imploring him to get himself a strong bowl of noodle soup or a cutlet set (he would not have dared asked to go eat with him and the other never invited him to join).

Then one day out of the blue, V announced that his current roommate was leaving (backpacking, Cambodia, indefinitely) and Maury wondered if this was a report of no particular weight, though he knew his new friend was socially cunning enough to not drop such a driblet by mere conversational chance. So he mentioned that he'd been thinking that after all these years in his room alone, some company might not be unwelcome. Provided the individual could respect his need for quiet (and cleanliness, of course). Depositing the statement as mock-innocently as V had deposited his. He could not guess at all how the suggestion would be received. Perhaps the other was too prideful to become a man's kept man. Perhaps he worried about tarnishing his 'reputation.' Or perhaps in this convalescing time, he'd appreciate an older benefactor who had no desire to beat around the bush or play love games.

Still he knew that to anyone (V included) he looked nothing more than a tattered, cracked old foreigner. Certainly nobody who could walk you around the shopping promenades by Kawaramachi and flash you on their arm. But money he had. In fact, the unassuming oldest tenant of their house had plenty to offer: the polyglot son of diplomats, Sorbonne-educated, the beneficiary of a generous inheritance, and a modest success as a novelist (on permanent hiatus and retreat) who still collected a regular royalty check he spent on absolutely nothing. Temporarily aligning with him wouldn't be glamorous nor would it lead to a visa, but it wasn't tactically the most unsound move for a youth with no prospects and a madly ticking biological clock. To attract, one must be attractive. And the upkeep of that took a certain fee.

A week after the offer was extended, V moved in.

As Maury suspected, he was easy to live with, on the right side of hygienic, and would occasionally even abide an older man's overtures. Not that he would ever initiate, or treat such things as anything more than the due for his keep, but Maury knew better. When he was in him, the other's whole body would seize, and his pores would seep that shimmery substance he remembered from their first night— As ashamed as he himself was to admit it, Maury was entirely captivated. At his age! But he knew that despite all the good he did, and all the odd chemistry they had, the other would never forgive him for being a man—a drabby one, at that. Yes, he could be very cold. Maury would diffuse his moods with laughter.

–I'm not one of your ladies you've got twisted around your finger, so you can check your high tone at the door, my dearest. And a mea culpa, mea maxima culpa if I ever presumed to have anything beyond money to even temporarily capture a prince's attentions!

The slavish patronizing would further irritate V, and to outright offend him, the older needed only to suggest that he take the active sexual role. The first time he made such a proposal, V gave him the unironic, disturbed stare of one who just discovers that he lives with a senile man. The look said: Maury may well be his lackey in bed if that pleased him to do, but *his* adoration would only and ever be bestowed on a woman.

Not misogyny nor masculine pride but, it seemed to the older man, a deep vein of *misandry* throbbed in him, through and through. His strange, bristly vanity Maury found particularly backward and childish and he could not help but laugh at him more.

Aid doesn't always come in the form we'd like, V-sama. So let's never forget. We all need to eat and we all bleed clear when we are fucked. Even you.

The younger man would not engage though. Maury learned, like a taunted cat that does not strike back, merely jumps to a higher place to put themselves out of reach, as if the taunter was beneath them and beneath all notice. So he wouldn't get angry when the other mocked him; rather, he'd move to the window, sit, chew on a nail, pick sores on his face and stare down at the street. When he did this, always, the older man would be abashed. Rather than victory, this last stanza of Rilke's poem would hover in his mind:

> Nur manchmal schiebt der Vorhang der Pupille
> sich lautlos auf --. Dann geht ein Bild hinein,
> geht durch der Glieder angespannte Stille--
> und hört im Herzen auf zu sein.[64]

[64] Only occasionally does the curtain of the pupil glide open silently–.
Then an image goes in,
Goes through the tense silence of the limbs–
And in the heart ceases to be.

-From Rilke's 'The Panther'.

And so, the season moved into deep winter, and the young man's health would not improve. If anything, it deteriorated further still. He quit smoking, claiming it simply didn't feel good. His appetite was bad, his hair dull and his nails grew long and brittle. The constant gnawing did not help them, and the ends of his fingers were chronically infected and bleeding. On the days he had to tutor someone, he would pull himself together, even cover the ugliest lesions with a bandage, but any other time, he would sit, unkempt, in a loose tied yukata, the grey planes of his sternum poking out from behind the two slashes of fabric, his green eyes almost glassy in his head. He had taken to wearing the silver necklace Maury had discovered back then in his pocket, despite the tender raw welts the metal plating left on his skin, and seemed perpetually preoccupied by it. One time in bed, the older man, who always positioned himself behind, accidentally grabbed at the chain when trying to grip his neck. He had never even seen him angry before—now the young man turned, fast as a cobra and practically pushed him to the ground.

–Do not *touch that!* –he snarled.

Maury stared, genuinely stunned.

–I'm... sorry, boy. It was an accident, so don't lose your mind over it.

–I *will* lose my mind if you fucking break it!

Other times, he would lie on his stomach for hours on the floor, reading one of Maury's French novels, twisting the necklace around on his own neck, sighing. He stayed in this state for weeks and weeks, and Maury could not tell if it was the young man's ill health that had started to poison his mind. Or if it was a poisoned mind that continued to wreck his body's health.

One day, he awoke rather early to find the other already fully dressed, pulling on the thin athletic jacket he always wore. The air in their room glowed, odd, lunar—it had snowed the night before. A generous blanket of white covered the window sill outside.

–Where are you going this early? –he asked, checking his own phone. It was not even eight yet.

–To Ootsu.

–Ootsu? Whatever for?

–I have a lesson there. This is our first meeting. They called me through the international house, I'm not clear on all the details. –He coughed here, and the hacking shook every centimeter of his lank frame. Maury looked over, thinking he wouldn't have been surprised to see the young man spotting a handkerchief with blood.

–All the way to Ootsu? In this weather? But they said last night it will snow again at noon. You should call them and cancel.

–A walk in the snow would be good for me.

–I don't see how, –the older man argued. –You're not well, you know. You've been coughing and your jacket is not thick enough for this weather. If you go out now, you'll catch your death.

–I should be so lucky, –the younger hacked spitefully, and Maury gave him a disapproving look.

–Oh, come! Enough self-pity to drown in!

–What self-pity? –he grumbled. –This could be a long-term job if they like me, and the money will be good. I'm glad to have a prospect, that means I'll be spending less of *your money*, so you should be happy too. Everything is good. No self-pity here, none at all.

–But you cost basically nothing beyond your phone, so it's really no worry. You need to focus on rest right now, not money.

–No, money is *exactly* what I need to be focusing on. –The other shoved his phone into his pocket. –I need to get out of here as fast as possible.

Maury's rheumy eyes widened slightly.

–Why though? If you are ill, then rest. I have everything taken care of. Or what, don't tell me this is about something else? Do you need to escape before I chip away your *manhood*? –When he saw the young man tinge red at the last word, he laughed dryly. –Honestly, that's it? I would have never expected *you* of all people to be hung up on such prudish, old-fashioned ideas!

The other stopped stiffly:

–You have no idea how old-fashioned I am, Maury. None at all. I've figured it out, it's staying here in this room that's keeping me sick.

The way he said it implied a throwaway remark of no particular depth, yet the older man stiffened here too. He had long imagined he'd be a dupe to expect affection returned, or even much gratitude for the money and care he'd spent—why should the younger one be grateful? They both knew, no muse had ever been plucked out of the muck from *altruism*. So he was surprised at the low, seeping ache he registered emanating through him, from his heart, to his mid-section, down to the groin, that dreary, shameful sting that confirmed that only God's most beaten, most sentimental imbeciles tie a hope on a Stockholm romance. And he knew that erotic dependency was one thing, but if he belied even a crumb of *this*, revealed a single rent or tiniest hole in the skin of his soul, the other would walk straight up and jab one of his elegant, broke-tipped fingers *right into* that hole without a second thought. All justifiably. And yet. And still. He found himself asking out loud:

—So it's really been so awful living here? With me?

The other looked away. Avoided the older man's watery eyes. Bit his chapped lips. And for once, had nothing clever to say. He hurried out the door, citing the impending lesson as excuse and Maury waited until he was down on the street, watching through the window the navy-blue jacket get swallowed by white. He went back to bed, though he could not fall asleep. Near noon, he got dressed and went outside himself. Normally content with the selection the Family Mart offered on the corner, and the few small fruit vendors and patisseries in the area by the boarding house, today he went downtown despite the snow. He wandered into some department stores by Shijou, even debated buying an expensive winter coat. Went all the way to the men's floor, to a store clerk for assistance—then stopped himself. No, he told the clerk, it would be best to come back with his nephew, he didn't want to buy the wrong fit. Thank you. And left. Ate a simple lunch of udon soup with fried shrimp (the hot, clear soup was good in such weather, with a generous sprinkling of shichimi) and went to the Book Off and foreign language bookstore to buy himself a few volumes. Then took a taxi home. By four that afternoon, the room gleamed in the eerie dusk of snowy nights. The other was not yet back.

Maury found himself glancing down into the street, again, again, until he pulled the curtain away roughly. Stepped aside. He told himself, he would not fret by the window like some lornly young bride. The other had made money today, no doubt a good amount if he was willing to go so far, and it was all too possible he was now trawling the town, looking for a woman to scatter it on. Spend the night in a hotel to reassure himself of something. Maury told himself that was well and not his affair. He would not expect him back tonight—so he was surprised when their door slid open half an hour later, and the younger man walked in. His hair was slightly wet at the tips (suggesting he had just come back from the bathhouse) and he carried a long package in his hands and a sizeable paper box. He placed them both on the low table and hung his jacket in the wall closet. Murmured a tadaima and nothing more.

–And? Did you get the job? –Maury asked, once it was clear the other would not speak first. –What is it that you brought?

The younger man looked over at the packages as if he too had just noticed them himself.

–I got the job, yes. ...You can open those, if you like. They're for you.

For me? Maury walked to the low table, earnestly curious.

In the longer package, he found an expensive bottle of cognac, and inside the flatter, square box, nestled with characteristic local meticulousness, were eight exquisite slices: classic strawberry cream, rich chocolate mousse, forest berries on custard, mango cheesecake, raspberry tart, Mont Blanc, maccha cream roll, studded with azuki beans. Mille feuille. He remembered two passing remarks he had made in the past—that it had been too long since he'd had a nice cognac, and that the cakes they made here really transcended any he had eaten, in any place in the world.

    –Eight pieces! Are we expecting guests?

    The other turned his face.

    –I don't know what you like. So I just got the ones I thought looked good.

    Imagining the youth going out of his way to find a pastry shop, then awkwardly looming over a well-groomed cake clerk as he poked at the slices he wanted through the viewing glass, made Maury smile.[65]

    –I... well. This is a surprise! I haven't had a cognac in over ten years. This all must have cost a fortune.

    The desserts and the fine bottle sparkled on the table, out of place luxuries in their Spartan room, and Maury tried to remember the last time he had been gifted anything at all. Perhaps from his daughter or son, a decade of Christmases back, when they were living on one continent and still in touch. He couldn't help but wonder if the younger man had spent everything he'd made today on the gesture. A modest thank you would have been a shadow of what he wanted to express: to throw his hands in the air. Or to embrace the other and kiss him on the lips. It seemed either reaction would be a disaster, so he said nothing.

    V left the room to bring plates, and forks, and little sake cups from the upstairs kitchen. Once he returned, Maury opened the bottle and poured. He made black tea as well from the water in the electric kettle, and though he half-expected the other to reject the offer of a drink, the younger man took the little cup of cognac without a word.

    –To your new job.

    –Yes. To my new job. 「Kanpai.」

    「Kanpai!」 –How was it, anyway? Ootsu! That's quite a ways.

    The other sipped—explained his immense luck. A

[65] Not the joyous wastrel he had once imagined, since living together, Maury had noted: V seemed to never buy himself anything out of spontaneous pleasure.

family of four—the father, to be transferred to his company's Brussels branch in a year—the wife had decided to go with him and their two children, but she wanted all three of them to speak French with some degree of competence before next year's move. She didn't want to bury herself in the expat community. The family was comfortable, money was not an issue, but their original tutor had left suddenly—a personal emergency. They did not think they could find anyone else willing to commute so far from Kyoto—they were all very happy. He would go to their house three days a week, and they would compensate not only for the lessons, but for the time spent commuting and the train.

–An amazing prospect, my boy. I'm glad for you.

They ate cake. Sipped tea. Drank cognac. The alcohol was rich and went straight to Maury's head. Combined with the sugar, one little cup was enough to make him feel intoxicated. He never drank anymore, not cognac nor anything else. Next to him, the young man talked and seemed himself for the first time in weeks—he even smoked a cigarette, taking it to the window, to ash out on the ledge. Snow started falling again. He watched it fall, and said:

–You know what it is? This sound in your room. Wrecks my nerves.

–I don't hear anything but quiet.

–No, there's a sound. There's a white sound and a grey sound and the electricity from outside. We had a radio with Rodrigo, but it broke pretty much right after he left.

–Ah yes. Rodrigo-kun. I remember him well. You two were inseparable when he still was here. –The other made no comment. –I am guessing you threw the radio away?

–The broken one? No, it's downstairs, where everyone stashes their junk.

—Bring it up tomorrow. If Sachiko-san has a toolbox, we should be able to fix it. But if not, I will buy a new one.

They did not drink more. Neither of them was drunk, and neither wanted to be. Maury cleared up the forks, and the remaining cake was left in the box, pushed to the end of the table. V went and brushed his teeth, then said good-night. Lay into the futon, towards the wall. It was early, but Maury was not surprised. Today had been the other's longest outing in a month. He himself went to the bathroom, deciding he would sleep early as well. His body throbbed from the cognac, but not unpleasantly. Once he brushed his teeth and washed his face, he walked back and stepped into their darkened room. Stopped in the door. He was expecting the other to be already asleep, deep under the duvet; instead he found him waiting on the top cover of the futon, his naked upper torso framed in a square of snowlight. It would be the only time his young lover would solicit him. So Maury walked over to the bedding, lowered his body down to his. Kissed him on the bare shoulder.

Sighed and put his own heart into a box.

February came. The plums bloomed. The river widened. The color came back into V's cheeks. His nails were still wrecked, but a sheen returned to his hair and eyes and skin. With his Ootsu family and some other pupils he had gathered, he made enough to move back into a single room, if he wanted. To move out of the boarding house all together. Maury prepared himself for the inevitable announcement that the other was leaving. He waited for it week by week, but it did not come. That whipped mid-winter desolation had melted, like the snow off of their window's ledge. They lived together well and the young man seemed cheerful enough—at night, they talked sometimes, played chess on a magnetic board V had liberated from the common room, or Maury would read while the other hunched by the window on his heels—smoking out of it with one hand, tip-tapping on his phone with the other, with the radio playing softly in the background. As for their conjugal issues, even those settled. When Maury desired something from him, he would leave a nice bill pinned under the ashtray on the low table and for an hour that night, the young man was his. No more discussion; no crisis and no discord.

Then one day in late March, Maury returned from an appointment at the shiyakusho. The room was light when he stepped in; every window thrown open, every curtain pulled aside, the beaten old table wiped and spotless, the futons aired, put away. The young man lay in the center of the room, staring up at the ceiling, smoking. The ashtray next to him bespoke he had been smoking nonstop for an hour at least. He wore a clean white shirt, open at the collar, what he always wore when he went to teach a lesson; the silver heart glinted on his collarbone and he stared at the ceiling, blowing lazy flaxen rings. Not even aware the other had come in. Worry closed the older man's throat. *He is out too much and it will make him sick again.*

–You all right, boy? Did you go to Ootsu today?

The other turned his head languidly.

–Oh. Yes. I got back a while ago. I cleaned up.

–Yes, the room looks wonderful.

The young man's eyes glittered unhealthily; his neck looked flushed, dappled with sweat, and Maury stepped over to him.

–Are you okay? Did you take a jacket?

–Stop fussing like an old woman, it's unbearable. I'm fine. –He smiled here and even reached out and playfully cuffed the older man around the ankle. The other jumped back, startled.

–Stop... that. You should really take that necklace off, by the way. The silver is irritating your neck. And you need to dress properly, you should not be leaving without a jacket. It still gets cold when it rains. I'll go down to the drugstore and get you some...

–I'm not sick, so don't bother with any of that. I don't need drugs or tea––

–Maybe you're not sick, but you don't look well, either...

–I'm very unwell, –he said happily. Like being unwell was the happiest thing in the world. The young man lay on the tatami, his features blurred in a haze of neon pink smoke. –I met someone on the train today, Maury. Je suis tellement amoureux.

I am so in love.

343

TWENTY-ONE

THE LIFE OF AN AMOROUS MAN

The river stays the same, but he is not the same anymore. Or maybe he has always stayed the same and change could only be measured in the subtle shifts of the river's level, water, color, swiftness. In the way birds come to it.

Now it is late spring again. Almost June. He walks south from his apartment in the north, coming all the way along from the lonelier banks further up. As he walks, he passes the path where he would have veered off towards the bridge, on to the road that would lead to the boarding house. It's been less than two months since he moved out, but the memory has blown away. Like the moulted skin of a snake, left behind once it's become too small for the growing body, that life has been shed, like all the lives before it. The direction doesn't even get a glance.

Instead, he faces forward, keeps walking, whistling a little. The buildings become more dense to the right and left, as he slowly reaches the central and southern banks near downtown. This is where friends congregate in the afternoon, where immortals drink and dance, where school kids skip class to walk and smoke and flirt. He walks until he comes to the big station and then turns off, towards the hill rising up to Kiyomizudera. He walks until he reaches Sanjuusangendou.[66]

The temple is a long wooden structure and one of the few popular places he likes to visit. Today, it is so grey; the soft, mysterious rain of tsuyu has come early this year. Days ago, it pelted the pregnant trees relentlessly, until they threw down their pink coats in a few afternoons, ruining many a blossom viewing party. Now the people

[66] Sanjuusangendou, along with Kiyomizudera and Kinkakuji, is one of the most famous and well-known temples in all of Kyoto. Sanjuusangendou is known for (amongst other things) housing one thousand nearly identical, life-sized, and yet individual images of the bodhisattva Kannon, the Goddess of Mercy and Compassion.

This is also the temple where 17th century Saikaku's sex-obsessed heroine in "The Life of an Amorous Woman" comes to pray for the souls of her aborted children and finds the faces of all her lovers in the statues instead.

walk furtively in the stuffy wet. Their umbrellas bob up and down as they pass over this rotting mauve carpet, and he slips between them without an umbrella and steals into the temple.

A party of students from Tokyo is finishing a tour and as soon as they shuffle out, the hall is deserted, musty. Almost quiet for once. The one thousand life-sized statues stretch out on the risers going all the way the length of the structure, like a god-choir. From where he stands, he cannot see the end of the progression.

He walks slowly down the line, looking up at the straight rows, the diagonals, all Kannons.[67] Some look softer, some austere, some are serene, others more warlike. A face stops him: More definitively male, round. Peacefully resigned. Yet with a touch of mockery around the fuller lips. He stares at it for a few moments. Stops quickly again at a more narrow face; beautiful, feminine. Narrow. Just below it stands a statue with a younger face—with an expression as sardonic as a holy statue can muster.

He swallows, moves, stops for a moment in the break of the risers: an enormous central figure gazes down at him, the 1001th face. He walks past it quickly, following the line of gold statues, until one makes him stop abruptly. It is in the third row up— A face slightly more rounded than the surrounding ones. Line eyebrows more horizontal than arched, and eyes that are wide and serious. The mouth is full, the expression grave. But with the hint of a smile. A child goddess. He keeps looking at it, wishing he could step up on the risers to it, noting the details of the statue's headdress, and the thirty-three arms which are in fifty universes (making them one thousand). He wishes he could, but he cannot take a picture or get closer to it. Overcome by an urge to write an ema, he remembers he won't find a booth selling them outside and leaves quickly.

[67] Kannon has thirty-three faces with which to see you and one thousand arms with which to catch you. They are the goddess of mercy, but a male bodhisattva. The name means the one who is all seeing, all hearing. Or the one who sees sound. Kannon appears across East Asia, depicted sometimes as male, sometimes as female. Sometimes as androgynous, to signify that enlightenment is genderless.

The street is glossy with humidity. He feels it might have gotten even warmer while he was inside. In the city of a thousand temples it takes less than one minute to find another one. One street up, there is a humble jinja with a garden, well-tended, but with no priests or temple girls present. He walks into the garden and then up to the main image. Tosses in one hundred yen and claps twice. Says a little prayer. By the offering box is a smaller box, set up with charms and ema. A rusting coin drop and a yellowing, laminated price sheet. He looks at the charms for Traffic Safety, Harmony in the Household, Academic Success, Good Health. Love. The love amulet is a tiny pale pink cloth bag, with the character ai[68] embroidered in silver silk thread, perhaps for a girl to hang off of her school bag. He pockets the amulet, then looks through the ema. They are simple and he selects one with some god on the front that he can't identify. The name of the jinja is also printed on it; he seems to have found his way to the Shrine of the Serene Water. He takes out 2,000 yen and tucks it into the offering box, then takes the permanent pen tied to the string. In his sloppy hiragana, he writes 「Harmony in the Household」 on the front, and the year. Then he turns the plaque around.

Thinking for a long time, he finally writes in his old language, then looks around the yard. On the far wall, other ema are hanging in the soaked air, rendered blurry by the moisture, and he walks over to them, attaching his in a free spot. It hangs to the far left of the middle bottom, between *May my baby be born healthy this fall, Aki* and *May I do well in my exams and get into Kyoudai next spring, Kazuhiko*. With the Japanese characters facing front, his plaque blends in perfectly with the others. He wonders how long they will all hang there before they are all burned.

By the far gate, a small group of school kids walks in.

[68] Ai – 愛

They appear to be on an organized tour. Some are ringing the bell, some are taking pictures of the yard. Their teacher stands off to the side. Now that they have come, the space constricts—the excessive component is himself. He nods at the teacher, then takes his leave.

But can't go yet. Standing on the uneven foot stones, he pulls out a cigarette, leaning his forehead against the cold cobalt shadow of the stone wall right outside the shrine's gate. He hears the drone of students from inside and the eerie whine of electricity in the air. The narrow street is desolate. He lights up then turns inward, his forehead searing against the slick wall, his eyes closed. At first there is only him and whatever he is considering, but then the click of low heels invades his head. Click. Click. Click. An umbrella is moving closer from down the street, closer. Closer. Finally, the figure stops next to him. He ignores it, but then her voice casts away the soft grinding between his ears. That pearly murmur, like the inside of a conch:

「Oniisan, hi wo kashite kuremasen ka?」

The umbrella closes and a girl's face is looking up at him, extending an unlit cigarette questioningly. A heart-shaped face locked in shockingly short hair. Her features are carved not from the hardness of ivory, but from the finest soap. He breathes out smoke, unmoved.

「Sorry and no.」

「But... you're smoking.」

「Look, here's the most I can do.」

He holds his smoldering stick out to her, and she drags from it. When he takes it back, there is a slight hint of vanilla where her polished mouth touched the filter, and the taste blends pleasantly with the tobacco. He puts his head back to the wall, dizzy. He needs the entire space of the street to himself.

But the girl won't go away.

「You could just give me a light. There's no one else around to ask.」

「Well, sorry, but I don't give lights to kids.」

「Excuse me, who are you calling a kid? I'm almost 23! I mean, how old are *you*?」

She says *you* like others say *asshole*. Now he smiles into the wall.

「I just turned 27. And that's not a very nice way to talk to a stranger—Miss... erm...」

「Ayumi.」

「But your friends call you Ayu, deshou?」

「How would you know?」

「I'm good at guessing things. I suppose you are too, because you skipped the English intro.」

「I dunno. I had a hunch you live here. Where are you from originally though?」

He turns to her, talking with the cigarette still in his mouth.

「You know, I really don't remember anymore. I think I might actually be from Kyoto. For real. Ayu-san, do you think that's possible?」 He smiles at her openly for the first time and Ayu's head falls to one side in perplexity.

「Anything is possible. You could be from Kyoto, you could be a psycho killer, what do I know? You don't look like a killer though.」

「No. But I have been accused of looking like a liar.」

「Oh, well that's not so bad. Everyone lies once in a while. But what are you doing here, anyway?」

If he had thought for a hundred years, the word wouldn't have come out of him. But he doesn't think. Maybe that's what makes it true. He says,

「Mourning.」

The answer surprises them both. The young woman steps back.

「What? Here, on the street?」

「Is there a better place?」

「Ok, I get it, you're teasing me.」

「No, not at all.」

「I'm sorry then. ...For whatever it is. But you don't look sad.」

「Because there's nothing to be sad about. *It's all done and gone.* And you? Coming to the temple?」

「Oh no, I was just on my way downtown to pick up a book. It's for my university. I'm getting ready for a proficiency test at the end of the summer and it's supposed to help me with the test questions.」 She addresses him here, with the confidence of fluent speakers. —Parlez-vous français?

Her accent is excellent, and her French chirrup is one of the most enchanting sounds he's heard in a long time. He shakes his head with a regret so genuine, it convinces even himself, and Ayu frowns once more.

「That's too bad. My next hunch was that you spoke French, but I guess not a lot of foreigners do. It's always so hard to find a good language tutor.」

「I can only imagine.」

Right as he says that, the sky shakes its pelt, and they both put their hands out, touching drizzle with their fingers. She squints upwards.

「It's going to rain again soon.」

「You look prepared.」 He glances at her umbrella.

「But you don't. I know a nice place not far. Instead of standing out here in the rain, we could talk a bit more inside, if you like. Want to go? They have good tea and cake there.」

He really, really wants—tea and cake.

「I'm sorry, but I probably shouldn't.」 Seeing her poise momentarily rattled, he adds, 「please, you seem like an interesting person, and I don't mean to be rude, but you know—⌋

Ayu opens her umbrella dramatically and twirls it around her head. Moisture flicks from the plastic, onto his face, and she laughs, her well-shaped head and posture cutting a perfect tableau with the street. He pictures her on a Vespa, zipping down the treacherous, cobbled waves around Gion, a silk scarf at her throat. A truculent Audrey in *Kyoto Holiday*. He wants her on a postcard.

Audaciously, she raises an eyebrow at him.

⌈Just say it. You have a girlfriend. Well, I'll tell you right now that I have a boyfriend. And so? I'm talking about getting *coffee*, not jumping into bed! Or are you the type who thinks a man and a woman are incapable of having a simple conversation, no strings attached? Why are you looking at me like that? That *is* what you meant, isn't it?⌋

A familiar melody plays in his head, this one lemony sharp in its variation. Another vector.

He looks over, letting her defiance weaken into mist. Letting himself imagine a long kiss against the stone wall. Eating the food of all young things. Tea, coffee, cake, candy, cigarettes. Lighting her each and every one, if that's what she wanted. Her skin, colder than poured milk. An afternoon spent in bed, whispering the most combustive French he knows. Falling in love, love, love. Again, neverending, forever.

⌈I'm sure a person like *you* could.⌋ He says *you* like others say *sweetheart* and throws his cigarette butt on the ground. It sizzles and dies on the stone. ⌈I'm not worried about *your* intentions, but with a bijin like you around, my own might get... problematic. Alors, bonne chance avec le français, Ayu. Sayonara.⌋

And then he's gone, and the heat rushes in to fill the vacuum left by his body. She stares after him, dumbfounded, and he walks away, because today is for someone else. But tomorrow though, who knows?

Anything is possible in a beautiful world.

He leaves the shrine, the ema, the street, Ayu behind, and walks towards the middle of town, into the crowds. Nodding at the young women, nodding at the old men, taking tissue packs from the hand-out person on the corner. The crush is part of him, removed from him. He buys a drink (the signs all say *cold* once again); flips out his keitai and writes a message to a pupil. Another message to his girlfriend. He's fed; he has money in his pocket. He loves beauty just as much as he used to, but maybe more cleanly. Or is it more guarded? He loves the rain—the warm rain comes down to wash the streets. It washes the faces of the people walking in it, and he imagines it cleaning his as well. Adding more water to the sacred river.

The Kamo is right there. It flows and changes and unchanges and moves. The river is the seasons. Alive. It won't stay in your hands. And looking at it gives him silence—that he understands. Not with his mind, but something more primordial. It's basic. He bites his nails while he walks and smokes with visible pleasure. People stare at the young man with that fatal serenity on his face. What could he possibly be thinking about, they wonder. With an expression like that, he could very well be contemplating any number of high themes, from godliness and peace, to harmony and beauty. But how could we know what it was? He could have very well been thinking about any of those things.

Or, knowing V as we do now—he could have just been thinking about H.

H – May be the most enigmatic letter to be imported into Japanese. Written sometimes as just the letter, or written out as 'ecchi,' it can be a verb, a noun, or an adjective, all referring to sex, desire, eroticism, or perversion.

In Closing

Okada Ayami graduated D— High School in 2006. Though they stayed friends, she broke up with her boyfriend Kurotani Kiriya to officially be with her high-school classmate Yamada Ren instead. After graduation, they went to Paris together, and Aya felt a great satisfaction when they kissed on top of the Eiffel Tower. They currently live in Osaka, where they co-own a fashion boutique and share a flat, with two cats.

Rodrigo Alfonso Emmanuel Cabral da Costa graduated with top marks from the University of Lisbon, eventually moving on to get his doctorate and finally becoming a professor of linguistics. He went back to Japan four more times, once with his wife and three daughters.

Okada Yukiko divorced her husband of seventeen years, moved back in with her aging mother and started teaching in a small school on the outskirts of Kyoto. She never remarried, choosing to focus on work and travel instead.

Marid 'Maury' Hamou continued to live a reserved life in Kyoto, publishing two more novels that achieved a modicum of success back in France. He eventually reconnected with his daughter when she relocated to Shanghai.

V------ (------) ------ --------- was on Kyoto's Keihan Line when he fell asleep against Kuromori Ai's shoulder on the way to Ootsu. Though she was quite taken and he was devoted, she was fully convinced only once her condition became imminent. Her aghast family helped him enter a language and translation school. A student visa is in the mail. He waits for it and for the birth of their first child. Blissed.

THANK YOU

To Kyoto, my most favorite city on this planet.

To Gordy.
To Jun, who is the light of my life. Here's to the Three
Robe Life. To Nazghul, the mini light of my life.
To Clarissa, a bright star.
I don't think I would've looked at this again without you.
To Csibe. To Ori.
You won't read this. But hi.
To Luvan, for the French help.
If mistakes remain, it's my fault.
To Dale Stromberg, my final editor.
You have the wisdom and the wit of a monk, and were
the PERFECT editor for this book.
To Jun again, for all his patience and technical support.
To Hazel Ang, for all the enthusiasm and energy she had
for the story and the original design of this book.
I am so in love with this layout, and I have you to thank.
To Bryan Cebulski, for valuable insight and comments.
To Mordor and the others in the Night Beats collective.
Your enthusiasm gave me the energy to push
for that last 3%. Thank you all.
To the wonderful people I met in Japan, and the
wonderful Japanese friends I've had out of Japan.
To Christoph R, who was the very first reader way back
when. I appreciate the effort you put in.

A time-capsule novel is a tricky affair because the urge to go back and retroactively inject your characters with the wisdom you possess now is almost irresistible. These days though, I try to accept that it's as important for a story to be dated as it is for it to be timeless, and that some writing needs to remain the unenlightened, greasy fingerprint of a Moment.

This book is a modern riff on Saikaku's 17th century novel "Life of an Amorous Woman" (Kyoto edition) topped with a generous sprinkling of (c)harem anime. It's a literary shitpost (predating the word shitpost) that is, despite an inverse on a fantasy, a snapshot of a definite place and time. That place is Kyoto, Japan; that time was the early 2000s. Specifically, 2003–2004, when the city was packed with tourists who were almost exclusively Japanese people from other parts of the country; a Docomo keitai could do things you'd never seen a phone in the west do; and hardly anybody spoke English, yet the DESIRE to, vibrated everywhere. Tech was advanced but social media nascent. Weeb yet to be coined. It is this narrow and highly specific window I wished to focus on.

When I first wrote this, I was roughly the same age as the protagonist and had nothing in common with him. My original inspiration was extremely loosely based on two actual people I had met in a Kyoto boarding house (they did not have the Golden English Goose), and the story was to be an homage to some of my favorite places and pulp-lit tropes: thirst lit, the Kamo river, rootless beings, social alienation, adult coming-of-age (i.e., inching towards thirty and still no clue), beautiful stranger ruins your life, and the floating world. Important also, I wanted to write an off-the-wall chronic foreigner story that operated outside the normal frame of expat culture and English language proselytization; where culture clash and does the e x o t i c locale satisfy or break the western (lowercase) preconceived notion was not on the table. With all this in mind, I wrote—a novel. It was kind of good. Kind of crap. And then, time flowed, life happened, I wrote other things, I stopped writing. I forgot about it entirely. A trip back to

Kyoto some years ago made me remember this story. A meeting online with another writer who has become a wonderful friend made me take it out again.

Reluctantly.

I'd changed so much and it had been so long, I was sure I'd be wanting to burn it. To be clear, I was still ashamed of it, but also struck by how relatable I found the characters (more so than when I had written them), and how the writing seemed both literary (??) and trashy. And unsaddled by the complexes and inhibitions social media brings to writing, as I had, at this point, not engaged with any writing community for over a decade. The story was, for better and for worse, a pure snapshot. Wanting to show it to aforementioned writing friend, I decided to revise it. Tried to preserve the naive tone; trim the suck, and flesh out the parts that were undeveloped. Much has changed, but much of the text and general structure is as it originally was. But what would I do once revisions were done?

I am torn about this novel. It is chronologically the first major thing I've ever written. This book is handsome, stupid, fun and sad; my most exuberant piece and an unapologetic, self-indulgent nerd out. It was written by a person who loves to read and write and play with language; for people who also love to read and write and play with language. I believe it strikes an interesting chord of irony, earnestness, social reality and fantasy; says something potentially universal about relationships and sex and gender, despite being stuck in such a specific time and place, aaaaand parts of it make me very uncomfortable.

Option one was go back and change the red-card parts. But as the book examines socially and morally unaware people (and a more socially unaware time in general), that would have destroyed it completely. Which brought me to option two. Destroying it completely. Deleting it. I could not bring myself to do that either. So why keep it at all? As one of the main characters says, maybe that means that somewhere, I believe the book is not 'really' wrong? And my only answer to that is well, I think it is wrongright. Or rightwrong.

My compromise is that I took out some of the more offending parts (and added parts that are possibly even more offensive, but I digress). And anyone seeking a sharp moral line drawn in the sand, and the characters, narrator, and reader firmly placed somewhere to the right or left of that line, will have hated every minute of this.

Now, I've explained what led up to this existing; what I thought I was doing when I revised it. But what is actually *there?* James Baldwin wrote: "When you're writing you're trying to find out something which you don't know," and there is much I did not know at the time of writing this that has only become clear to me looking back with time and distance. Again, however tempting it would be to establish certain points as canon and reinterpret with my current knowledge, that would feel like an act of cowardice towards ambiguity.

So, whatever I see today in this story's reflection will stay with me and I will resist the urge to try to explain or exonerate myself. What this says regarding sex (the act, but also the gender), sexuality, misogyny, or finding the social category, country, or relationship where you can belong, remains up to the reader's imagination.

Inspiration and references

I think few books capture so brilliantly that inexorable and humbling pilgrimage from desired to desiring, virgin to vampire, as James Baldwin's *Giovanni's Room*. Though that is not the theme the book is most known for, it is the one that resonated with me most strongly when reading and rereading it. Other books on my mind when writing this one:

Osamu Dazai's *No Longer Human*. (Or *Human Failure*, how I personally would translate it.)

Ihara Saikaku's *The Life of an Amorous Woman*.

And of course, Arthur Rimbaud's delirious and sweaty prose poem, *A Season in Hell*.

Italicized French texts on pages 127, 129, 146, 182, 236, and 264 are directly taken from Arthur Rimbaud's poetry, notably from his prose poems *Bad Blood* and *The Foolish Virgin*.

On Edo Period Sexuality and Amorous People In General

Japan's Edo Period (1603–1868) was perhaps more erotic than our modern brains would imagine. Traditionally, Japanese society was divided into four classes: warrior (samurai); farmer; craftsman; and merchant; with their order of social importance ranked as such. Outside of these classes were eta (those performing tasks forbidden by Buddhist law and thus considered unclean); and artists, performers, entertainers and pleasure workers (existing on the periphery of society in the *water trade* or *floating world*—so called because of its instability).

While merchants held the lowest status of the four official classes, they rose to become the wealthiest—but were not allowed to use their wealth for ostentatious display. The pleasure quarters (originally set up for samurai to use while visiting (ahem, under house arrest by) the Shogun in the capital of Edo (today's Tokyo)) became a place for merchants to sink their riches, and an unrestrained sexuality was born.

Seventeenth century writer Saikaku Ihara (born into the lowly/ rich merchant class) wrote many pieces on lust or amorousness. His novel, *Life of An Amorous Woman*, describes the trials of a woman ruled by desire. The story depicts many instances of passionate highs and lows, and when the aging woman encounters all the ghosts of her aborted children after a lifetime of unbridled sexuality, she goes to Kyoto's Sanjuusangendou to pray for her sins. She ends up seeing all her lovers in the Kannon statues—and finding—enlightenment?

aho Fool, dumbass.
Aho yanee ka? You fkn idiot. (Rough male
form).

ai Love. 愛

aishiteiru I love you.

anata You. (Generally, women to men.)

anta You. A more familiar form; can be rude or
dismissive.

ara ara A feminine expression. Something like,
Tsk, tsk, what have we here?

arara Also very feminine, to express
amusement/confusion.

are That. (As in 'this or that' but can also be
a euphemism for any number of things,
including sex.)

arienai/ Unbelievable, outrageous.
arienee (Male form rhymes with a pure vowel
'neigh,' not 'see.')

bijin Bi = beautiful, jin = person.
Used for a beautiful woman;
also, binan/bidan (beautiful man).

castera/ castella	A popular Japanese sponge-cake inspired by a cake first imported by Portuguese merchants in the sixteenth century. Tenpura is another dish popularized by Portuguese influence.
cherry girl	(or boy) A phrase taken from English and Japanized to cheri gyaru. A virgin.
daiai	Big 大 love 愛. So big love, consuming love.
daikon ashi	Legs like the thick white radish, i.e., thick, shapeless legs.
daisuki	Big like, so love.
dasai	Corny, embarassing.
do S (esu)	A big S (esu), i.e a major sadist. Do M (emu), a big masochist. ('O' more like 'doh,' not 'moo.')
ema	A wooden plaque purchased at a Shinto shrine. A wish is written on the plaque, which is then hung in the temple's yard and later burned in ritual fire.
ero-	A prefix indicating someone/something sexual/perverted, e.g. erojiji = dirty old man, eromanga = lewd comics.
futon	Duvets laid directly on the tatami floor for the night, then usually folded up and put away during the day in a wall closet. (Not the low frame beds/folding couch beds in the west.)

fusuma	Paper doors, made of more substantial material than shouji.
gaijin	Gai = outside, jin = person, i.e. foreigner/non-Japanese person. A bit of a loaded phrase and some prefer gaikokujin (outside-country-person). However, gaikokujin often denotes a non-Japanese (but visibly East-Asian) person, so many go back to gaijin for a not East-Asian-looking foreigner.
girochin	Guillotine. And a chinchin is a...
geesen	Gaming arcade. (G and ee like the pure vowel sound of 'game,' not the sound of 'jeep.')
hostess/host (bar)	Attractive young women (or less often, men) who make conversation and flirt with patrons at a bar. Since workers earn money from commissions on drinks, charisma, convincing patrons to buy more alcohol, and holding your liquor is important. A water trade job.
ike ike	Go go! Happy-go-lucky party girls (can also mean a chug party).
inchiki	Fake, low-quality, sketchy. An inchiki Prada bag.
izakaya	A place for food and drinks that is open late and popular with students; relatively cheap.

jinja	A Shinto shrine (as opposed to an otera, a Buddhist temple).
Jizou	A deity in Japan considered to be a guardian of children, specifically children that have died early in life, were miscarried, stillborn, or aborted (so-called mizuko—water children).
	Jizou is said to help the children in Sai no Kawara (a kind of purgatory), by shielding them from demons and helping them build stone towers. In Kyoto, there are many roadside shrines with depictions of Jizou (usually with a little apron to keep the statue warm, because Jizou is often portrayed as an infant).
(o)jousama/ (o)jousan	Miss, young lady.
jyuku	Cram school, usually taken by students in the evening as a supplement to regular class.
kaishounashi	Lit. cannot provide. A good-for-nothing, useless man. 甲斐性無し
kami	God(s), spirit(s). 神
kao ga ii	Lit. his face is good. Attractive, handsome (used for men/boys).
kappa	A water sprite from folklore that makes mischief, but does occasionally eat a choice pet, child or person. (Also the name for a cucumber roll in sushi, kappa maki.)

karaoke	Done in a rented private room, only for the company of your personal party. As it is private, dark and inexpensive, with food, drinks, even alcohol brought directly to your room, it is a popular date activity.
kebai	Adjective for heavy makeup.
keitai	Mobile phone.
	Though not yet smartphones, early 2000s Japanese flip-phones were light-years ahead of their western counterparts and already a necessity for daily life.
kibi dango	Pounded rice (mochi) balls on a skewer, glazed with a sweet and savory sauce.
kimoi	Creepy (as in a creepy guy, not 'dark/scary' creepy).
kinpatsu	Blond/a blond. Gold kin 金 hair patsu 髪
koan	A vague or sometimes absurd short story, used in some Buddhist sects to encourage enlightened thought. Many Zen gardens are intended to be contemplated as a koan, a subtle question with no easy or tangible answer.
kun	A name suffix used by women towards men roughly the same age/status as them, teachers to students, and bosses to subordinates. Parents to male children. More familiar than san.

love hotel	Or rabuho. Rent by the hour hotels made specifically for sexual encounters. Not considered particularly sleazy or seedy (though of course, quality of hotel varies).
man	One man = 10,000. 20,000 yen = two man yen. Pronounced 'mahn'.
mate	Pronounced mah-teh. Hang on there just a second, tiger.
matsuri	Festival, generally held at a shrine or temple, with music, events, and booths selling traditional foods.
(o)miai	A marriage arranged through dates controlled by parents and matchmakers. Still sometimes used in modern day by professionals too busy to date.
(o)mikuji	A fortune bought at temples and shrines. If the fortune is good, you keep it, if it is bad, you tie it to the pine tree in the temple yard. The fortunes range from extremely good (daikichi, big blessing) all the way to extremely bad (daikyou, big curse).
moshimoshi	Hello? (Phone only.)
nandeyanen	A colloquialism unique to the Kansai (Osaka-Kyoto) region. What the hell???
(o)neesan	Older sister. Also used to address a young(ish) woman. Similarly, (o)niisan is used for addressing younger men, meaning older brother.

nomiya	Nomi 飲み drink ya 屋 store. A pub.
noren	The canvas curtain used by traditional businesses to cover their entrance and advertise the establishment.
nurikabe´	A plaster wall, but also a monster from Japanese folklore. It is an invisible, endless wall that can trap travelers late at night.
o- (prefix)	A prefix in front of many nouns that is a mark of softer, polite speech (and/or women's speech). (O)saifu (wallet).
OL	**Office Ladies**; the young women in offices who (generally) are only working until they can get married and quit.
oujisama	A prince.
purikura	Before smart phone selfie filters was purikura: with flattering lighting and customization options, these picture booths would instantly print out tradeable sticker sheets of your photos. Super popular for friends and dates.
ryoutoutsukai	Uses both swords. A bisexual.
sama	A name-suffix denoting high respect. e.g. Kamisama (God).
sawarantoite	Don't touch me. Literally, leave me untouched.
sefure	A portmanteau of the English words *se*kkusu = sex *fure*ndo = friend. Sex friend, f--- buddy. セフレ

seishun	Or aoi haru (blue spring). A period of innocence and vitality, considered to end in the early twenties.
senpai	A person with more experience or seniority.
shikkari	firm/firmly Shikkari shite yo! (Imperative. Pull yourself together. Get a grip.)
shikkusu nain	69 シックスナイン
Shinto	Shin (gods) to(u) (way) Way of the Gods. A set of practices, stories, and beliefs, including the belief that the kami, i.e. gods or divinity, manifest in the natural objects around us. There are many natural places in Kyoto considered to be a manifestation of the kami, including the Kamo river.
shouji	Traditional walls made of rice paper.
shouchuu	A potent schnapps (usually drunk mixed with water).
tabehoudai	Tabe = eat, houdai = limitless. i.e. all you can eat
torii	Vermillion gate marking the entrance to a Shinto shrine.
tsuyu	The rainy season in summer. Characterized by extreme humidity and rain. 梅 Tsu = plum, 雨 Yu = rain.

yabai	Dangerous, or, so good/tasty, it's dangerous, or, oh crap.
yankee	A punk, characterized by rough speech, rowdy behavior, and bleached hair.
yare yare	A phrase of defeat. Man oh man, etc.
yarichin	A portmanteau of the verb yaru (to do (in this case, to f***)) and chinpo (dick) (or manko (p***y)). So, a guy who is always getting 'done.' A man slut (and a woman slut would be a yariman).
yukata	A traditional light summer garment, often worn to festivals or more casually at a traditional bath house. Much less elaborate (and expensive) than a kimono.
yume	Dream. 夢

ABOUT THE AUTHOR

He is a mysterious creature, but if you leave a cup of coffee on a stump in the woods, you may see him scurry out to get it. He's lived on three continents, speaks four languages badly, and has worked as a cook, a mannequin, a translator, and a freelance illustrator. His favorite shape is the hexagon.

ABOUT THE PRESS

tRaum Books is a queer micro press dedicated to publishing literature that quietly and loudly fucks with binaries (especially those of gender and sexuality). Established in 2021, the press has published a variety of fantasy, horror, uncomfortable and absurdist fiction, with a focus on trans narratives and authors.

You can find more of our books at www.traumbooks.com

www.ingramcontent.com/pod-product-compliance
Lightning Source LLC
La Vergne TN
LVHW030814220425
809226LV00014B/391

* 9 7 8 3 9 4 9 6 6 6 3 7 7 *